A PLUME BOOK

THE END

SPARKPIX

G. MICHAEL HOPF is the bestselling author of *The End: A Post-apocalyptic Novel.* He spent two decades living a life of adventure before settling down to pursue his passion for writing. He is a former combat veteran of the U.S. Marine Corps and a former bodyguard. He lives with his family in San Diego, California.

G. MICHAEL HOPF

THE END

A Postapocalyptic Novel

• • •

BOOK I OF THE NEW WORLD SERIES

A PLUME BOOK

PLUME

Published by the Penguin Group
Penguin Group (USA) LLC
375 Hudson Street
New York, New York 10014

USA | Canada | UK | Ireland | Australia | New Zealand | India | South Africa | China
penguin.com
A Penguin Random House Company

First published by Plume, a member of Penguin Group (USA) LLC, 2014
Previously published in digital and print formats by the author.

LIBRARY OF CONGRESS CATALOGING-IN-PUBLICATION DATA IS AVAILABLE
ISBN 978-0-14-218149-2

Printed in the United States of America
10 9 8 7 6 5 4

Set in Minion Pro
Designed by Eve Kirch

To Tahnee

Acknowledgments

Everything in life starts out as an idea, but only through applying massive amounts of energy do those ideas manifest into reality. The journey from idea to reality is a part of the process and usually requires assistance and support from others. This book is not unlike that; it all began one day in my head, and then I took time to sit down and begin what you are now reading. I didn't complete this without the love and support of the following.

Tahnee, your love, support, and guidance helped from day one and continues till this day. You are always there for me with an encouraging word and sound advice. I love you. The day you entered my life it was destined to be blessed and enriched. Thank you.

Judy, you never waver in your support; you are always there to assist me in anything that I do. You have graced my life with your generous spirit and love. Thank you.

Mike Smith, you gave this book the polish and touch that all books need. Thank you for your valuable time and efforts. Now onto the screenplay!

Scott Wilson, your professional eye made the words go from manuscript to novel. Thank you, you're the best!

Mom, Dad, John, Becky, Billy, Neal, Uncle Rod, Aunt Jeri, Travis, Steve, Nicole, Nick & Wags, thank you for your love and support through this journey.

THE END

OCTOBER 15, 2066

• • •

Olympia, Washington, Republic of Cascadia

Haley stood, staring through the thin pane of glass that separated the chilly sea air of the Puget Sound and the warmth of her living room. She looked at the capitol building in the distance. Its sandstone dome towered over the other buildings in the city, as it had for the past 138 years. At one time, it was the capitol of a single state; now it was the capitol of her country, a country born out of chaos and destruction.

She tore her gaze away from the distance and looked down at the photo she held in her hand. She touched the faces of the family depicted. Tears began to well up in her eyes as she passed her fingers across the photo. It contained four smiling faces; a portrait of a once-happy family, her family. More tears came as she thought back to the day the picture was taken. She remembered it vividly, as though it were that very morning. Haley closed her eyes and pressed the photo against her chest; the tears ran down her cheeks and hung from her chin. She remembered her father holding her tight as she sat on his knee; he kissed her many times on her head and told her how proud he was that she had tied her own shoes that day. She longed for that innocent time when she had no concerns or cares. She longed for the days when her family was together and happy. Not long after that photo was taken, her innocent world collided with the harsh realities of mass murder and apocalypse. Her family was to be ripped apart by this new reality, and what remained would never be the same.

A knock at her front door jolted her back to the present. She quickly wiped the tears from her face and placed the photo in the pocket of her sweater. She walked toward the front door, but before she opened it, she turned to the mirror that hung on the wall in the foyer and looked at herself. She made sure she had wiped away all the tears and fixed her graying hair.

"You can do this, Haley," she said, attempting to reassure herself of the difficult task she had before her.

She turned and opened the door. On the porch before her were three people. The first was a man in his thirties, John, the lead reporter for the *Cascadian Times*. He was accompanied by two photographers, neither of whom could be more than twenty-five years old. They were all postwar babies; none of them knew the horror and brutality of the Great Civil War.

"Mrs. Rutledge?" John asked as he reached his hand out.

"Yes, please call me Haley." She grasped his hand firmly and shook.

She greeted the other two and invited everyone into her house. They shared small talk as the photographers set up equipment for the photo shoot that would follow the interview.

"Mrs. Rutledge, when you're ready to begin, let me know," John said.

"John, please, call me Haley."

"Yes, ma'am," he answered with a sheepish grin.

Haley sat nervously, her hands rigidly clasped on her lap. She rubbed her fingers in anticipation of the first question.

"Haley, first let me thank you for letting us into your home. It is an honor to be able to speak with you and to get your personal story and perspective."

"You're very welcome, John. I have to admit, I'm a bit nervous. As you know, I don't like the limelight nor have I ever been one for doing interviews. If it weren't for your family connection you wouldn't be here. I knew your father; he was a friend and colleague to my own father. It was only when I heard you would be the one conducting this interview that I agreed," Haley said. She sat very straight and looked at John directly.

"I do know that our families have had some connection in the past and, again, thank you. Let me then get right into this."

Haley just nodded her approval.

"Next week marks the fiftieth anniversary of the Treaty of Salt Lake. It was that treaty that gave our young republic the formal victory over our opponents and gave birth to our country. Your father was in Salt Lake for that signing. What can you tell me about him?"

Haley chuckled a bit before she answered. "Wow, that is quite the question. What can I tell you about my father? Where do I begin?" She paused for a moment before she continued. "Are you asking me about how he was then?"

"I can see how that can be a vague question, I'm sorry. Let me start again. Your father was very instrumental in the founding of this country; he is one of our founding fathers, as some would say. While many praise him for his sacrifice, there are some now that question some of his actions during the Great Civil War. How would you describe him?"

"I have heard some of those revisionists who now, in the protection of our hard-fought freedom, question the means by which it was gained. To them I say, 'You didn't live it, you were not there.' It is easy to sit in the comfort of liberty handed to you, swaddled in the bloodied cloth of our revolution," Haley said firmly. "If you are here to question my father's actions, then I feel we should start with who my father was and where he came from. The man I knew was a loving and protective man. He cared for me and the rest of his family and was willing to do whatever it took to ensure our survival. Many look back on history without looking at context. You have to have lived it to truly understand why anyone did what they did. My father was a pragmatic man who took direct action when it benefitted those whom he pledged to protect. He was not always a pragmatist, though." Haley paused; she shifted in her seat and then continued with a softer tone in her voice. "Daddy was very open about his life. He told me stories from his past. Many times, he told me that life will show up and change the way you look at the world; that there would be incidents that would shake you to the core and shift your way of thinking. My daddy had a few of those moments, the first one I can remember him telling me happened back when he was a Marine in Iraq. What happened there changed him as a person and set him on the course that would lead us to this living room today. I hope you planned on being here a while, because I am going to set the record straight."

NOVEMBER 16, 2004

• • •

Be polite, be professional, but have a plan to kill everybody you meet.

—Marine General James Mattis to his Marines in Iraq

Fallujah, Iraq

"Target acquired!" yelled Sergeant Gordon Van Zandt, his face planted firmly on the day sight of the TOW antitank missile system.

Gordon could hear gunfire cracking around him. He focused on the target he had acquired, a small window. Inside, an Iraqi sniper was pinning down a squad of Marines farther up the road. The glint of the sniper's scope and an occasional flash from the muzzle gave away the sniper's position.

After the pinned-down squad was notified that no air support was available, Gordon's TOW squad was called up to take out the sniper's nest. TOWs had been initially designed to destroy armored vehicles; the previous Gulf War had proven their farther-ranging battlefield application, bunker busting.

Gordon steadied his breathing and kept the crosshairs on the target while his driver, Lance Corporal Bivens, crouched outside the vehicle, alongside the rear driver's side with his SAW machine gun against his shoulder.

Bivens yelled, "Back blast area all secure!" Bivens was not your poster model of a Marine physique. He was small in stature, lean, and stood only around five feet six inches. But his nickname, "Pit Bull," said more about him than anything else could; he was a staunch fighter and had proven himself a worthy opponent in hand-to-hand combat.

Immediately, Gordon reached up with his right hand, lifted the arming lever, and shouted back, "Gun up!"

He placed his hands gently back on the traversing unit's control knobs and with his right thumb flipped up the trigger guard.

Just then, he saw the sniper's rifle barrel emerge from the shadows of the small room he occupied. Not willing to waste another second, Gordon yelled out, "Fire in the hole!"

He pressed down on the trigger.

A loud pop and whiz came from the TOW. Within a couple of seconds the loud blast of the missile leaving the tube on its way to the target rattled Gordon's ears. He tracked the missile through his sight as it flew to its target. After only a few moments, he saw a flash of light. The missile had struck its target. All Gordon could see now was dark smoke billowing out of the room.

"Impact, target destroyed!" he yelled out. He reached up, released the bridge clamp unlocking the missile, and tossed the empty tube onto the ground.

Bivens slung his SAW and quickly opened the Hummer's rear hatch. He grabbed a new missile and handed it to Gordon, who loaded it into the launch tube with precision speed and closed the bridge clamp down. He jumped behind the scope, assessed the damage, and looked for more targets.

After feeling secure, he looked up from the gun and shouted out to Bivens, "We got that fucking Muj, jump back in, and let's drive up to assist the grunts."

Bivens jumped back into the driver's seat and proceeded toward the Marine squad.

"Bivens, radio the Battalion Forward HQ and order a medevac."

"Roger that," Bivens replied, grabbing the radio.

Bivens and Gordon pulled up to the Marines.

Grabbing his M-4 rifle, Gordon jumped off the top of the Hummer. He looked back to Bivens. "Stand watch while I attend to these guys."

"Roger that," Bivens replied as he crawled up into the hatch.

Gordon saw before him chunks of building, combat gear, and discarded weapons. Among the debris he also found eleven Marines, some battered and bloody. Some were sitting up against the wall of a building in an alleyway, but others just lay on the ground motionless. He couldn't tell if they were dead or not. Gordon could remember the first time he took fire; the sights of destruction and death were surreal then. Now, they had become commonplace.

Gordon approached the first Marine, knelt down, and asked, "What's your condition?"

"Shot in the gut. This really fucking sucks," the wounded lance corporal muttered.

"Listen. We'll get you out of here soon," Gordon assured him as he lifted up the bandage on the first Marine's stomach.

"Corpsman? How's it looking here?" Gordon shouted over to the Navy corpsman attending to another wounded Marine.

"Much easier without that fucking Hajji shooting at us," the corpsman responded while bandaging another Marine.

"Thanks for blasting that Muj. You were a godsend," a second Marine told Gordon as he walked over.

Gordon looked up at the second Marine and noticed blood running down his leg and all over his left arm.

"How you holding up?" Gordon asked.

"Shit, Sergeant, I've seen better days, but I'll live."

"Good, man. Who's in charge here?"

"Well, it was Corporal Davies, but the sniper took him down first. A shot through the head," the second Marine explained, gesturing toward his squad leader's lifeless body lying in the alleyway.

"What's your unit?" Gordon asked.

"First Squad, third platoon, India Company, three-one, Sergeant, and I'm Lance Corporal Smith. Just call me Smitty."

"I'm Sergeant Van Zandt, Weapons, three-one, nice to meet you, Devil Dog," Gordon said, patting Smitty on his good shoulder.

Gordon proceeded to check on each wounded Marine. The Marines of Third Battalion, First Marines had been fighting their way toward their objective for almost ten days now. The fight was tough, but these men were Marines. Even though they had suffered casualties they were determined. The Thundering Third would reach their objective or die trying. However, dying wasn't an option for any of these Marines; it was their job to ensure it was the enemy who died for his cause.

Gordon came upon a Marine who was severely wounded; he dropped to one knee and examined the man's wounds. Gordon could tell from the markings on his bloody uniform that the man was a private first class; he couldn't be any older than twenty. Gordon couldn't help but make the grim prediction that this young Marine probably wouldn't see his twenty-first birthday. Gordon grabbed the Marine's hand and asked, "How you doing, Marine?"

Without opening his eyes, the young PFC whispered, "I'm cold . . . very cold."

Gordon could see the large pool of blood collecting under the wounded Marine. He bent down to his ear and whispered, "We got the fucker that did this and we'll get you out of here soon, I promise."

A Hummer rumbled to a stop in front of the squad. Two Marines sprung from the rear doors, stretcher in hand and ran to the wounded Marines. One by one, they loaded the most critical into the vehicle.

Just as they began backing away from the scene, a black streak from the south soared toward the Hummer and struck its cab. The explosion knocked Gordon to the ground.

• • •

Gordon opened his eyes. He wasn't sure how long he had been unconscious. The yelling, screaming, and gunfire seemed strangely faint and distant. His eyes burned; all he could see was deep black smoke billowing over him. He tried to get up, but intense pain shot up his back.

"Goddamn it!" he screamed. He took a deep breath and forced himself to sit up. His movements were slow, but he knew he needed to get up and start doing something. He looked around and found Bivens behind the TOW, scanning the area. The burning chassis and four smoldering tires of the ambulance were still there, but not much else. All on board were definitely dead; he could make out two burning corpses in the front seats. The charred bodies were slumped over, flames dancing out of their open mouths.

He saw the squad's remaining Marines taking cover and engaging something down the street. Gordon rose to his feet, balanced himself, and headed toward his Hummer.

"Bivens, if you got a shot, take it!" he commanded.

"Nothing, Sergeant. My visibility is not that great with all the smoke. Wait a minute . . . I see the fucker. Target acquired!"

Gordon looked to the rear of the TOW. He didn't see anyone and yelled back, "Back blast area all secure!"

"Gun up," Bivens hollered, and not a second later he bellowed, "Fire in the hole!"

After its familiar pop and whiz, the missile propelled out of the tube. Almost instantly, it reached its target, a minaret of a mosque. The missile struck the minaret squarely, and it crumbled and fell to the ground.

The Marines cheered, but the engagement wasn't over. They had taken out the insurgent in the minaret but were still taking small arms fire from the mosque.

Gordon and Bivens worked to get the TOW back up while the remnants of First Squad were engaging, slowly eliminating the Iraqi hostiles holed up inside the mosque.

As Gordon and Bivens readied the TOW for more action, the second vehicle in his team pulled up. Gordon looked up to Corporal Nellis, who was manning the "Ma Deuce" .50-caliber machine gun affixed atop the Hummer.

"We have some Muj in the mosque that is located on the left about a block and a half down. Provide support with the fifty to the grunt squad," he instructed Nellis before running back to his vehicle to grab a radio.

He contacted Battalion Forward Headquarters to request additional support and another medical evacuation team.

Gordon was really starting to feel the toll from the blast. After radioing the headquarters, he noticed blood on the handset. He checked his hands, discovering that they, too, were covered in blood. He glanced down, wiped them off on his trousers, and saw more blood drip from his chin onto his boot. He wiped his face with his hand and looked at it. A thick layer of blood again coated his palm. He examined himself in the side mirror of his Hummer, discovering bloody pockmarks all over his face. He had taken shrapnel from the blast. He used his sleeve to wipe off more blood. Knowing there was no more time to waste on his face, he headed back into action.

The .50 caliber, with the help of a few M203 grenades, did its work on the mosque. The area fell silent, save for some gunfire in the distance.

"What do you see, Bivens?" Gordon asked.

"No movement, but you know those motherfuckers."

The mosque stood eerily quiet; no movement or gunfire came from it. Looking up the street, Gordon could see what was once a thriving marketplace on the right and a soccer field on the left. Now, debris littered the street, all the buildings were shot up, and a few small fires burned on the vacant sidewalk. Gordon wanted to ensure the mosque was secure, but the only way to do that was to take it.

"Stay in the gun and provide support if we need it. I'm going to take these Marines up the street and take the mosque," Gordon said to Bivens. He reached into his Hummer and grabbed a few more magazines and as many high-explosive grenades as he could carry.

"Roger that," Bivens confirmed.

"Actually, change that. Turn the gun around and watch our six," Gordon commanded Bivens. He then turned to Nellis and ordered, "Nellis, provide overwatch as we move up the street."

"Roger that," Nellis responded.

Gordon ran up to Smitty. "You and these Marines okay enough to go take that Hajji temple down?"

"Yes, we are!" he said with a smile.

Gordon led the Marines through the commercial buildings on the right side of the street, clearing each one. He navigated up-down, down-up, crossing over from one building to the next from the rooftops. The front glass of the last building had been blown out and the entire structure was riddled with holes. He grabbed one of his high-explosive grenades and tossed it through the open window. The explosion was followed by a scream from inside. While the Marines were stacked up along the side of the building, waiting to go, Gordon stood back, kicked the door, and ran inside. The Marines followed, each peeling off into a separate room.

Gordon had gone in and immediately went left into the remnants of a café. Tables and chairs were scattered, along with empty brass casings.

"Sergeant Van Zandt, Sergeant Van Zandt!" Smitty hollered from a room farther inside the building.

Gordon could hear Marines shouting and someone yelling in Arabic. Upon entering the room he met Smitty, another Marine, and two Iraqi insurgents. One was alive, wearing a white, deeply blood-stained thobe. The second insurgent lay motionless on the floor. The room had pockmarks from shrapnel and bullets, there was debris and trash all over the floor, and three AK-47s were leaning up against a wall. Smitty and the other Marine shouted to the wounded insurgent, demanding he keep still with his hands in the air.

The insurgent shrieked back in Arabic. Gordon couldn't know for sure, but after already spending a tour in Iraq, he had picked up some of the language and he thought it sounded like "Don't shoot."

All the yelling was becoming distracting; Gordon knew he needed to take charge and process the prisoner ASAP.

"Everyone shut up! Smitty, process the guy and check him out for any intel. The rest of us will head upstairs." The Iraqi kept screaming. Gordon turned and yelled, "Shut the fuck up! That's enough! No one is going to shoot you!"

The Iraqi fell silent, as if he understood Gordon's words perfectly. He quietly sobbed as he rocked back and forth, shaking in fear.

Gordon left the room and started slowly upstairs. His progress was interrupted by Smitty's panicked voice: "The other fucker—"

A loud explosion shook the room.

Gordon whipped back around. Chaos had erupted downstairs; the two Marines who had been following Gordon were now yelling, though he couldn't make out their words.

Gordon headed back downstairs, into what was left of the room. The wounded Iraqi was now blown apart. A Marine had also been torn up by the explosion, but he couldn't tell who it was.

Gordon heard a voice from the hallway. "Sergeant!"

Gordon turned and saw Smitty lying on the ground, covered in the blood of four people, including his own.

"What happened?" Gordon asked, kneeling next to him.

"The motherfucker on the ground wasn't dead. He turned over and had a grenade. He blew up Grebbs."

"Dirty motherfuckers!" Gordon cursed.

Just then, another squad of Marines emerged from the entrance of the building. They were followed by an embedded reporter and his camera crew.

A corpsman followed behind and immediately started to look over Smitty.

"Suicide bomber killed a Marine in that room," Gordon informed the new squad of Marines, pointing to the room. "Upstairs is not clear yet. Let's go."

Gordon and the new squad proceeded upstairs and cleared the area. On the roof, they could see the mosque. There was still no apparent movement.

"Let's go take it," Gordon said to the Marines. They rushed back downstairs and out across the street. The reporter and his camera crew followed closely.

Smoke flowed from a few windows on the south side of the mosque. The entire south and east sides were riddled with bullet holes. Gordon and the squad approached the front door and stacked up along the east side. Gordon kicked the door, but it did not break down. He kicked it twice more. Nothing.

"Sergeant, I have a shotgun," a Marine in the squad offered.

"Okay, get up here."

The Marine shot the door handle twice with his 12-gauge shotgun and backed away. Gordon took a step back and kicked the door; this time it flew open. He tossed a high-explosive grenade through the open door and stepped back, leaning against the wall. The grenade tumbled and rolled down the narrow hall and into the large great room of the mosque. The explosion shook the ground. As was standard operating procedure, he and the Marines proceeded into the mosque after the grenade detonated. The reporter and camera crew followed right behind the last Marine.

The first room on the right side was full of munitions and small arms. The room on the left was vacant except for soiled mattresses. The men proceeded down to the great room, where they found a few Iraqis leaning up against a wall. The Marines loudly demanded they stay still. They all appeared alive but wounded.

"Do not fucking move, fucking stay put!" Gordon yelled at them. He quickly assessed the situation in the room.

In the background, Gordon could hear the reporter talking to a rolling camera.

"I'm here inside a mosque in Fallujah with the Marines. The battle has been fierce and the Iraqis have put up a tough resistance. In the end, though, they are no match for the superior firepower of the United States Marines. These wounded Iraqis here have managed to survive the heavy onslaught and are requesting aid—"

"Requesting aid? They haven't said a fucking thing!" a Marine from the squad snapped at the reporter.

Gordon, with his rifle firmly planted in his shoulder, kept scanning over the half-dozen Iraqis. From the corner of his eye, he saw the Iraqi at the end of the line move his arm toward something on the ground.

Without hesitation, Gordon turned and fired off a single shot, hitting the Iraqi in the head. The sound from Gordon's gunshot echoed through the great hall.

"Did you get that? Did you get that?" the reporter asked his cameraman.

"Yes, I did," the cameraman responded, turning the camera on Gordon.

"That Marine there just shot an unarmed and wounded Iraqi," the reporter said to the camera, pointing directly at Gordon.

MARCH 17, 2014

• • •

Other things may change us, but we start and end with the family.

—Anthony Brandt

San Diego, California

"Pink or purple?" Gordon's five-year-old daughter, Haley, asked, showing him two different bottles of nail polish.

"I like purple, but I prefer pink," Gordon said, looking at his daughter as she started to shake the bottles.

"Can I have a snack after we're done, Daddy?" Haley asked, slowly applying polish to Gordon's fingernails.

"Yes, of course, what did you have in mind?" Gordon replied in a soft tone.

"Fruit leather, I want a fruit leather and then I want to watch *Octonauts*!" Haley squealed, looking up. She smiled at Gordon and brushed some hair out of her face.

"Okay, fruit leather it is." Gordon smiled, looking at Haley.

Haley was small for her age, very girly with long, blond curly hair and very fine features. She was definitely all-girl and loved everything princess.

Gordon adored his family and felt blessed to have his two children. Hunter, his seven-year-old son, and Haley were his pride and joy. His entire life revolved around them and Samantha, his wife.

He had met Samantha about a year after his tumultuous departure from the Marines. They were married after a year and had Hunter within the next. He was happy, secure and lived each day in the now. He never thought too much about his time in the Corps and when he did, it seemed like it was a different life entirely; almost as though it wasn't even his life, but someone else's.

Though his time in combat didn't come to mind often, his everyday life was still influenced by his two tours in Iraq. The experience had shifted his priorities and shaped his perspective. He was no longer the idealist who believed in helping all. Instead, he had become more pragmatic and only wished to take care of his family. He was done sacrificing for those he considered "clueless."

"After you're done in the salon, meet me outside," Samantha said to Gordon as she passed the doorway on her way to the kitchen.

Gordon looked over his shoulder. "Okay, but are you sure you don't need a mani-pedi too?"

Samantha shouted from the kitchen down the hall, "Maybe later. Haley needs a little quiet time, and you and I need some adult time."

"Adult time? Like 'adult time' or adult time where you have to tell me something and have my full attention?" Gordon yelled back while watching Haley finish applying nail polish to his last finger.

"You'll find out later," she hollered from the kitchen.

"You're such a tease," Gordon shot back.

"What is a tease, Daddy?" asked Haley.

"Well, honey, it's when—"

"Haley, it's when we play jokes on one another," Samantha interrupted, now standing in the doorway of the playroom.

Gordon whipped his head back over his shoulder. "Gosh, you move so quickly and stealth-like." He winked and noticed a semi-irritated look on her face.

Samantha stood there, looking at her husband. She loved him so much. She felt so blessed to have such a good man and good father to their two children. She couldn't think of too many men who would subject themselves to having their nails painted pink. She was so proud that he actually took an interest in his children and loved how important they were to him.

She continued admiring Gordon. He fit her perfect profile of a man. He was tall and ruggedly handsome with a chiseled jaw, light eyes, and broad shoulders. Haley looked so small next to him, dwarfed by his strong, muscular build. She knew from the first time they met that he would always take care of her. She felt safe with him.

"Done, Daddy! Now can I have my snack?" Haley asked sweetly as she closed the nail polish bottle.

"Of course," Gordon answered. He started to blow his fingers dry but paused when he noticed Samantha still staring. He looked up to her and asked jokingly, "Does the pink bring out the blue in my eyes?"

Haley jumped up and ran out of the room, down the hall toward the kitchen. Gordon jumped up and followed, of course mindful of the wet nail polish he had on his fingers.

"So what's up?" he asked Samantha before leaning forward to kiss her on the lips.

"Let me set up Haley for quiet time and I'll meet you outside on the patio in, say, five minutes," Samantha responded, then kissed him back.

• • •

Gordon sat on the patio and waited for Samantha to come out and join him. He leaned back, kicked his legs up onto the outside coffee table, and let the mid-afternoon sun warm his face. While he had a love/hate relationship with Southern California in general, he definitely loved the weather. He preferred smaller towns, and San Diego definitely wasn't a small town anymore. All in all, though, life was good. He enjoyed a comfortable lifestyle, a nice group of friends, and the family he had around him. The one family member he wished was around more often was his little brother, Sebastian, who had joined the Marines four years after Gordon had left the Corps. His brother originally followed in his footsteps and became a TOW gunner, but it proved a bit boring for him. Being a man of adventure, he would now try out to be a Scout Sniper.

Gordon's slumber in the sun was interrupted when he heard Samantha come outside. He opened his eyes to find her hovering over him.

"Are you enjoying yourself?" she asked, looking down on him, her arms crossed.

"Why, yes, I am, thank you for asking," Gordon replied with a grin on his face.

"When were you going to tell that your brother was coming down tonight for dinner?" Samantha asked, taking a seat across from him. "You know I need notice so I can get the house ready."

"I thought I told you. I'm sorry," Gordon said, sitting up more in his chair. "It is okay, right? We don't have anything else going on, do we?"

Gordon looked at Samantha sitting across from him. He had fallen for her instantly when they met. He loved everything about her, from her small frame and long, wavy blond hair to her light green eyes and full lips. For him she fit the portrait of the perfect woman.

"No, we're fine; I just need to know next time. Had I not checked the voice mail, I never would have known. Just promise me you'll give me some notice next time."

Gordon stood up and walked over to Samantha. He softened his voice. "Absolutely, honey."

He bent down and gave her a big hug and kiss and whispered into her ear, "How about I apologize more upstairs?"

Samantha, a bit stubborn, pulled back and said, "You know I have things to do."

"All things can wait," Gordon said, even softer, knowing his wife too well. He followed up with a proposal. "How about I help you with your stuff later if you help me with my stuff now?"

Samantha raised her eyebrows and smiled mischievously. "Deal!"

She grabbed his hand and they both ran upstairs.

• • •

"Someone's at the door!" Hunter yelled excitedly.

"Go ahead and get it; it should be your uncle Sebastian!" Samantha said from the kitchen. She was too busy preparing a salad to go to the door.

"Gordon, I think your brother is here!" she called out to Gordon, who was in his office working. Samantha loved Sebastian but didn't always like his visits. It wasn't Sebastian's fault, but just having him around made Gordon act differently. She knew that Gordon would be very distant in the days after Sebastian's departure.

"Uncle Sebastian!" Hunter screamed as he opened the door. Hunter and Haley loved his visits; they always had the best time when he was around.

"Uncle Sebastian, Uncle Sebastian!" Haley screamed as she bounded down the stairs.

Sebastian stepped inside and picked up Hunter. Haley made it down the stairs and grabbed his leg.

"Hey, guys, how are my favorite niece and nephew?" Sebastian asked. He squatted down and picked up Haley with his other arm. He walked into the kitchen where Samantha was still rushing around, preparing dinner.

Sebastian was tall and, as they say in the Corps, "lean and mean." He and Gordon looked very similar; there was no mistaking they were brothers. The major differences came from their seven-year age gap: Gordon was slowly getting a widow's peak and a bit of gray on his sides. Sebastian had a full head of thick brown hair and no gray. While he was a hard charger, he didn't go for the flat tops or high and tight haircuts; he liked his hair and made sure it was just regulation or longer if he could get away with it. Sebastian always had a smile on his face and took life more lightly, as opposed to his brother, who had a more serious and stoic persona.

Sebastian wanted to have kids himself one day, but for now he enjoyed the life of a single Marine. He still had the adventure bug, and with the Corps being tough enough without a family, he thought it not fair to start one. So for now, Sebastian took what family life he could get with his brother's family.

"Hi, Samantha!"

"Hi, Sebastian, how are you?" Samantha replied, looking flustered trying to get everything finished. Samantha was a perfectionist and needed everything to look perfect for guests. She stopped for a few seconds to give Sebastian a quick hug and peck on the cheek, though. "Gordon is out in his office finishing up a project. Go ahead on back."

"I think I'll do that"—he looked down to the kids in his arms and raised his eyebrows—"but first I have a couple of monkeys on me that need to see what Uncle Sebastian got them."

Both kids squealed, “Presents!”

He let the kids down and squatted so he could look at them eye to eye. “Go out front and you’ll see two bags on the table out there. The green one is Hunter’s and the pink one is—”

“Mine!” Haley cried out, already running to the front door. Hunter did not hesitate either and took off.

Sebastian stood up and approached the kitchen island. “Wow, something smells great! I’m hungry.”

“I hope you are, we have tons of food and Gordon ran out a bit ago and picked up your favorite tri-tip.”

“You guys are great, thank you,” Sebastian said, looking at Samantha, happy his brother had found such a wonderful wife. It made him smile when he thought about how much his brother deserved this life, especially after everything he’d been through.

Samantha had the TV on in the background as she cooked; it was really the only time she could catch up with the news. Her two kids were a full-time job, demanding more than a fair share of her day.

On the TV, Bill O’Reilly was interviewing the Republican speaker of the house, Brad Conner, and Democratic California representative Shelly Gomez.

“The president is clearly failing in ensuring our country is safe. Allowing Iran to manufacture nuclear fuel and only slapping their hands will not keep us safe. The Iranian regime cannot be trusted. We need—”

“—need what, Mr. Speaker, another war?” Representative Gomez shot back.

“We must keep everything on the table and we need to project strength, not telegraph the fact that he will not use force.”

“Speaker Conner, you are a proponent of pre-emptive strikes. Do

you favor striking Iranian nuclear facilities if we had solid intelligence that they were making nuclear weapons or selling weapons-grade fuel to terrorists?" asked O'Reilly.

"Bill, Iran is a terrorist state. To answer your question more directly, yes, I would."

"Ms. Gomez, what say you?" O'Reilly asked quickly.

"Mr. O'Reilly, we must always keep every option on the table. However, we cannot sidestep diplomacy and we must ensure that we have exhausted all attempts at a peaceful solution."

"So you would favor a military strike?" O'Reilly asked her directly.

"What I am saying is that we should never pigeonhole ourselves into one solution."

"It's a simple yes-or-no question, Ms. Gomez," O'Reilly shot back.

"Mr. O'Reilly, diplomacy is more dynamic than a simple yes-or-no answer," Gomez challenged, looking agitated.

"I understand that, Ms. Gomez. Let me make the question clearer. If you exhausted all diplomacy and the intelligence stated that Iran would develop a weapon or was prepared to sell weapons-grade fuel to a known terrorist group that would use it as a dirty weapon, or even worse, they were to sell a nuclear weapon, would you support a military strike?"

"I think you have to define 'exhausted all diplomacy,'" Rep. Gomez answered.

"Really? Really? Ms. Gomez, you can't answer that question?" O'Reilly pushed further, looking a bit disgusted.

Speaker Conner interrupted. "I can answer the question, Bill. Yes, I would strike them and strike them hard. Bill, Ms. Gomez is aware of the threats, the real threats that our country faces. She is in the briefings, she knows. But what do she and her colleagues do? They vote every time to weaken our defenses or to not fund projects that can harden our defenses."

"Mr. Speaker, what is one threat that faces our nation that most Americans are not aware of?" O'Reilly asked, looking to wrap things up.

"What I fear the most is a rogue nation or terrorist group attacking us with an EMP or an electromagnetic-type weapon. We are not equipped for this; it would destroy our entire power grid. The Iranians, for one, have stated their awareness of this weakness and want to exploit it."

"There you go again, Mr. Speaker, spreading fear," Gomez disdainfully accused.

"Fear? Ms. Gomez, you have seen the reports regarding this specific threat. Even some in your own party realize the threat and have courageously put forth bills that never made it out of committee. I am now pressing Congressman Markey to put forth the same bill again. I will work hard to ensure the bill at least gets the up or down vote it deserves," Conner spat back, obviously irritated.

"Ms. Gomez, you have the last word. Please respond to what the Speaker just said."

"Mr. O'Reilly, this administration is doing an incredible job at defending our nation. After almost ten years of war, it is time to take care of the homeland by addressing domestic issues. We have everything under control as far as defense. We need to get issues like education and health care in the forefront."

"Well, I have to leave it there. Ms. Gomez, Speaker Conner, I appreciate your time. Next on the lineup we have retired General McCasey here to talk about the recent terrorist attacks in Paris and London."

Samantha grabbed the remote and turned the TV off. "Sorry, it's the only time I can listen to what's happening. It's scary out there right now with so many attacks happening overseas; I just feel it's only a matter of time before it comes here."

"Yeah, maybe so; I wouldn't focus too much on that; I think we're pretty safe here. As far as the talking heads on TV, I just don't listen at all. Sounds like a bunch of hot air to me," Sebastian said.

"Can I grab you a beer?"

"I'll get it, I know where they are. Can I grab you one too?" Sebastian asked, opening the fridge.

"Why, yes, thank you."

"Get one for me too!" Sebastian recognized his brother's voice. Gordon was grinning from ear to ear as he entered the kitchen; he was always thrilled to see his little brother.

"Gordo!" Sebastian boomed, setting the beers down on the counter. He approached his brother and gave him a big hug. "Great to see you, thanks for the invite."

"Of course, little brother. We just wish we saw you more."

Gordon turned to Samantha and asked, "Where are the kids?"

"Outside, playing with the toys Sebastian brought for them."

"Tell me what's up with you?" Gordon asked Sebastian after taking a swig from his beer.

"I guess I need to ask you that," Sebastian replied, pointing at Gordon's fingers. "You know, if it was the 'Don't Ask, Don't Tell' policy that made you leave the Corps, you're good to go now."

"What?" Gordon asked, puzzled for a second by Sebastian's comments before realizing he still had on the pink fingernail polish from earlier.

"Kids," he explained, shrugging off the comment.

Gordon walked over to the fridge to get the meat for the grill. "Well, Mr. Smartass, how about helping me with this outside?"

"Roger that."

• • •

"Dinner was great. I'm stuffed," Sebastian said, leaning back against his chair.

"I'm glad you liked it. Why don't I clean up and you boys go enjoy a beer and chat?" Samantha said while stacking plates.

"Are you sure?" Gordon asked, looking up at her from his chair. Gordon respected Samantha and looked at his relationship and the responsibility of parenting as a true partnership. He never wanted to take her for granted.

"Yes, I'm sure. You boys go be boys. Drink some beers, talk shit, and solve the world's problems. I can take the kids upstairs to watch a movie." She gave him a kiss on the cheek. "I love you, baby."

"I love you too, sweetie."

Sebastian watched their interaction and smiled. When it was time for him to settle down, he wanted exactly what his brother had. Of course that wouldn't happen for a while since he had another year on his enlistment and life was just too much fun.

Samantha grabbed the remaining dishes and walked back into the kitchen. The brothers could hear her talking to the kids. After a minute of squealing and cheers from the kids, the house fell silent.

"Let's grab those beers and go to the back patio." Gordon stood up and Sebastian followed him to the fridge before heading outside.

"Here." Gordon handed his brother a cold beer and sat down.

"Thanks. So what you been doing lately?"

"You know, the usual. Oh, I have been getting to the range more lately."

"Good, any new acquisitions?"

"Yeah, when I was in Idaho I stopped by a gun show and finally bought an M-4 and another Sig."

"You were always more of the collector than me, you and Dad were alike that way," Sebastian commented, then took a drink.

"So, tell me more about Scout Snipers," Gordon asked, kicking his feet up on the table.

"I really want it; I get to try out in a couple of weeks. I've been training, so we'll see."

"As long as you're clear," Gordon said, looking down at his beer in his hand.

"What does that mean?" Sebastian asked, raising an eyebrow.

"Just that."

"Listen, don't project your anger with the Corps onto me," Sebastian said with a bit of attitude.

"I'm not projecting anything. I just want to make sure you're making the right decision. I don't think you made the right decision by signing up for six years initially. All you had to do was sign up for four, and if you liked it, go for another enlistment," Gordon admonished.

Sebastian stared his brother down, frustrated. He loved him so much but hated when Gordon acted like a parent. He figured that after two combat tours, one in Iraq and another in Afghanistan, his brother would finally treat him with respect. He knew it stemmed from two things, one being that Gordon and Sebastian's parents had died a few years back. Gordon took it upon himself to fill that role for his much younger brother. The other issue was Gordon's anger toward the Marine Corps. He felt betrayed after the incident in Fallujah ten years before.

"Gordo, I know what I'm doing. Scout Snipers are a tight unit, professional and motivated. I wish you would stop second-guessing me. I know you asked me not to join the Marines, but I did. Then you were against me signing for six, but I did that too. I needed to guarantee the job I wanted. You were against me being a TOW gunner and now you're second-guessing this. I'm a man; I know what I'm doing." Sebastian sat straight up in his chair and looked his brother directly in the eye.

"Okay. Okay," Gordon replied, waving his left hand in the air and rolling his eyes.

"I'm gonna make a head call." Sebastian put down his beer and walked inside.

Gordon rested his head on the back of the chair and looked up at the stars. He thought back to that day in the mosque in Fallujah. In the years immediately after, he'd mentally replayed the incident over and over again. Every time, though, he'd concluded that he'd do it all the same. It frustrated him to no end, the ridicule and hatred he received. The investigation from the NCIS team proved he made the correct decision, but those stories are not interesting and always land on page D9 of the newspaper. Stories of Marines shooting "unarmed and wounded" prisoners, on the other hand, make for headline news and political fodder. He hated the politics most. The entire situation changed how he looked at his country and countrymen. When his time for reenlistment came around, he opted to get out. He could no longer risk his life to defend a country wherein half the citizens either hated him or, only slightly better, thought nothing of him.

Gordon had joined the Marine Corps right after the attacks on September 11. He dropped out of George Mason University in his third year because he felt it was his generation's calling to serve, walking away from a full academic scholarship. At the time it felt like the right thing to do, but now things had changed.

He often questioned why he had sacrificed so much. For what? So people could hate him? So people could take their freedom for granted? For all the lazy asses and all the dumb shits who want to sit around and do nothing? Fuck them, he thought. Never again would he sacrifice himself for anyone but his family and friends. Now his brother was putting himself in harm's way so those same worthless people could sit back and enjoy their freedoms and abuse their rights.

Sebastian knew how he felt, but he was never the idealist Gordon once was. Sebastian loved his country, sure, but he was in it more for the adventure. He loved the action. Sebastian felt lucky that people would pay him to blow things up. He never thought much of politics, thinking it was a waste of time. Gordon would love to share his brother's outlook, but how could the country survive if all anyone did was look out for themselves? Ideologically, he was conflicted. Practically, though, until his anger went away, he would not put anyone else before himself or his family.

Sebastian's return interrupted Gordon's train of thought.

"Here, bro," Sebastian said, handing over another beer.

Sitting up and grabbing the beer, Gordon said, "Thank you. Look, I'm sorry if I seemed like I doubted you. I do respect you and I don't look at you any other way than as a man. You know how I feel about the Corps and everything else. I really don't want to get into it again. I just don't want anything to happen to you."

"I know, I know. Listen, I'll be in good hands. By the way, I forgot to tell you, we just got a new commanding officer," Sebastian said after drinking some beer. He had a big smile on his face.

"Who is that?" Gordon was interested.

"Barone!"

"Major Barone?" Gordon's eyes widened.

"Yeah, but he's a light bird now."

Again, Gordon's memory flashed back to the time after the Fallujah incident. Major Barone was one of his staunchest defenders. He stood by him while the other brass were ready to offer him up to appease the politicians and media. The press had a field day with the story and was bloodthirsty in its reporting on the shooting. For all intents and purposes, he had been publicly convicted before any investigation had even been completed.

Comforted by the memory of a loyal friend, Gordon said, "That is great news. He's a great man. You are definitely in good hands with him."

"I knew you'd be happy to hear his name again. I haven't had the chance to actually meet him, but I hear he loves his snipers. I'm pumped. Now, all I have to do is make the cut."

"It really does make me happy that he's in charge and will be taking you guys back into the mix on your next tour," Gordon said. He felt relieved that his brother would be in such trustworthy company.

Gordon was very happy to have that bit of news. Regardless of his brother's confidence, he would always worry and look after him. Sebastian was his little brother and, as the oldest, he felt a bit responsible for him even if it meant being accused of acting like a parent. Gordon was also concerned because of the increase in terrorist attacks against military installations around the globe. Over the past few months, there had also been an uptick in attacks against civilian targets in Europe. He and Samantha often talked about how strange it was that the terrorists had never attempted those attacks in the United States. With the porous border to the south, he just felt that the U.S. would not always be so lucky. He knew that eventually the terrorists would come back and the next large attack could be so damaging it could bring the country to its knees.

Gordon put aside the thoughts about the harshness of the world and refocused on having a good time with his brother. After a few more beers, some laughs, and a brief trip down memory lane, the brothers said good-bye to each other.

After walking him to the front door, Gordon gave Sebastian a hug and said, "If you ever need anything, you call me; don't hesitate. We're here for you."

"I will, Gordo. I love you, brother." Sebastian always felt bad when he had to leave. He hated good-byes.

As Sebastian walked down the sidewalk Gordon yelled after him, "Stay frosty, Marine."

DECEMBER 4, 2014

• • •

Fear is pain arising from the anticipation of evil.

—Aristotle

San Diego, California

"This is a CNN News Alert. A series of explosions have gone off in downtown Seattle inside of CenturyLink Field, home of the Seattle Seahawks. The number of casualties is unknown at this moment. We go to our local affiliate, who is reporting from a helicopter above the stadium."

"Oh my God," Samantha gasped. She placed her hand over her mouth in shock.

"Mommy, where's Hunter?" Haley asked.

"He's upstairs playing in his room; now please be quiet for a moment," Samantha said, not looking at Haley.

"Mommy, Mommy, I want juice," Haley said, tugging on Samantha's pants.

"One sec, Haley," Samantha replied to her daughter.

"Mommy!" Haley yelled, ignoring her mother's dismissal.

"Haley, please, honey, one second!" Samantha raised her voice. "Mommy is watching something very, very important."

Samantha could not take her eyes off the scenes coming from the television. Columns of smoke were pouring out of the stadium. Sadly, these images were becoming common now.

Beginning on September 6, there had been ongoing attacks across the country. From car bombs and suicide bombers to gunmen walking into malls, violence had become almost a daily occurrence. From Miami to, now, Seattle, it seemed as though no place in the United States was safe. The president tried to calm the nation the night before with a nationally televised address. He promised he was using every resource available to stop any future attacks.

Unfortunately, though, these attacks were happening so frequently across the country that many resources were being stretched thin. The various intelligence agencies had been successful in stopping a few incidents, but due to their sporadic nature, it was impossible to stop them all. Every American felt on edge. Many had completely stopped frequenting crowded public places, but some people still braved it. Samantha and Gordon were among those who avoided going out at all. When they did venture out, it was only to get what they couldn't order online, and they never took the kids with them. The tension was very high and the economy was suffering from the repeated attacks.

"Gordon!" Samantha yelled.

A minute went by without a response from Gordon. She yelled again even louder than before. "Gordon, come here!"

"What's up?" he yelled back from his office at the end of the house. Gordon was fortunate; he worked from home for a Web design company. After he left the Marine Corps, he didn't know what to do; he didn't want go back to college but needed a trade. He had been working toward a degree in computer science before he joined the Corps and was very computer savvy. While in college, he designed sites to help pay the bills, so it seemed natural to gravitate to something familiar.

He enjoyed the work, but enjoyed the freedom that came with working from home more. It gave him more time to spend with his family. Now, with all of the attacks, he was especially glad he wasn't going back and forth to some cubicle somewhere, becoming a possible target.

Gordon walked into the living room. Samantha was sitting on the edge of the couch, leaning forward with her elbows on her knees and her hands covering her mouth.

He recognized the desperate look on her face and glanced toward the TV for confirmation. "Shit, really? Another attack? Where?"

"Seattle." She finally lowered her hands from her face.

"What happened?" he asked.

"Gordon, be quiet, I can't hear." Samantha sounded very upset and looked stressed.

He walked over to her and sat next to her on the couch. He grabbed her hand. She turned to him; she had tears welling up in her eyes. Her voice cracked. "I'm scared, Gordon. These attacks just won't stop. We knew they'd come here, but they are relentless!"

"I know you're scared, honey. I'll do whatever I can to keep us safe, trust me. I'll do whatever is necessary to protect you all," Gordon said, squeezing her hand and looking into her eyes. With his free hand, he wiped away the tears that started to flow down her cheeks.

"I know, but promise me again that you'll do whatever is necessary to take care of the kids."

"I promise you." He placed his hand on the back of her head and pulled her gently toward him. He leaned in and kissed her. He could taste the saltiness of her tears on her lips.

"Daddy, why is Mommy crying?" Haley asked, leaning up against Gordon.

"Come here, honey." Gordon reached out and grabbed Haley and brought her closer. He hugged them both and said, "We are going to be okay, I promise you. No matter what happens, this family will be okay."

On the TV, the reporter on the scene in the helicopter finally started to provide some preliminary information.

"What appears to have happened is three different suicide bombers have blown themselves up. We are being told that the first explosion happened at a security checkpoint. Apparently, the security staff had noticed something odd about someone in line and when they approached him, he blew himself up. The other two explosions happened within a minute of the first. As of right now, we are getting conflicting numbers of casualties, ranging from fifty to maybe one hundred and fifty. It is just chaos here right now."

Gordon squeezed Samantha and Haley, his eyes glued to the news report. As he watched smoke pour out of the stadium, he felt such anger. While he had prepared as best he could, there was only so much he could do. The attacks had been going on for months.

He hadn't told Samantha yet, but recently Gordon had been considering taking his family to go stay in their cabin in McCall, Idaho. Feeling vulnerable, he thought McCall's tiny population of about twenty-five hundred people wouldn't put it on a terrorist target list.

After the first week of attacks, Gordon stopped letting Hunter go to school, or anywhere else for that matter. He tried his best to explain what was going on without scaring them, but they were only kids and could only understand so much.

Gordon did feel secure in their North County San Diego neighborhood. They lived in a pristine gated community, but he felt like his family was imprisoned in their own home.

He had kept in close touch with Samantha's parents through all the attacks. Samantha's parents lived in Kansas City, Missouri. Her father was ill and needed a lot of medical attention, so there was no convincing them to go to Idaho. He was concerned for them, but his main priority was Samantha, Hunter, and Haley.

Musa Qala, Helmand Province, Afghanistan

Sebastian was positioned in an observation post at the south edge of Forward Operating Base Musa Qala. He had just heard about the new bombing in Seattle. In some ways, things seemed safer in the Helmand Province than in the big cities back at home. He knew Gordon and the family were okay, but many of his fellow Marines were very anxious about their own families and wished they could be back home keeping them safe.

Sebastian was very tired and couldn't wait for his watch to be over so he could catch some sleep. His sniper team had been busy since their first day in country back in late August. Most snipers, including him, had dozens of confirmed kills each. While Musa Qala was not as violent now as in the past, it still provided a target-rich environment for the snipers.

Sebastian loved his new life as a Scout Sniper with Second Battalion Fourth Marines; it was everything he wanted it to be. They were under the command of Lieutenant Colonel Barone, who was a Marines' Marine—his reputation preceded him. He took care of his Marines and always backed up his snipers.

Sebastian remembered back to an incident that occurred when they had just arrived in country. They had conducted a reconnaissance of the valley looking for signs of Taliban. During the briefing to the Regimental Combat Team's S-2, his team's intelligence was challenged by an administration officer. Barone jumped to his team's defense, telling the officer that his snipers were the best in the field and that if Corporal Van Zandt said they had gathered intel on the Taliban's movements, then goddamn it, it was correct. Sebastian would never forget Barone telling that major that he, a corporal, knew more about what was happening in the field than the major did. That moment would forever be etched into Sebastian's brain. That incident and others like it gave Barone the unwavering loyalty of the Marines in his battalion; they all were willing to do whatever he needed.

Washington, District of Columbia

Upon exiting the Rayburn House Office Building, Speaker Brad Conner ran right into several reporters who were braving the cold December day, waiting for a chance to ask him questions. He was in a hurry, but he stopped to answer what queries he could in reference to the latest bombing in Seattle. Conner was not of an impressive physical stature. He was neither tall nor well built, but he had a presence about him. When he walked into a room, people would take notice. His hair was short, black, and receding, a style fit for a conservative politician. In college, some twenty-eight years before, he had been more active and played baseball, but the days of working out gave way to many hours behind a desk. He would joke that he gave up his six-pack for a pony keg.

"Mr. Speaker, Mr. Speaker, do you have the votes in the House to pass the Vigilance Act?"

"I have been staying in close contact with the whip and we are talking with each one of our members as I know the minority leader is doing the same. I, as well as many other colleagues, have some concern about the act but realize the pressing issues we have before us, magnified by the most recent attack in Seattle," Conner explained calmly but forcefully as he put leather gloves on his hands.

"Mr. Speaker, we understand the president has requested to hold a joint session of Congress so he can speak to you and the nation concerning these attacks. Is that going to happen?" a reporter from the back of the group yelled, waving his hand in the air.

"I have received the formal request from the president and we will honor his request tomorrow evening."

"Will you be present for this joint session in light of the personal situation involving your son back in Oklahoma City?" another reporter asked, pointing his microphone toward Conner.

"As you all are aware, my son was involved in a car accident in Oklahoma City just this morning. His mother is there with him now and I am leaving to go be by his side. I am planning on being back in Washington tomorrow evening for the president's address. So I hope you can understand that will have to be the last question. Thank you all very much," Conner finished. Quickly he pushed his way through the group of reporters and down the stairs toward his limousine.

Conner stepped into the car and closed the door. His top aide was inside already and said, "Your flight is on schedule, sir, and the latest from your wife is that your son has stabilized."

Dylan McLatchy was not only Conner's top aide but in many ways was Conner's right-hand man. Dylan had started as a page when he was in college and now had moved through the ranks to become a trusted aide for the third-most powerful man in the world. Dylan was small, only topping out at five feet five inches. He prided himself on his looks and tended to be as trendy as one could while also maintaining a conservative enough look. The black-framed glasses he wore looked large on his face. His jet-black hair was always kept cropped and neat. Conner liked Dylan a lot because he was always available. No matter what time he called, Dylan was always ready to help.

"Thank you, Dylan. Let's hurry please," Conner said loudly enough for the driver to hear.

The limo sped off down C Street toward the airport.

DECEMBER 5, 2014

• • •

Hell is empty and all the devils are here.

—William Shakespeare, *The Tempest*

San Diego, California

It was another beautiful December morning in Southern California; unlike most of the country, it was a nice sixty-one degrees with blue sunny skies. Perfect for Gordon's morning run. He cherished his daily run; even just twenty minutes to clear his mind while the rest of the neighborhood headed to work was enough to make him content. As he ran, he thought about his conversation with Samantha the night before. He told her he was taking the family to Idaho so they could safely wait out the nonstop attacks and be in an environment where they could relax. She completely agreed and was already packing for the trip. Even though it meant leaving behind San Diego's perfect weather for feet of snow, he couldn't wait to get there. He and Samantha only needed a couple of days to plan and pack, so they could be there by the weekend. They had told the kids this morning about the trip, using the prospect of a white Christmas as their excuse. The kids were very excited; they loved Idaho and looked forward to playing in the snow.

Gordon stopped at a busy intersection, pressed the crosswalk button, and waited patiently for the red "Do Not Walk" signal to change. He took the time to stretch; he bent over at the waist and reached for the ground, stretching his lower back and hamstrings. He straightened up and checked the sign; it was black, no red or white. Suddenly, two cars collided in front of him. Before he could shake the shock of the first crash, another car slammed into the first two. He watched as even more cars stacked up on one another. It had been a while since he had seen an accident. Gordon stood looking at the wrecked cars, then slowly noticed that no cars were moving on the usually heavily trafficked road. He then noticed that all of the lights in the area were blacked out, not flashing red as they normally would during an outage. He looked left up the road and saw all the cars stopped or slowly coasting. Looking right, he saw the same thing. He raised his eyebrows with curiosity.

"What is going on?" a clearly disgruntled driver said, slamming his car door and looking around.

"My car just died and now it won't start," another driver said to the first.

Gordon was just standing there taking in everything around him.

"What's that?" someone yelled loudly pointing to something in the eastern sky.

Gordon followed the man's finger and saw a source of light in the sky, smaller than the sun and not quite as bright.

As he stared at the glowing orb he could hear others commenting on it, while the people involved in accidents yelled. He heard people complaining that their mobile phones and cars were not working.

"Oh my God, it's going to crash!" a woman screamed from down the street, standing outside her car.

Gordon turned to the woman and followed her sight line back up to the sky. A plane was free-falling. It was far away, but close enough for him to see that it was a commercial airliner. The plane looked like a toy as it fell from the sky. The whole scenario felt surreal. He just stood there, frozen, watching the plane fall until it crashed into a distant hillside and exploded into a fiery red ball of carnage.

Screams of horror followed the crash of the plane. Many of those around Gordon were, like him, frozen by what they had just witnessed. Finally breaking his temporary paralysis, Gordon started to run for home. He knew he needed to get back as quickly as he could.

As he ran toward his house, Gordon's military training kicked in. He started to assess the situation and bits of information began falling into place. His heart was pounding. Everywhere he looked, people were standing outside their cars holding their mobile phones in the air. It all seemed so unreal, but he had a feeling he knew what might be happening.

It was obvious his hometown had been attacked, but he didn't know if something worse was coming. As he crested a hill that had a commanding view of the area for miles, he saw smoke in the distance and, in one area, what appeared to be large flames licking the sky. The fire and smoke were miles away, but something dynamic had happened. When he came to the intersection that led into his community, he saw those streets were littered with stalled cars, broken glass, and other debris from numerous car accidents. The lights were not working and the guards at the gate were just standing there talking to the owners of the stalled cars. Nobody was moving.

As Gordon ran past them he overheard a guard state plainly,

"Ma'am, we have experienced some power and phone outages; I am sure it will be back on shortly, so let's not panic."

Reaching the pedestrian gate, he unlocked it with his hard key and kept running. Finally making it to his street, he saw neighbors outside staring at the mobile phones in their hands, pressing buttons, apparently attempting to power the devices back on.

Without slowing his pace, Gordon shouted, "Get back inside now! Get inside and take cover!"

No one listened to him; they all stayed put looking confused and bewildered.

After many hard miles, he made it to his front door. He was breathing hard, shaking, and trying to focus as he grabbed his keys. His hands and fingers were slippery from sweat, making it hard to steady the right key.

"C'mon, damn it!"

As Gordon still fumbled his keys, the door opened. Samantha stood in the doorway, with Haley on her hip and Hunter hugging her leg.

"What's going on? Nothing is working!" Samantha exclaimed urgently. She was clearly nervous; the past months of attacks had already put her on edge. This did not help.

Gordon walked in and told her sternly "Follow me" as he passed her at the threshold.

She did so without hesitation, but kept asking, "What is going on?"

"Samantha, I don't have time to explain everything. Please just listen to me." Gordon guided them to the built-in desks in the kitchen area. "I need you all to get under there now and stay until I get back."

"Gordon, why? Please talk to me." Samantha's eyes were wide

open; her fear was visible in her expression. Hunter and Haley could pick up on the tension and urgency. Haley started to cry.

Samantha kissed her and said softly, "Everything will be okay, honey, I promise."

"I'm scared, Mommy," Haley said, burying her head in Samantha's shoulder, arms wrapped around her neck.

"Me too, Mommy," Hunter said soon after. He wasn't crying, but Gordon could see the fear on his son's face.

"Please, Sam, just listen to me and trust me. Get under there and wait for me."

"Where are you going? Why are you leaving?" Samantha asked, refusing to let go of his arm.

"Honey, I'm not leaving the house, I'm just prepping some things. I'll only be a few minutes."

"Please, Gordon, don't leave us," Samantha pleaded, desperately tightening her grip on his forearm.

Gordon knelt down and hugged his whole family. "I promise you, I'll be right back." He kissed Samantha, jumped to his feet, and walked briskly into the kitchen.

Gordon plugged the sink and turned on the water, then ran into the closest bedroom and did the same to the sink and tub in there. He proceeded to run throughout the house, closing every drain and turning on every faucet. Coming back into the kitchen, he saw his family tucked neatly under the desk all huddled together. They peered out at him; their distress evident.

"Almost done, guys," Gordon yelled a little too cheerfully attempting to calm them as he walked into the pantry.

Gordon grabbed every open jug, container, and glass in the kitchen and filled them all with water. His hands were shaking. He was scared, too, but he knew he had to get this done. He needed to save as much water as possible. His hunch about the attack would mean that water would soon be a rare commodity.

Gordon thought of the many times he had been tempted to buy a five-hundred-gallon holding tank of potable water, but never actually did. Before any guilt could set in, he forced those thoughts out of his mind. Times like this were not about looking backward with regret but looking toward securing the present and winning the future. After filling all the containers he went back to his family.

As he sat on the floor next to them, Samantha grabbed his hand and asked again, trying to seem calm, "Gordon, what's going on?"

As badly as Gordon wanted to be reassuring, to soothe his wife's anxiety, he felt a responsibility to be honest. "There appears to have been some sort of attack that has disabled the power and all electrical devices. These sorts of attacks usually precede a nuclear attack."

She squeezed his hand hard and they met each other's eyes. "Is this it? Is this how it ends?"

"I don't—" Gordon paused. "Sam, I seriously don't know. All I know is what I remember reading and some training I went through years ago. I love you. And if this is it, then at least we're here together."

Hugging each other, they said nothing else, and listened to the surrounding silence.

An hour went by and nothing else had happened that they could tell. Gordon assumed the other shoe wasn't dropping.

"I think it might be okay," he said as they crawled out from underneath the desk and stretched.

"Now what?" Samantha asked.

"Mommy, I have to go potty," Haley said, grabbing herself.

"Okay, honey, go ahead," Samantha told Haley, patting her on the head.

"Hey, guys, this time will be okay, but we will have to look at not using the toilets anymore," Gordon said.

"Why?" Samantha asked, looking bewildered by Gordon's statement.

"Because if what I think has happened, the waste treatment systems will soon start to back up and not work properly. Plus, we should preserve as much water as possible."

"So what do you suggest?" Samantha asked, now sounding irritated.

"Hey, Sam, I don't like it any more than you do, but we might have to create a latrine outside."

"What? You want us to start going to the bathroom outside?"

"Until we can figure out what's going on, yes," Gordon answered bluntly.

"Gordon, that's ridiculous!" Samantha snapped back.

Gordon walked over to the sink and grabbed one of the many glasses of water and drank it. He set the empty glass down and said, "Samantha, enough; something bad has happened, you either adapt to the situation or you die."

"Die?"

"Daddy, are we going to die?" Hunter asked, still standing next to the desk.

"No, honey. I didn't mean to say that to Mommy," Gordon replied softly, changing his tone completely. Gordon walked over to Hunter and knelt down. "Can you take your sister and go play in the playroom while Mommy and Daddy talk, please?"

"Okay, Daddy, but can I have some juice first?"

Gordon thought of his children's innocence. Hunter had no idea that he could be facing the end of the world; he wanted juice. Gordon touched his son's face. "Sure, son, go grab a couple of juice boxes in the pantry."

Hunter grabbed two juices and headed toward the bathroom to wait for Haley to finish. When she opened the door, he grabbed her hand and walked her into the playroom.

"So, let's talk," Gordon said to Samantha.

They went over to the couch and sat down. Neither could relax; they sat rigidly on the edge of the cushions.

Gordon started in hastily, "Here is what I think is going on. Obviously, you're more than aware of all the terrorist activity we've been having over the past months. Well, today we were attacked with a much larger weapon. When I was out running, I saw cars stall and stop working, street lights go out, and planes fall out of the sky. Here at home all the power is out, your phone doesn't turn on. Nothing works. I think someone hit us with some sort of EMP weapon."

"EMP?" Samantha stopped him.

" 'EMP' stands for electromagnetic pulse," he answered directly. "It essentially overloads anything electrical and fries it; that's why your phone, the lights, and cars don't work. I am guessing the entire local grid is down. I don't know the extent of the damage because I haven't gone out to see what's going on, but I think I'm right."

"So, when will the power come back on?"

"It all really depends if this is a local thing, regional, or national. Worse case is it's national and power could be out for months, if not a year."

Samantha interjected impulsively, "A year! How will we survive? What will happen?"

"Samantha, like I said, I don't know. One thing I want to do is see if by chance our car made it or not. Then, since there's daylight left, I want to try to go to the store and pick up anything we will need for the long haul."

Gordon slid closer to Samantha and put his hand over hers. She was clearly upset and he needed to at least appear calm; he needed to be the rock. Comforting her, he said, "We will make it through this, I promise you."

Musa Qala, Helmand Province, Afghanistan

"Van Zandt, get off your ass; we have a battalion formation, right now!" said Gunny Smith, kicking his cot.

"Roger that, Gunny," Sebastian said, swinging his legs off the cot.

When he left the tent, he noticed a sense of excitement on the base. Seeing Master Sergeant Simpson about-face, Sebastian knew he needed to hurry. As soon as he made it to his unit he saw Barone approach Simpson.

"Battalion all present and accounted for!" Simpson said while saluting.

Barone saluted him back. "Thank you, master sergeant." Simpson brought his salute back and marched off. Looking out over the men all standing at attention, Barone finished by yelling, "Battalion at ease!"

Barone was a tall and sturdy-looking man. He had a rugged face, light eyes, and thick, dark hair that he kept groomed with a flattop haircut. His stature coupled with his personality made him appear like a giant to some of the Marines. He looked out on the fifteen hundred Marines in front of him. While Marine life was difficult for many, it came easy to Barone. This occasion was different, though; to have to address the Marines about any situations back home was difficult. The whole reason these Marines traveled so far from home was to defend their loved ones, but now their homeland was threatened, their loved ones in harm's way, and they were about as far away as they could be from them.

"Marines, I am not going to stand here and bullshit you. You know me well enough to know I am a plain-spoken Marine. I tell it like it is. I don't sugarcoat it. I don't glaze it over." Barone began walking back and forth in front of the assembled Marines. "So I will tell you right now that our mission here has ended, effective immediately."

The Marines of 2/4 all started looking to one another for clarification. They still had four more months on their deployment, so they all knew something significant must have happened.

Barone stopped his pacing to drop the real news. "Marines, initial reports suggest our country has suffered a massive attack. What we do know is coming from assets we have in the air over the country. The intelligence we have received so far indicates that some type of nuclear event has occurred. One struck Washington, D.C., and another device detonated in the atmosphere above the Midwest. It also appears that major communications are down with our allies in Europe and Asia."

Sebastian was in shock. His mind immediately raced to Gordon, Samantha, and the kids. He couldn't believe it, the bastards had done it; they had finally done it, they had gone nuclear.

Barone continued on. "Marines, it has not been confirmed. Let me say it again, this has not been confirmed, but with the nuclear attack on our Capitol, our commander in chief, the president; the vice president; and the entire Congress may be among the casualties. If this is indeed the case, our enemies have effectively cut the head off of our government. At this moment, we are operating under procedures put into place in anticipation of a situation like this. Marines, it appears that we are in the midst of World War Three. We do not yet know who actually orchestrated the attack, but I can tell you this, we will find out and when we do, they will have to face the United States Marine Corps!"

Some Marines started yelling "Ooh Rah!" in response to Barone's address.

"Marines, we have to clear out of Afghanistan immediately. We have birds coming in tomorrow morning at zero-six-hundred. They will take us to ships positioned in the Arabian Sea. From there, we'll sail to the East Coast of the United States and assist with the search and rescue efforts around Washington, D.C."

He looked around at all the Marines in front of him and then continued.

"Marines, I know all of you are concerned for your family members back home. I'd be lying if I said I wasn't, too, but we have a mission; we are United States Marines and we must not fail. Our country needs us now more than ever! We must be vigilant. Tonight, pack your gear and be ready to depart this wasteland tomorrow!"

Barone walked back to his position centered on the battalion, stood at attention, and yelled, "Battalion attention!"

Master Sergeant Simpson walked around Barone until he faced him, and then saluted.

Barone saluted back and said, "Top, give final instructions to the company first sergeants and get these Marines prepared to ship out at zero-six-hundred tomorrow."

"Yes, sir," Simpson replied.

Barone finished his salute and walked away.

Oklahoma City, Oklahoma

"Nurse! Nurse!" Brad Conner yelled down the darkened hall of the hospital. The power was out everywhere, but most disturbingly the power was off to his son's life-support system.

The stress was visible on Conner's face as he continued yelling for assistance, receiving no response. All he could see was hospital staff scrambling in the partial darkness, frantic and confused. Other voices echoed from rooms up and down the ICU wing.

"Bobby, it will be all right," Julia Conner whispered to her son, who lay motionless in the hospital bed. Tears streamed down her face. "Brad, anything? Is anyone coming? What happened to the power?"

Conner turned and looked back at his wife. "It will be okay, the emergency generators will kick on any minute." He started to fear the worst but kept telling her that everything would be fine, even though he was concerned. The pain on Julia's face was something he'd never seen. Her dark brown hair hung down, covering her fine features. She was always put together, never one to be seen without her hair done or makeup on outside of the house. Julia always wore the best in clothing and had maintained an attractive figure throughout her life.

He allowed a few more moments to pass without any hospital staff checking in before storming down the hallway toward the nurses' station. As he approached, it became apparent he would find no help there. What little staff remained was hopelessly trying to see if anything would come on. He overheard several nurses mumbling to themselves that the emergency generators should have come on by now.

"Excuse me," Conner tried to interject, but no one paid him any attention. "Excuse me!" this time at full volume.

One nurse stopped her conversation with a doctor to shoot back plainly, "Sir, we are working on the issue and will have the power back on very soon."

"That might be fine for you and me, but my son in room 303 has no life support and I need your assistance now!" He slammed his hand on the counter. "NOW!"

The nurse turned to him, visibly irritated by him and frustrated by the greater situation. She repeated, with attitude in her voice, "Sir, the power will be on soon. We will go check on your son very, very soon."

"Listen, you don't know who I am; I am the Speaker of the United States House of Representatives. I am not asking you, I am telling you, to go down to room 303 and check on my son, now!"

Her eyes opened wide. She was visibly disturbed by his last statement. "Take me to your son's room."

She came out from around the counter at the nurses' station and ran beside Conner, down the hall to room 303.

When they entered the room, Julia was sobbing uncontrollably, her head placed against Bobby's limp hand. The nurse immediately approached their son and checked his pulse. She reached over him and grabbed a stethoscope and put it on. She continued checking his vitals, listening intently but hearing nothing. The nurse dropped the stethoscope and ripped open Bobby's hospital gown to administer CPR. Julia, with tears streaming down her face and gripped by fear, sat frozen, watching the nurse desperately try to revive her son. Conner came to her side and put his hands on her shoulders.

The nurse administered CPR for what seemed like forever, pausing every few minutes to check his vitals. Eventually, she ran to the loud and chaotic hallway and yelled, "Dr. Rivera, Dr. Rivera!"

"He's down here in 311!"

"I need him in 303, stat!"

No reply.

The nurse turned back to Bobby. She again checked his vitals and continued the CPR. Another few minutes passed and, after checking Bobby's vitals one last time, she turned to Conner and his wife and whispered, "I am so very sorry."

"No, no! You keep trying, don't you stop!" Julia screamed hysterically. "That's my only boy there, don't you stop!"

"Ma'am, I have tried; I could give him more CPR but he's gone, there's nothing more I can do," the nurse replied, her voice subdued and defeated.

"Goddamn you! Get someone else in here who will try," Julia yelled at the nurse. She turned to her husband. "Brad, goddamn it, do something!"

"Julia, I think he's gone," Conner said sadly to his grieving and hysterical wife. He then lowered his head in sorrow.

"No, no!" she said, hitting her husband in the chest twice. She pushed past him, walking toward the nurse who began to back away, apprehensive about what was coming toward her.

"Get out of my way!" Julia said to the nurse. She then bent over and placed her ear against her son's chest. She started to try to perform CPR herself; it was obvious she did not know what she was doing.

Both the nurse and Conner watched Julia, stunned. Conner stood there for a brief time before motioning for the nurse to leave. He walked over to his wife, who was still unsuccessfully attempting CPR, and placed both arms around her. She tried to shrug him off at first but eventually gave in and collapsed onto her dead son. The hospital's chaos faded as they sank into their own despair.

Musa Qala, Helmand Province, Afghanistan

"Holy shit, I cannot believe this is happening," Sebastian said to Lance Corporal Tomlinson while stuffing his sea bag.

"I know; I'm shocked too; I just hope my folks and girlfriend are cool. My parents live up in northeast PA and you know my girl is out in O'side."

Grabbing more gear and forcing it into his bag, Sebastian said, "Whoever did this needs to die, all of them need to die. I just hope I get them in my scope; I'll fucking kill them."

"Yep, I hope we get a chance. I want to put one in their nasty grape too," Tomlinson said.

"I just wish we weren't going to the East Coast. I wish we were going back home. I know my brother will take care of everything, but I want to be there to help him. God knows what kind of crazy shit is going on," Sebastian said.

"What do you mean, bro?" Tomlinson asked, sitting down on his cot next to his half-filled sea bag. He pulled a tin of Copenhagen out and began tapping it. Tomlinson was tall and very thin. He had reddish hair and fair skin. His face was covered in old scars from acne. He didn't take much pride in his appearance. He was the opposite of Sebastian, who made sure he was always squared away and put together.

"Look at what happened to New Orleans after Katrina or what kind of crazy shit happens during blackouts. People go fucking crazy when the lights go out and stay out. There's no law and order. It's a recipe for disaster and mob rule."

"Really bro, you think people will start going crazy back home?"

"Yes, I do. Most people are idiots, so if there is no power, there is no water, no food, no medical supplies, the list goes on. This is not good. Everything will go south, trust me, and here we are in fucking Afghanistan, heading to the East Coast. We need to be going back home to help our friends and family."

"You're right, bro. My girlfriend can barely even program the DVR to watch her stupid *House Hookers of Orange County* show.

Not to mention she never keeps food in the house," Tomlinson said with a chuckle.

"Tomlinson, what has happened is bad, very bad. An EMP destroys everything electrical. Millions and millions of people will die and the only way to help our families, friends, and stupid girlfriends is to be there, not all the way on the other coast." Sebastian was getting himself worked up. He tossed the items he had in his hands onto the cot.

"Well, not much we can do, Van Zandt; we have our orders and it's back east," Tomlinson stated, shaking his head side to side.

"I know, and I fucking hate it." Sebastian sat down on his cot, clearly angry and frustrated.

San Diego, California

"The car is dead. The battery still works but the car won't turn over," Gordon told Samantha as he walked in from the garage.

"So what are we going to do for transportation?" Samantha asked.

"Here's my plan. Right now it's been about two hours since the attack. Most people don't know what's going on. I'm going to take advantage of the ignorance and go to the store and get as much stuff as I can before people start to freak out and clear it out," Gordon said as he walked toward his office.

"How are you going to get there?" Samantha followed him into his office.

Gordon grabbed his desk chair and positioned it underneath attic space opening. He stood on the chair and pushed it open. Dust and insulation fell onto his face.

"Damn it," he sputtered in between coughs as he spit out debris.

He reached up and fished around till he felt what he was looking for.

"What are you hiding up there?" Samantha asked curiously.

"Something we'll need," he said, stepping off of the chair and placing an ammo can on his desk. He looked at Samantha, winked, and opened the can.

"Cash? You hid this from me? You never told me you were hiding cash and, by the looks of it, a lot of it."

"I may not have been prepared for this type of situation, but I prepared for an economic crash. Good thing I was paranoid about that, because now it will at least come in handy until people realize that it has zero value," Gordon said, pulling out stacks of cash.

"How much do we have?" Samantha asked, picking up a stack and thumbing it like a deck of cards.

"About seventy-five thousand," he answered.

"What? Where did we get that?"

"It's our retirement money," he answered, feeling a bit guilty. He had taken it out in October before the markets crashed. With hindsight on his side, his guilt melted away and he felt proud of his decision.

"I knew you were getting nervous, but when were you planning on telling me?" Samantha reached into the can and pulled out another stack.

"I don't know, but does it really matter now? I need to take some cash with me to the store and buy as much as I can," he said, putting a small stack in his pocket. He put the rest back in the ammo can, closed it, and placed it back in his hiding spot.

"So here's the plan. I'm going to ride my mountain bike to Albertson's. I'm going to wear a pack, attach the basket from the kids' playroom on the front handle bar, and attach the kids' trailer on the back. That will give me a lot of space to bring food and supplies back. What I need from you is to make sure the kids do not use the toilets anymore. And keep this in close proximity," he said, handing her his favorite Sig Sauer handgun. Then he started for the garage to prepare for his trip.

Oklahoma City, Oklahoma

"Excuse me, sir," the hospital administrator said, looking nervous about interrupting Conner and his wife, who were still sitting next to the bed that held their dead son. But he felt he needed to because the situation in the hospital was deteriorating. He hoped the Speaker could leverage his power and influence to get something done.

Conner lifted his head and looked toward the door.

"Yes," Conner said. His voice was labored and his face was filled with sadness.

"Sir, excuse me for the interruption at this most painful moment; but I was wondering if I could have a minute of your time?"

Julia did not look up at all; she rested her head against her son's hand. Conner stood up and walked toward the hospital administrator.

When Conner reached him, he put his hand on his shoulder and led him out of the room into the still-dark hallway. The hospital was even more chaotic than before. Everyone was panicked and confused; flashlight beams darted around in the darkness. Everyone was busy, but no one seemed to actually be accomplishing anything.

"Yes, how can I help?" Conner asked.

"Sir, let me again express my condolences for your son's loss. We are trying as hard as we can to get power back up, but nothing is working."

"What is wrong with the generators?" Conner asked.

"That's just it: The hospital's generators are hardwired into the electrical system and they won't turn on; they're dead. The other troubling thing, sir, is that no one's phones will work. That includes our staff's personal mobile phones. Their cars don't start either. We tried to send some of our staff to Home Depot to buy some portable generators, but their cars just won't start."

Conner interrupted him and asked, "Nothing works?"

"Yes, sir."

Conner had been so consumed with his son's death that he had lost track of time and what was going on. He grabbed his own mobile phone from his pocket and glanced at the screen; it was completely dead. He tried turning it on, nothing. He then started walking down the hallway to the nurses' station.

"Sir?" the hospital administrator asked, following him briskly.

When he reached the station he leaned over and grabbed a phone, it was dead; he started clicking around to get a line, nothing. He dropped the phone and walked to a large window in the elevator lobby, which looked out over the large parking lot. He saw people by their cars, hoods up. Nothing was moving at all. He then looked at the horizon and noticed the smoke rising from various parts of the city.

As he scanned up and down the lot, he saw movement; an old pickup truck pulled up to the hospital ER entrance. He looked closer; it was an old F-100 Ford pickup. The driver jumped out, ran over to the passenger side, and started pulling someone out who obviously needed medical attention. He stood there for another minute before he finally snapped out of his trance and realized that something very serious had happened. As he turned and ran, he bumped into the administrator, but continued down the hall to his son's room.

"Julia, Julia?" he said as he ran into the room.

"What?" She looked up quickly; she could tell by the sound in his voice that something was wrong. "Brad, what is it?"

"We have to go!" he said authoritatively. "NOW!"

"I am not going anywhere," she said, squeezing her son's hand tighter. "What's wrong?"

"Julia, I need you to come now!" he demanded, grabbing her arm.

She pulled away from him and protested, "No, I'm not leaving Bobby!"

"Listen, we have been attacked. The city has been attacked!"

"What?"

"That's why there's no power. We've been attacked. We have to go."

"Brad, I am not leaving. You can go and come back for me later; but I'm not leaving until we make arrangements for Bobby."

He paused, frustrated and unsure of what to do. He considered forcing her, but that would only cause problems. She'd at least be safe at the hospital, and he'd come back for her as soon as he could. "Okay, you stay here, but I need to go back to the hotel and get Dylan and find out what is going on. I'll have the hospital make the arrangements to move Bobby's body to Tinker Air Force Base as soon as we can find transportation that works."

Defeated and tired, Julia sat back down next to her son's bed. "Okay," she replied without even looking at Brad.

Conner stood for a brief moment, feeling torn. He wanted to stay but knew he must go. Knowing something terrible had happened, he needed to find out what. He turned and left the room. Finding the hospital administrator, he gave him instructions on how to handle his wife and pledged that he would return with support. Time was of the essence. Remembering the truck from moments before he ran toward the bay window and looked down. The old truck was still there. Not wasting a moment, he located the staircase and ran for it.

Cautiously moving down the darkened stairwell, he thought to himself that maybe this one time he should have had his protective detail with him. Leaving them at the hotel with his aide made sense before, but now he regretted that decision. Reaching the ground level, he opened the door and ran down the hall. The scene downstairs was similar to that of his son's floor, complete disarray. People were all around looking at their phones, many lined up at the information station asking questions of a couple of overwhelmed volunteers who were just stating the hospital's canned response that the power would soon be restored. He knew better. He found an exit and made it out onto the curb. To his right, the old truck sat idling in front of the ER entrance. He ran to the truck, peered inside, and saw blood on the passenger seat. The driver's window was down and he saw the door was unlocked. Without hesitation, he grabbed the handle, swung it open, and jumped behind the wheel. He threw it in gear, slammed down on the accelerator, and took off out of the hospital parking lot and toward the hotel.

San Diego, California

"Here, Daddy, let me help," Hunter said, walking into the garage and toward Gordon.

Gordon was pumping up the tires on his mountain bike; he stopped and looked up. "Okay, son, come here; fast now, I have to go."

Hunter walked over and placed his small hands on top of the manual pump. Gordon slowly brought the pump handle down and up, the tire expanded, and the joy of helping his father was making Hunter's day. Together they pumped up the tires on the bike and trailer.

Looking at Hunter, Gordon felt proud. His son wanted nothing more than to contribute. He tousled Hunter's brown hair. Hunter had Gordon's look, light-colored eyes and dark hair. He was tall for his age, but had a strong, lean build for being only seven years old.

"Thank you, Hunter; here, finish up by putting the pump back."

"Okay, Daddy," Hunter responded, cradling the pump and walking it over to the cabinet.

"Hunter, when you're done with that I need you to help Daddy with something else."

Hunter quickly put away the pump and came running over. "What, Daddy?"

"I am leaving in a few minutes to go get some things at the store. Please promise me you'll help Mommy with anything she asks and take care of your little sister. Okay?" Gordon knelt down to meet Hunter's eyes.

"Okay, Daddy; when are you coming back?"

"Soon, son, I promise. Now can you promise me what I asked?"

"I promise." Hunter felt important since his father had given him some responsibility.

"Thank you," Gordon replied. He gave Hunter a big hug and kissed him on the cheek. "Run on in now and see what you can do to help your mother."

Hunter opened the door and stepped in, but before the door could close behind him, he poked his head out again. "Daddy, can you get some ice cream?"

"I'll see what I can do," Gordon said with a smile. This made Gordon feel more protective; he wanted to ensure his kids' innocence remained as long as it could.

Gordon stuffed some cash into a fanny pack that already held his Sig Sauer P239 pistol. He also packed a small first aid kit, water, and a headlamp. He put on his pack and walked the bike with trailer out of the garage. After manually closing the garage door behind him, he looked down his street. Many of his neighbors were out in front of their homes. Some were holding their phones, still attempting with no luck to get them to work; others were working on their cars. It was now late morning and people still had no clue what was going on. He knew he had a small window of time to get more supplies before the real panic set in. He climbed on his bike and started his trek toward the store.

As he rode, he kept going over a mental list of what he needed to get. He wanted to make sure he picked up what was important and what would last. He wasn't sure how long it would be before all hell broke loose and everything would be gone. His quick thinking about the water could help them last longer. He knew he should tell his neighbors, but not until he returned from the store with what he needed first. As he rode on, he passed disabled car after disabled car. Most had now been abandoned.

When Gordon pulled into the Albertson's parking lot, the scene was basically the same as on the streets. He saw many cars with their hoods up. People just standing around and talking; they all just seemed to be waiting for the power to come back, something Gordon knew that would not happen anytime soon. He quickly thought to himself about how as a society we all had become dependent and interdependent on our system and the comforts of having easily available electricity. Once people found out what had happened, he knew widespread panic would descend upon the city. This was Gordon's only opportunity to secure vital resources.

The front doors were shut with a handwritten sign taped on that read, "Closed Due to Power Outage."

He parked the bike next to a large column, jumped off, and walked quickly back to the trailer; he opened a pouch on the side and pulled out a small chain and lock. He chained and locked the bike and trailer to the column. With most cars not working, his bike might be tempting to steal.

He walked up to the doors and looked inside; it was hard to see far. He looked from left to right, seeing if anyone was still in there. He started to knock loudly. After a full minute of knocking, someone finally emerged from the darkness and walked up to the doors. The gentleman looked like he might be a manager. He pointed at the handwritten sign. Gordon acknowledged that and then held up a wad of cash. The man stared at Gordon's hand, wide-eyed, paused, and then pried the doors open.

"What can I help you with, sir?" the grocery store manager asked.

"I need to get some supplies. I understand you're closed but I have cash and I can pay extra . . . if you know what I mean," Gordon said quietly, leaning in close to the manager for the last part.

The store manager looked left and right then whispered, "You aren't an Albertson's employee or something, are you?"

"Nope," Gordon replied.

"What do you need?"

"Canned food, batteries, a few propane tanks and whatever else I see. I have plenty of cash to go around," Gordon said, waving the stack of bills.

"Listen, put the cash down and step inside," the manager said after looking left and right again.

"Can I bring my bike and trailer in? It will help to load up everything directly," Gordon said, pointing toward the rack to which his bike was chained.

Looking over Gordon's shoulder, the manager said, "Sure, but hurry."

Gordon didn't hesitate; he turned around, unlocked the bike and trailer, and walked them into the store. He put on his headlamp, knowing he'd need it as they got farther into the store. He was familiar with its layout and went right for the canned food aisle. He started to fill the trailer up with canned vegetables, tuna, chicken, and fruit. The manager showed back up with a notepad and was writing everything down. Gordon didn't say a thing to him. He took every battery he could get his hands on. He found the nuts and grabbed all the dry roasted almonds, peanuts, and cashews they had. He then proceeded to the pharmacy area. Most of the over-the-counter drugs were locked up, but he was able to grab bandages, Band-Aids, antiseptic ointments, painkillers, and antihistamines. He essentially grabbed anything he thought they could need to last them for years.

"Looks like you're stocking up for the end of the world," the manager quipped.

"Well, you never know. I like to be prepared," Gordon replied without slowing down. He darted over to another aisle and grabbed every box of powdered milk and powdered Gatorade in stock. He finally paused for a moment, just to pull his checklist from his pocket. He then inspected the trailer and all the contents he had so far. He needed a bit more room for some propane tanks but then decided it would be better to have more food than fuel for cooking.

He returned to the canned food aisle to grab more and more. He cleaned off the shelves of tuna, meat, sardines, and salmon.

After a solid forty minutes of "shopping," the trailer, basket, and backpack were full. The tires on the trailer stressed under the weight.

"What do I owe you?" he asked the manager.

"Let's go to the customer service desk and I'll grab a pad."

Gordon followed him toward the counter where he saw a display of Albertson's baked goods. He paused and looked at the doughnuts and ginger snap cookies. He had always had a sweet tooth and any sort of treat would be scarce soon. He grabbed as many doughnuts and packages of cookies as he could squeeze into the limited space of the trailer.

While the manager scribbled numbers on his pad, Gordon checked and double-checked his trailer and the store shelves around the customer service area. He noticed a few pegs filled with lighters and tossed the whole lot onto his pile of goods.

"Sir, your total is one thousand, eight hundred and seventy-five dollars," the manager said looking down at his notepad and writing the amount down.

"Will three thousand work? The rest is a tip," Gordon said, handing the man over a small stack of hundred-dollar bills.

"Yes, it will," the manager said, excited and surprised.

As the money changed hands, a loud knocking from the store's front doors startled them both. The manager quickly pocketed the cash and made his way toward the front. "Stay here," he instructed as he walked away.

Gordon took a few steps away from the counter so he could see the front doors. He saw the manager doing exactly what he had done when Gordon knocked. He didn't say a word, he just pointed at the sign. The person on the other side shrugged his shoulders and walked off. The manager came back and said, "Listen, I don't need any trouble, so follow me to the back and go out that way."

"I can do that," Gordon agreed. He followed the manager to the back of the store, through the warehouse, and to an emergency exit. The alarm didn't sound when the manager opened the door, and Gordon quietly navigated his load through the opening.

Gordon shook the manager's hand, jumped on his bike, and pedaled off. The bike was very heavy now, which meant the ride home would be slower than the ride to the store. As he rode, he felt proud of himself for his quick thinking under pressure. He might have just given his family a longer lease on life. The regret he had earlier for his overall lack of preparedness was eased now.

Oklahoma City, Oklahoma

The atmosphere of the hotel parking lot was similar to that of the hospital. Scattered throughout, cars sat still with their hoods raised and people meandered, confused. Conner turned into the lot, hastily parked the truck, pulled the keys from the ignition, and jumped out of the cabin. He locked the truck, hoping to provide some security for one of the only operational vehicles around. He noticed everyone in the lot was staring at him and his operational truck.

He ran to the emergency stairs and up to the second floor. He went directly to Dylan's room. Once he reached the room, he furiously rapped on the door until his trusted aide answered.

"I've been trying to reach you," Dylan said, feeling relieved to be face-to-face with the Speaker.

"Grab what you can, get the two Capitol Police officers, and meet me down in the parking lot in five minutes. Please hurry,"

Conner ordered, then turned away, leaving Dylan standing there bewildered.

Conner darted down the hallway toward his room. He pulled out his key card, hoping it would work despite the power outage. He slid the key into the card slot above the doorknob, but nothing happened. Unsurprised, he took a step backward and kicked the door as hard as he could. The door hardly budged. He gave it another shot; this time, it buckled under the force of his kick and flew open. He bolted inside, grabbed his briefcase and a small piece of luggage, and immediately left.

"Mr. Speaker!" a voice yelled down the darkened hallway.

Conner turned around. He couldn't see anything down the near-black corridor, but he heard footsteps approaching.

"Mr. Speaker!" the voice said again.

"Agent Davis, is that you?" he asked.

"Yes, sir, it's me and Jackson."

From the darkness, two large-statured men wearing suits approached Conner.

"Have you been able to communicate with anyone in Washington?" Conner asked.

"No," Davis responded

"Nothing, sir," Jackson answered, shaking his head. "None of our equipment will even power on. We went down to the front desk and everything is down."

"Listen, go back to your rooms and grab what you will need and meet me out front. I have a working vehicle."

Both men acknowledged Conner and ran back to their rooms. Conner headed for the stairwell and quickly made it back to the truck. Seeing the truck as he exited the lobby, he breathed a sigh of relief. He tossed his bags in the back and got in. So much had happened in a day. Just yesterday he and Julia were at a charity luncheon in D.C. when they received word that Bobby had been in a near-fatal car accident.

"Mr. Speaker?" Dylan asked, puzzled by the fact that his boss was sitting behind the wheel of an old, beat-up pickup truck.

Conner opened his eyes. "Throw your stuff in the back and get in the cab, but don't get blood on you."

Dylan obeyed and climbed into the passenger seat nervously after taking notice of the blood on the inside door panel and side of the seat.

"Where did you get the truck?" Dylan asked, looking around inside.

"That is a long story and it doesn't matter. As soon as Davis and Jackson get down here we are heading straight for Tinker Air Force Base."

"Mr. Speaker, may I ask where your wife is?" Dylan asked hesitantly.

"She's still at the hospital with my son. Once we get to Tinker and I can find out what is going on we'll send someone back to get both of them. The priority now is to see if we can find out what is happening. It seems the entire power grid is down, and I can only assume there's been some type of attack."

Davis and Jackson suddenly emerged out of the front of the hotel running with their small carry-on bags. They tossed them in the bed of the truck.

"Jump in the back, gentlemen," Conner yelled.

Davis and Jackson climbed in and Conner sped off. Driving through downtown Oklahoma City was like playing a video game; he was swerving around and narrowly missing stalled, abandoned cars all along West Sheridan and down South Robinson toward Interstate 40.

"Sir, this is really strange. I understand the power being out if someone took down the power grid, but why are all the cars stalled?" Dylan pushed for some information, frustrated by Conner's prior refusal to answer his questions.

Paying close attention to his driving, Conner quickly answered, "There are only two things that could do this type of damage: a nuclear weapon detonated high in the atmosphere or a massive solar flare."

"A nuclear weapon?"

"I'm not sure what is going on exactly, Dylan, but this is why we need to go to Tinker—to find out."

The drive to the Air Force base was slowed down by the constant dodging of stalled cars along the interstate. As they drove, the men did encounter a few more operational vehicles; all appeared to be early vintage cars.

Coming off the exit for Tinker Air Force Base, both Conner and Dylan could see movement all around the base. There were moving vehicles, but people were clearly scrambling. As they slowly approached the front gate, several military police pointed their rifles and ordered for them to halt.

"Put your arms up, Dylan," Conner instructed as he stopped the truck just before the first barriers to the entrance off of the exit ramp. "Davis, Jackson, put your arms up!" Conner yelled.

Both Davis and Jackson complied and held their arms up. A single military policeman approached the truck.

"What is your business here?" the officer asked, pointing his rifle right at Conner.

Conner could see the other two policemen spread apart from each other and take positions with their rifles trained on the truck.

"Airman, I am Speaker of the House Brad Conner. May I reach in my pocket and get my ID?"

Conner slowly put his right hand into his jacket pocket and pulled out his wallet, then pulled out his Congressional ID and driver's license and held it out the window.

The MP took a few steps and grabbed the cards. He inspected them both and looked at the Speaker. He then shifted his gaze to Dylan and both men in the bed of the truck.

"Who are the other men, sir?"

"Dylan McLatchy in the cab with me, and in the back are Special Agents Davis and Jackson; they are with the U.S. Capitol Police."

"Sir, I need all of their IDs as well," the officer requested.

"Airman, this is the Speaker of the House of Representatives and we need access immediately," Dylan demanded.

"Hold on, Dylan, let the man do his job and check us out." Conner knew everyone was on edge and he didn't want to make matters worse by forcing his way in. "Everyone get your IDs and hand them to the airman."

Dylan and the two special agents did just that. The airman gathered all the IDs, looked at them, and then looked at each man; he then stepped away from the truck. "Sir, I need to go back and send someone to HQ as our comm is down; we are not allowing anyone onto base due to the national emergency."

"Wait a minute, airman, what national emergency?" Conner asked.

"The EMP and nuclear attack sir," the MP answered, then jogged back to the guard shack.

The MP conferred with his counterpart at the guard shack. The MP who had the IDs kept pointing toward the truck. Finally, he jumped into a jeep and headed into the base.

"Sir, looks like your hunch was right," Dylan said.

"Yeah," Conner whispered. He lifted his head and stared outside of the driver's side window.

Ten minutes later, the jeep returned. The MP jumped out accompanied by another man. As the second man approached the truck, Conner could see he was a general.

The general stepped up to the truck and saluted. "Welcome, Mr. Speaker, General Daniel Griswald at your service." He turned to the MP and instructed them to open the gate. "Sir, I apologize for the wait but after what has happened, we are locked down."

"General, I can appreciate that and understand. Please take me somewhere secure so we can be briefed."

Griswald quickly walked back to the jeep, the MP jumped back in, and they turned around. Conner navigated the barriers and Jersey walls set up at the entrance and followed the jeep.

Conner looked around as they drove down the main road. He could see that even the Air Force base was not immune to the EMP attack.

They reached the headquarters building and quickly exited their respective vehicles. As they walked toward the building, the general made his way over to the Speaker.

"Sir, how is it that you're here in Oklahoma and not in Washington?

"My son was involved in a car accident, so my wife and I came here to be with him."

"I am sorry to hear the bad personal news, sir. I hope he is doing well," Griswald said.

Deliberately avoiding the subject of his son, Conner asked, "How much damage does the base have from the EMP?"

"Well, sir, most vehicles and electrical systems as well as the generators are down."

Griswald continued to explain some of the challenges they were having at the base while he guided Speaker Conner to the secure briefing room. Conner took a seat while Griswald talked to a few other personnel.

"Sir, just another minute, we are waiting on Colonel Jameson with Seventy-second Wing."

Conner acknowledged with a nod.

A few minutes passed and a burly man walked into the room. Colonel Jameson was short and robust, a contrast to Griswald's tall and lanky figure.

Jameson carried a stack of binders. Other staff came in with a paper map that was attached to an old chalkboard. He walked over to Conner and put out his hand. "Mr. Speaker, Colonel Todd Jameson, pleasure to meet you."

Conner stood and shook his hand. "Same, Colonel." He looked to Griswald and said, "General, I don't want to wait any longer. What has happened? I need to know now." His patience was wearing a bit thin.

"Sir, we are ready and I apologize for any delays. Let me debrief you on what we know so far," Griswald began, standing at the front of the room in front of the map of the United States.

Conner leaned forward and placed his elbows on the table with his hands clasped.

"At approximately ten-thirteen hundred hours local, a high-altitude electromagnetic pulse device was detonated approximately three-hundred-plus miles above Kansas. The resulting effects from that EMP caused massive and catastrophic damage across the entire national grid. The estimated diameter of the EMP stretched from one coast of the continental United States to the other. From what we can tell now, with the scarce intelligence that we have, is that the EMP burst shut down the country's entire power grid from the East Coast to the West Coast. Sir, I know you are aware of the last Congressional Report put out about this type of attack and it appears the scenarios and estimates of damage were either incorrect or the device that hit us was huge. Now we believe—"

"What do you mean our estimates were wrong?" Conner interrupted.

"Sir, I know you have heard of a 'Super EMP,' correct?"

"Yes, General, I have."

"Well, sir, based upon reports we are getting from the field and from our own experiences so far, this EMP strike took everything out. You are aware that our testing and estimates showed that a standard nuclear detonation high in the atmosphere would have taken out most of the power grid but other damage would not have been universal. This detonation seems to have taken every modern vehicle out, most electrical equipment, et cetera. None of our testing showed damage this widespread. So without truly knowing, we can only assume it was a device designed to emit a greater amount of gamma radiation, or in layman's terms, a Super EMP."

"How do you know that the grid is down across the nation?"

"Sir, we still have communication with assets across the country using SIPRNet."

"Sipper what?" Conner asked, confused.

"Sir, it's the DOD's secured Internet and the servers connected to many of them are hardened."

"Well, thank God for that," Conner exclaimed. "What are we doing about the power outages? How are we supporting government?"

"Not much right now, sir. Everybody is running around with their heads cut off. It's chaos on all bases. Plus, with what happened back in Washington . . ."

"Let's get to that now, then. What else happened?"

"Ahh, sir," Griswald replied. He looked at Jameson and then back at Conner and paused.

Conner noticed the glance to the colonel; he looked directly at Griswald and asked firmly, "What is it, General? What else has happened?

"Sir, we have confirmation that there was a second attack. This was a low-yield surface nuclear explosion. The ground zero of the detonation was Washington, D.C."

"Are you sure?"

"Sir, we have received confirmation. We currently have communications with an E6-B from Naval Air Station Pax River. They have flown over the area and Washington, D.C., has been attacked." Griswald paused and then finished. "Sir, Washington, D.C., is gone."

San Diego, California

Gordon's ride home from the store was taking a lot longer than he thought it would. His first downhill slope didn't go well; the weight of the full trailer made it intensely difficult to control his speed. That weight made uphill rides completely impossible. So Gordon had to push the bike and trailer for the rest of the trip. Sweat was pouring off his face and drenching his clothes. All along Camino del Sur, the main road to and from his neighborhood, abandoned cars filled every lane. Most of the owners had now given up and walked home. Though Gordon had stayed in decent shape after leaving the Marine Corps, pushing the bike was proving to be quite the challenge.

When he crested the hill at the intersection of Camino del Sur and Carmel Valley Road, he finally took a break. He sat down on the sidewalk and drank some water, thinking to himself that maybe he should go to another store after this trip. The more he could supply his family, the longer they could hold out. He knew eventually he would have to tell his neighbors what he knew, but not until he could secure as much as he could for his own family. He sat on the sidewalk with his head down, watching the sweat drop off his face and chin and onto the sidewalk. As he felt the cool breeze hit his hot face, he became aware of the unusual silence for the first time. The hum of cars was replaced by the sound of birds flying. How strange, he thought. How peaceful it seemed right at this moment. He knew the peace would end soon, once people realized what had occurred.

Gordon had never really feared death, but now he did. If something were to happen to him, how would his family make it? Samantha was as tough as they came. She had been a top producing sales person for a large firm. Her reputation in the corporate world preceded her, she was aggressive and no-nonsense, all business, and didn't take shit from anyone. That type of toughness was great in an insulated environment, but this wasn't about being tough in a boardroom. The true realities of what was coming were frightening; the way people lived would forever change and only those who could adapt quickly would survive.

If Gordon's fears proved correct, then in an instant, the United States had been transported back to before the Industrial Revolution. There would be a fight for resources, specifically food and water. Electricity had enabled the country and society in general to feed many people, but without power this equilibrium would stop immediately. The area they lived in would not be able to support the 3.2 million residents. Soon, the water would dry up, and then the food. Gordon couldn't bear to think about it anymore; he needed to keep moving. He decided to attempt another trip today, which wouldn't be possible if he didn't make it home quickly.

As he started to push the bike, he heard a familiar sound coming from behind him. It sounded like a car, something with some real horsepower. He stood still, waiting. The sound grew louder; the car was coming his way. At the top of the hill, emerged a cherry red 1957 Chevy truck. He had seen that truck before; he put out his arm and waved. The truck pulled up right next to him.

Gordon bent over and peered through the passenger window. The driver leaned over and started to crank the window down.

"Hey, buddy," the driver said.

"Jimmy, what's up?" Gordon asked.

"This is some shit, isn't it?" Jimmy replied, then pointed to Gordon's bike and trailer. "What's going on here?"

Gordon paused and considered whether he should he answer his friend's question honestly. As he played out the scenario in his head, he started to realize that if he and his family were to survive long-term, they would need cooperation with others.

"I went to the store to get supplies," Gordon answered. Leaning farther into the open window he followed up with his theory. "Jimmy, here's what I am guessing: We've been hit with some type of nuke."

"Nuke?"

"I know, you think that a nuke just blows everything up and it does if it blows up on the ground or just above it, but if it blows up high in the atmosphere it causes what they call an electromagnetic pulse. Essentially, it fries everything electrical."

"Gordon, you're confusing me, slow down."

"Jimmy, it's pretty much the end of the fucking world right now, trust me on this. I know for sure that this isn't some blackout like a few years ago. This is everything electrical, cars, phones, everything," Gordon said, speaking faster and faster.

"I need to get home, then," Jimmy said, placing his hand on the gear shift.

"Wait a minute. I'm sure your family is fine. What you and I need to do is team up and get supplies as fast as we can. There is some low-hanging fruit out there that we need to pick before panic and total fucking chaos erupt."

Jimmy looked back at Gordon and asked, "Are you sure about all of this, Gordon?"

"I'm not sure about the size of this attack, but you see me here, pushing this thing." Gordon pointed to his overflowing trailer.

"Gordon, I need to get home to check on my family."

"I understand, but do this as soon as you get home. Fill every tub, sink basin, jug, whatever you can with water. Soon, water will stop flowing. Once you feel secure, come to my house and we'll head out to another store to get food and more supplies."

"Okay, I'll see you soon." It seemed as though Jimmy sped off before he even finished his sentence. Gordon looked on as he accelerated down the road, zigzagging around the endless obstacle course of stalled cars. He then realized he and Jimmy weren't thinking clearly as Gordon should have asked him for a lift.

"I'm such an idiot!" Gordon said out loud as he watched Jimmy's truck vanish over the hill.

It took Gordon another thirty minutes to complete his journey home. He parked the bike in front of his house and ran to the door. The ride had really taken a lot out of him, but he needed to unload as soon as possible so he could go back out.

He opened the door and yelled for Samantha. He walked down the hallway to the kitchen and grabbed a towel. He was drenched with sweat.

"Daddy, Daddy!" Haley yelled from upstairs.

He could hear her running down the steps.

"Daddy, Daddy!" Haley yelled again as she ran into the kitchen.

Gordon bent down and opened his arms. Haley ran straight into him.

"Yucky, Daddy, you're all wet!" Haley squirmed away from Gordon.

"Sorry, sweetie, Daddy was working."

Samantha walked up to Gordon and hugged him too. "Thank God you're safe."

"Thanks, honey. Not to cut the homecoming short, but I have to get the bike inside, and Jimmy's stopping by anytime."

"Why is Jimmy coming by?" Samantha sounded very curious about this newest development.

"I ran into him on the way home from the store. By the way, the trip was a huge success. I told Jimmy my theory on the situation. He has a working vehicle, so we're going to take it to Ralph's in 4S Ranch to see if we can get more supplies," Gordon said, wiping sweat from his face as he laid out his plan.

"What should we do while you're gone?"

"Why not go down to Jimmy's house and spend some time with Simone? The kids will love it and you can help her with any prepping she hasn't done," Gordon said. He tossed the towel down on the counter and walked to the garage.

He manually unlocked and pushed up the garage door. Just as he stepped outside an elderly neighbor from two doors down ran up to him.

"Did you hear?" The man was very clearly stressed. "The blackout is due to some sort of terrorist attack."

"How do you know that?" Gordon asked. He placed his hands on his hips and looked at the older man, feigning skepticism.

"I have a hand-crank radio and heard the emergency broadcast system put out an alert. They've been repeating it every few minutes. Something about an attack on the power grid and some kind of attacks back east. Right now the info isn't clear."

"What else did they mention?"

"That's it; they recommend that we all stay inside and that the power may be out for a few days or more."

Gordon scoffed to himself, knowing that it would be a lot longer than a few days; then he remembered that the man mentioned other attacks on the East Coast. He wondered what that meant. Knowing the news would eventually get out and once it did it would spread quickly; he couldn't waste time.

"Maybe I can come over and listen with you later or maybe you could help keep me informed if you hear anything else," Gordon said to his neighbor as he stepped over to his bike.

"Looks like you were thinking this thing could last longer," his neighbor commented, noticing all the food and supplies.

"I always like to be prepared," Gordon answered; he still couldn't come to an agreement with himself whether or not to share his opinion until he could secure more food and supplies.

The rumbling of Jimmy's truck interrupted their conversation. The neighbor turned quickly, surprised.

"Your truck works?" he asked while jogging up to Jimmy.

Gordon parked his bike inside and noticed Samantha standing there with Haley.

"Where's Hunter?" Gordon asked.

"He's upstairs standing watch," Samantha said.

"Good," Gordon said, nodding.

Gordon then heard his neighbor ask, "Can I go with you?"

Gordon turned around and shook his head at Jimmy. Jimmy

raised his shoulders and told the neighbor, "Not enough room, sorry."

Jimmy was short, lean, and always looked like he had slept with his clothes on. His shoulder-length brown hair was hardly ever styled. Gordon just assumed that Jimmy's focus was not on himself but on his business and family. Jimmy ran a successful business near downtown San Diego.

"Gordon!" Samantha said loudly.

Gordon turned back around to face Samantha and walked up to her. He stood in front of her and whispered, "We don't have the room—"

"We have to start helping our neighbors," Samantha said, interrupting him.

"We don't have the room, Sam. We need to get as many supplies as possible. He is not my concern right now, you and the kids are."

"I'm sorry, Gordon, this is not how we'll survive. We need to help our neighbors," Samantha said.

"Sam, I don't even know his name, do you? Listen, I need to get going and get more supplies. Please trust me and don't interfere."

"I think you're wrong, but I'll leave it at that. I'm going to go inside and get Hunter. We're going to go over to Jimmy and Simone's house." Samantha turned and walked back into the house with Haley.

Gordon watched her walk back inside. He respected his wife, but he would not budge on this. Protecting his family was his priority; helping neighbors would come a distant second.

"Sorry. Maybe we can pick you up some ice, but we don't have room for you," Jimmy kept insisting to the neighbor standing outside his truck.

"I'm sorry, I'm Gordon," Gordon said, walking back up to his neighbor with his hand stretched out.

“James,” the neighbor said, shaking Gordon’s hand.

“What do you need? Maybe we can pick up some items for you. That’s if we can even get in a store; it could be closed.”

“I want some ice for my freezer items and some batteries, Ds and AAs,” James answered.

“Okay, we’ll see what we can do. We’ll let you know when we get back,” Gordon said.

“Thank you. Can I give you my credit card?” James asked.

“Don’t worry about it, let’s settle up later.”

“Thank you very much,” James said, then walked off toward his house.

Watching James, Gordon thought that he would soon have to let everyone know what he thought, but that would have to wait till tomorrow. Today and tonight were about getting more supplies for his family.

Gordon turned toward Jimmy and said, “Give me a minute.”

Gordon then jogged into the garage, closed it behind him, locked the door, and made his way to his office. He unlocked his armoire and pulled open a drawer; inside were several handguns. He grabbed an HK 9 millimeter and two full magazines. He tucked it into his pants and locked the armoire back up.

On his way out the front door he ran into Samantha. She was bringing the kids down the stairs.

“Sam, I heard you out there. I know you think that I don’t listen sometimes but I do. I hear what you’re saying, and my plan, our plan, is to eventually come together as a community and work together to survive this,” he said with a softer tone than he had spoken to her just moments before.

She reached the landing of the stairs holding Haley in one arm and a bag in the other. Hunter was following close behind with a small backpack. “Sweetie, I get it. I do understand what you’re doing and I appreciate you for doing it. I never doubt your commitment to this family. I guess I just hate knowing that others will suffer and here we are stocking up."

"It does suck for them, but they are not my responsibility. You all are," he said, looking and feeling better now that she was on board.

"Stop wasting time and get back out there," she said with a grin.

"Roger that. I love you," he said, winking at her. He walked up to her and kissed her, then kissed Haley.

"Love you, Daddy," Haley said, then followed up with a quick request. "Can I come with you?"

"Not this time, sweetie, sorry. Go with Mommy and visit your friend Mason," Gordon answered, petting Haley's head. He looked at Hunter, who was standing on the step behind Samantha. "Big guy, remember, take care of your ladies while I'm out."

"Yes, sir, I will," Hunter said. He was a bit tired now. "Can I play Xbox later?"

The question broke Gordon's heart. All the little luxuries to which his kids had become accustomed were gone in a flash.

"Sorry, buddy, but the power is out and will be for some time. Why don't you grab a few of your Star Wars figures to play with at Mason's?"

"Okay," he answered, disappointed.

"Okay, babe, I'm out. We'll probably be a couple hours, maybe more. We should be back by late afternoon."

He ran to Jimmy's truck and jumped into the passenger seat.

"Here," Gordon said, handing the HK to Jimmy.

"Whoa. Really? You think it's going to be that bad? You know I'm not a big gun guy," Jimmy said, taken aback by the sight of the handgun.

"Listen, I don't think it will be that bad at Ralph's but you better get used to it. I believe shit will hit the fan and you better know how to use this thing. Remember what happened after Katrina hit New Orleans or the chaos in the Northeast after Hurricane Sandy? This is like a million Katrinas. Jimmy, you're going to have to change your perspective. Your business is gone; your job now is to find food and water for your family daily. I don't mean to preach, but you need to wake up. the lights are probably not coming on for a long, long time." Gordon didn't mince words.

"Okay, give it to me," Jimmy said reluctantly. He grabbed the handgun and slid it between the seat and the center console.

"Enough bullshitting, let's go get some food," Gordon said loudly.

Jimmy started the truck. It had a deep exhaust sound. He put it into gear and accelerated quickly, causing a brief spinout. They headed west, toward the slowly descending sun.

Musa Qala, Helmand Province, Afghanistan

"Van Zandt, you awake, bro?" Tomlinson asked. The tent was pitch-black except for a slight haze coming from the old halogen lights outside.

"Yes," Sebastian answered from the darkness.

"I'm really worried for my girl. You think she's okay?"

"I'm sure she's fine; just probably laying around with a candle lit, thinking of you," Sebastian answered.

"Yeah, you're right." Tomlinson sounded a little more relieved.

Sebastian tossed and turned. He couldn't sleep for two reasons: the loud sound of heavy machinery outside his tent, and the never-ending thoughts about Gordon, Samantha, and the kids. He felt that he needed to be there with them and was considering voicing his opinion on the topic. He finally made the decision, and since he couldn't sleep he sat up. He felt around in the dark until he located his boots, put them on, and left the tent heading directly for Gunny Smith's tent.

Even though it was very early in the morning, there was a lot of activity going on at the base. Everyone was prepping for the move out. Heavy equipment moved items onto pallets and everyone was abuzz.

It didn't take Sebastian long to make it to Gunny's tent. He was about to poke his head in and wake him, but paused. Thinking that complaining would get him nowhere, he changed his mind and walked away.

"Corporal Van Zandt, did you need to see me?" asked Gunny.

Sebastian turned around to see Gunny Smith walking toward his own tent.

"Yes, Gunny, I was looking for you." Sebastian walked toward Gunny. Sebastian felt very nervous and now wished he had never decided to do this.

When the two reached each other, Sebastian stood for a brief second, silent. He was still contemplating whether he should voice his concern.

"Well, what is it, Van Zandt?" Gunny asked, hands on his hips.

"Gunny, I'm trying to figure how to put this. May I speak frankly?" Sebastian asked.

"Let's go into my hooch, we can have a conversation in there, but please make it brief, we have a lot of work to do," Gunny said. He walked over to his tent and went inside. "Come on in, Corporal."

Sebastian followed.

"Sit down over there on that cot," Gunny said, pointing at a cot up against the left side of the tent.

There wasn't much in the tent: two cots, a makeshift desk with a chair, and a few boxes of Meals Ready to Eat rations. Gunny took off his cover and tossed it on the cot and sat down in the chair.

Gunny just stared at Sebastian, waiting for him to talk. He was of average height, lean, always tan, and had the scars of war already on his body from his face down to his arms.

"Okay, Corporal, what's on your mind?"

"I'm going to be blunt."

"Please do, Corporal."

Sebastian kept hesitating, but he knew he was committed to speaking his mind now; he just wanted to phrase it right without looking like a whiner.

"Gunny, I don't like this idea of going to the East Coast while our families are on the West Coast, possibly in harm's way."

"I understand your concern, Corporal, but our mission is to go support recovery efforts on the East Coast around D.C. You're a Marine and your orders have been given."

"I understand that, Gunny, you know I do, but has anyone else voiced these concerns to the battalion commander? I can't imagine I am the only one who has this concern. These attacks on the homeland are unprecedented and put all of our families in life-and-death situations," Sebastian said. The tension could be seen in his body as he spoke.

"Yes, your concerns have been expressed. However, we have our mission and we cannot deviate from that. Our new mission is like any other we have taken. We will do it and do it like U.S. Marines. I do appreciate you coming to me and you always know my door is open. I trust that even with your concerns and disagreement with our new mission that you'll perform your duties like you always have?" Gunny asked as he stood up from his chair.

"Yes, Gunny, of course," Sebastian assured him, standing up as well. Sebastian walked to the entrance of the tent.

"Make sure your team is ready to go, we have company formation at oh-five-hundred," Gunny told Sebastian.

"We'll be ready, Gunny," Sebastian replied. He exited the tent.

Walking back toward his tent, he felt conflicted. The Marine Corps meant a lot to him, but knowing his brother and family were in harm's way changed everything.

"Van Zandt!" Gunny yelled at Sebastian as he was walking away.

Sebastian turned around quickly and saw Gunny Smith standing just outside the entrance to his tent. Sebastian walked back to him.

"Van Zandt, if you're concerned about your brother, don't be; he can handle himself."

"You know my brother?" Sebastian asked, surprised.

"Yes. I never thought to mention it before, but I met him in Iraq back in 2004. We fought together in Fallujah."

"You were with him in Fallujah?" Sebastian asked. He had never known this and was even more shocked by Gunny's bringing it up.

"Yes, I knew him for a very short period, but in that short time he proved to be a very capable Marine and NCO. I know your brother will be fine; he will have no problem taking care of himself and his family. He'll do what is necessary now, just like he did in Fallujah."

"I hear ya, Gunny. I just feel like we need to be with our families and protecting them now. I'm a faithful Marine, but my family is important to me," Sebastian said.

"Like I said, there are others who feel the way you do and have expressed these concerns with just as much passion, but unless our orders change, we must push forward."

"I know, Gunny. Thanks again and thank you for mentioning my brother. I do feel better now that we've talked," Sebastian said.

"Not a problem. We're a big family here too and we must take care of our Marines when they have a legitimate issue or concern," Gunny said, placing his hand on Sebastian's shoulder and patting it.

Sebastian turned around and walked away. He really did feel better knowing that the Gunny knew his brother and appreciated his affirming that Gordon was very capable. However, the conversation didn't relieve his overall issue with the new mission. As he walked back to his tent, an unfamiliar, unexpected thought popped into his mind. Should he abandon his unit and find a way home?

Tinker Air Force Base, Oklahoma

"Sir, based upon mounting evidence and credible intelligence, we have concluded that Washington, D.C., has been destroyed and all remnants of our government there has gone with it. At this time, it is monumentally important that we maintain continuity," Griswald explained, placing his pointer down on the table in front of him.

"What do you mean, General?" Conner asked.

"Sir, our intelligence indicates that both the president and vice president were killed in this morning's attacks. We must get you sworn in as soon as possible and transport you immediately to a secure underground bunker."

"General, before you go any further, I need to be excused for a moment. Where's the closest bathroom?" Conner stood up, overwhelmed by this staggering revelation.

"Just down the hall, sir, on the left," an Air Force officer answered.

"Thank you, I'll be back in a few." Conner stepped away from the table and walked quickly to the door. He pushed it open and made his way as quickly as he could to the bathroom. He went inside the bathroom and called out to make sure he was alone. He opened all the stall doors to double check. Once comfortable that he was truly alone, he walked to the sink and turned on the cold tap. He cupped a handful of water and splashed it on his face. After a few more splashes, he stared into the mirror at his own reflection. As he watched the water drip down his face, he noticed dark circles under his bloodshot eyes.

"Oh my God," he said to himself, unable to break his gaze into the mirror. The weight of everything that had happened over the past eight hours was unbelievable. It felt surreal. He reached over and grabbed a paper towel from the dispenser and dried his face and hands. He then paced around the empty bathroom for a minute before he approached the mirror again. He bent over, grabbed the sides of the sink, and stared at his reflection again and said, "Brad, pull yourself together. Your country needs you. Be the leader you know you can be. You have a responsibility to lead this nation. Stop freaking out and pull it together."

He stood up straight, taking a final glance at himself, then left the bathroom. When he walked back into the briefing room, all conversation halted and everyone looked over to him.

"General Griswald, I need you to coordinate a team to go retrieve my wife and my son's body from St. Anthony's Hospital. Once they are secure, we shall leave."

"Yes, sir, but can we swear you in now?"

"Not until your team gets my wife. Do you understand?"

"Yes, sir." Griswald turned to his aide and shot him a commanding look. The aide jumped up and left the room, followed by Agent Davis.

"Please keep me briefed on my wife's situation at all times. I have another request, General. Go find a judge and get me a Bible."

San Diego, California

As soon as Jimmy made the turn into the Ralph's parking lot, he and Gordon could see the crowd gathered outside and commotion erupting. As they drove closer, they could see people hauling items, pushing full shopping carts out of the store.

"Looks like the word has gotten out," Jimmy said aloud.

"Yes, it does," Gordon replied, nodding his head in agreement. "Listen, I don't feel safe leaving the one and only operational vehicle out in the open. Pull up over there and I'll go see what I can get inside by myself," Gordon told Jimmy, pointing over to an area in the parking lot that had few cars and few people.

As he slowly weaved around parked cars toward the area Gordon indicated, Jimmy noticed many in the crowd looking and pointing at the truck. He felt uneasy and was now glad Gordon had given him the gun.

"Make sure you park in a spot that you don't have to back out of," Gordon recommended, pointing to a spot next to a line of shopping carts.

"Good idea," Jimmy said as he took a left into the spot.

"I don't know how long I'll be. With all this going on it might be hard to get what we need," Gordon said while checking his cash and gun and grabbing his pack. He opened the truck door and stepped down. Before closing the door behind him, he bent over, looked into the car, and said, "Stay frosty, my friend."

"Stay frosty?" Jimmy asked.

"It means stay alert," Gordon said, and shut the door. He grabbed a cart and started running toward the front of the store. People all around rushed in and out of the store. Some people were pushing full carts; others just were running out with arms full of groceries. He pushed his cart directly into the crowd and pushed his way through. After a minute of pushing and elbows he made it inside. He stopped, put on his headlamp, and headed for the canned food area.

Inside, people were running all around, groceries were all over the floors, and people were yelling and screaming. Gordon ignored the commotion and went directly for the aisle he needed. Once he reached the canned food section, he saw that many of the shelves had been stripped, but not completely bare. Not wanting to waste any time, Gordon started to toss in whatever he could get his hands on.

He made his way down the aisle and cleared what he could. His makeshift plan was to fill up the cart, go back to Jimmy at the car, leave the cart for Jimmy to unload, grab a new cart, and do it all over again. What was becoming more problematic every passing moment was the setting sun on the horizon. Gordon was getting a bit concerned for Jimmy outside by himself. He followed his plan and with no altercation he left the store and dropped off the cart.

He grabbed a new cart and made his way back into the store, keeping aware of his surroundings as best he could in the semi-darkness. He heard people falling into shelves and displays as they stumbled through the store with no light, tripping over loose cans and other items dropped by previous looters. He remembered judging people he'd seen on TV, looting stores after natural disasters. He felt a bit hypocritical, but this was a life-or-death situation.

Four trips later, the truck was filling but the store had been all but stripped bare. The sun was very low on the horizon now and Gordon knew it was time to get home.

"Well, I better start to like canned corn," Jimmy said, looking at all the Ralph's brand canned corn piled in the bed of his truck.

"Not too much to choose from, buddy. Kind of slim pickings."

"What a mess," Jimmy said, nodding toward the groups of people darting in and out of the store.

Out of nowhere, someone rushed the truck on the driver's side.

"Help, please help me!" a man shouted. His shirt was bloody and he was sweating badly.

"Whoa," Jimmy said clearly shocked by the bloodied man knocking on his window.

"Get away from the truck!" Gordon yelled.

"Please help me, my wife; I need someone to take her to the hospital!" The man frantically banged on the hood and glass of the driver's side of the truck.

"Stop hitting my fucking truck, dude! Back off!" Jimmy yelled back.

"Listen, back off!" Gordon yelled again.

"I need your help, my wife is having a baby and she's bleeding badly; I need someone to take her to the hospital."

"What should we do?" Jimmy asked Gordon.

"Start the truck and leave. We can't help him or his wife," Gordon said firmly.

"Please help me!" the man screamed. He was starting to get crazed and looked desperate.

"Maybe we should help him," Jimmy said to Gordon.

Gordon pulled out his Sig and pointed it at the man, who immediately backed away.

"I need help, please don't shoot me!" the man said, backing away slowly.

"Now start the truck and get the fuck out of here," Gordon yelled in a commanding voice to Jimmy.

Jimmy didn't hesitate; he started the truck, put it into gear, and started to pull away. He looked at the man again and saw him just standing there, arms slumped forward, defeated.

"Let's move, Jimmy. It's getting dark and we need to get back," Gordon said.

"Okay," Jimmy responded. His heart was still racing from the incident with the man. He gripped the steering wheel tight as he maneuvered the truck through the people and cars in the lot.

"What's going to happen to us?" Jimmy asked Gordon as soon as they cleared the parking lot.

"I don't know, Jimbo. I don't know. What I do know is that I plan on making sure my family survives."

"How long will the power be out? I just can't believe that our government or the military are down. I'm sure they'll help soon, don't you think?"

"Again, I don't know if this is an isolated situation, but it sounds like it may not be. If this is a large-scale EMP attack, then more than likely the entire power grid in the U.S. is down. Just dealing with getting the power back up by itself is a huge issue. Now add insult to injury and have everything electrical from cars to phones to generators—everything is down, and how do you repair or replace those systems on the power grid? Jimmy, I fear we may be in for a long haul; we may not see the lights come on at all for a very, very long time. When they do, there's a good chance the world we knew before will have been lost." He turned away from Jimmy and stared out the window of the car. Everything looked the same, the mountains were still there, the roads, buildings, and houses, but nothing worked.

"Do you have any type of plan?" Jimmy asked.

"Yes and no. Was I really prepared for something like this? No. Do I have everything we need? No. Do I plan on getting it? Yes," Gordon said, turning back to his friend.

"What do we need?"

"Food, water, medicine, fuel, and ammo are our basic needs. Precious metals, gems, and cash for a short time will help us secure more of those needs. We have a very short window before all the food is gone," Gordon said.

"What about our neighbors?"

"I haven't figured that out yet, but we should all get together sometime tomorrow and attempt to have a community meeting. The truth is this: Not all of us are going to survive this. It will take three days, tops, and San Diego will be out of food. The water will start to dry up too. In about a week, we could start to see wandering bands of people looking for food in our neighborhood. We'll have to secure our community, lock it down."

"Should we leave?" Jimmy asked with concern in his voice.

"My gut says yes, but at the moment we have only one vehicle between us. We need to find more vehicles. Until we can put everything together, we should focus on food and water so our families don't starve."

"Okay, just take the lead, Gordon, and tell me what needs to be done; you seem more ready for this than me."

"I wish I were more ready, but we have no choice but to go forage every day," Gordon said. "How are we looking for gas?"

"I have half a tank, it can last us tomorrow depending on how far we go, but we'll need to get some more soon," Jimmy said.

"I agree. Once we off load all the food and divide it up, let's make a plan."

"Sounds good," Jimmy replied. He was feeling better knowing that he had Gordon as a friend. Gordon was taking charge, and Jimmy didn't mind. This survival stuff was not up his alley. He didn't know what lay ahead for all of them but he felt better knowing that they had an advantage.

• • •

“How long will they be gone?” Simone asked Samantha. Simone and Jimmy had known each other since high school. The love they felt for each other ran deep. She had short dark hair and was petite. She had been raised in the Northeast and had the typical northeastern accent that accompanied her sweet but hyper personality. Simone was more on edge than usual because the blackout had stopped her from taking her and Jimmy’s son, Mason, to his doctor’s appointment. They had recently been informed that he had asthma.

“I don’t know, but I’m sure they’ll be fine,” Samantha answered as she poured some lukewarm milk for Haley. Samantha was nervous too but didn’t want to show it. Simone, however, was visibly freaked out.

“When will the government come and get this all straightened out? I’m sure this is only temporary,” Simone said aloud just to reassure herself. She was pacing in the ever-darkening kitchen.

“I’m sure you’re right. Soon all of this will be over and we’ll be back to normal,” Samantha answered, even though she knew better. Everything that Gordon had told her made it sound as if the power might be out for months.

“Mommy, can I have my milk?” Haley asked, walking into the kitchen.

“Here, sweetie,” Samantha replied gently to Haley, handing her the cup she had just filled.

Haley grabbed the milk and ran down the hall to the playroom.

Samantha watched as Haley ran on and was deeply saddened by what was happening. She was scared most for her children and what they might have to experience. She then thought of Simone and her son, Mason.

"How has Mason been?" Samantha asked.

"He's okay. We've explained to him what he has and he kind of understands. We have been drilling into his head to make sure he has his inhaler wherever he goes."

"I'm so sorry for you all."

"I just feel better knowing what it is; the unknown is what scared me the most. At least now we can tackle it and move down a road of treatment."

"How has work been for Jimmy?" Samantha asked, almost ashamed by how mundane the question was.

"Business has been up and we are hoping to secure a new contract with a large client soon. Jimmy has been working on it all month. He's put a lot of time into it and has been working so many late nights to make sure it happens."

"That's great," Samantha replied. She could not stop thinking about Gordon. The small talk wasn't helping her forget what was happening. She trusted Gordon above anyone else and knew he was a capable man. She was just feeling very insecure now and wanted him home.

Her thoughts were broken by the flash of headlights cutting across the room. She and Simone looked at each other excitedly. They both jumped up and walked to the front door.

Simone opened the door just as Gordon was walking up the path.

"Hi, Gordon. Everything okay?" Simone asked.

"Yes, we're all good. The trip went well. I need to go and open the garage door." Gordon walked briskly by Simone and Samantha. Even back at the house, he was certainly a man on a mission. He wanted to get the truck in the garage as soon as possible to get it unloaded.

Gordon made his way into the garage, found the cord that disengaged the automatic garage door, and pulled it, releasing the lock. He lifted the door manually.

Jimmy slowly drove the truck into the garage. Gordon stepped outside and looked both left and right to see if anyone had seen them. He couldn't see much now that the sun had set and it was getting dark outside. The neighborhood seemed eerie and unnatural with no sounds or lights. After his quick scan of the neighborhood, he pushed the door back down.

With the garage door shut, he turned to Jimmy and said, "Let's get this unloaded."

Simone had come in the garage with a lantern that painted the garage with a yellow glow.

Both Jimmy and Gordon wasted no time in unpacking the truck. The wives stood in the doorway to the garage. Gordon noticed Samantha and stopped for a brief moment to look at her. They made eye contact and Gordon smiled, then went back to work unloading.

"Well, Simone, I hope you like lima beans and Spam!" Jimmy said jokingly as he stacked a case of Spam on top of the case of canned lima beans.

"Was all of this necessary?" Simone asked, helping grab loose cans and items. "This is a lot of food. How long do you think the power outage will last?"

Jimmy looked nervously to Gordon. Gordon stopped unloading and answered her question. "Simone, this could last a while. After we're done unloading, I'll explain what I think is going on."

Gordon went back to stacking when they heard a knock at the front door.

"I doubt it's the pizza guy," Jimmy joked as he headed into the house.

He opened the door slightly and peeked out. His neighbor Melissa stood on his porch holding her newborn baby.

"Hi, Jimmy, I'm sorry to bother you, but have you seen Eric?"

"Uh, no. Sorry, I just got home myself."

"I can't reach him, my phone won't work, and my car won't start. I'm kind of freaked out," Melissa explained intensely. She was rocking back and forth attempting to soothe her baby, who was making some noises.

"Uh, come on in. I'm sorry, come on in," Jimmy said, fully opening the door.

"I don't want to impose. Do you have a phone that works?" she asked.

"No, sorry; our phones are down too. Now come on in."

"Maybe for a minute, thank you."

Stepping inside the foyer, she held her baby close. Just as Jimmy shut the door behind her, Samantha walked in from the garage.

"Hi, Melissa! How are you doing?

"Hi, Samantha. I'm fine; just haven't heard from Eric since the power went out. It's getting late and I don't know what's going on."

"Come on in, sweetie," Samantha said. She walked up to Melissa and put her arm around her and walked her down the hall to the living room.

Jimmy watched as the two ladies walked down the dim, candlelit hallway before he proceeded back into the garage.

"That's it, all unloaded," Gordon said, placing the last can of food on top of the stack.

"Wow, that's a lot of food," Jimmy remarked, looking at everything they had brought back.

"Not nearly enough, pal. We will definitely need to go back out tomorrow."

"How is that not enough food?" Simone asked, staring down the impressive stacks of food.

"Let's go inside, grab a drink, and I'll explain."

They all marched into the house.

• • •

The group all gathered in the living room. Gordon sat down in a large cushioned chair in the corner. It wasn't until then that he realized how sore and tired he was. He took a drink of the Knob Creek bourbon Simone had poured him and closed his eyes briefly. When he opened them, everyone was staring at him expectantly.

Gordon sat up and said, "Well, I assume since everyone is looking at me, they want to know my thoughts on all of this?"

Simone nodded, then said, "Yes, 'cause I'm kinda freaking out here." There was a frantic tone to her voice.

Jimmy reached over and touched Simone's knee. She brushed his hand away and snapped, "Listen, I need to know what's going on. Why all the food, what's up?"

"Just relax. He'll explain," Jimmy said, reaching back, squeezing her knee.

"Don't tell me to relax! Something is going on and it doesn't sound good," she shot back at Jimmy.

Knowing their back and forth was not productive, Gordon interrupted. "Simone, you're right, something has happened and it's not good."

"Okay. I'm listening," Simone said.

"We must accept that our way of life has been altered and prepare for a life without any of the luxuries of modern society, like electricity. I don't know the extent of the problem or what is happening outside of our city, but I'm guessing it's widespread."

"What does that mean, you're 'guessing it's widespread'? What has happened?" Melissa asked, seeming annoyed but really more nervous and scared.

Gordon continued. "Everything I'm about to tell you is an educated guess. I do not know exactly what happened, but what appears to have happened is that we've been attacked by an EMP bomb."

Simone nervously interrupted again. "EM what?"

"EMP; it stands for electromagnetic pulse. One can be produced by detonating a nuclear bomb."

Simone gasped, "Oh my God!" She reached over and grabbed Jimmy's hand.

Gordon continued on. "An EMP is just a super charge of electricity. Anything that is electrical or has circuits gets fried within a millionth of a second."

"What about radiation?" Melissa asked.

Gordon acknowledged her concern and answered, "From my knowledge on the topic, there are no effects from radiation. The bomb was probably detonated a few hundred miles in the air. The strategy behind an EMP is to wipe out everything electronic. This is where it becomes a major problem. Everything in our lives runs off of electricity, everything! With no power or transportation, all food and water supplies will dry up, fast. A single grocery store will only have about a three-day supply of food. Without trucks bringing in new supplies, that's it. Water will stop flowing as well, because we get water pumped to us from somewhere. Without power, those pumps will cease to work. We should not expect to get help from anyone, because the government and law enforcement are in the same situation: no operable cars or power. Depending how large and where the bomb was blown up, this could be affecting the entire country."

"How long will we be without power?" Simone asked, terrified. She was gripping Jimmy's hand very tightly.

"Simone, that's a good question. Worst case could be six months or more."

"What?" Simone couldn't believe his answer.

"If the power stays off for longer than a week, we will start to see society collapse, plain and simple. The life we knew before is gone and I don't know if it will ever come back."

Simone put her head in her hands and started to cry. Jimmy put his arms around her and tried to comfort her.

"What do we need to do?" Melissa asked.

Gordon was staring at Simone. Then he turned to answer Melissa. He thought to himself how interesting it was how each individual responds to situations. He admired her pragmatism.

"First thing is not to worry too much about Eric. He's probably finding a way back home now. Unfortunately, that probably means walking back. That could mean he won't show up until tomorrow sometime, so don't panic if you don't see him tonight. While you're waiting for him, you need to go back home and fill all of your tubs and sinks with water. Make sure you clean them out as well as you can before filling, of course. Do not use the toilets from now on. Eat the food in your freezer and anything that is perishable first. Keep your canned foods for last. Locate all of your fuel if you have any; candles, matches, lighters, flashlights, et cetera. Use all of them sparingly."

"What about Sophie?" Melissa looked down to her baby in her arms.

Gordon paused and looked at Melissa rocking Sophie. "She'll be fine. You're breast-feeding, right?"

Melissa nodded.

"Then she'll be okay, as long as you take care of yourself. Do not give her any water unless you know it's clean. I recommend you go home now and start prepping. We'll keep an eye on you from here. If you need anything, come by."

Jimmy reassured them. "Yes, Melissa, don't hesitate. Come by if you need anything, anything at all."

Melissa stood up and started for the door. Gordon followed her out.

"Melissa, if you need anything please let us know. I'd say call, but . . ." Gordon made a weak attempt at humor.

Melissa smiled and said thank you. "I'll let you all know when Eric makes it back."

Gordon watched as she walked off into the darkness toward the sidewalk. He closed the door and went back into the living room. Jimmy was trying to console Simone, who was still very upset. Not wanting to intrude, he left the room and walked down the hallway toward the playroom. He saw the small light flicker off and on in the room and heard laughter. He walked up to the doorway and looked in. The kids were under a blanket with the flashlight; they were turning it off and on.

He then realized Samantha hadn't been in the living room when he walked in on Jimmy and Simone. He assumed she'd be in the kitchen, but when he checked, it was empty. He spent the next few minutes looking for her. Finally he checked the garage, saving it for last because he couldn't think of any reason she'd go in there by herself. He opened the door and, sure enough, there she was. She was holding a notepad, taking an inventory of the food they had just brought back.

"What are you doing?" he asked, already knowing her answer.

"Taking inventory; it needed to be done. Why don't you go and get the bike and trailer and bring it back so we can take our half home," she suggested, not looking away from the notepad.

"That's not going to happen. I am sore as hell and like my grandad used to say, 'work smart, not hard,'" Gordon replied.

Not looking at him she responded, "However you get this home, just get it done."

"Yes, ma'am." He walked over to her and stood behind her. He reached around with his arms and brought her close to him. "I love a take-charge woman."

"Gordon, now is not the time," she said, shrugging him off.

"Okay. I just love it when you start to bark orders," he said, and then slapped her on the butt.

She stopped writing for the first time since he walked into the garage and snapped at him. "Really, you think this is an appropriate time?"

Gordon stepped away and said, "It's okay, I know where you live."

She rolled her eyes and shook her head.

Gordon went back into the living room. Jimmy was still on the couch but Simone was gone.

"Where did Simone go?" Gordon asked

"She went to go check on the kids."

"Hey, I'm going to load up my supplies in your truck and take them to my house, okay?"

"You do that," Jimmy responded. He reached down and grabbed his glass of bourbon and tossed it back, downing the whole glass.

Gordon looked at his friend for a moment, then headed back to the garage. He was tired but there still was a lot of work to do before he would rest.

Tinker Air Force Base, Oklahoma

Flanked by an entourage of people, Conner walked briskly toward the aircraft waiting on the tarmac.

"How is it this plane is operational?" Conner asked, pointing at the aircraft.

"It's an E-6 Mercury, sir," Griswald answered loudly. He almost had to yell as they grew closer to the plane. The high-pitched whine of the plane's engine made it hard to hear. "We did do something right, sir. We have a fleet of these that are hardened against nuclear or EMP attacks. They are a mobile command post to be used for incidents just as this."

"Glad to hear some of our money was spent wisely," Conner responded.

Standing at the base of the stairwell, he looked up contemplatively. He'd walk through the door as Speaker of the House and out as the president of the United States. Grabbing the rail, he jogged up the stairs. A uniformed officer saluted and led him to a furnished conference room on board.

Griswald and a few members of the entourage followed Conner into the conference room. Conner turned to Griswald and asked, "Any update on my wife?"

"No, sir, not yet. Sir, we have not been able to track down a judge but we do have a Bible. May I suggest we get you sworn in so we can proceed with any response we may have to these attacks?" Griswald implored.

"Okay, let's do this," Conner said, standing up.

Griswald turned to his aide. "Give me the Bible and the oath of office."

The aide stepped forward with both requested items.

"Stand there and hold the Bible," Griswald instructed his aide.

Conner placed his left hand on the Bible and raised his right hand.

Griswald proceeded, "Mr. Speaker, please repeat after me. I, Bradley Raymond Conner . . ."

Conner repeated, "I, Bradley Raymond Conner . . ."

". . . do solemnly swear . . ."

". . . do solemnly swear . . ."

". . . that I will faithfully execute the Office of President of the United States . . ."

". . . that I will faithfully execute the Office of President of the United States . . ."

". . . and will, to the best of my ability, preserve, protect, and defend the Constitution of the United States. So help me God."

". . . and will, to the best of my ability, preserve, protect, and defend the Constitution of the United States. So help me God," Conner finished, overwhelmed with emotion.

Griswald put his hand out. "Mr. President."

Conner took his hand and shook it, then gave his first order as president: "General, I need an up-to-date briefing on the status of everything."

"Yes, sir," Griswald answered enthusiastically.

All those in the room took their seats. Griswald sent his aide to find out what new information might have come in since their last briefing more than an hour ago.

"While we wait, can you tell me now how our forces are positioned around the globe?" Conner asked.

Griswald turned on the large flat-screen monitor at the head of the room. He pulled up a map of the world and started to touch options on the side. With each tap on the screen, avatars representing military units began to appear on the map.

"Sir, what we know as of this morning is that we have carrier groups positioned here and here. We also have two Amphibious Ready Groups positioned here and here. Each ARG represents a reinforced battalion of Marines and all the air assets they would have to accompany them. In Afghanistan, we have two more battalions of Marines. Our land-based Army units in Europe have been unresponsive. This is due to an EMP detonation over central Europe that has destroyed the entire power grid from England to central Russia. All military units in the contiguous United States are down. We have been able to reach Hawaii and Alaska. There we have a mix of Army, Navy, Air Force, and a Marine Infantry Brigade located in Hawaii. Many of our attack and ballistic missile submarines are fully operational and are located here, here, here, and here."

Interrupting Griswald, Conner asked, "General, tell me what you think happened or how it happened."

"Sir, we believe that the EMP bomb was deployed on a missile and fired from some type of ship-based platform."

"What happened to our missile defense systems?"

"Sir, we don't know why the missile was not intercepted or if an attempt was made to intercept it. We strongly believe it was fired from offshore, probably on board a container ship."

"Why do you believe that?" Conner asked, leaning forward and placing his elbows on the table.

"One reason is that the ship would have to have been large. We did not have any intelligence on any large, state-flagged military ships nearby, so this was probably a container cargo ship. It would have had to be large enough to hold the missiles and ordinary enough not to be noticed. We are not sure if both missiles were deployed from the same ship or separately. We have to assume the missile that hit D.C. was fired from somewhere in the Atlantic. This would have reduced the distance and time for the missile to travel, increasing their odds of success. Now, if they both weren't shot from the same ship, then a likely location for launching the missile that had the EMP would be the Gulf of California."

"Do we have any idea who did this?"

"No, we do not know for sure."

"Answer this question with all honesty: With the entire power grid down across the country, when can we get it back up and what can we expect from the loss of the grid?"

"Sir, based upon all estimates, it would take as little as six months to as great as eighteen months to get the grid back up. The main problem is that all the power plants are down; we have no means of direct communication to speak with them. We don't have the assets in country now to bring in supplies to get them back up. Without power and without transportation assets, it's not just the power grid that is gone but the entire interstate infrastructure that supplies critical food, water, and medical supplies. The general population, specifically those located in major cities across the country, will start to feel the strain from the lack of food and fresh water within days. Local authorities have no means of assisting their local populations because all of their assets are down too."

"Okay, so no power for a while. The main issue I'm hearing from you is a lack of food for the general population."

"Yes, sir."

"What can we do?"

"Not much right now, sir. What I suggest is we recall all of our military assets from across the globe. Bring them home. They have operational equipment and can assist in resupply to local municipalities."

"How do you propose that?"

"You asked me to be honest, sir, and, honestly, I don't know even where to begin."

Conner sat back in his chair. He was deep in thought. He then propped back up and asked, "General, without power, food, water, and medical supplies, what do you estimate will happen to the general population?"

"Sir, we have done those studies before." He got up from his chair and approached the screen. He tapped a few buttons and pulled up a timeline. "Before I begin, sir, let me start by saying that right now there is not a lot we can do to assist the general population. Right now they are on their own. What we must focus on is getting the grid back up and maintaining the continuity of government. Once the grid is up, we can start to focus on supplying the general population."

"I don't agree with you completely, but I hear what you are suggesting. What I am asking is what are we looking at in terms of casualties?"

Griswald turned around and tapped the screen; a graph came up. "Within the first few minutes of the detonation of the EMP, we estimate that approximately one hundred and fifty thousand people died."

"What?" Conner said loudly in disbelief.

"Yes, sir. Based upon the detonation time we can estimate that approximately three thousand aircraft were in the sky at that time across the country. Assuming the average passenger load would be fifty people, you get to our estimate pretty easily. The EMP would have knocked out the aircraft's engines and they would have fallen to the ground."

"Good God, that many people?"

"Sir, it's just the beginning. The nuclear bomb that struck Washington, D.C., was an approximately one-hundred-kiloton bomb. The epicenter of the explosion was near Kingman Park in the District. Everything within one mile of the explosion was completely destroyed. The Capitol and White House fell just outside of that zone, but a couple of aerial photos, seen here, show those structures are just about leveled."

Conner sat silently in awe of the photos he was seeing.

"Mr. President, the initial loss of life estimated in Washington due to the nuclear attack is probably in the one hundred thousand range. We estimate another hundred thousand will perish due to radiation exposure, dehydration, and starvation." Griswald paused, allowing the information to settle with Conner, while trying to process it emotionally himself. He then continued. "Mr. President, I need to warn you, the following numbers are staggering. Within the first month, the total loss of life will be about three to five million, within three months about fifteen to twenty million. By the six-month mark another fifty million, and, if nothing changes, within a year, ninety percent of the United States population will be dead."

"Ninety percent! I don't understand; why so many?" Conner asked, exasperated.

"Mr. President, in the first month with no power and with a lack of a constant flow of adequate food, water, and medical supplies, all of those Americans who are hospitalized or have any sort of special needs will most likely perish. Starvation starts to take its toll around month two and mass starvation will start to hit by month six. This doesn't take into account the civil unrest that will kill tens of thousands."

"What can we do? We must do something."

"Mr. President, there isn't much we can do for the average

American. The best thing we can do is reestablish the continuity of government, and, from there, we can start to get the infrastructure back in place. I recommend we find a vice president for you as well as a cabinet. We can then set up teams to go to the state capitals and make liaison with governors. With the U.S. capital destroyed, we will need to find a new seat of government for us. I recommend a military base that is secure with an underground bunker."

Conner just sat back in his chair. He folded his arms and concentrated on this overwhelming flow of difficult information. He leaned forward and asked again, "General, do we know who did this? If so, what are your recommendations for a response?"

"Mr. President, we do not know exactly who is responsible for these attacks. We obviously have suspects, but no one has stepped forward to accept responsibility, nor do we have access to any intel that lets us know."

"Okay, based upon whatever intel we do have, how are our allies doing?

"Sir, it appears that similar attacks were conducted against Europe, the Pacific Rim, and an attack was stopped in Australia."

"How did the Aussies stop their attack?"

"We do not know; we have received intel from them that they were able to seize a ship that had a nuclear weapon aboard it. We are working with them to see what intel we can gather from their interrogations of those captured."

"How did the Aussies manage to stop the attack and not us?" Conner was getting a bit indignant.

"All we can assume, sir, is that our resources were stretched thin with all the recent attacks—"

"That's it! The other attacks were just to bog us down so they could orchestrate this attack."

"Yes, sir, that sounds like exactly what happened," Griswald answered back.

• • •

Griswald continued his briefing for another half an hour. The more information he presented, the more helpless Conner felt. He had become the most powerful man in the world but without the power.

"Sir, what would you like us to do?" Griswald asked.

"I need to process everything. I need you to get me a list of possible suspects and I want to speak with the prime minister of Australia as soon as possible. I want you to get all of our military assets back into the United States as soon as possible. I want some of them on the East Coast to assist with recovery efforts." Conner paused, thought for a minute, then looked back at Griswald. "Once my wife is on board, let's depart."

"Sir, where do you want to go?"

"Florida."

"Florida, sir?" Griswald asked, confused.

"Yes, Florida," Conner said, standing up.

"Why Florida?" Griswald asked with a puzzled tone.

"You said I need a VP, didn't you?"

DECEMBER 6, 2014

• • •

Here is a test to find out whether your mission in life is complete. If you're alive, it isn't.

—Richard Bach

Musa Qala, Helmand Province, Afghanistan

"Get your asses on that bird, boys, go, go!" Gunny yelled at his Marines.

The CH-53 was waiting, ramp down and props moving. Sebastian stood in his designated stick, weighted down by his gear and his thoughts. As they boarded, the crew chief pointed for them to go directly to the front of the helicopter.

All the Marines in his squad sat down one after another without much thought; this was a normal drill for them. Sebastian turned and peered through the small window behind him. He saw one helicopter after another spread out along the flat plain with lines of Marines slowly boarding. He looked past the choppers to the mountains; he thought that he'd probably never see this place again. How strange, he thought, that the U.S. spent so much blood and treasure to help create a new democracy while theirs at home was now in peril. Looking back now it seemed like such a waste. He turned his head back around and looked at his fellow Marines all sitting on the webbing. After Gunny boarded, the crew chief lifted the ramp and readied the chopper for liftoff. Like he always did, Sebastian said a ritualistic prayer. As he finished his prayer, he felt the chopper start to lift. There is nothing like flying in a chopper; the combination of the sound and smell was unique. He quickly turned around again and looked through the glass. The glare of the sun first blinded him, then, as the chopper banked, the mountains came into view again. He wanted one last look at his home away from home. Facing forward, he settled in for what he knew would be a long ride by tipping his helmet to cover his eyes and going to sleep.

Sebastian's slumber was interrupted by Tomlinson tapping his arm.

"Hey, corporal, we're getting close!" Tomlinson yelled.

Sebastian sat up and looked over his shoulder out the window. All he saw was blue sky and blue water below. Then the ships came into view when the chopper banked to the right.

There below him was the *Makin Island* Amphibious Ready Group. On board was the 11th Marine Expeditionary Unit, who has been at sea for months now in the western Pacific and the Indian Ocean. His unit would be sharing quarters and the ship's amenities with a bunch of grunts from 1st Battalion 1st Marine Regiment, a sister unit from Camp Pendleton.

• • •

"Let's go, Marines, move!" Gunny hollered. Sebastian and his team of Marines stood up and walked off the chopper. They proceeded down the ship's tarmac toward the aft of the ship. The cool ocean air felt good and helped to mask the strong smell of fuel. Sebastian could also smell the saltiness of the ocean. He loved ship life, and especially loved the port calls; unfortunately there would not be liberty anytime soon. The days of pulling into foreign ports and enjoying the local flavor were over.

Not long passed before they were led off the flight deck and into a passageway. After maneuvering through tight, narrow hatches and down steep stairwells loaded with their gear, they finally reached their new home. Upon entering they could see that it hadn't been vacant for long.

"Nice of them to clean up for us," a Marine said sarcastically.

"Gunny, what's up with this shit? We get left with cum-stained sheets and a head that's totally unsat!" another Marine hollered, after exiting the head.

"Marines, I understand you're upset, but this isn't the Ritz. Get this place cleaned up before chow at seventeen hundred. Corporal Van Zandt, come here," Gunny said in his loud and commanding voice.

Sebastian dropped his pack on a rack and walked up to the Gunny.

"Yes, Gunny."

"Grab a working party of three Marines and make sure our gear that's coming in gets down here. Once that's done, make sure you get some chow, okay?"

"Copy that, Gunny," Sebastian said. He turned around and walked back to his rack.

Tomlinson looked at him. "I'll help out."

"Thanks, go get Morris and Randall too," Sebastian said.

• • •

As Sebastian and his working party were making their way through the maze of passageways toward the flight deck, they ran right into some unexpected commotion. A group of armed Marines were forcibly escorting some naval officers down the narrow passageway.

"Step aside, coming through!"

Sebastian and his Marines stepped back out of the way as best they could as the armed Marines quickly passed by. Sebastian noticed the officers were a high-ranking bunch. He had been in long enough now to know something was up and that he had never seen a Navy captain being escorted away by a group of enlisted Marines.

"What was that all about?" Tomlinson asked aloud.

"I don't know, but it didn't look good," Sebastian responded. "Let's get topside and see if something is going on."

They hurried the rest of the way without further incidents, opened the hatch to the flight deck, and stepped out. The bright sunlight blinded them all as they stepped over the hatch entrance onto the deck outside. There was a flurry of activity on the flight deck with more choppers coming in.

Sebastian recognized a Marine from S-4, his unit's logistics and supply unit. He approached him and asked, "Has the gear started arriving yet for the STA platoon?"

"No gear has arrived yet, we're just getting the last of the personnel, then the gear will follow; probably within an hour or so," the S-4 sergeant answered.

"Thank you," Sebastian said. He turned back to his Marines. As he was walking back, he looked up toward the superstructure and saw Barone just outside the bridge talking with another Marine. The other Marine was waving his arms around in what appeared to be anger.

Sebastian, walking back to his Marines, said, "Look there," pointing toward Barone.

All the Marines turned around and looked up.

"Something doesn't seem right now, does it?" Sebastian said.

"If I were a betting man, which I am, I would say it looks like the colonel is getting his ass chewed," Tomlinson said jokingly.

San Diego, California

Gordon shot up in his bed, awakened by cries from down the hall. He tossed off the covers and got out of bed.

"What is it?" Samantha said, a bit alarmed.

"I think it's Haley. I'll go get her; I think she's having a nightmare," Gordon said quietly. He cautiously walked down the darkened hallway to her room. When he got to Haley's bedroom door, she let out another cry.

"Mommy, Mommy, Mommy!"

He quickly opened the door and stepped inside. "It's okay, sweetie, Daddy's here."

"Daddy, Daddy," Haley said with a terrified and sobbing voice. She was sitting up in her bed and staring into the darkness of her room.

Gordon sat down on the bed, grabbed her, and brought her close. He hugged her and kissed her head. "It's okay, sweetie. Daddy is here now. It's okay."

"It's so dark," she said, still sobbing. She had lost some of her breath with all of the heavy crying.

Haley's room had a night light before, but with no power it was completely dark.

"I know, honey, but it's okay now. Do you want to come and sleep with Mommy and Daddy?"

"Yes," she answered. Her face was planted against Gordon's shoulder.

Gordon could feel her wet tears on his shoulder. He patted her head and back and then whispered to her, "Daddy's here, I will never let anything hurt you."

Gordon stood up, still holding Haley close, and walked back to his room. He climbed back into bed with Haley clinging to him.

"Come here, honey," Samantha said sweetly and softly to Haley.

"Momma," Haley said, reaching out to Samantha.

"She was afraid of the dark," Gordon told Samantha.

"I figured as much."

Gordon stood back up and was walking for the bedroom door when Samantha asked, "Where are you going?"

"I'm going downstairs; I don't think I'll be able to sleep now."

He carefully made his way down the stairs to the kitchen. Out of habit, he attempted to turn on the kitchen light, but the reality of the event yesterday suddenly came back when the lights did not turn on. Finding his way to the couch, he sat alone in the dark and thought about the events and the future. Today would be a busy day again. Knowing he couldn't hold back what he thought was happening, he planned on informing those in the community today. He was sure by now that most knew something was terribly wrong but many were not aware of how severe it was. Looking outside, the setting crescent moon took him back to the day he first met Samantha. Sitting back comfortably in the couch he thought about the weekend they had met. His thoughts raced back to that Friday afternoon more than nine years ago.

Gordon had just gotten out of the Corps and was staying in Southern California. He had no interest in going back east. He had created a small group of friends, some in and some out of the Marine Corps. One of those friends was Nelson Williams, a firefighter in Oceanside. Gordon had met Nelson while going through a water safety qualification course back in 2002. Nelson was also an Oceanside lifeguard and an instructor for the Marine Corps' Water Safety Course. Gordon and Nelson had hit it off right away. They were both the same age and had identical views of the world and politics. Nelson was throwing a party for Gordon and some of his fellow Marines from 3/1. It promised to be one of those parties that lasted all weekend. Nelson had two different reasons for throwing a party for Gordon. The main one was to introduce him to his girlfriend's best friend, Samantha. Nelson's girlfriend, Seneca, knew Gordon's type—short, blondish hair, curves, with a bit of sweet and feisty thrown in. Fortunately for Gordon, Seneca's friend from school, Samantha, fit that description. Nelson knew they would be a match and he couldn't have been more right.

Gordon's thoughts were jolted back from the past when he felt a touch on the shoulder.

"Oh my God, you scared me," Gordon said with a hushed voice so as to not wake the kids.

"Are you okay? I wanted to check on you after I put Haley back to sleep."

Gordon could see her partially illuminated by the faint moonlight coming through the door.

"I was just relaxing and thinking. Come here, sit next to me," Gordon requested.

Samantha took a few steps and then Gordon grabbed her by the waist and swung her down onto his lap. He put his arms around her and gave her a kiss on the lips. She then rested her head against his shoulder.

"I was thinking about when we met," Gordon said. "Remember that weekend?"

"I sure do," she said softly. "I knew when I first saw you that we'd be married."

"I lost all of my mojo when I saw you. I knew after our first conversation that you were a keeper, but what sealed the deal was when you saved my ass," Gordon said with a chuckle.

"Your ass needed saving. Plus, I wasn't going to let four guys beat up my future husband."

Still chuckling, Gordon followed up by saying, "Nelson still mentions that fight every time we get together. Unfortunately I didn't get to see it, but I am reminded often. You have quite a right cross when you're holding a bottle."

"I told them to get off of you, but they didn't listen," Samantha said with a sweet and soft voice.

"Please remind me to always listen to you, okay?" Gordon said, hugging Samantha tighter.

"What I need to remind you of is to stop taking on groups of people by yourself at one time."

"Wait a minute, I didn't take them on or start it. It all started when they wanted to kick Sebastian's ass for flirting with one of their girlfriends. I thought I had smoothed everything over, but those college frat boys thought they had us outnumbered six to two. When that guy laid hands on Sebastian, all negotiations ended," Gordon said, sounding more defensive.

"I remember, but I also remember you not liking it when they called you 'Scarface,' " Samantha said, rubbing Gordon's arm.

"I don't care what people say to me. But Sebastian always gets himself into trouble. That's not the first time I've gotten him out of a rough patch. He just opens his mouth and says shit he shouldn't and it goes from there. He's the one that starts it with people; I just usually have to finish it for him."

"Well, that time at the beach, I think they got the upper hand."

"I know. It irritates me still to this day that I didn't see that guy to my right."

"Honey, you can't get mad; he hit you with a two-by-four. Anybody would have dropped from that."

"I'm just glad that you smashed him in the head with that bottle," Gordon said. He paused for a moment, then continued. "Where would I be without you? You have been taking such great care of me since then," Gordon said, embracing her tighter.

Samantha was running her fingers through his hair and said softly, "Of course I take care of you. You're my man and you take such good care of me and the kids. I will always have your back."

Samantha then lifted her head and kissed him passionately on the lips.

38,000 feet over Alabama

"President? I'm president of the United States?" Conner said out loud to himself after waking from a restless sleep. He looked over at his wife's empty cot. He wondered where she might be. So much had happened in one day to the both of them. In one day he had lost his son, hundreds of thousands of Americans were dead, and his country was plunged into darkness that would last for months if not years. Over the next weeks and months, more and more Americans would die from dehydration, starvation, lack of medicine, disease, and violence. He was now the one responsible for protecting those 315 million Americans. The questions started coming to him. *Was he up to the task? How would he respond? How would he ever know who did this? What about further attacks? How could he stop those attacks?* The questions kept pouring into his mind.

The overriding question was, *How can he protect the American people in such a weakened state?* He knew then he must respond soon. The United States had many enemies, and they would definitely attempt to capitalize on their weakened state.

Standing up with renewed purpose he walked out of the room and down the narrow hallway to the communications area. He needed to speak with Griswald immediately.

Opening the door to the Communications Central Area he found Griswald talking with his aide.

"Mr. President," Griswald said, standing up quickly.

"Sit down, General," Conner said, closing the door behind him. "General, what assets do we have at our disposal this minute?"

"Sir?" Griswald asked, looking confused.

"The overriding question that I keep asking myself is, how can we protect the American people from further threats or from our enemies taking advantage of our current state?" Conner spoke quickly, almost in a ramble of thoughts. "General, how can we prevent our enemies, like North Korea or Iran, from attacking us? We are paralyzed here. Why wouldn't they take advantage and move on us? Why wouldn't they attempt an invasion or work toward doing more damage? How can we rebuild with that threat hovering over us?"

"Mr. President, those are all good questions. Why don't you take a seat and we can discuss this?"

"I don't need to take a seat! What I need are answers!" Conner snapped.

Griswald looked surprised by Conner's behavior. "I suggest we first gather our cabinet and conference with what military commanders we have and then sit down to analyze these threats to see what we can do and how we can move—"

"We don't have time to gather a cabinet and analyze data!" Conner yelled.

"Excuse me, sir," Griswald said, looking a little taken aback as he relaxed more into his chair.

"General, I need a briefing in thirty minutes on what assets we have from as simple as a grunt on the ground to where our nuclear subs are located."

"Yes, sir, I will have the information for you as best as I can, but nothing has changed with our forces since yesterday." He then looked at his aide, who nodded.

"Just do it, General!" Conner barked.

"Yes, sir," Griswald said.

Conner looked at Griswald briefly, then turned around and left the room just as abruptly as he had entered moments before.

Griswald looked at his aide again and said, "See what we can find out from our units around the world; do the best you can do."

"Yes, sir," the aide said, standing up.

"One second," Griswald said.

"Sir?"

"Does it seem like the president is a bit overwhelmed?"

"Sir?" the aide asked, looking confused.

"Nothing. Now go get me that information and confirm our transport once we land," Griswald said, pointing toward the door, motioning his aide to leave.

"Yes, sir," the aide said, leaving the room.

Griswald sat back in his chair. He wondered to himself what type of response they could muster with what available and operational assets they had around the world. He wasn't sure what kind of response the president wanted when they didn't know who attacked the country. He understood that the new president had a lot on his plate, but he also knew that what steps the United States took next must be carefully calculated.

San Diego, California

Gordon awoke suddenly. He opened his eyes to see Haley with the remote for the TV.

"Daddy, can I watch TV?" Haley asked, looking innocent and holding the remote in front of his face.

Gordon had fallen asleep on the couch with Samantha but she was nowhere to be seen. Looking outside, he saw the grayish sky of a typical Southern California morning.

"Where's Mommy?"

"Mommy is upstairs sleeping. TV, please," Haley said, still holding the remote in Gordon's face.

Gordon sat up, stretched, and said, "Honey, I'm sorry but the TV doesn't work. Can I read you a book?"

"No, I want TV," Haley said, looking disappointed.

"Honey, like I said, the TV doesn't work," Gordon said, looking at his determined daughter.

"Can you fix it, Daddy? I want to watch Disney Junior."

"Sweetie, if I could fix it I would," Gordon said as he reached over and picked her up. He kissed her on the cheek and forehead. "Believe me, honey, if I could fix it I would."

"I love you, Daddy," Haley whispered to him.

Gordon's eyes teared up as he hugged her even tighter.

"I love you too, sweetheart; you're my baby girl and I'll do anything for you. I will fix the TV, I will do what I can to fix it all, I promise you," Gordon said hugging Haley tight as tears slowly rolled down his cheek.

"Why are you crying, Daddy?"

"Because I love you so much," Gordon replied, not telling her all the reasons he was crying. He kissed her again on her head. He then said, "Run upstairs and get your three favorite books; I'll read them to you."

"Thanks, Daddy!" Haley said, jumping off of Gordon and running toward the stairs.

Gordon watched her as she ran. He felt like the world was on his shoulders. Today would be a big day for him and his family. He would finally reach out to his neighbors and inform them of what he thought had happened and try to start coordinating a community-wide effort for mutual survival. All of this would happen, though, after he spent a few moments of quality time with his daughter.

His thoughts were interrupted with Haley jumping into his lap. She held more than three books under her arms.

"Here, Daddy!"

"What's this? Looks like more than three books," Gordon said, smiling.

"Read to me, Daddy!" Haley said with excitement in her voice as she rested against his chest.

"Looks like five books."

"Please, Daddy, read them all!"

Gordon chuckled and said, "Sure thing, honey." He opened the first book and began to read.

USS *Makin Island*, Arabian Gulf

The level of activity had been at an all-time high on the ship since their arrival earlier in the morning. Some typical, but also some unusual, but these were unusual times. Sebastian's unit had already settled into their new home aboard the USS *Makin Island*. He and his team of snipers were relaxing in the berthing area and using the break to play spades.

"Are you fucking kidding me!" Tomlinson yelled as Sebastian threw down the ace of spades and took the last trick.

"Sorry, buddy, but you dealt them," Sebastian said, winking at Tomlinson as he picked up the cards.

"I dealt you like every spade in the deck. Such bullshit!"

"I think this last hand has given me the game and that twenty spot," Sebastian said, reaching over and grabbing the twenty-dollar bill next to Tomlinson.

"Want to go again?" Sebastian asked Tomlinson.

"Why not, what good is the money now anyway?"

As Sebastian was shuffling the deck of cards, the berthing area hatch opened and Gunny appeared.

"Marines, listen up!" Gunny hollered with his scratching voice.

Everyone stopped talking and all eyes focused on Gunny.

"Marines, we have a ship-wide formation on the flight deck in fifteen minutes. Get your asses squared away now, be up there in ten, do you hear me?" Gunny yelled.

Various Marines acknowledged by yelling back, "Yes, Gunny!"

The snipers began collecting themselves and putting on their blouses and boots.

"I wonder what's up now?" Tomlinson asked out loud.

"There's going to be a lot of these, I suspect, so get used to it," Sebastian replied. He put on his blouse and grabbed his cover from his rack.

When Sebastian and Tomlinson walked through the hatch they ran into a line of Marines trying to go up the ladder well. They waited a few moments and lost their patience.

"Fuck this, follow me," Sebastian said.

Tomlinson followed Sebastian down the narrow and busy passageways. They came to a closed hatch and opened it, but were quickly stopped by an armed Marine on the other side.

"Off limits," the Marine commanded.

"Off limits?" Sebastian asked.

"You heard me, corporal, this passageway is closed off," the Marine said.

"Come on, sergeant, let us cut through here so we can get to the formation, all we need to do is go up that ladder well right there," Sebastian said, pointing over the Marine's shoulder at a ladder well just a few feet away.

"No, corporal, this is off limits. I suggest you turn around and find another way."

"Come on, Sergeant . . . Devonshire," Sebastian said, pausing to look at the name badge on his chest.

Sebastian then heard some loud commotion down the passage and saw two Marines wrestle another Marine to the ground. A fourth Marine, an officer, entered from an adjacent hatch near the fight and helped the two Marines. The officer then looked down toward Sebastian and yelled, "Sergeant, shut that fucking hatch now! This area is secure and off limits!"

"Sorry, corporal," Devonshire said, quickly closing the hatch in Sebastian's face.

Sebastian turned to Tomlinson and said nothing. They both stared at each other for a moment and then Tomlinson said, "What the fuck is going on?"

"I don't know, but let's get topside," Sebastian said.

When they both finally reached the flight deck their platoon was already formed up, as were thousands of other Marines and sailors.

They quickly ran over to their platoon and got in the last row. Gunny Smith turned to them and just leered.

"Marines and sailors of the USS *Makin Island*, attention!" Master Sergeant Simpson yelled, and turned around. Barone approached the master sergeant and returned his salute. Simpson stepped to the right and marched off.

"Marines and sailors of the USS *Makin Island*, at ease!" Barone yelled. "You all know we are living in unprecedented times. Our country has suffered an attack that has brought it to its knees; our families have suffered and are suffering right now. Many thousands have already died. We have lost our entire federal government to an attack on our capital. The president and vice president are dead. There is a new president; Speaker of the House Conner was sworn in just hours ago. We still do not know who committed this attack, but we do know that they also succeeded in Europe and over China. We have learned that there was an attempt over Australia but our Australian brothers stopped it. With many of our allies down and our enemies still out there, we have been ordered to go back east to assist in the search and rescue efforts while our families suffer at home without our care. Since yesterday, I have been approached by many platoon commanders expressing your concerns, specifically your concerns for your families, wherever they may be. I am here now holding this formation to inform you there have been some changes to our mission again." Barone paused and looked around at all the Marines and sailors before him. He looked down at his boots and then looked back up and continued.

"We are not going to the East Coast; we are going back to California! I stand here before you, letting you all know that I have listened to your concerns; I heard you! We are going to go home to take care of our families!"

Many Marines and sailors started yelling their approval to what they were hearing.

Barone raised his arms and yelled, "At ease, at ease!"

The hoots and "Ooh rahs" stopped after a few moments with the assistance of platoon commanders yelling for everyone to be quiet.

Once the quiet returned, Barone continued. "This change in mission does come at a price. I started this formation by telling you that we are living in unprecedented times and unprecedented times sometimes require unprecedented actions! Sometimes we must look at what is happening around us and make decisions that at first may seem incorrect but are really the correct decisions. I have made a decision that may not seem to some of you as correct, but which I know is the right one. I have made this decision and I am willing to suffer the consequences of it. I am now going to ask you, not tell you, what you need to do. I am not ordering you to make the same choice I made, I am asking you to come with me."

Many of the Marines and sailors were looking around. Whispers and murmuring could be heard everywhere. Marines and sailors were accustomed to taking orders; now they were being given the ability to choose.

"I have secured command of this ARG; I have arrested those commanding officers who would not join me in our new mission. To some, I am committing mutiny! But in my heart I know what I am doing is right for our families regardless of what they call it."

The sound of talking and murmuring grew louder as the shock of what Barone was saying began to sink in.

"I have heard your needs and desires, I have turned us around, and we are heading for San Diego! Those of you in formation who wish to join me and go back to California so you may be with your families and protect them from the dark days ahead will be rewarded. If your family is not there but you wish to join us on the trip there you are welcome. If you do not wish to continue with us once we make landfall, you may depart then with no questions asked. Now, if you do not wish to join us at all then we will drop you off on Diego Garcia."

Barone took another pause and looked around.

"I feel it is important that in order for me to lead you on this new mission I should explain how I came to this decision. I have been a Marine for eighteen years. I love the Marine Corps. I love my country and I love my Marines and their families. I cannot in good conscience lead us to the East Coast to clean up something that I feel is a total loss. I cannot lead you knowing that your families are at risk. Our federal government is gone; those authorities back in California are also gone. Without power and equipment our families are being left to fend for themselves. Our mission back east is to dig up dead bodies. By the time we make it back home we would be doing the same thing, but those bodies would be of our families and friends. This is why I have done this. I ask you to join me on this new mission. It will not be easy, and we will be alone, but I do not see our country being the same again. I have given you the new mission; I am giving you the choice to join me. We are now living in a new world. Who out there will join me?"

Thousands of Marines and sailors yelled in unison, "Me, sir!"

"Who will join me?" Barone repeated even louder.

"Me, sir!"

Sebastian just stood there stunned and confused; he liked what he heard from Barone but he also felt that by joining him he'd be turning his back on his country. He then thought of Gordon, Samantha, and the kids. When the colonel again yelled, "Who will join me?" Sebastian raised his right arm and yelled, "Me, sir!"

Dade County, Florida

Conner could hear all the activity outside on the tarmac. Their landing had gone smoothly; in fact everything seemed to be moving too smoothly. While they waited for the convoy that would take him to meet his new vice president, Conner and Griswald were just finishing up a briefing.

"General, thank you for putting this all together so quickly," Conner said.

"Mr. President, you're welcome. I hope this has helped you understand how we sit and what options you have when you make the decision to respond. What are your thoughts on a response?" Griswald asked.

"General, I think it's important to respond very soon. I believe we can't wait too long. When I spoke with the Australian prime minister, they hadn't gotten much of anything from the individuals they had captured on that container ship. The main concern I have is that whoever committed this might attack us again, and soon. I also don't believe this was a rogue group. I believe it was orchestrated by a nation-state. What we do know is that these attacks only targeted us and our allies. China and Russia were also affected but you know who wasn't? South America, Africa, and the Middle East were not attacked. I don't think that was accidental. I feel whoever committed this came from there or was supported by a country in that area."

"Sir, I would agree with you that more than likely a nation-state like Iran or Pakistan was behind this."

"I wanted to bring this up earlier but you didn't mention our nuclear forces."

"Our nuclear forces?"

"Yes, General; I believe the only acceptable response would be to respond with a nuclear attack. We do not have the time or the resources financially to commit air or ground forces. I say we nuke the bastards and move on!"

"Mr. President, while I agree we should respond with the same force, I have to ask, who do we use them against? We don't know who attacked us."

"That, General, is the question, and one we may not be able to answer anytime soon, if ever. I ask you this: How can we even think of rebuilding if we might be attacked again? What we do know is there are many countries that do not like us. Many have worked against us before; they have supported terrorist organizations openly and have wanted our demise. If they didn't directly take part in this, haven't they indirectly supported it?"

"Mr. President, are you suggesting that we nuke them all?"

Conner sat there for a brief second looking at Griswald. There was an odd silence in the room. The air was thick with tension. All eyes were on the president, waiting for him to respond to Griswald's question.

"Yes, General, I am suggesting we nuke them all! We have to assign blame and make it happen. Our countrymen would demand an immediate response."

"Mr. President, do you know what you are asking? By unleashing our nuclear arsenal we will kill millions of innocents."

"Are there innocents anymore? What about those innocents in our country? What about them? We can't invade these countries and spend years attempting to seize them. We need to neutralize this threat once and for all. And that is by killing all of them!"

"I understand you are upset, Mr. President, but maybe a more measured response like airstrikes or cruise missiles."

"There cannot be a measured response; we must once and for all destroy our enemies. Here is what I want now. What would it take to destroy our enemies in Iran, Iraq, Pakistan, North Korea, Yemen, Libya, Egypt, Syria, Afghanistan, and Somalia?"

"All of those countries? You want to attack all of those countries with our nuclear forces?"

"I want to look at our options, General."

"Mr. President, I am concerned about this approach."

"I respect your concern, but please get me the information as soon as you can." Conner just looked at Griswald, then continued by pivoting the conversation. "Have you secured transport for me to go meet Governor Cruz?"

"I believe so."

"Great, thank you. I want to leave in twenty minutes," Conner said, standing up. "I hope to return with Governor Cruz and his family. From here, we'll go to Colorado. Thank you again," Conner finished and left the room.

Griswald stood up and watched Conner leave. After he left, Griswald turned to General Houston, the commanding officer from Homestead Air Force Base, and said, "Are you as concerned as I am?"

"Gris, look, our country has been hurt badly. I agree with the president. We have to have a firm and prompt response. Waiting only invites further attacks," Houston said with his southern drawl.

Interrupting him, Griswald fired back with anger, "What will the world think of us if we wipe each one of those countries off the map? There has to be another way."

"As I see it, we should get all of our troops who are left overseas back here to help support getting this country back on its feet. The world is a different place now; I don't know when it will recover. We have a chance now to take out once and for all those countries that dislike us and seek to do us harm. We have the legitimacy for this attack based upon what has happened here."

Griswald, looking frustrated and angry, stood up from his chair and pushed it back hard against the wall. He paced back and forth and then responded to General Houston's comment. "General, with all due respect, that is a piss-poor reason to kill millions of innocent people. While I somewhat agree in the use of our nuclear forces against those who actually perpetrated this act, we must determine with confidence who actually did it! We cannot and must not kill millions of people out of the excuse that we have been attacked and we do not get along with those people!"

"Well, Gris, at the end of the day, it's not your decision; it's the president's."

Griswald just looked at Houston with a blank stare. He then looked at the map on the table and said, "You're right, Houston; those decisions are always left to whoever is the commander in chief."

Houston cocked his head a bit, not sure of the tone in Griswald's comment.

Griswald then continued by saying, "Let's go make sure the convoy is ready to take President Conner." He immediately left the room, followed by his aide and other officers who were in the room for the briefing.

Houston, still sitting in his chair, leaned forward and rested his arms on the table. Placing his head in his hands, he took a long sigh and said, "May God save us all."

San Diego, California

Gordon's senses were alive with the sounds, smells, and feel of nature unfettered by what had happened to mankind. The birds were still chirping, the wind still had that cool ocean feel to it, the sun's warmth was still there along with the smell of sage that permeated the air. What was missing was the daily hum of traffic, the loud lawnmowers or leaf blowers. Those sounds were replaced by the sound of people walking, talking, and kids playing in the street. Many people now spent time outside their homes; no longer were they able to hide inside with their TVs, computers, and other electrical devices. Electricity created the modern world and had given people many luxuries, but it had also divided and made them a people who interacted only online. There was peacefulness about it all that Gordon liked.

He knew it would not last; he knew eventually people would start to tear at one another for what few resources were left. He had returned from another successful trip to a grocery store. Their cache of food and supplies were now enough to keep his and Jimmy's family alive for about a year. Upon their return, he stopped by each house in the neighborhood and dropped off handwritten notes. The note asked everyone to meet in the central park later in the day. He was now en route to go meet with Mindy Swanson, the HOA president. He wanted to sit down with her to explain his theory and present his solutions to confront the problem. Gordon knew that for long-term survival the neighborhood needed to come together so they could coordinate efforts to collect food, water, fuel, medicine, and other items. Pooling the talents of his neighbors was critical to his plan.

Standing nervously in front of Mindy's door, he took a deep

breath and knocked. He had known Mindy for three years. They had met within a week of their moving into the neighborhood but he never really got to know her except for her reputation as a tough-as-nails person. She usually got what she wanted and was someone who wasn't afraid of speaking her mind. They initially had a cordial relationship but had a falling out eighteen months ago because of his response to a rash of break-ins in the neighborhood. Even though Rancho Valentino was gated, thieves had managed to gain access and break into homes. He had written a letter to Mindy and the board recommending some action be taken. With no response, he went to the next board meeting and laid out his recommendations. All at the meeting expressed support for his plan but decided not to approve it because of how it might look. This angered him; they were more concerned with appearances than results. Instead, they opted for an approach of posting signs and creating an open channel of communication with police. He argued that wouldn't stop the break-ins; unfortunately, he was correct. Within days of the signs being posted two more homes were broken into. Taking it upon himself he conducted foot patrols. One night, he managed to catch those responsible. What he thought would be praise from Mindy and the board turned out to be condemnation and ridicule. She expressed openly at the next meeting and through a letter to all homeowners that she and the board did not appreciate or condone what they called his "vigilante" behavior. Gordon never forgave Mindy for the way she treated him. The entire incident split the community and created an atmosphere of mistrust that still existed.

The door opened and there stood Mindy. She was in her early Rancho Valentino forties, average height, slender with shoulder-length black hair.

"Gordon, hi," she said, looking surprised to see him.

"Hi, Mindy. I want to talk to you about the blackout," Gordon said, trying to be very professional. "Is now a good time?"

"Sure, come on in," she answered, opening the door fully.

Gordon walked in and stood just inside the foyer.

"Let's go into the living room. Can I get you water or something else to drink? Not cold, of course."

"Water would be great."

Gordon walked over to the couch and sat down. She came over with a warm bottle of water and handed it to him.

"Thank you."

Mindy took a seat in the leather chair across from him and asked, "So, how is your family?"

"They're fine, thanks. Listen, I'd like to cut straight to the situation, if you don't mind," he said as he sat up on the edge of the couch and put the water on the table next to him.

Mindy's body language signaled that Gordon made her uncomfortable.

Nodding, she said, "Sure, go for it."

"Mindy, what we are experiencing now, this blackout, is not a normal blackout. I'm sure you have now heard the rumors of an attack. What I wanted to share with you is that I think I know what happened. I believe we have been attacked with some type of electromagnetic pulse weapon; it's the only type of weapon that can cause this type of blackout. We've had blackouts before, but now our cars don't work, cell phones don't work, nothing electronic seems to work at all. What could have caused this are two things: a major coronal mass ejection from the sun, or an EMP detonation. I am guessing we would have been warned about the CME, so the EMP makes more sense," Gordon said. He was speaking quickly, and Mindy was trying to take it all in.

"Wait a minute; what you're guessing is that we've been attacked with some type of magnetic weapon? This is why nothing works?"

"Yes, we have been attacked by a nuclear weapon that was blown up somewhere in the high atmosphere."

Not letting Gordon finish, Mindy yelled out, "Gerald! Gerald! Come down here now!" Gerald was Mindy's husband; he was a lanky tall man in his mid-fifties. He was a very successful financial analyst in Rancho Santa Fe.

"Gordon, if you could wait a minute, I want Gerald to hear this."

"Sure, no problem." Gordon reached over and grabbed his water.

Gerald walked into the room and approached Gordon with his hand outstretched. Gordon stood and shook his hand firmly.

"Good to see you, Gordon," Gerald said.

"Nice to see you too."

"Gerald, please take a seat. I'll just quickly tell you that Gordon has stopped by to give us his opinion on what he thinks is going on with this blackout," Mindy said to Gerald.

"Oh, really?" Gerald said, looking over at Gordon, then taking a seat in the other leather chair next to Mindy. "What do you think is going on, Gordon?"

"I have been explaining to Mindy that this is not a normal blackout. My experience and training, coupled with what has happened, leads me to believe this situation has all the trademarks of an EMP bomb."

"EMP?" Gerald asked.

"Sorry, electromagnetic pulse. Essentially, someone has detonated a nuclear bomb high in our atmosphere. The resulting effect fries everything electrical. What I don't know is if this is more local, regional, or nationwide."

"What does all this mean?" Gerald asked, looking very interested.

"That is a good question. If this is widespread, then we must come together as a community and work toward securing as much food, water, medicine, and other resources as we need to survive." Leaning forward toward Gerald, Gordon looked intense and finished by saying, "Gerald, what you do for a living is now over for as long as the lights are out, and with all power out across the area our focus has to be getting and stocking up on the items I mentioned. I feel it is important that we move now, not tomorrow. This is why I have had flyers circulated across the neighborhood today calling everyone to come meet in the central park this afternoon."

"Why didn't you come to us first before taking it upon yourself to circulate a community meeting?" Mindy asked, looking a bit put out.

Gordon looked at Mindy and said, "Mindy, please don't take offense, but I thought I needed to act. I feel this is a life-changing event and we must act now. I am not trying to step on anyone's toes here."

"I am the HOA president and I feel it's important that I was informed before you decided to organize a community meeting. What if you're wrong? By having a meeting and announcing to our friends and neighbors your theory you could start a panic," Mindy said in a scolding way.

"Mindy, please stop, just stop. This isn't necessary," Gerald pleaded.

"No, Gerald, I won't. I am the head of this HOA and I feel it is important that we should have vetted his theory before we just jump to conclusions," Mindy continued.

"Gordon, I appreciate your theory, but we should wait a few

more days to make confirmation of it before we make any announcements and plans within our community," Mindy said firmly.

"Sorry, Mindy, I will not stop my meeting. I have the right to talk to whomever; those who decide to come to my meeting, I will give them the truth. This is not some average situation. We do not have the luxury of waiting a few days. There are only a few days of food to go around in grocery stores as it is, and that counts the perishable foods. If this community is to survive till help comes, we must act now. I will not wait for you. I thought it prudent and respectful to come to you, but I can see that you still hold a grudge after the last incident. I'm not here to usurp what power position you think you have; I am here to ensure that as many people survive what is coming!" Gordon said. He was clearly disturbed by Mindy's attitude. He stood up and continued to speak. "You can join us at three p.m. in the central park. I'll announce to whoever shows up what I know is going on. Then I'll begin to organize efforts for our collective survival. You're more than welcome to come and participate but if you don't that's fine too."

"Gordon, wait," Gerald insisted. He looked at Mindy and shrugged his shoulders.

Mindy just sat; she was tapping her fingers on her crossed legs. Her anger was just hiding behind her pursed lips. She let out a deep sigh and said, "Gordon, I like you; I do. I just think that you approach things differently than most people. You're kind of a bull in a china shop. I prefer the way of careful and diligent thought versus shoot-from-the-hip decision making; however, I would agree that something is different with this particular situation and I will come to this meeting. I will trust your instincts on this one and only hope that you are not right for all of our sakes."

"Thank you, your support will be helpful. With that said, then should we go over what I propose?"

"Sure," Mindy said, nodding her approval.

Gordon sat back down and pulled a pad of paper out of his backpack.

"I have drawn up a plan for us to work from, and I made you a copy," he said, handing her a second pad of paper.

She took the pad and reviewed them. "Well, based on what you have here, I would have to say this is a serious situation." She handed the pad to Gerald, who looked it over and handed it back to Mindy.

"Look at page two, item seven."

"Thank you, Gerald, yes, I saw that. So, Gordon, looking at this, it appears you are recommending we become, essentially, our own town?"

"Yes and no. We have three hundred and twenty-four homes in our neighborhood. Without most vehicles and specifically without support from anyone we have to tackle all the responsibilities that a town must. . . ."

"Like having a sheriff?"

"Yes, I just used that for lack of a better word, but we will need a sheriff, militia, or security force to protect what we have."

"And who do you recommend for that position?" Mindy asked with a rhetorical tone.

"Without knowing everyone else in the community and their specific talents, I would volunteer myself for that position."

With a slight grin, Mindy said, "Of course."

"Mindy, if that's a problem then we can hold an election and see who our neighbors think would be best suited. Listen, I'm not here to gain position; all I want to do is survive this."

"Gordon, let me contact the other board members; have a quick meeting. We will all be at the three p.m. gathering today. Okay?" Mindy stood up and Gordon followed. She walked up to Gordon and put out her hand. "Thank you for informing us of what you think is going on."

Gordon took her hand. "You're welcome. I'll just show myself out." He turned and left. After closing the door, he murmured, "What a bitch." As he walked off, he thought to himself how clueless and insecure some people were. He looked around the neighborhood and everything looked normal per se, but it would change and change soon. He hoped he was wrong, he longed for his theory to be completely wrong but knew he was right. He thought that for too long many Americans had taken everything for granted and assumed life would continue on uninterrupted. But history shows that it doesn't; all throughout time civilizations have risen and fallen, and now this could be the end of the American Dream.

USS *Makin Island*

Sebastian stood on the railing of the USS *Makin Island* and looked at the white heads of the waves of the Indian Ocean. The cool breeze felt good on his face in contrast to the warmth of the waning sun. He looked across and saw the USS *New Orleans* just in the distance; the entire ARG was now heading in a southerly direction toward Diego Garcia. After the stunning announcement at the formation earlier, Gunny had collected his entire platoon in the berthing area to see what each Marine felt about their new mission. The decision was unanimous; all were in support of it and wanted nothing more than to get back to California. There were rumors of a few Marines and sailors being taken into custody because they disagreed.

This was done as a procedural maneuver to prevent any type of conflict. Sebastian felt good that the decision-making of possibly leaving was taken away from him. No one knew what the future held, but when you're in the Marines there never is a guarantee of anything.

The hatch behind Sebastian opened and Tomlinson stepped out. He pulled a pack of cigarettes from his blouse pocket, lit one, and leaned on the railing next to Sebastian.

"This is all really somethin', isn't it?" he asked.

"Yes, it is. I agree with Barone, we have to get home. We have to take care of our own, period," Sebastian said.

"I'm nervous about my family back east, but I guess there wasn't much I could have done even if we went to the East Coast."

"At least your girl will be fine," Sebastian said, turning to look at Tomlinson.

"How do you think we'll be able to get into Diego Garcia without causing a problem?"

"I don't know," he said, looking up at the bridge of the ship. "But I bet they have a plan."

• • •

"Major Ashley, how are things proceeding?" Barone asked his young executive officer. Major Ashley was a handsome man with light brown hair. He stood six feet tall and was chiseled. He graduated Quantico top of his class and went through the ranks very fast due to his superior intelligence and political prowess.

"Sir, two-four's company commanders are reporting that we have seventeen Marines who are not in agreement with our new mission. Those Marines have been taken in custody."

"Captain, what about one-one?" Barone asked, turning to Captain Tetter, who was 1st Battalion 1st Marines liaison on the *Makin Island*. He was as wide as he was tall. He was the kind of guy you'd find in the gym twice a day, but with his shaved head not one you'd want to meet in a dark alley.

"Sir, we have thirty-eight Marines. I believe that is because you are the one taking control."

"Do you have any recommendations?" Barone asked

"Yes, sir. I do. You need to have a joint formation with Lieutenant Colonel Silver and show that there is solidarity between both battalion commanders."

"Okay, let's do that immediately. I won't have a formation but a joint announcement and have us both speak about the new mission. Please make it happen when you get back to the *New Orleans*."

"Yes, sir," Tetter said.

Looking to the lone naval officer in the room, Barone asked, "How is the Navy looking?"

"Not good, sir; we've lost about twenty percent of our personnel across all ships. We've had some altercations and it might inhibit our abilities to operate the ARG effectively," Navy Lieutenant Montgomery said. Montgomery was of average height with sandy blond hair. Not of impressive stature, he made up for it with his cockiness and straightforward style.

Barone had been pacing the room for the entire briefing. He finally walked to his chair and sat down. He turned to Montgomery and asked, "What are your suggestions?"

"Sir, I don't know. Many of the men feel like you have taken their ships. The talk is that these are Navy ships and the Marines have stolen them. We also have the issue that not everyone has family in California. Some actually had family back east."

"I realize that not everyone has families in California, but many do. I can't make everyone happy. Going to California is the best plan. Like I said, once we land, if anyone wants to go on their own they can. We will give them a weapon and some supplies. I think we should also offer an incentive. All men in the end have something they want, everyone can be bought. In my announcement with Silver I will announce that all those who join us will receive bonuses."

"Bonuses?" Montgomery asked.

"Yes, we need to incentivize them. At the moment we cannot offer pay. But soon we will have things of value."

"What will that be, sir?"

"Gold and land," Barone said.

"Really?"

"Yes, that will be our plan for payment for their loyalty. We will find gold and we have land back at Camp Pendleton that we will give to those who join our cause. We will give each a house and an acre of land."

"How the hell can we do that?" Montgomery asked.

"Mr. Montgomery, we can do anything we want right now; we are Marines and we have three thousand plus well-armed fighting men who want to get home and want to know they will be taken care of. We will figure out the land issue later and the gold will come."

All men at the table were looking at one another.

Ashley asked, "Sir, what is our objective in going to Diego Garcia? I have to assume it's more than just dropping off those who do not support us. It's a risky operation, you must know that."

"Gentlemen, in order for any army or navy to operate we must have food, water, fuel, and supplies. Diego Garcia has all of them, plus the Second Squadron of MPS ships are there. We need those ships and we will take those ships."

All the men in the room nodded.

"Smart move, sir," Major Ashley said, still nodding.

"From there we'll head back north and cut through the Strait of Malacca toward the western Pacific."

"Will we stop in Hawaii, sir?"

"Not a chance. That would be a bad move. By then the word will be out that we have mutinied. I don't want to engage in combat operations against fellow Americans. That's something I wish to avoid at all costs. All I want is to go back home, defend our families, and help rebuild."

"So then the plan after we hit Diego Garcia is to head nonstop for San Diego."

"Correct. That is the plan, but as usual plans can change and we need to be flexible." Barone looked around the table and asked, "Is that all, gentlemen?"

"Sir, what are we calling this mission?" asked Ashley.

Barone sat for a second, then responded, "We will call it Operation Homestead."

Dade County, Florida

Conner could see why so many people moved and retired in Florida. The weather was perfect; it was December and the temperature was in the mid-seventies. The convoy of jeeps pulled up to the front gate of Governor Cruz's house. Conner jumped out of the jeep and walked up to the gate. He was met by two guards.

"May we help you, sir?" one of the guards asked.

"Yes, you can. I need to speak to Governor Cruz immediately," Conner said, standing there alone with his convoy behind him.

"Sir, may I ask who wishes to see him?" the guard asked, looking over Conner's shoulder at the small convoy of jeeps with armed soldiers and plainclothes men accompanying this stranger.

"Tell him it's Brad Conner and that it's a matter of national security."

"One minute, sir," the guard said. He backed away from the gate and approached his colleague. They whispered to each other before one of them started to walk briskly back toward the house.

Dylan stepped forward and handed Conner a binder and said, "Mr. President, what else should I bring with us for the meeting?"

"Nothing, Dylan. I won't need anything and I'll go by myself. This needs to be a private meeting. I've known Andrew since college and the best way to get through to him is to have us talk privately."

"Yes, sir," Dylan responded, and walked away from Conner.

Conner walked back and forth in front of the gate, thinking about what he would say to Andrew. They had met each other in graduate school at the University of Iowa. They both were pursuing their master's degrees in American history. They both instantly clicked and spent a lot of time together. Not only did they share the same views on politics, they shared the same interest in sports and good beer. After grad school, they both found themselves successfully entering politics, with Andrew ascending to the governor's office for two terms in Florida. Andrew had been term-limited out of office and had since been spending his time writing his memoirs. If he could convince Andrew to become his VP, he would have a trusted ally and friend to help lead and rebuild the country.

Conner's thoughts were interrupted with seeing Andrew walking down the driveway along with one of the guards.

Andrew Cruz was the same age as Brad Conner; in fact they

were only months apart. Andrew was of average height and very slender. While Brad did not take good care of himself physically, Andrew made running a daily part of his lifestyle. His hair was black and full, his eyes brown and his skin an olive tone that hearkened back to his Cuban ancestry.

"Open the gate," Andrew ordered.

Both guards manually opened the gate and Andrew stepped through and gave Conner a big hug.

"When my guard told me that you were at my front gate, I said, 'Who?' Brad, what are you doing here? What's going on?" Andrew said after embracing his old friend.

"Andrew, it's good seeing you, especially with all that's happening. Can we go somewhere private and talk?"

"Absolutely, follow me," Andrew said, motioning Conner to follow him inside the gate.

"So how is the family, Brad?"

"Not good; my son, Bobby, is dead."

Andrew stopped walking and responded to the shocking news. "What? Oh my God, Brad, I'm so sorry. How did it happen?

Conner had also stopped; he was looking down at the ground. The loss of his son was visible on his face when he looked up. He opened his mouth to speak, but his voice cracked.

"Brad, come over here, sit down." Andrew motioned to a bench in a garden.

"No, not necessary," Conner said, forcing the words to come out. He cleared his throat and said, "Andrew, there's been a couple of major attacks against the United States."

"Yes, I had been watching the news until all the power went out yesterday."

"No, Andrew, not those small car bombings or mall shootings; someone has detonated an EMP bomb over the U.S. They also detonated a nuclear weapon in Washington, D.C.," Conner said, his face now clear of the pain from his son's death.

"What?" Andrew asked with shock on his face.

"The president, vice president, and all of Congress is gone. We have not been able to get on the ground in D.C. to get a confirmed report, but our aerial photos show the city leveled. If someone has survived, they'd be lucky."

Andrew was in total shock. He walked away from Conner to the bench he had pointed at earlier and sat down.

"Andrew, I'm here because I am now the new president and I need a vice president. I need someone I can trust, someone who thinks like I do but also has a good head on his shoulders. I need you right now. Your country needs you right now. We need to get this country back up."

"Brad, this is unbelievable. So the lights are out because of the EMP burst?"

"Yes, it appears to have been a super EMP, because its effect is continent wide. It's really bad, Andrew; the entire power grid across the country is down, and whoever did this to us also attacked Europe and Asia. Australia managed to thwart the attack."

"Brad, I'm in shock. I don't know what to say right now," Andrew said, looking flabbergasted.

"Andrew, say yes. I need you. We don't have much time. I need your counsel as I need to make a crucial decision very soon. We must respond! I have a plan, but I want to run everything by you. I also need to create a line of succession if I die. I wouldn't want anyone else to succeed me but you."

"Brad . . . I," Andrew said and then paused. He then stood up and put out his hand. Conner grabbed it and shook it firmly. "I'm with you; what do we need to do?"

"You need to go inform your wife, gather your family and everything you'll need to bring with you. I don't know when we'll ever come back here. From here we fly to Cheyenne Mountain in Colorado. Can you get everything done in an hour or so?"

"An hour? I don't see why not," Andrew said, and stepped away. He then stopped and turned and said, "Brad, we can fix this together; thank you for allowing me to serve my country."

"Andrew, I wouldn't have called on anyone else."

San Diego, California

Gordon looked at his watch; it was 3:10 P.M. and only about one hundred and fifty people had gathered so far. He was willing to wait a bit longer but he couldn't believe people wouldn't come, when the announcement was clear that it was an emergency community meeting.

Jimmy walked up and patted Gordon on the shoulder. Looking out on the crowd of his fellow neighbors chatting and kids playing, he asked, "Where's everyone?"

Looking perturbed, Gordon said, "I don't know; but I do know that I can't wait for everyone, and someone that is also notably late is Mindy and her cohorts."

"Hey, that was a good haul we had this morning, good job on getting in through the shipping doors. I have to say I've only seen people shoot locks on doors in movies, now I know you can really do it," Jimmy said. He was in a good mood. The past day and half had made him feel alive in a way. He was enjoying the adventure of it all.

"How's Simone doing?"

"She's good, man, no worries; thanks for asking."

"Glad to hear it," Gordon said. He then looked at his watch

again and saw that it was now 3:14 P.M. "I'm going to start. Screw Mindy and her bullshit."

"Hey, bud, her timing is impeccable. Over there," Jimmy said, pointing to the far corner of the park. "Here she comes with her entourage."

Gordon saw her leading a group of people. As they came into focus he could see the board members following her.

Mindy walked up to Gordon and said, "Hi, Gordon. Sorry we were late, but the meeting lasted longer than we had expected." She looked around at the group gathered and then finished her thought by saying, "Thank you for waiting for us." She then turned away from Gordon and spoke loudly, "Neighbors and friends of Rancho Valentino, thank you for coming to this emergency meeting!"

Everyone in the group started to quiet down and all turned their attention to Mindy.

"I need everyone to listen, so please pay attention!" Mindy said. The last murmurs and chatter stopped after a brief moment.

"Friends and neighbors, we have called this emergency meeting to inform you of some troubling news. This blackout we are experiencing is not normal and unfortunately may not end anytime soon. With that in mind, we feel it is important to look inward and work together as a community to confront this problem. We do not know when the power will come back on, but it might be weeks if not months. Without power and more importantly without operational cars, the access to those things we need like food, water, and medicine will be restricted. Your HOA board feels we need to come together now and work to limit our exposure to this issue."

All eyes were on Mindy, including Gordon's. Gordon was just amazed by Mindy; he didn't understand why she never pursued real politics.

"We are working on a final plan and will present that to each homeowner very soon. What we recommend is to conserve water and to ensure you eat those foods that are perishable first. If any of you have any questions, please ask them."

A gentleman in the crowd raised his hand.

"Yes, go ahead," Mindy said, pointing at him.

"Mindy, what do you know about this? You seem to know more. . ."

Mindy paused and looked around at the board; she then turned and looked at Gordon.

Someone else then shouted from the crowd, "Tell us what you know!" Then someone else yelled, "If you know something, tell us!"

Mindy looked back toward the crowd and then to the man who had asked the first question. "Ahh, yes, well, we have a theory, or I should say that Mr. Van Zandt has a theory about what might have happened. We, meaning the board, are not sure about this theory, but felt it prudent to act because this blackout is unique." Mindy looked nervous and out of sorts.

Someone from the crowd yelled, "What is it? What is this theory?" Then another person yelled, "C'mon, we have a right to know!"

Mindy, looking more uncomfortable, turned back to Gordon and waved for him to approach. She then turned back to the crowd and said, "Mr. Van Zandt will tell you his theory."

Gordon walked up and looked at Mindy, who backed up a step. Gordon turned and began to address the crowd.

"Friends and neighbors, I hate to be the bearer of bad news, but this blackout we are experiencing is not going to end anytime soon. Based upon the facts, nothing more, I believe we have been attacked with some type of electromagnetic pulse weapon, or EMP.

What an EMP weapon does is fries everything that is electrical. This is why our cars don't work or our phones or anything that we have that is electrical even if it was on batteries. I know my neighbor, James—James, are you out there?" Gordon asked, peering into the crowd looking for his elderly neighbor.

"Here, Gordon!" James responded from the back of the group.

"Yes, James there has heard the emergency broadcast system on his radio announcing that we have been attacked." Gordon paused for a few seconds then continued. "An EMP is a very destructive weapon, depending on where it was set off and how large of a weapon it was; this blackout could be local, regional, or even nationwide."

Dozens of people in the crowd started talking among themselves. The chatter became louder and louder.

Gordon continued. "I approached Mindy late this morning and informed her of my theory and presented her with a plan to survive this."

"Survive?" someone yelled from the crowd.

Looking very serious, Gordon yelled back, "Yes, survive! People, let me explain. There is no help coming anytime soon; if my guess is right we are on our own. We must act now to secure as much food, water, and other supplies as we can to get through this. If this attack was nationwide, the lights will not come on for possibly years. Let me just lay it out to you. We live in a city of about 2.3 million people. San Diego is a semi-arid desert; there is not a lot of agriculture around, at least not enough to support 2.3 million people for a sustained period of time. Right now, grocery stores are not being restocked; they have but a day or two of food in them. Water will soon dry up because the pumps that bring it in are down. We must act now to get as much of the supplies we will need to last us at least a year, if not more. We should prepare ourselves for the fact that some of us will die."

"Gordon, that is enough, now you're just scaring them!" Mindy snapped at him.

Gordon ignored her and continued. "There is not enough food and water for 2.3 million people in this area. If you want to survive what is coming, we must start today to go out and get these supplies. We cannot wait for the board to come back in a few days."

"Gordon, that is enough!" Mindy snapped again, this time walking up to Gordon and taking his arm forcefully.

Gordon looked at her and said, "Let go of my arm."

Mindy looked out into the crowd and said, "I am sorry for Mr. Van Zandt. We on the board feel he is being a bit sensational and we must think clearly before we overreact."

"Let him speak!" someone yelled from the group. "What about my husband?" someone else yelled. "He hasn't come home yet from downtown."

Gordon shrugged off Mindy's grip and answered the woman who asked about her husband. "Your husband is probably fine; it just takes a while to walk here from downtown. Friends and neighbors, I am not overreacting; this situation is not normal. Who out there happened to see that commercial airliner fall from the sky yesterday?"

About a dozen hands raised.

Gordon, sensing he had an upper hand with the group, pressed his case further.

"You're right, that is not normal; typical blackouts do not cause cars to just stop working, cell phones not to turn on, or planes to fall out of the sky! I know this is hard for everyone to deal with, but our life, the life we knew before, is over. The jobs you had before, they are gone. We must start now to go out in organized groups to secure these resources before others do. The plan I gave Mindy addressed the things we need to do. We first must start with a headcount to see how many people we have in the neighborhood, how many are on medications, any with medical issues. We need to know what talents or trades you have that will benefit us."

Gordon turned and looked at Mindy, who had hate in her eyes. He turned back to the crowd and finished by saying, "Please line up in a single file line. I will take your name down, how many in your household, address and talents that can serve our community. So please form a line over there, okay?"

People started to move and the line started to form. Gordon turned back to Mindy and said, "Sorry, but your typical bullshit won't fly here; I won't allow it. We have to act now. So you can either work with me or get the fuck out of my way." Gordon walked away and approached the first person in line.

Jimmy stepped up next to him and said, "You the man, great speech."

"Help me. Take this notepad and form another line or we'll be here all day."

Gordon and Jimmy worked until the sun set. They tried to help answer as many questions as they could. The back and forth with Mindy was noticed by all and even commented on by some. Gordon had not wanted the meeting to go in that direction, but he knew he was right and that Mindy seemed more concerned about pretense and procedure than about getting things done. Even in his frustration with her, he felt a bit sorry for her. How could she grasp the magnitude of what had happened and what would happen? Most people had never experienced the things he had. He had traveled the world, seen combat, seen death, and taken life himself. He knew that when the sun was rising in the morning that he needed to be out with Jimmy and others looking for food. Even though the sunset signified the day was over, his work was not. He would have to go home and pore over all the info and start to form the teams. Two of the other major problems were getting the rest of his neighbors on board and helping find those who had not made it home. He also knew that he would have to go back to Mindy and make amends; in order for the community to move forward everyone needed to work together. He would give her a few days; he knew that eventually she would come over to his side. What she probably needed was to see the reality start to hit home. Until then, he was the leader of the community and that brought responsibility. He was used to leading and in some ways was happy to do so.

As Gordon was walking into his house, he heard a voice he had not heard in a long time. Looking down the candle-lit hall he saw Nelson.

"Nelson?"

"Yep, it's me, good buddy!" Nelson yelled.

"Oh my God, am I glad to see you!" Gordon exclaimed.

Nelson greeted him with the same upbeat and humorous attitude that was his trademark. "Hey, man. Great to see you! How about paying the electric bill?"

Gordon smiled and said, "Nelson, my man, it's going to take more than a check to get the lights back on."

Nelson was tall with an athletic build. His hair was a light brown with natural highlights of blond from spending so much time outside. He was a very active person; if he wasn't working at the firehouse, he could be found on his board in the ocean, surfing. He was generous of spirit and with anything he had. He felt it important to give to his hometown; this is why he became a fireman and EMT. Gordon liked Nelson for his fun-loving and carefree attitude as well as his strong family values and principled beliefs. Nelson had resented how San Diego had changed since his childhood; gone in many ways were the days of flip-flops and beach shorts. He felt San Diego had become just a mini-L.A., or, as Nelson put it, Hell A. Nelson and Gordon got along from day one, they appreciated many of the same things, like good beer, great whiskey, and a lifestyle that was about working and playing hard.

While the events of the day could be measured as positive, the sight of Nelson made the day perfect. Gordon hoped Nelson wasn't just passing through. He needed quality people on his team, and Nelson had the skills needed and the right attitude to see any job done.

"Can I get you a drink?" Gordon asked.

"I can never say no to you."

"Not until you eat some dinner," Samantha said from the kitchen.

Gordon turned his attention to Samantha, who was busy making dinner on a Coleman stove that sat on top of the old burners of their electric range. Four lanterns provided adequate light for her to work.

"How long before dinner?" Gordon asked, walking into the kitchen and kissing Samantha on the head.

"Almost done. Can you please put the paper plates and plastic utensils out?"

Looking over at Nelson, who winked, Gordon replied, "Sure."

• • •

"Samantha, I'm amazed by what you can do with only candlelight and a propane stove. The stew was great," Nelson said, relaxing into his chair.

"Thank you, I'm glad you liked it. I have to say I miss my salads but hopefully in a few months we'll have some fresh veggies."

"Hey, sweetie, I was going to take Nelson to my office to discuss some things, okay?"

"Sure."

"Follow me; let's go to my office so we can chat."

Gordon grabbed a lit candle and escorted Nelson across the house to his office. Along the way Gordon grabbed two glasses and a bottle of Maker's Mark.

As Gordon poured a glass of bourbon for Nelson, he said, "I have to say, my friend, seeing you is really good."

"Same here, buddy. I'm glad you all are okay," Nelson said, now settled into his chair.

Gordon sat down and asked, "So I know you're not here just for the whiskey. What's up?"

"Remember all those conversations we had over a glass of good bourbon like this? Well, as soon as the lights went out I knew some shit had gone down so I decided to check on you."

"You made the right call. What are your plans?"

"First, I'd like to know what you make of all this."

"To make a long story very short, I think we've been attacked by an EMP and this is all the calm before the shit storm begins," Gordon said, then took a big drink of whiskey.

"I figured something like that happened, so let me ask you the same question: What are your plans?"

"Well, right now I'm hunkering down with my family; we have stocked up on food and water. Now I'm trying to get the neighborhood organized. Things are going to get real bad and we need to be ready for when it does."

Nelson took a drink and said, "Damn, I love Maker's." He looked at the glass and then asked with a slight grin, "I suppose offering someone a little ice would be out of the question?"

Knowing Nelson's sense of humor Gordon played along. "I only serve ice to my upstanding and reputable guests."

Nelson smiled and said, "So what do you think is going to happen?"

"Before I answer that, what's up with your firehouse? What have you heard?"

"Nothing, just rumor; the station is completely down, no power, trucks don't work. I stopped by and only the chief and another guy were there. Their replacement shift never made it in. The chief asked me to stay, but I told him I had things to do and that I'd swing back around to see what I could do for them. I have to admit, it kinda seems useless now, based on what you're guessing happened. If we don't have operable trucks and such, what's the use of a fire department? I'm tellin' ya, Gordon, this is some crazy shit. I knew you'd have a good feel for what was happening since you were Special Forces and all."

"I wasn't Special Forces, just a grunt, buddy."

"So tell me, what do you think is going to happen now?"

"Well, that would have to be the golden question; you remember what happened after Katrina and Sandy, don't you? Well, it will be a thousand times worse but there will be no National Guard or police to come help. This thing has paralyzed everyone. I guess for now the local and county governments are scrambling but they will soon break down under the stress of it all. I guess after only a few days all government will be gone."

"Really, that soon?"

"Yeah, let's face it; we are humans and for one, how do people get to work? How do they do anything even if they make it to the offices? If local government lasts a few days, that would be a generous. Now, some of the military locally might have been hardened against the attack but they will first take care of their own. That leaves all two-point-whatever million out there fending for themselves with enough food to last three days at most. The wheels of this bus will come off fast. It's very simple, Nelson. We need to move on this fast and get as much as we can. That then leaves me with asking you, what are your plans? We could use you around here."

"Well, now that you've left me with a warm and fuzzy feeling, I don't know."

"We could really use someone of your talents here. You can stay here, and to be honest we could also use your vehicle. What we can provide is a secure area with food and water. You can help with our community clinic or hospital. I understand that you may want to go stay with your family, but what if I sweeten the pot and offer them all sanctuary here behind our gates?"

"Well, your gates aren't all that," Nelson said with a chuckle.

"What?"

"I made it in here now, didn't I? And I'm not Special Forces like you."

"That will end soon. The gates were left open right after the attack. My plan is to lock this place down and create a mini-city state. My plan calls for all services that a town has, from hospital to militia."

"Damn, man, you don't waste time," Nelson said as he leaned forward and poured each of them another glass full of Maker's.

"This is life and death, Nelson, truly life and death. Please say yes and let's get your family here ASAP. We could use good people like you here."

"I'm tempted; let me sleep on it. By the way, is it cool if I crash here tonight?"

"Of course you can stay. Even though you haven't given me an answer, let me show you my detailed plan and get your thoughts."

Gordon spent the next hour covering in great detail his plan for Rancho Valentino while also dropping hints to Nelson to stay on board. He needed more people he could trust, and people with strong skills like Nelson. The world was different now; the skills needed to survive were in only a few hands. The skills of yesterday were now worthless. The skills needed in a cubicle were of no value, a degree in human resources or marketing wasn't going to cut it in this new economy. In one flash, the world had gone back to the eighteenth century, but without the knowledge of those foregone years. Once the war over resources began, things would be violent and bloody and Gordon not only needed food and water, he needed all the able-bodied people he could get to protect what they had.

DECEMBER 7, 2014

• • •

Decisions determine destiny.

—Frederick Speakman

Cheyenne Mountain, Colorado

Conner sat in his quarters staring at the stark gray walls. The air was stale and cold and the lights gave off an eerie luminescence that fit his mood. He had just come back from burying his son. His wife was able to keep a sense of composure during the ceremony, but now she sat in the other room sobbing. Her sobs echoed off the concrete and steel walls of what would be his home for a long time. He had attempted to console her, but his attempts failed. He knew it would take time for her to get over the death of their only son.

While she did not find fault with him, she was angry that he did not show more emotion. If only she could read his mind, he thought; the sense of loss, anger, and sadness filled him up, but he also needed to suppress it so he could be effective as the new president.

His mind then started to focus on the task at hand. He needed to lead his country through this catastrophe and hoped that on the other end there would still be a country. He did not want to leave her during this time, but he knew he must go meet with Griswald and Vice President Cruz to discuss their next move. During the flight to Colorado, Griswald was able to report that all military in Afghanistan had made it out safely and that they were heading directly for the Eastern Seaboard.

Conner had also been able to speak with the Australian prime minister again. He had pledged their full support to assist the United States. The prime minister still was unsuccessful in garnering more information on the attacks. Conner felt anxious; he felt he needed to act quickly to show those responsible that while they had hit the United States hard the country was not out. Conner and Griswald had gotten into another back and forth over the use of their nuclear arsenal against those enemies. What Conner did not expect is that his new VP sided with Griswald. Cruz's support of what they called a more "diligent and cautious" approach had taken Conner by surprise; he had just assumed that his old friend would agree with him. Conner had decided not to make any decisions until he could process Griswald's and especially Cruz's objections. When he stood up to leave his quarters he thought of going to his wife but stopped himself short and just left. He walked down the dimly lit passageways of the bunker toward the command post. He had called another meeting to give his thoughts on what type of response should be given and when.

When he approached the door to the command post, he heard someone call his name. He turned and saw Cruz coming from the opposite way. They both greeted each other and Cruz asked to speak with him privately.

Without knowing another place to go, they both decided to just find the closest closet and chat. After checking several doors they found a small storage closet that would suffice.

"Brad, I've thought a lot about our meeting last night and while I have reservations I'm with you on whatever decision you make; however, I am concerned about General Griswald."

"In what way are you concerned?" Conner asked, crossing his arms and looking curious.

"I can't peg it, but I think I overheard him say something like *'I won't let this happen'* in relation to your proposal."

"Really? Hmm. Well, let's not jump to any conclusions. The general seems like a good man and I understand his concerns; I have them too, but I have a responsibility to take care of this country and to ensure we can rebuild without the threat of further attacks. Now, if that's it, let's go to the meeting."

Both men left the closet and went to the command post. It was a large room staffed by more than a dozen Air Force and Army personnel who sat behind computer consoles. All along the wall were large monitors, many of them were dark. No one in the room seemed to take notice of Conner or Cruz. It might be that they did not know who they were. They both walked past everyone and into the briefing room that looked over the command post. Inside the room was a large table like any boardroom would have. There sat Griswald and his staff. When both Conner and Cruz walked in, the general and his staff stood up. After a few pleasantries everyone sat down.

Griswald started the meeting by saying, "Mr. President, I have compiled everything you asked for yesterday concerning a nuclear strike plan."

Leaning forward on this table Conner said, "Great, General. Please proceed."

"Mr. President, we have available to us the weapons to strike multiple targets in each of the following countries: Iran, Iraq, Pakistan, Afghanistan, North Korea, Yemen, Somalia, Libya, and Syria."

"Once ordered, how long for the strikes to be over?"

"From start to finish, about thirty minutes, sir."

"Okay, good; let's move on. Have we been able to reach the prime ministers in Turkey and Israel?"

"Yes, sir, we have. They are pledging whatever support they can. Israel has expressed their concern for their own safety, of course, and cannot at this time devote any military assets to us."

"What about our neighbors to the south?"

"Sir, you mean Mexico or South America?"

"Both."

"We have been able to contact the military in Mexico and they are dealing with the same situation we are; Mexico City was not affected, but easily half of the country was. I haven't been able to reach the Mexican president. We have reached out to your counterparts in Central and South America and they wish to express sorrow for the attacks and want to give us as much support as possible.

"Please set up conference calls with all the leaders you can get and patch them through to my office directly after this meeting. I want to talk to each one and attempt to get what support we can get."

"Sir, can I be frank?" Griswald asked.

"Sure."

"If you go through with these nuclear strikes, I am not sure how much support we will get from the rest of the world."

"I understand your concerns and you might be correct, but what are we to do, nothing?"

"Of course not, sir, but we should make sure we know who did this before—"

Stopping Griswald mid-sentence, Conner started yelling, "General, how many times do I have to hear you make this same concern? I have heard you! We do not have the luxury of time or the assets at our disposal now to conduct a full investigation. What we do know is that in order for someone to carry out this attack, they had to have substantial resources; and while this might have been a terrorist group they were financed and provided direct support by a nation-state. We know who our enemies are; they are on that list. Our enemies are laughing at us right now and who knows, they are probably plotting further attacks!" Conner finished yelling and then slammed his fist against the table.

Everyone in the room and around the table just stared. They were all a bit taken aback. Conner sat there fuming and looked at each person in the room. Griswald sat motionless at the opposite end of the table.

Conner started to speak again, this time loud and determined: "General, your concerns have been noted; I appreciate you and respect those thoughts but you stress the need for more information; what you don't offer is a plan. While it is easy to give critique and criticism of my potential plan, you offer none of your own. I alone hold the responsibility for this country's safety." Conner finished and turned and looked directly at Cruz, who sat next to him.

Cruz returned the look and said, "Mr. President, I have expressed similar views myself, but whatever decision you make, I will support."

Nodding his approval, Conner turned to Griswald and asked, "What about you, General?"

Still sitting in awe of the lambasting he had just taken, Griswald did not respond right away. The silence in the room made many feel uncomfortable. Finally he answered, "Mr. President, I am sworn to follow and obey the commander in chief and I will do so; whatever you decide I will follow."

"General, please put our nuclear forces on standby for now."

"Yes, sir."

"If there is nothing else, I think this meeting is over. Please put me through to all of my counterparts, starting first with any NATO allies we have and then with those leaders in Central and South America."

"Yes, sir," Griswald answered.

Conner stood up and left the room. After closing the door, he stood just outside the room for a moment. Some of the military personnel behind their monitors looked at him; he wondered if they had heard his tirade. He ran through the events that had just transpired in the briefing room. He did not want to kill millions of people, but he didn't know what else to do. He thought of those dictators and mullahs in Iran and how they were probably celebrating the fact that the United States had finally fallen. That thought alone made Conner angry; he could not escape taking the attack personally. His thoughts then went to Griswald and what Cruz had mentioned. He did not want to consume himself with Griswald's supposed comment, but he was a bit nervous. These were unprecedented times and right now anything could happen. He planned on keeping an eye on Griswald.

San Diego, California

Gordon yawned and stretched his tired and achy body. The sun's initial rays were pushing their way through the eastern clouds.

Gordon and Jimmy were staged at the central park waiting for his scavenger party to show up. Gordon had stayed up into the night working on a plan that would ensure their survival. Three two-man teams would scavenge daily for food, water, fuel, medicines, vehicles, and weapons.

He assigned each team a specific task: one was to go get food and medicines, the second water, and the third to find vehicles and weapons. The hours would be long, but what else did they have to do now? Beyond the scavenger teams his plan called for a hospital, a team of gardeners that could start to work on converting one of the parks into a garden, perimeter security, and school and community maintenance teams. The community would meet daily to get their rations delivered to them based upon what they found the day before.

He was concerned about Mindy and the board's cooperation. Not everyone had shown up yesterday to be added to the list, so he wasn't sure if everyone would be in agreement with his plan or if he would have a divided neighborhood, something he desperately did not want.

He and another team convoyed to the Carmel Mountain Plaza, a large series of strip malls about five miles away from his neighborhood. There they split up so they could adequately cover more territory. He sent Nelson with another man to recon a potable water reservoir close by. If his hunch was correct, there could be water in the tank. If there was, they would seize it, isolate it, and conduct daily water runs.

During the drive, Jimmy just chatted about nothing and Gordon took the time to relax. It wasn't long before his relaxation turned into sleep.

Gordon was jolted awake by Jimmy punching him in the arm and yelling at him to wake up.

The first store, a grocery store, was teeming with people. Mobs were carrying out armfuls of food and supplies.

"What should we do?" Jimmy asked, leaning against the steering wheel looking at the people running around.

"Ahh, let's see," Gordon said, sounding a bit foggy from his short nap.

"Bro, that looks like a cluster fuck."

"I think you're right, but I need to go in and see what I can get. Keep the truck back," Gordon said.

Pulling his pistol out of his shoulder holster he press-checked it to confirm it was loaded. After ensuring Jimmy was armed and prepared, he left for the store. Gordon counted dozens of people coming in and out. All along the front of the store and into the parking lot, debris and crushed food items were strewn. Gordon wore a large backpack and made sure he kept his jacket unzipped so he could get his gun if needed. To Gordon the mob was proof positive the word had gotten out. Knowing his odds of securing a large cache of food and supplies was limited, he still had to go get what he could.

Upon entering the darkened store, his assumptions proved correct. Walking briskly down the empty aisles, he grabbed what lone can or packet of food he could find or pick up off the floor. Seeing the pharmacy right away, he proceeded toward it. The pharmacy shelves were stripped bare too. Jumping over the counter and into the pharmacy was easy since someone had smashed the windows. He picked up what he could and stuffed it into his pack. Feeling frustrated after spending twenty minutes with not much to show for it, he left the store.

He exited the dimly lit chaos of the ransacked store to witness what would soon become the new normal. Jimmy and the truck were surrounded by three men. They were rocking the truck back and forth, all the while taunting and yelling. Jimmy returned the taunts and screams. He also was threatening them with his gun, but the threats didn't stop them.

Gordon began to run toward Jimmy. He unholstered his Sig, held it above his head, and pulled the trigger. The sound of the gun made the men stop. They turned and looked at Gordon, who pointed the gun at the closest one and yelled, "Back the fuck off! Step away from the truck!"

"Hey, bro, chill!" yelled the man whom Gordon had the gun trained on.

Gordon's situational awareness was still there. While he kept his gun on the one man, he was also tracking the other two. He noticed the other two took a few steps back but the one man did the opposite. He took a step toward Gordon.

"Get the fuck out of here now!" Gordon yelled at him.

"Hey, bro. This your truck? Let us borrow it."

"Get the fuck out of here NOW!" Gordon yelled again.

Taking another step closer to Gordon, the man yelled something in Spanish to his two friends. Gordon didn't understand what he said, but whatever it was made the other two start to advance again.

"If you don't listen and back away from the truck, I'll shoot you!" Gordon commanded.

Gordon was feeling a way he hadn't felt in a long time: fear coupled with anticipation. Time started to slow for him. His eyes shifted from the man to his front to the other two and back again. His hands were firmly grasping his pistol. He then noticed the man was looking over his shoulder at something behind him. Sensing that he needed to look, he glanced back quickly to see three other men running toward him. They were forty feet away but closing fast. Gordon instinctively looked back to confront the original three just in time. The first man had closed the distance and was feet from him. Without hesitation Gordon shot the first man in the face. The back of his head exploded then he fell to the ground with a thud. Gordon advanced, stepping over him, and took aim on the next man. He squeezed the trigger, unleashing another 9-millimeter round. The bullet ripped through his chest and the man fell back. The third man turned and ran. Showing no mercy, Gordon aimed and shot him between the shoulder blades. Knowing that a threat still existed, he swung around to address the other three, but they had stopped their advance and were running away. The distance was too great for the capabilities of his pistol, so he didn't waste the bullets. The shooting had slowed the looting and ransacking of the store. People were standing in the parking lot staring at him. The voyeurism lasted only moments before everyone went back to looting.

Hearing the truck door behind him, he turned and saw Jimmy slowly getting out of the truck. His face told Gordon the state he was in. He looked over the three lifeless bodies that surrounded his truck. Only in movies had he ever seen anything like this before. In fact, he had never seen a dead person except for his grandparents a few years before.

Gordon re-holstered his Sig and walked up to the first man he shot. He knelt down and started to check the man's pockets.

"What are you doing?" Jimmy asked, clearly looking disgusted.

Not looking up at Jimmy, Gordon responded, "Seeing if he has anything of value."

"Are you serious, man?"

Gordon looked up at Jimmy with a blank stare. "Jimmy, you

better realize that this is the new world we're in. They might have something that we could use. Now go check that one," Gordon ordered, nodding in the direction of one of the dead men.

Jimmy looked at the body next to him and said, "Fuck that, man, I'm not doing that."

Finishing his search of the first man, he walked up to Jimmy. "If you're not going to help, then step aside."

Backing away to let Gordon pass, Jimmy walked back to the truck and got in. He watched in bewildered amazement as Gordon searched the dead men. Only two days after the attacks and the world was going to shit. His thinking had not caught up with the realities of the new world, as he thought Gordon did not have to shoot all three. The entire situation made him feel very uncomfortable and out of place.

Gordon got back in the truck. He began to wipe blood on his pants. "Not much on those guys. I have an idea, though; there's a Home Depot just down the street. I want to go there and get seed for our gardens."

Jimmy sat motionless and quiet.

"Jimmy, snap out of it; we need to go."

"I just don't understand why you had to kill the other two guys. The first one, sure, but the other two had stopped," Jimmy said, speaking in a low tone.

"I can see why you would think that, but I will say it again. What you saw out there is just the beginning. We will have to kill more people just like that. I did us a favor by killing them now. Hell, I might have saved a life. Those guys were up to no good. I only wish I had a rifle. I would have shot the other three."

Looking over at Gordon, Jimmy queried, "Seriously? You would have killed the other three guys?"

"Yes, Jimmy, I would have," Gordon said, not pausing a second to think of the answer.

"What happened to you over in the war, man? Did it fuck you up?"

Gordon looked down at Jimmy's shaking hands, then stopped defending his actions. He knew he needed to help his friend, as Gordon just realized he was in shock.

"Hey, buddy, I know this is tough for you. But please trust me when I tell you I did it to protect us all, especially your family. If they could have they would have probably killed you," Gordon said with a softer tone.

Jimmy kept seeing images of what just happened over and over in his mind.

"Let me drive, okay?" Gordon said.

Jimmy just nodded and got out of the truck. Gordon slid over behind the driver's seat and started it. He watched Jimmy slowly walk around and get back in. The drive to Home Depot was quiet as both men processed in their own way the events that had just occurred.

USS *Makin Island*, Indian Ocean

"Yes!" Barone yelled, responding to the banging on the hatch to his quarters.

The hatch opened and a young Marine lieutenant stepped inside.

"William, my boy, so glad to see you, son," Barone said with happiness in his voice as he stood and approached the young Marine. They both embraced, patting each other on the back.

"Dad . . . I'm sorry, Colonel; good to see you too."

"Billy, it's just Dad when we're together; you know that," Barone said back. He motioned for his son to sit down at a small table in his room. "I'm so glad you could make it for dinner with your ol' man."

Billy was Barone's only son; he had a daughter too, who was still in high school back in Oceanside. Billy looked very much like his father but with a slender, athletic build. Billy had followed in his father's footsteps and joined the Marine Corps after college. While his father went on to become an infantry platoon commander out of school, Billy saw his future in the air. He became a fighter pilot, flying AV-8B Harrier Jump Jets. It was just a coincidence that he was onboard the *Makin Island*. Billy had been on a West-Pac deployment with his unit as part of the 11th MEU. Barone could not have been more excited to have his son with him as they started this new mission together. He had not had a chance to speak with him since they arrived, and now they'd be able to catch up. Billy always looked for his father's approval and did what he could to always support and make his dad proud.

"Dad, I have to say, it would have been nice to see you before you made that huge announcement."

"Sorry, son, timing was everything; I knew you'd be with me and I had to move fast the minute we boarded the ships," Barone said.

"I understand. I just got some heat from some of my colleagues."

"So, tell me, are they on board with this?" Barone asked, looking concerned and earnest to hear his son's thoughts.

"At first there was shock, but everyone agrees that our mission should be back in California, not on the East Coast."

"I'm sorry, son, can I offer you a drink?" Barone asked, pointing to a bottle of Jack Daniels sitting on his desk.

"That would be great, thanks, Dad."

Barone stood up quickly and grabbed the bottle and two plastic cups. As he poured, he asked what was a sincere and sensitive question for him: "Billy, tell me honestly. Do you agree with this decision? You can be honest with me; I trust and respect your opinion."

Billy raised his eyebrows in surprise; it was not often that his father asked him about a decision he had made. This really struck him as odd, but he also felt proud that his father trusted his thoughts enough to ask. "Dad, I don't know how it could have gone any different. I look at what's happened and think we need to be home protecting our families. So, yes, I agree with your decision; I know in some people's eyes we are now traitors but I know enough about history to know that we will be judged by those generations later who have a clear view of everything in its context."

"Thank you, son, I appreciate your candid thoughts. It wasn't an easy decision, but I just couldn't go along with leaving our families defenseless at home; I only wish we could get back sooner. I estimate that if all goes smoothly, we should be pulling into San Diego within three weeks. From there we'll be in a better situation to assess the situation on the ground."

"Dad, what happens to us once the president finds out?"

"Billy, you don't have to concern yourself with that now. I will take full responsibility once and if, I emphasize if, we are charged with anything."

"Why would you say 'if'?"

"Because I don't know if our country will survive this. I fear it will rip itself apart and when it comes back together it may not look like the country we left."

"So in some ways we aren't risking it all, because there may not be a country to mutiny against in the end," Billy said, nodding. All of a sudden the bigger picture was becoming apparent to him.

"Right now, our concern needs to be getting to Diego Garcia, where we will try to drop off those who don't want to go with us. We also need to pick up additional supplies and from there we'll head onto San Diego," Barone said, before he took a drink of his Jack Daniels.

"Dad, whatever you need from me, let me know. I support you one hundred percent."

Barone reached across the table and patted his son's hand and said, "Thank you, son."

They enjoyed the rest of their dinner together with conversations about home. After Billy left, Barone sat back down and poured himself another drink. He looked around his stateroom, the cold, gray steel walls and piping that zigzagged across the ceiling. He liked his life in the Marine Corps; a room like this had been his home on and off for a long time. Upon their return to San Diego, he wasn't sure when he'd set foot on a ship again. The journey home would be full of potential surprises and possible conflict. The paradox of it all was that the worst case for him personally was that the country returned to normal. He would surely be arrested, court-martialed, and jailed for a long time. He wasn't hoping for the country not to recover, but he was betting it wasn't going to. He longed to be with his wife in Oceanside, who was alone. He could not bear to think of what might happen to her and his daughter, Megan. He had been married for twenty-eight years and wasn't going to leave her alone and in need. Everything had become complicated, but he felt what he was doing was just. He decided he wasn't going to concern himself with the distant future; whatever would happen, would happen. After pouring another drink, he looked at it before he quickly drank it down with one gulp. The effects of the whiskey were starting to take hold. He welcomed the feeling. He wouldn't have very many breaks, so getting a bit drunk was his way of escaping the realities of his self-imposed situation.

San Diego, California

Gordon's Home Depot plan had proven to be a good decision. As Gordon liked to say, "It was a target-rich environment." He gathered every packet of seed, batteries, flashlights, gardening tools, junk food, drinks, and miscellaneous supplies he could take. The way the ransacking was going at the strip malls that day, he was surprised that no one had broken in yet. It took him fifteen trips and two hours to bring everything back. The darkness of the stores made the scavenging difficult. Gordon laughed to himself about how finding things in Home Depot was tough when the lights were on. Each time he returned with a full basket he could see the shock wearing off of Jimmy. They exchanged some casual banter back and forth. Gordon had liked Jimmy from the first time they met. They both shared similar values and raised their children in the same fashion. Gordon also appreciated Jimmy's sense of humor and respected his business prowess.

"How are we looking for fuel?" Gordon asked, after dumping his backpack of candy bars into the bed of the truck.

"We could use some, let's top off over there," Jimmy said, pointing to a new model Chevy Tahoe.

"Sure, pull the truck over there and get the siphon going. I'll grab some empty gas cans and toss them in the back too," Gordon said, putting his pack back on and heading to the store again.

Gordon gathered up all the gas cans he could find and came out to find Jimmy petting a dog.

"What a sweet dog," Jimmy said, crouched down petting the gray pit bull.

"I think that's it," Gordon said, tying down all the scavenged items in the bed of the truck. He ignored Jimmy and the dog.

Jimmy kept petting and talking to the dog in a high-pitched voice.

"Let's head back, make a drop, and see if we can make it back out maybe somewhere close before it gets dark," Gordon said, walking around the truck to talk to Jimmy.

Jimmy was still petting and talking to the dog.

"Helloooo," Gordon said.

"Yeah, I heard ya," Jimmy answered, then followed up with, "Do you think he's lost?"

"No, I don't. He's just scavenging like us, now let's go. We're wasting time."

Jimmy gave the dog one last pet and kissed the top of its head before getting behind the driver's seat. He started to pull away and saw the dog starting to follow them. As he weaved around parked and stalled cars in the parking lot the dog kept following. This happened for about two minutes before Jimmy stopped the truck and jumped out.

"What are you doing?" Gordon asked, looking agitated.

Jimmy grabbed the dog and put it in the cab with them. He then looked at Gordon and said with a grin, "I promise I'll feed him."

"Whatever, just remember that dogs use resources," Gordon said, shaking his head.

The dog leaned against Gordon and licked him.

"Mason will love her. Plus, this will help him with everything that is going on."

Jimmy put the truck in gear and drove on, heading west toward their community.

Driving on the freeway was not easy; the constant weaving in and out made driving slow. Gordon noticed several other cars operating on their way back, all were older models. People were walking the highways in greater numbers than just the day before. They were peering into abandoned cars, looking for what they could take. What he couldn't understand is that people were stealing TVs and stereo equipment. They held the belief that those items still held value. They didn't know that those things weren't worth the plastic they were made with. The economy had changed and the only things of value now were those items that could keep you alive. He wondered how the other two teams made out. If Nelson had secured the water tank that would make the day a huge success. The only issue would be holding it; they would have to use additional manpower and resources to keep it.

When they pulled up on the main gate, one of the new guards opened up the gate manually and let them in. They drove in and saw a large gathering in the central park.

"What's going on there?" Jimmy asked out loud.

"Not sure, pull up over there," Gordon said, pointing to an area next to the park.

The gathering consisted of about fifty or more people, and Mindy was standing at the head talking to them.

"Great!" Gordon said loudly and sarcastically as he finally saw who was speaking.

They pulled up and Gordon jumped out before the truck even came to a final stop. He approached the group at a quick pace.

"I want to thank you all for coming out and for your trust. Your board will work to make your lives better and keep this community functioning properly," Mindy said. The crowd's applause turned to loud chatter when they saw Gordon.

Mindy saw Gordon too and turned to greet him. "Mr. Van Zandt, I am so happy to see you," she said, putting out her hand.

Gordon didn't shake her hand. He quickly stepped beside her and quietly asked, "You're not causing trouble, are you?"

"Gordon, I am not here to cause trouble but wanted to explain myself to whomever would hear. I first want to apologize to you for my words and doubt yesterday. I also want to say that we want to work with you to make this transition go smoothly."

Gordon was surprised by Mindy's comments. He hesitated before saying, "Mindy, I'm glad to hear that, thank you."

"When you have time, I'd like to see what you've done so far. Can we help with the administrative side of it?" Mindy asked.

"Sure, I'd love that; let me unload what we were able to get today and talk with our other two teams before, okay?"

"Sure, take your time. Just meet me at my house later," Mindy said, smiling.

Gordon felt surprised and relieved. Just a day ago it looked like getting the entire community together would be an issue and only complicate what was a complicated problem. Gordon watched Mindy stride away with her typical confidence.

As the sun began its westerly descent, it proved that regardless of the bombs, death, and chaos around them, Mother Nature still was able to show her beauty. It made Gordon feel small knowing that nature did not care what humans did to themselves. The sun had been rising and setting for billions of years and would continue to do so for billions more without them.

Gordon's thoughts were interrupted by the wetness of Jimmy's new dog licking his hand.

He squatted down and started petting the dog. "Hey, girl, how ya doing?" The dog didn't have a collar but must have been someone's dog by the way it displayed its affection. Hearing the truck horn, he knew it was time to get back to business. Walking back to the truck he went through a mental checklist of everything that had occurred so far that day: *food, check; seed, check; batteries, check; tools, check; dead bad people, check. . . .*

DECEMBER 11, 2014

• • •

Where there is no vision, the people perish.

—Proverbs

Diego Garcia, British Indian Ocean Territory

Sebastian looked over his shoulder to see any sign of the ARG. Nothing. They were out there somewhere hiding in the darkness. Operations such as this, while new, were not something that made him nervous, but he couldn't fight that feeling. He peered through his scope onto the decks of the two MPS ships that were docked. There wasn't a lot of movement, but he didn't expect to see much at 0215 in the morning.

Sebastian's sniper team was assigned to provide overwatch for the half-dozen twelve-man teams of Marines and sailors that were coming ashore at 0315 to seize the two MPS ships. Sebastian's nervousness sprang from the fact that what they were doing was stealing two large cargo ships from an American base. The questions ran through his mind. What if it doesn't go smoothly or they resist? It was one thing to shoot and kill a Taliban fighter, but to shoot an American Merchant Marine who would be doing nothing but defending his ship just did not sit well with him. Sebastian and his spotter, Tomlinson, were hidden in a grove of trees on the south side of the port. The sun would be rising within a few hours and they needed to have the ships under control and underway by 0445. The pre-raid briefing estimated that the six teams could have complete control of both ships within forty-five minutes and be under way shortly after that. The plan called for no air support, so it would be man against man.

Sebastian kept looking at his watch like a novice chef would watch water boil. He was growing impatient and more anxious as the minutes ticked away. He looked through his scope again. All was quiet and no movement around or on the ships. He could hear the hum of machines in the distance and the air was cool and smelled salty.

"Damn, I gotta piss," whispered Tomlinson.

"Piss then," Sebastian told him.

Tomlinson rolled a couple of feet away and undid his trousers.

"Ahhh, nothing like taking a piss after you've held it forever," sighed Tomlinson. "It just feels—"

"Shhhhh," Sebastian snapped as he heard a truck coming. He peered through the scope till he finally saw it. A gray pickup truck was speeding toward the MPS ship *Bennett*. When it reached the gangway of the ship it stopped and two men got out and ran up toward the quarterdeck. Sebastian sensed something was wrong. He thought to himself, Had their mission been compromised? Only a few minutes went by before he heard the general quarters alarm sound on the ship.

"Shit!" Sebastian said out loud.

"What's up?" Tomlinson said after rolling back over and grabbing his binoculars.

"We've been compromised, Tomlinson; contact the *Makin Island* and let them know."

"Roger that," Tomlinson said, then pressed the mic of the radio. "Charlie Papa, Charlie Papa, this is Sierra Tango One, over."

Sebastian now saw the decks of the *Bennett* spring to life. The two men who had obviously sounded the alarm ran down the gangway and got back in their truck; they sped off toward the *Stockham*, which was moored next to the *Bennett*. Their trip was unnecessary, though, as Sebastian heard the general quarters alarm begin on the *Stockham* too.

"Charlie Papa, Charlie Papa, this is Sierra Tango One, over," Tomlinson said again into the mic of the radio.

Sebastian looked at his watch; it was now 0306. The raiding party would be hitting the shore any minute now.

"Charlie Papa, the two targets have been alerted to our intentions, over," Tomlinson said to someone on board the *Makin Island*.

Sebastian could see the men on board the *Bennett* preparing to defend the ship. Just what he had feared was coming true, American against American.

"Roger that, Sierra Tango One, out," Tomlinson said, finishing his conversation with command on the *Makin Island*.

"So what's up?" Sebastian asked. He didn't take his eyes away from the scope.

"They want us to proceed with the raid and that the rules of engagement are the same."

"Damn it," Sebastian said with frustration in his voice.

In the distance, Sebastian then heard more vehicles coming. He turned his rifle toward the sound and looked through his scope. What he saw confirmed his fears. Three trucks of armed military police were coming toward the ships.

"This is going down very badly," Sebastian said.

"Yep, sure is," Tomlinson said, agreeing with Sebastian.

"Van Zandt, I see our raiding party; they're heading toward the *Stockham* now!" Tomlinson said, peering through the binoculars. He wasn't the only one who had seen them either. Within seconds, yelling started to come from the ship as spotlights splashed down on the advancing Marines and sailors.

"What do we do?" Tomlinson asked.

"First we need to slow down these reinforcements," Sebastian said as he placed his finger on the trigger and started to squeeze. He thought to himself that as soon as he squeezed off this shot, there was no going back. The seconds it took to fire the first round off seemed like forever. Sebastian's training had paid off, and with precision he hit the front tire of the first truck. He cycled the bolt of his rifle with speed and took aim on the second truck's front tire, and within three seconds he fired his second shot, striking his target. He repeated this one more time and took out the third truck's front tire. His accuracy had worked; the first truck lost control and almost crashed, but the driver maintained control only to have the second truck ram him. Just after he had taken his third and final shot, the third truck swerved to miss the accident and lost control due to its flat front tire and turned over. The men violently flew out of the open back onto the road. Sebastian wasn't sure if anyone was dead, but he had slowed them down and helped assure the success of their raiding teams.

Sebastian now turned his attention to the action happening over near the *Stockham*. When he looked through his scope he saw a couple of Marines lying on the ground. The crew of the *Stockham* had managed to bring enough gunfire to hold back the advancing Marines. He scanned the decks of the ship looking for the shooters.

Finding one near the bridge with a rifle, he placed the crosshairs on the man's chest and started to squeeze the trigger. He then paused. His previous thoughts came to him again. This is an American! He took his gaze away from the scope and looked down. Tomlinson could hear him exhale deeply and turned to him.

"Corporal, you okay?"

Sebastian did not respond, he just looked down.

"Corporal Van Zandt, you all right?" Tomlinson asked again.

Clearing his thoughts and getting back behind his rifle, Sebastian replied, "Yeah, I'm okay."

He soon found the man with the rifle on the bridge and took aim again. He placed his finger back on the trigger and squeezed; this time he aimed for the man's head. His thoughts were that if he was going to kill him he'd make it a clean shot. He applied more steady pressure to the trigger till it went off. The round hit the man in the head. Sebastian could see his head explode and the man fall backward.

"Good shot!" Tomlinson said.

Sebastian took the butt of the rifle out of his shoulder and took a deep breath.

Tomlinson was busy looking for more targets through his binoculars. "I have another shooter, three o'clock to the last guy; distance is the same, windage is the same. Take the shot."

"I don't know if I can do it," Sebastian said, exacerbated.

"What?" Tomlinson asked. He put the binoculars down and turned to Sebastian.

Sebastian was not feeling right about any of this. "Tomlinson, what are we doing? We're killing Americans now. All I wanted to do was go home; now we're in Diego Garcia killing Americans."

"Listen, Corporal. I hear ya, but it's on now. We are committed and now it's us or them."

"I don't know if I can do this," Sebastian said again.

"Can you at least spot for me?" Tomlinson asked.

Sebastian handed the rifle to Tomlinson, who didn't waste time. He took aim on the last target he had spotted for Sebastian. It took him only seconds before he squeezed off a round, killing the man.

Sebastian's and Tomlinson's accurate shooting had provided enough support for the raiding party to make ground and advance toward their objective.

Tomlinson was not waiting for Sebastian; he was identifying his own targets and taking the shots. Sebastian was watching it all happen before him through the lenses of his binoculars.

Then he heard what sounded like helicopters. Sebastian lowered the binos and looked into the darkness beyond the ships and the gun battle before him. Moments later, two Cobra attack helicopters came racing above the two MPS ships and took position hovering over the bay. It appeared the call to have no air support had been changed. Sebastian knew the targets they were going after. Seconds later, the Cobra gunships opened up their 20-millimeter mini-guns and blasted the reinforcements that were in the trucks. The mini-guns laid waste to the vehicles and what men were still in the area.

"Fuckin' A, get some!" Tomlinson said loudly with excitement.

Now Sebastian knew that his whole world had officially changed; he now was a rebel, a traitor, a mutineer. If Barone was wrong and the world they went back to came back to normal, they all would be arrested and possibly hanged for treason. As these thoughts raced through his mind, he asked himself if he should go through with it or just stop now. He couldn't turn back now; he had already killed one American if not more in the trucks. Following Barone was the only direct way back to Gordon and his family. He finally decided to be committed to this for now; but he didn't know if he would do it past landing back in California.

He turned to Tomlinson and said, "Okay, T; I'm good now; let me get some."

"That's music to my ears," Tomlinson said, handing him back the rifle.

Sebastian took the rifle, cycled the bolt, and placed his face against the stock and looked through the scope. Tomlinson said, "Look aft on the *Bennett*, we have a guy up there with a rifle."

Sebastian searched for the man till he saw the muzzle flash of his rifle. He took aim on his head, squeezed the trigger, and shot him dead.

Cheyenne Mountain, Colorado

"Mr. President, thank you for coming so quickly. We have an incident that needs your attention, sir," Griswald said.

Conner took a seat at the table in the command post briefing room.

"No problem. What do we have?" Conner asked. The lack of sleep was taking a toll on Conner. He had large black circles under his eyes and he was losing weight; not from lack of food but from his lack of eating.

"Sir, we just received word that two Maritime Prepositioned Ships were just seized in Diego Garcia."

"By whom?"

Griswald looked at his colleagues before he answered Conner. "Sir, by U.S. Marines."

"What?"

"Yes, sir; I'm surprised by this too, but what we have heard is that a Lieutenant Colonel Barone with support of his officer corps have taken control of an Amphibious Ready Group. They sailed the ships to Diego Garcia, refueled, resupplied, and then after they left, they attacked the island and seized two MPS ships."

Conner just sat looking stunned. He shook his head and asked, "Where are they now, where are they headed?"

"Sir, I do not know. Their orders were to head to the East Coast to help support the recovery effort in Washington, D.C. Where they are heading is unknown for now."

"Do we have any satellite support at all?"

"Yes, sir, we do; most of those survived the EMPs due to their Medium Earth Orbit. But it appears that Barone has disabled us from tracking the ships."

"Okay, let me make sure I understand what has happened. A rogue Marine colonel has taken an entire ARG, then sailed it to Diego Garcia where he stole two MPS ships. He is now sailing for God knows where."

"Sir, that is correct. It appeared to the U.S. command element on the island that they were just stopping by to get refueled and resupplied before heading east. After the ARG had departed the island, the command on DG had been notified by someone on the ships that Colonel Barone had mutinied and taken the USS *Makin Island*, the USS *New Orleans*, and the USS *Pearl Harbor* and had plans for seizing the MV *Bennett* and USNS *Stockham*. DG command attempted to thwart the seizures but overwhelming force by Barone's men stopped any resistance and both ships were taken. DG command reports forty-two personnel KIA and twenty-three WIA. They also reported that Barone lost six Marines."

"Where is Barone based out of?" Conner asked.

"Sir, he commands the Second battalion, Fourth Marine Regiment out of Camp Pendleton, California."

"Then, General, I would guess California is where he's headed. What assets do we have in the area?"

"For what, sir?" Griswald asked, not sure of how to answer the question.

"I'll just cut the bullshit right here, General. We cannot let this stand, we cannot have Marine colonels or anybody just stealing our ships and resources. This man and his men must be dealt with. Find me some planes or a goddamn carrier group to go after this man and his pack of traitors. They must be stopped."

Griswald looked around the table and then back to the president. "Sir, yes, sir."

"Let me know as soon as you find someone to intercept them—" Conner said, pausing mid-sentence. A new idea came to him. "General, do what you can to contact this colonel; I wish to speak to him."

Raising his eyebrows curiously Griswald replied, "Yes, sir."

"Thank you, General. Now, if that is all, I will retire back to my room," Conner said, then stood up, turned, and left. As he walked back to his room, thoughts of how fast things were falling apart consumed him. He had never thought that military commanders would start to disobey orders and mutiny. It had not been a week since the attacks and things were deteriorating quickly. They still did not know who had attacked them and they still had not responded. He knew that his time to make a decision was running out; he knew in order to show his enemies he was serious he would have to act soon.

Entering his room, he could hear his wife sleeping. He wanted to wake her up and tell her about his day; he missed her so much. He needed her more than she needed him at this moment. She had closed herself off since the death of their son. Even though he was being ignored, he felt it important to just love her regardless of what she gave in return. He hoped that eventually she would come back to him, but until then he would have to love for two people.

Conner not only had to support his country in this dark hour, he had to take control of his marriage too if it was going to survive.

San Diego, California

Gordon loved his coffee. In fact, if he didn't get his "fix" he would get headaches. The smell of fresh brewed coffee was one element of his past life he missed. So while he didn't enjoy the cold, bitter coffee, he enjoyed it better than a headache.

The search for food was becoming more and more difficult every day. They had to keep going farther and farther only to find less and less. The community teams he had set up had been working. Their little community was functioning like a town. After each scavenger team returned, they would inventory and store their findings nightly. The following day it would be distributed evenly to each household. Rancho Valentino was fortunate because they had a diverse cross-section of people, from doctors and nurses to engineers and even a horticulturist. Gordon had taken direct control of the community's security forces. He saw that they were trained, armed, and given the support they needed to protect the community. He had set up guard positions at each gated entrance and on several rooftops that had commanding views of the area.

Gordon and the other scavenger teams started to see an increase in violence on the outside. They had been fortunate to have enough arms to give to all of his security forces, but there was not enough to protect from an all-out assault if attacked by a well-armed enemy. He needed to find weapons and ammunition. He had conducted a meeting with his security force team leads comprised of Jimmy, Nelson, and a cop named Dan Bradford. Gordon did not think highly of Dan. Maybe it was that he had the responsibility of protecting people but didn't have the discipline to take care of himself. He was overweight and slovenly. Coming highly recommended from Mindy did not help. Whatever the reason, Gordon just didn't quite trust Dan, nor did he care for his arrogance; but Gordon had dealt with a lot of egos in his life and he would just have to deal with Dan.

All the team leads decided that they needed to create two new three-man teams, one headed by Gordon and the other by Dan, to find weapons and ammo. They had identified locations where they might find them; Dan would take his team to different police stations while Gordon would go to gun stores.

Each morning before Gordon left for the day, he went and kissed his kids and made sure he told them he loved them. Dan was taking his team south into Mira Mesa; the area was heavily populated and was sure to pose potential problems. Gordon stressed to Dan to get in and out as fast as possible. They had a clear objective, no detours or sightseeing. Gordon was taking his team north just a few miles to a sheriff's depot, then on to Solana Beach if they could fit it in.

Gordon walked back into his bedroom after visiting his children. As Samantha was getting dressed, he walked up behind her and put his arms around her. Embracing her tightly, he kissed her neck and whispered in her ear. He loved her so much; she had adapted quickly to the new reality and had volunteered to be a teacher in a school that they had put together. The idea of the school was Samantha's; she thought it best to ensure the children were still educated. The school also gave the children something of structure and the comfort of routine.

Holding her tightly, Gordon said, "Love you, babe."

Samantha leaned against Gordon and replied, "I love you too."

"I just wanted to give you a kiss before I left."

"Where are you going?" she asked.

"Nowhere special," Gordon said. He never got into too much detail with her over his daily missions and he never told her about any incidents; the last thing he wanted to do was make her any more nervous than she was.

Samantha turned around and faced him. She looked up at him and asked, "Gordon, how long can we do this? How long can we keep this all together?"

Looking down at her, he stroked some hair away from her face. "As long as we have to."

"That's not an answer, Gordon."

"Sam, all I know is we don't have a choice but to keep doing what we're doing. Things seem to be working, and if we can keep finding food then we will be okay," Gordon answered. He had a hard time keeping a straight face, as he didn't believe the words that came spilling out of his mouth.

Looking more deeply into his eyes, she asked, "Really?"

Putting his hand on her cheek and bringing her lips to his, he kissed her. He then looked at her green eyes and said, "Yes, we will be okay." Gordon was unsure of what the future held. His nightly sleep was interrupted with nightmares of losing his family to this new world. He struggled but had been successful at keeping those thoughts out of his mind. "Honey, I have to go; I'll see you tonight." He kissed her again and left.

Walking the neighborhood, he noticed a transformation in the community. Dozens of people were walking the streets coming and going, clotheslines now stretched in backyards, tarps were hung to capture the morning condensation, five-gallon buckets were positioned under rain gutters to gather runoff, smoke billowed out of chimneys. Gone were his neighbors exercising or mothers casually pushing their strollers while talking on their phones. Most people had pushed their unusable cars out into the street to open up more space in their garages.

As he walked he looked at everyone. They no longer seemed to care about appearances. Most of the women had their hair pulled back while men wore hats and were unshaven.

Each scavenger team brought back food, but it was never enough to feed the more than seven hundred people who lived in their community. The gardening might work but it would be slow, it would take months before the gardens would be producing any real amount of food. Water too would become an issue; they had secured the large tank but that would only last for a couple of months before it ran dry and then there was the issue of medicine; some in the community had ongoing medical issues that required daily medications. Jimmy's own son had to have an inhaler due to his asthma. Fortunately, the teams had been very successful with securing large caches of medications, but that too would eventually dry up.

Gordon had a lot on his plate, but he was committed to making it work; at the moment he had no other choice unless he was going to leave and risk it on the road.

Gordon's thoughts were interrupted when Melissa hollered his name from a distance. "Gordon!"

He looked around and saw her waving; returning the wave he wondered what she might want as she jogged up to him.

"Hi, Gordon, how are you and the family?"

"I'm good, thanks for asking; how are you doing?"

"Good—well, as good as can be with the circumstances. As you know, Eric finally made it home the next day. He had to walk all the way from downtown," Melissa said. She appeared nervous; she crossed her arms when she wasn't talking.

"I had heard, I knew he'd be fine." Gordon tried to keep his answers short because he now was late to meet his team.

"I'm sorry; I know you're busy, Gordon, but I'm really here to ask a favor and not to have small talk."

"Okay, so how can I help?"

"Eric has just been at home with the baby and not doing anything; I've been doing some volunteering at the school with Samantha, as I'm sure you're aware."

"Yes, I know," Gordon said.

"You see, it's about Eric; he's kinda in a funk," Melissa said. She was not really looking Gordon in the face when she talked and her nervous behavior increased when she mentioned her husband.

Sensing her nervousness, Gordon reached out and touched her arm and said, "What is it, Melissa?"

Giving a sigh she said, "Can Eric join your teams? He's really smart and he's strong; he rowed in college and he's athletic. I know he's just an accountant and has no military experience, but he can use the guy time and he needs to get out of the house and do something."

"Why isn't Eric here asking me?" Gordon asked.

"Because he was afraid you'd say no."

"Oh my God, not at all; I need smart guys like Eric. I don't care what he did before as long as he can handle himself outside the gate."

Melissa's face lit up and she said, "Great! I'll let him know. When can he meet you to go over any details?"

"How about you come over for dinner tonight? I'll pull him aside to chat. How does that sound?"

"Sounds perfect, Gordon. Thank you so much," Melissa said, now looking happy and relieved.

"Not a problem at all. But if you'll excuse me I do need to go," Gordon said, pointing to his team waiting on him.

Melissa turned in the direction he was pointing and then turned back and said, "No problem, thank you again. I'll see you tonight."

Gordon walked off and then stopped. He turned back and said, "Please let my wife know we're having you all over for dinner tonight."

"I'll let her know at school," Melissa said. She then waved and turned around.

Gordon started walking toward his team. He liked Eric; he didn't know him that well, but Eric impressed him as an educated and smart man. He was a second-generation Chinese immigrant. His parents had come to the U.S. with nothing and opened up a small bakery. Pouring their heart and soul into it, they made the bakery successful enough that they could afford to send Eric to Harvard. Eric followed his parents' entrepreneurial spirit and opened his own accounting firm after getting an MBA. He was average height and very lean. He was five years older than Gordon and about ten years senior to Melissa. Gordon would get a better feel for Eric's spot on the teams tonight over a drink. Always needing good people, Gordon looked forward to sitting down with him.

Gordon finally reached the vehicle and tossed in his gear. Today he was going out with Max and Jerrod. Jerrod was a former Army

Ranger and veteran of Iraq. He was tall and muscular, with thick brown hair and brown eyes. With the last name of Hernandez, Gordon laughed to himself that Jerrod was not a very Hispanic first name. Before the attacks, Gordon knew him only in passing when he'd see him out running in the neighborhood. Jerrod was married and had a two-year-old son.

Max was short in build but made up for his height by having quite the "colorful" personality. Gordon thought he fit the perfect image of a suave Italian single guy. He kept his full head of short, black hair combed back. He was one of the few single people who lived in the neighborhood. Gordon had never met Max before the attacks but knew he was an attorney for a law firm downtown.

Both men had proven to be quite competent and capable. Max was a bit of a hothead and had a short temper, but he had proven he could fight and Gordon liked that.

"You gentlemen ready?" Gordon asked.

"Yes, sir," Jerrod said.

"Yep," Max answered, leaning against the Chevy Nova. The Nova was Max's car. He loved old classic muscle cars and he let everyone know that his car was fast.

All three men got in the car with Gordon riding shotgun. After they cleared the main gate, Max asked, "Where to?"

Gordon looked both ways and said, "That way. Hopefully we'll come back with a lot more guns. Keep your fingers crossed, boys, and stay alert, we're going farther than we have before."

Max slammed the gas pedal down, causing the Nova to spin out. They accelerated quickly and disappeared over the hill.

USS *Makin Island*, Indian Ocean

Sebastian sat outside getting some cool ocean air when the hatch opened, bathing him in the red light from the passageway. Tomlinson stepped out of the glow and approached Sebastian.

Tomlinson pulled out a pack of Camel Lights and offered one to Sebastian. "You look like you could use one of these."

"No, but if you had a drink I would take that," Sebastian answered. He stared out into the moonlit waters of the Indian Ocean. The saltiness of the air and the sounds of the waves soothed his troubled mind.

Tomlinson sat next to him and lit his cigarette. He took a drag and asked, "So tell me, what happened out there this morning?"

"I don't want to talk about it," Sebastian said, not looking at Tomlinson.

"Well, I'll tell you this, if you ever want to chat, I'm here for ya, bro, as long as you're not going to whine."

"What do you think happens now?" Sebastian asked.

"Oh, I don't know; what sucks is that we have to be under way for the next three weeks with not a single port call," Tomlinson said, then took another drag.

"You do realize that if we get back to the States and everything is working fine or things go back to normal, we risk being arrested and possibly hung for what happened today?"

"Well, first they'd have to catch me and second I trust the colonel. I think everything is fucked and we have to carve out something for us now."

"I hope you're right, I really do."

"Seriously, man, what's your deal? I've never seen you like this before," Tomlinson said, then took his last drag and flicked the butt of the cigarette over the railing.

"I told you, I don't want to get into it right now. Let me process what happened today and then maybe we can talk about it, but please respect me and stop asking," Sebastian said, with a tinge of irritation in his voice.

"Okay, bro. I'll leave you be." Tomlinson stood up, opened the hatch, and walked back inside the ship.

Sebastian sat and plotted what he'd do once they reached California. He just hoped that they could avoid anymore engagements against other Americans before then.

San Diego, California

Gordon returned home safe but not happy. The journey into Solana Beach to gather arms proved to be a partial success. They had made it in and out without any confrontation, but the gun store had been sacked already. His team had managed to get some items that could come in handy, like body armor, clothing, boots, slings, holsters, and other accessories, but no guns or ammo. They did stop by another Home Depot and pulled more seed and some fertilizer but the food was gone. Gordon was shocked by how quickly the resources were drying up.

On their return, they had made a grisly discovery at a Von's grocery store. Dozens or more people had been executed outside of the store. Whoever it was had left their mark. The word "Villistas" was spray painted on the wall behind them. He did not know what it meant, but he knew it wasn't good. It appeared that gangs or armed groups were already coalescing together. Things were clearly getting more violent and desperate.

Gordon walked into the house tired and ready to eat. When he walked into the candle-lit foyer he could hear his kids playing and giggling down the hall and Samantha scolding them to clean up their mess. Gordon smiled. The sounds of normal family life were still there, even though the house itself was starting to go through a transformation too. The toilets had overflowed a few days before. Even though they had cleaned up the mess, taped the toilet lids shut, and secured the doors, a slight smell of raw sewage remained in the air. Samantha tried her best to cover up the smell with scented candles, but a faint aroma remained.

"Gordon, when you're done settling in, can you help clean Haley up?" Samantha yelled from the playroom.

"What happened?" Gordon yelled back bent over taking off his boots.

"She thought it was more fun to paint herself instead of the paper."

"Okay, babe; I'll get right on it," Gordon said after taking off his last boot and sitting back in the chair. He let out a sigh of exhaustion and rubbed his face.

Hunter ran up to him. "Daddy, you're home!"

"Hey, big guy!" Gordon exclaimed. He picked up Hunter and hugged him. "How were things today, anything to report?"

"No, sir, all good," Hunter answered as he saluted Gordon.

"Thank you for watching over the ladies of the house, I appreciate that," Gordon warmly told his son.

They began to walk down the hall when banging on the front door disrupted their family bliss. Gordon quickly put Hunter down and told him to go into the playroom immediately. Hunter listened and ran off. Gordon pulled his pistol from his shoulder holster and approached the door. All of his exhaustion had been replaced by adrenaline. Whoever was banging would not stop. Gordon slowly approached the door when a familiar voice cried out.

"Gordon, open up!" Jimmy cried.

Gordon quickly opened the door to see Jimmy before him with Mason in his arms.

"Jimmy! What's going on?"

"Gordon, it's Mason; he's having an asthma attack and we can't find his inhaler. I stopped by the clinic and we don't have any in inventory. I don't know what to do. Please help me!" Jimmy said with fear in his voice.

Gordon acted without thinking and asked Jimmy, "Is your rig out front?" Gordon thought that they had two choices: go door-to-door to see if anyone else in the neighborhood had an inhaler or take their chances outside the gate. He decided that they'd have better luck going outside the gate to a hospital or pharmacy.

"Yes, yes!" Jimmy said.

Hunter and Haley were peering from behind the door of the playroom. Samantha ran down the hall and stopped just behind Gordon. She could see Jimmy was on the verge of breaking down. Mason was pale and limp in his arms, almost lifeless.

"Come on, let's go!" Gordon said to Jimmy after just sliding his boots back on. He pointed outside and then followed up by saying, "We need to go out the gate to find an inhaler!"

Jimmy didn't say a thing; he just looked down at his son, whose arms dangled as he walked briskly behind Gordon to his truck.

When Jimmy reached the truck, Gordon held the door open. He lay Mason down across the bench seat and sat next to him. Jimmy put Mason's head on his lap and stroked his hair. Mason's breathing was very shallow. Gordon jumped behind the wheel and turned on the truck. He sped off toward the closest gate. When he reached the gate he yelled out the window to the gate guards to open the gate immediately. Gordon started to accelerate when he heard someone yell. He looked and saw Dan Bradford in the side mirror.

"One second, stop!" Dan yelled.

Gordon stuck his head out the window and replied, "Dan, we don't have time. We have to go; it's an emergency."

"Can I help in any way?" he said, after jogging up to the driver's-side window.

"Do you have an inhaler?"

"No."

"Then the answer's no. I need to go find one for Jimmy's son ASAP."

"Let me go to help as backup for you."

"Sure, jump in the bed," Gordon told him.

Dan jumped in the bed and immediately slapped the side of the truck, telling Gordon he was ready to go. Gordon sped off and headed north.

Gordon drove as fast as he could. All of the abandoned vehicles on the road made it difficult as they had to swerve to avoid them, causing him to slow down and speed up. Gordon focused on driving and Jimmy comforted his son and whispered to him that everything would be okay.

Gordon knew exactly where he was going and after twelve minutes of driving they pulled up to Sharp Hospital's ER entrance.

"I'll find an inhaler as quickly as I can, I promise," Gordon assured Jimmy. He then placed his hand on Mason's head and said softer, "I will find one, I promise you."

Jimmy looked up at Gordon. The lights of the dash cast a somber shadow across his face. "Please hurry. I don't know how long he can make it, he's barely breathing now." Gordon slammed the truck door and ran for the ER entrance with Dan.

Pulling his pistol out in anticipation that they might run into others, he approached the doors to the ER main entrance apprehensively. The doors were closed tight. Dan ran up and started to try to peel the doors apart. Gordon didn't want to waste time so he looked around for something to smash the glass and found a large paver brick; he picked it up and told Dan to step aside. He threw it as hard as he could, shattering the glass. Dan and Gordon cleared the remaining glass and entered the dark hallway. Immediately upon entering the hallway the smell of death wafted over them.

"Oh my God!" Dan said, placing his hand over his nose and mouth.

Gordon turned on his small Surefire flashlight and quickly proceeded down the hallway. The farther he moved into the darkness the stronger the smell. It appeared that no one had ransacked this part of the hospital yet. It looked in disarray, but that was due to the chaos created after the attacks. Gordon guessed that the hospital employees probably abandoned the hospital days after the attacks. Gordon's light illuminated the hallway and brought light to darkened spaces. He peered into each room to see what was there. The smell grew greater; he knew he would soon locate the source.

Gordon reached the end of the hallway. Casting his light inside the last room he finally found the origin of the rotten smell that filled his nostrils. Lying naked and now bloated was an old man who had been in his sixties or seventies.

Dan walked up just behind Gordon and said, "Nasty!"

"Well, I'm sure that's not how he wanted to go or be remembered," Gordon said. He then turned his attention away from the dead man and opened the swinging doors that led into a main corridor.

The doors hadn't closed for a few moments before Dan and Gordon heard a crash at the end of the corridor. They both flashed their lights and bathed the entire hallway in light. Another crash echoed, followed by angry yelling. They were able to pinpoint the noise from a room around the corner. With pistols drawn they proceeded down the hall. Gordon had no doubt it was someone scavenging like them. Gordon looked on the wall and saw a sign with an arrow pointing in the direction they were headed that said PHARMACY. He peeked around the corner of the corridor and heard the noise again. The sound came from the direction of the pharmacy. Gordon turned back to Dan and said, "Sounds like whoever is making that noise is in the pharmacy. We need to get down there and get what we need. This could turn ugly, so be ready."

"Okay," Dan said, looking a bit nervous.

They both turned the corner with their pistols raised and slowly made their way down the dark hall toward the sound. After only a few steps, they saw a light bouncing around a room on the left. Without notice, someone appeared from the room carrying a box. He turned away from Dan and Gordon and walked down the hall and exited on the right. Once the door closed behind the stranger Gordon stepped up to the room and saw no other lights. He turned on his flashlight and entered the room while Dan remained in the hall providing cover. The pharmacy had been almost stripped. Gordon immediately started to dig through the open boxes on the counters. Not finding what he was looking for made Gordon frustrated. He quickly began to look at each shelf and went through every drawer. After an exhaustive search he still could not find an inhaler.

"Damn it!" Gordon said aloud, pushing one of the boxes onto the floor.

"Just hold it right there," Dan ordered.

Gordon stopped his search and headed for the door.

"Don't make a move!" Dan yelled.

Gordon stepped out of the pharmacy and saw the man. Dan had the flashlight on him.

The man stood there with his empty hands up.

Gordon put his light on the man's face and said, "I need an inhaler; where are the rest of your boxes?"

The man did not say a word; he just stood there blocking the lights from his eyes.

"Where are your boxes?" Gordon again asked. "If you can't see let me just tell you that we are both armed."

Still the man just stood there.

"Fuck it!" Gordon said. He walked over to the man and pistol-whipped him in the face. The man fell to the ground.

"Stop!" the man screamed finally.

"Where are the rest of your boxes?"

"Out in my truck."

"Take us there now!" Gordon demanded. He pulled the guy up by the back of his shirt and pushed him through the door.

They walked through the hallway and came to an exterior exit door.

"My truck is out there," the man said.

Gordon kicked the door open and flashed his light outside. He could see what looked like an old farm truck. He pushed the man through the open door, causing him to stumble and fall.

Walking over, Gordon grabbed him again but this time was met with resistance. The man elbowed him in the crotch.

"Shit!" Gordon cried out in pain.

The man took off running toward his truck.

"Freeze!" Dan yelled.

Gordon stood up clearly hurting but ran after the man. Managing only to make it around to the driver's door, he stopped when Gordon fired a shot in his direction.

"Listen, I don't know what you're going to do to me, that's why I hit you. I don't know who you are; I'm getting this medicine for my family."

Gordon was seething with anger. Looking at the man, he yelled, "Step away from the truck!"

Dan came up alongside Gordon and ordered the man to get on the ground.

"Step away from the truck! I need to see if you have something we need!" Gordon barked.

"I don't want any trouble; I'm just getting this for my family. Please let me go," the man begged, then took a step closer to his truck door.

"This is a fucking waste of time!" Gordon screamed as he squeezed the trigger and shot the man in the chest.

The bullet hit the man with a dull thud. He instantly dropped to the ground, dead.

"Why did you shoot him?" Dan asked.

"We don't have time for this shit anymore. Mason needs the meds." Gordon re-holstered his pistol and started to rummage through the boxes in the bed of the truck.

Dan just stood there looking at Gordon in amazement.

After going through several boxes, Gordon exclaimed, "Here they are!" He pulled an inhaler out of a box and held it high. Not wasting another moment, he then took off running back to Jimmy and Mason.

When Gordon reached Jimmy's truck he could hear Jimmy wailing with grief. He could not see Jimmy, but the cries told him of a fate that should not have been. Gordon just stood in the darkness listening to his friend and wanting for the outcome to be different.

DECEMBER 12, 2014

• • •

**When men yield up the privilege of thinking,
the last shadow of liberty quits the horizon.**

—Thomas Paine

USS *Makin Island*, Indian Ocean

Barone was abruptly awakened by banging on his stateroom door. He sprang from his rack and opened the door. Wiping sleep from his eyes, he said, "What is it?"

"Sorry to disturb you, sir," a nervous lance corporal said.

"Well, what is it?"

"Sir, there is an important call for you."

"A call?" Barone asked, looking confused. He stepped away from the door and walked over to a chair in the room. "Come on in, Lance Corporal."

The lance corporal nervously stepped in.

"Since it required you to come down here and wake me up, who may I ask is on the call?" Barone asked, with a hint of sarcasm.

"Sir, it's the president."

Barone stopped tying his boots and looked at the lance corporal. A myriad of emotions came over him—shock, fear, anxiety. He went back to tying his boots and cleared his mind. Not wanting this young man to see him nervous he abruptly finished the conversation by saying, "Lance Corporal, you may leave. I will be there shortly."

Barone sat up and exhaled deeply. It was obvious that the call was prompted by the raid on Diego Garcia. He never expected he'd received a call from the president. He would have expected to hear from some general. If the president was calling then he assumed that they wanted to come to some type of settlement. Now curious to find out what the president wanted, he quickly grabbed his blouse and headed toward the CIC. The usual short walk seemed to take forever; his anxiety was at an all-time high. In his entire career he had never spoken to a president. Now he would, but the circumstances were extraordinary. When he entered the darkened command center all eyes were on him. Major Ashley stood up and said, "Sir, we have a secure line in the back room."

Barone just nodded to Ashley and walked briskly to the back room and closed the door. He looked down at the receiver on the desk. He paused for a moment to get his bearings. On his walk he had run through how the conversation would go. With anticipation that the new president would toss around words like "traitor" and "mutiny," he promised himself to remain calm and keep his composure.

He cleared the onslaught of thoughts, sat down, and picked up the receiver. Swallowing hard, he spoke: "Lieutenant Colonel Barone here."

Silence.

"Lieutenant Colonel Barone here."

Still silence.

"Is anyone there?"

"Colonel Barone?" a voice asked, breaking the silence.

"Yes, Colonel Barone here."

"One moment," the voice said.

Barone was tapping his foot with nervous energy. The anticipation was excruciating.

Seconds felt like minutes. Then a familiar voice filled his ears and brought back memories of a congressional hearing he was subjected to years ago. He now remembered he had met the president during a hearing about the shooting of an unarmed Iraqi in 2004. Barone had volunteered to testify on behalf of a Marine who had been indicted from his unit. He recalled that the president had been fair in his cross-examination and only wanted to get to the truth.

"Colonel Barone?" Conner asked.

"Yes, this is him."

"Colonel Barone, hello; this is President Conner."

"Hello, sir."

"Colonel, I don't know where to begin, so let's begin with what the hell are you doing?" Conner asked.

"Sir, first let me say that what I am doing is in the best interests of my men and their—"

Cutting him off, Conner asked him with a scolding tone, "What about the best interests of your country?"

"Sir, sending us back to the East Coast to dig up dead bodies is a fool's errand. You know the magnitude of what has happened. I voiced my thoughts before we made our decision but no one would listen. I therefore deemed it necessary to act in the best interests of Americans that are alive in the hopes of keeping them alive."

"So you thought that it more important to defy a presidential order and mutiny?"

"Sir, I—"

"So you thought you would seize U.S. naval vessels and then lead those ships in an attack against a U.S. military installation, stealing even more U.S. ships and property?" Conner asked, his tone becoming more aggressive and angry.

"I thought—"

"You thought what, Colonel? You are now an enemy of the American people; you have committed mutiny and treason!" Conner yelled.

Barone paused for a moment before he attempted to respond. His assumptions about the accusations he'd hear were correct.

"What am I to do with you, Colonel?"

Barone did not answer; he wanted to make sure he could answer without being interrupted.

There was an uncomfortable silence.

"Well, Colonel?"

"Can I answer without being interrupted?"

"Go ahead, Colonel."

"I looked at the entire situation and felt that"—Barone paused and then completed his thought—"No, I *knew* that going back to the East Coast to assist in a recovery effort was futile. What about our families back in California? Who is taking care of them? I feel it is more important to keep as many people alive instead of digging up dead bodies. I did voice my concerns, but the plan was in place and so I did what I knew was the right thing."

After Barone had said his piece, there was silence.

After thinking about what Barone said, Conner continued. "Colonel Barone, I have heard your excuse, I am giving you one chance to correct your errors and turn your ships around and go back to your original mission. As your commander in chief, I order you to do this. We will deal with you later. I need good men in the field and I need you to follow what is in the best interests of our country. Do you understand?"

Barone sat and thought about what the new president had ordered. He then felt in his heart that he was doing the right thing and told Conner, "Mr. President, I cannot. I have committed myself to my men and their families. I am sorry, but your orders to go back east are foolish. I cannot in good conscience follow those orders. I accept full responsibility for this and my men are doing this because of me."

"Colonel Barone, I am sorry to hear that. Here is what will happen. We cannot allow you to openly defy the government. We will be compelled to use force to stop you," Conner said coolly.

"Mr. President, I would ask that you let us go peacefully. Engaging in open conflict is not advisable."

"Colonel, you have done this, not us. We cannot allow this mutiny to go unchecked. We will stop you before you ever reach California."

"Mr. President, I'm pleading, don't take it to that level. We only mean to go home and take care of our families. We did not mean to get into a fight on Diego Garcia. We came under attack so we defended ourselves and will do so if we are attacked again. Sir, there does not need to be bloodshed. Please let us go freely."

"Colonel, you have twenty-four hours to accept my offer. If after twenty-four hours you have not turned the ships around, we will consider you a hostile to the United States and an enemy of the people. We will use whatever means necessary to ensure you do not land in California."

"Sir, I will not change my mind and again ask you for leniency. However, if attacked we will defend to the death."

"You have twenty-four hours. We will await your reply. Goodbye, Colonel Barone," Conner finished, then the line went silent.

Barone put the receiver down and sighed loudly. He needed to meet with his staff and work out a plan to avoid contact with any

U.S. military ships. He stood up, opened the door, and before he left he looked back at the receiver. He had finally talked to a sitting president but not under the circumstances he would have wanted over the eighteen years of his career. He chuckled to himself and closed the door.

Cheyenne Mountain, Colorado

Conner slammed the phone down. "Goddamn it!"

He looked around at the staff that surrounded him. No one said a word; they all just stared. They knew by hearing just his side of the conversation that Barone was not backing down.

"As you heard, I am giving him twenty-four hours to change his mind and change course. If not, we must stop him. General Griswald, if he continues, what are our options?"

"Sir, we have a carrier group located in Hawaii that we can use, and we have three attack submarines in the Western Pacific."

"General, contact our command in Hawaii and move some ships out of port and have them prepared to engage Barone and his ARG. Also contact those subs and get them in position as well."

"Yes, sir," Griswald said.

Conner looked at each person in the room. He then said, "We cannot allow this to stand; we must stop him. If we do not, this will encourage others to defy us. God damn him. We have enough to worry about, now we have to dedicate resources to stopping him."

"Mr. President, this is a wise decision," Griswald said.

"General, do we have any more information about the attacks? Our time frame to do something is running short."

"Sorry, sir, we are no closer than we were a day after the attacks. This will take time."

Everyone was getting accustomed to seeing Conner act out in anger. So seeing him again display his anger by slamming his fist on the table was not shocking.

Conner scolded Griswald. "We don't have much more time. Every minute that goes by without a response emboldens our enemies and makes them think we don't have the means or the guts to do something about this. I am only being patient for you, General; I need some answers and I need them soon."

"We will continue to keep working on it, sir," Griswald responded.

Griswald was not being completely honest with the president. He did not want to give him what he had found out from his counterpart in Australia. From his conversations over the past week, the Australians had managed to secure information from one of the prisoners. The prisoner told them that he had been trained in Iran. He did not know where the bomb had come from as it was already there when they arrived. While this information was valuable he did not want to give Conner the excuse to nuke Iran just yet. He felt Conner had an itchy trigger finger. Griswald wanted to see if he could build a coalition among the new presidential staff to his mostly diplomatic and limited military option versus the president's nuclear-only option. Griswald realized what he was doing could be considered a violation of his duty to the president but he felt that going along with the president's option would leave half the world a nuclear wasteland. He knew he didn't have much time, so he needed to act soon.

DECEMBER 13, 2014

• • •

The only cure for grief is action.

—G. H. Lewes

San Diego, California

Gordon sat on the edge of the bed, distraught. The thought of going to Mason's funeral was dreadful. He could not help but think that he could have acted quicker. Regret filled his mind as he doubted his actions. He doubted his actions and thought he had been too cautious while he searched the hospital. If he had acted more quickly, Mason might still alive. His thoughts were also plagued by the feelings of guilt. He cursed that he had not secured enough supplies beforehand.

He had not seen Jimmy since that night. The entire event had caused heartache and controversy in the community. All were saddened at the news of Mason's death and some had also used the incident for political gain by using it to strike out at Gordon. Dan had confronted Gordon later that night about the shooting of the unarmed man. As soon as Dan had finished arguing with Gordon that night he promptly went to Mindy's house to inform her of the confrontation, the killing, and Mason's death. Mindy, shocked by Mason's death, also saw it as a chance to publically condemn Gordon. She had called a special session of the board to meet after the funeral.

Life in Rancho Valentino had been insulated from the realities of what was happening to those outside the gate. Not realizing the harshness of the new world, Mindy was successful in sowing discontent against Gordon. He felt had they only been able to see the world outside they would see cause for his decisive action. Many in Rancho Valentino were spoiled and protected.

Those outside the gate did not have that luxury, and were scraping by or not at all. Many had already become victims of violence or lack of food and water. He now realized how important cooperation was in the community. Even those who disagreed with his actions he needed in order to have a successfully running community. However, Mindy had an agenda that was more personal. She had not been outside the gate; she had never had the chance to experience what was really going on. She wanted power and she wanted to humiliate Gordon. With the death of Mason, she would have her chance to publicly call into question Gordon's tactics and seek to have him replaced.

Gordon knew what was coming but didn't care, except for the fact that every minute not focused on resupplying was an opportunity lost forever.

Gordon stood up and stretched. He slowly walked into the dark closet and grabbed a pair of jeans and a T-shirt. Putting on the T-shirt, he noticed the absence of the fragrant smell so typical of his clothes. The softness also was missing, replaced with a stiffness in the fibers from being hung to dry outside.

When he exited he was greeted by Samantha. They exchanged the typical morning greetings. Samantha could see the weight of everything on his face and said, "Honey, come here."

"What?" he said, not looking at her.

"Come here, give me a hug," she said, grabbing Gordon and pulling him in close.

She just held him and kissed him.

"This is all so crazy," Gordon said softly.

Whispering into his ear, she said, "I know, but you need to keep moving forward. We need you; we cannot afford to have you down like this."

Gordon pulled away and looked at her.

Looking into his eyes, she could see the disappointment. She continued to console him by saying, "Gordon, I know you may have doubts because of what happened the other night. But believe me, I trust you, I believe in you. You did what was necessary to protect us and to get the medicine for Mason. It wasn't your fault he died."

"I could have—"

She stopped him from talking by placing her fingers on his lips and softly saying to him, "You did everything you needed to do. What happened, happened. It was not because of you."

Gordon kept staring at her. Her words of encouragement meant a lot to him. In many ways, they both shared the responsibility of being each other's "rock."

The tone in her voice then shifted. "I know that bitch Mindy is using this as a chance to smear you. I need you to fight back, we need you, and this community needs you. Don't take her shit. You're a fighter, that's why I love you. You never give up. I know you need this time to reflect, but this afternoon you'll need to let that go and defend yourself."

As the words came from Samantha, they gave Gordon the confidence he needed. He brought her in close, hugged her tightly, and said, "I love you, Sam."

"I love you too."

A moment passed as they both just held each other, and as in many times before their intimacy was cut short by the voice of one of their children.

They both laughed. Gordon looked at her and said, "Thank you."

Touching his face, Samantha finished their special moment by saying, "Now go put your boots on."

• • •

The funeral was tough on Gordon. Seeing his good friends go through the loss of their only child was excruciating. He could not imagine having to go through this with one of his own. He was given a brief moment to talk with Jimmy, who reassured him that he did not blame him. Jimmy really placed the blame on himself for not being more prepared. He had just assumed they had more inhalers. Simone could barely walk; Jimmy had to support her the entire time. She sobbed throughout the ceremony. Her sobs and wailing made many in attendance do the same.

They buried Mason in their backyard; the scene resembled something from the eighteenth century. An uneven hole was dug in the earth. Two shovels were sticking out of the pile of dirt that sat next to the hole and Mason was wrapped in his special Star Wars blankets that he loved so much. All who attended brought flowers with them and as they passed the open grave they tossed them in. After the last person came by, Jimmy approached the grave and grabbed one of the shovels. He gripped the handle tightly as he drove the shovel into the fresh dirt. After dumping the first shovel of dirt onto Mason he stopped. Overcome with grief, he fell to his knees and began to sob. Gordon could no longer just stand by idle. He stepped forward, grabbed the other shovel, and began to fill the grave. Gordon couldn't imagine the pain his friend was feeling; he fought back his own grief so he could finish.

When the ceremony ended, many just left. A few went up to

Jimmy and Simone and offered their condolences. There would be no food platters or drink to be offered. Simone sat in the weathered outdoor chair, staring blankly at Mason's now covered grave. Gordon was going to walk over and say something, but he felt it was time to leave; he took Samantha's hand and graciously walked out of the house. They had left the kids at home with Nelson because they felt the kids were too young to see their friend buried. They walked back to their house, holding hands. Silence was between them, no words could convey how they felt. Gordon looked at his watch; he would soon be pulled before the board and grilled about the events that night. He was ready for them; he was ready for the inquisition and spectacle that Mindy had in store for him.

The troubles of the day temporarily lifted when he and Samantha were greeted with joy by their two children. They both ran out of the house and into the arms of Gordon and Samantha. They both embraced their kids and held them close. Gordon held his little daughter and kissed her. She knew something was wrong and said to him, "I missed you, Daddy. I love you!" Those words filled Gordon with intense emotion. Hunter had heard Haley and he repeated the same thing to Samantha. Gordon looked over and Samantha looked at him. They both smiled. The love they felt for each other was present in that moment and more powerful than at any other time.

It was time for Gordon to go. Samantha grabbed his hands and looked at him. "Gordon, I love you. I've got it all covered here. Go and take care of this for us."

He smiled at her and said, "I will, honey. I'll be okay."

• • •

Gordon arrived at the community clubhouse a few minutes before the scheduled emergency board meeting. The room he was to be questioned in was also used to inventory the items his teams brought back daily. Boxes of food, water, supplies, and accessories lined the walls. In the center of the room were two long tables; they had been cleared and chairs set up. A single chair faced both tables. Gordon assumed that was for him. He smiled to himself then spoke out loud, "What a joke."

"What's a joke?" said someone behind him.

He turned and saw it was Eric.

"Hey," Gordon said, stretching out his hand.

Eric took his hand and said, "Hi, Gordon."

"What are you doing here?" Gordon asked curiously.

"I heard about this hearing and wanted to come support you."

Looking very surprised, Gordon said, "Thank you. I appreciate that."

Gordon hadn't been able to discuss Eric's new position on the security force that night because of the situation with Mason. Fortunately, Jerrod had met up with him the next day and took him out on a quick trip to the hospital where Mason had died. While Gordon had not been successful in getting the inhaler to Mason in time, the night proved successful for the community.

Gordon and Eric carried on a very casual conversation before Mindy, Dan, and the board arrived. They quickly took their seats at the tables. Not taking a seat, Dan stood off to the side of the room. Mindy carried a binder along with a mallet.

Sitting in the center seat, Mindy looked left and right to wait for her colleagues to sit before she gave her attention to Gordon.

Gordon just stood near the seat facing them and stared back at her. Seeing them all made him feel like being defiant.

Mindy grabbed her mallet, tapped the table, and said, "I hereby open this emergency meeting of the Rancho Valentino Board.

Would all present please take a seat." She looked directly at Gordon, who did not move. He just stared at her.

She tapped her mallet again and said, "Mr. Van Zandt, can you please take a seat now so we may begin?" She looked past Gordon and saw Eric. "I'm sorry, but this is a closed meeting."

Gordon turned around and gestured for Eric to leave.

"Are you sure?" Eric asked.

"I'll be fine." He then turned, looked at the board, and said, "I'm not worried about any of this."

Eric listened to Gordon and left. Not wanting to waste any more time, Gordon walked over his chair and sat down.

"Thank you, Mr. Van Zandt," Mindy said, taking off her reading glasses and placing them on the binder in front of her. She folded her hands, leaned forward, and asked, "Mr. Van Zandt, do you know why you're here?"

Gordon chuckled out loud, sitting straight in his chair. "Yes, you want to grill me about the other night. Then you want to embarrass me and ridicule my actions."

"Mr. Van Zandt—"

"Call me Gordon, I would prefer that."

"Gordon, no one is here to embarrass or ridicule anyone. We are here to investigate the incident that occurred the other night that resulted in the death of an innocent and unarmed man as well as the tragic loss of Mason Torrance. We have been briefed thoroughly by Mr. Bradford on the incident in question," Mindy finished. She picked her glasses back up. Opening her binder, she started to read the report that Dan had given the board. When she was finished she closed the binder and took off her glasses again.

"Gordon, we have all discussed the report we received from Mr. Bradford and we are concerned."

"Concerned about what?" Gordon snapped with a tinge of anger in his voice.

"We are concerned that you may not have the capacity to lead the security force. You have shown several times to have a short fuse and you react without due diligence."

"Short fuse? In relation to what?"

"As you know, Mr. Bradford is a trained police officer and he would have handled the situation differently. He feels it was unnecessary to shoot the man."

"Well of course he thought that, he's a cop," Gordon said with sarcasm in his tone. He looked over at Dan, who was standing to the side of the room with his arms crossed.

"Why do you say that?" Mindy asked.

"This whole episode is bullshit!"

"Excuse me."

"Listen, this is all bullshit. For one, Dan is a fat cop. Highly trained my ass; like most cops they feel they are only doing their job when they are harassing good people or attempting to find a way to ticket them. They are nothing but glorified tax collectors. Dan probably never pulled his gun out in his career and if he did it was when an eighty-year-old got pissed about the speeding ticket she was being given." Gordon was very upset, it could be heard in his voice.

The expression on Dan's face changed from smugness to anger after Gordon's diatribe.

Mindy tapped her mallet and said, "Mr. Van Zandt, stop your attacks on Mr. Bradford."

"Okay, I will. But I'm not done. I have a few choice words for you. You're nothing but a power-hungry, naïve bitch; you are wasting my time and wasting this community's opportunity to have as many of us as possible out in the field. I don't understand you. You need to go outside these gates to see what is going on. You're protected behind these gates and are still living in a pre-attack mindset. You need to open your eyes and realize that we must all work together to do this. You're still holding a grudge from the incident a few years back. Get over it and let me get back to work."

Not liking what Gordon had said, she fired back, "Mr. Van Zandt, your immature responses only prove that you lack the temperament to lead our community's security forces. We had thought maybe we could have you see the errors in your ways, but obviously you are a stubborn man. We have all voted and it is unanimous that you will be removed from the head of the security force and be held under house arrest for the murder of the unarmed man at the hospital."

"Are you crazy?" Gordon yelled.

"We know your history, Mr. Van Zandt. We know that your killed an unarmed Iraqi back during the war and it appears this is a common trait of yours—"

"Fuck you!" Gordon yelled. He stood up and pointed a finger at Mindy.

Dan took a step toward Gordon. Gordon turned to him, pointed his finger, and said, "You come toward me, I will ruin you!" He then turned his attention back toward Mindy. "You are making a huge mistake and I will not abide by this kangaroo court."

Mindy grabbed her mallet one more time, but this time she slammed it down. "Order, order; Mr. Van Zandt, sit down!"

Dan and Gordon were now cross talking over Mindy. Mindy kept slamming her mallet down but both men were not listening; they were yelling at each other.

Unexpectedly, the door to the room opened up and light washed across the room. Everyone turned to see Jimmy. The sight of him brought silence to the room. Jimmy walked in and stood next to Gordon.

Putting his arm around Gordon he said, "This man is my friend and he did what he needed to do the other night for me and Mason. We heard what was happening here so we all came to protest and stop this injustice."

"Mr. Torrance, I am sorry for your loss. Don't you think you should be home with your wife now?" Mindy asked.

Just then Simone walked in along with Samantha, Melissa, Eric, and another two dozen neighbors. Before long, Gordon was flanked on either side by dozens of supportive neighbors.

"Gordon is my friend and a trusted part of this community. Without his leadership we may not be in the shape we are today. I have been outside these gates, Mindy. The world has changed. We are not dealing with the world you think still exists. What Gordon did the other night, and his actions before, he did to protect us," Eric said eloquently. He stood on the other side of Gordon.

"I appreciate you all coming, but this is a closed-door meeting and you do not have all the information," Mindy said in a weak attempt to respond.

"This is our community, not just yours! You do not decide for all of us anymore! There are more of us just outside; we have gathered many in the community and they support Gordon. So maybe the people that should be getting fired from their jobs are YOU!" Simone exclaimed, her eyes still swollen from tears.

Mindy sat, shocked, as did the rest of the four members of the board. Looking confused and in disbelief they all looked to one another for an appropriate reaction.

From outside the room, someone yelled, "Gordon! Gordon!" Suddenly a chorus of people began chanting his name.

Gordon turned around to look at everyone; he was unaware that his neighbors felt this way about him.

Mindy looked defeated, and instead of attempting to quell the group she stood up, grabbed her binder, and stormed out of the room via a back door. The rest of the board, including Dan, followed her out. Gordon glared at Dan as he left. He knew that he'd have to deal with him again and soon. This fight wasn't over yet.

DECEMBER 16, 2014

• • •

Anyone can hold the helm when the sea is calm.

—Publilius Syrus

Cheyenne Mountain, Colorado

Griswald exited his room and closed the door, then looked up and down the stark and dimly lit hallway. He had become more cautious about his movements and surroundings since he had been meeting secretly with those he thought supported his opposition to President Conner's plans. With another meeting concluded, he was pleased to see his group grow daily. He felt soon he would have strong enough support to openly challenge Conner. With each new meeting he left feeling more confident. One topic that came up a lot in his meetings was what to do with Conner. Griswald's initial intentions were not to depose Conner but to convince him he did not have support and will of his staff. However, that position was shifting toward usurping Conner.

Griswald had been working nonstop since the attacks and had barely slept. The reports coming from the outside were frightening; the death toll across the country was growing each hour. Local small gangs and groups were taking advantage of the situation and there wasn't much anyone in government could do. They had been able to reach out to thirty-four different governors. They had pledged the support of the U.S. government, but all knew it was mainly talk. Each governor they spoke with asked the same questions. They wanted to know when that support would come and how much. All Griswald or anyone on his staff would say is "soon."

Even while the general was working behind the scenes against Conner, he did his appointed job. He didn't mean the new president ill will. He actually liked Conner personally but now felt he was not fit to lead.

Griswald entered the command post briefing room. Everyone looked up at him; he had never been late to a scheduled briefing. He offered his apologies to the president and all present and took his seat. The vice president continued his update on the calls he had just had with governors and how the situation looked in those state capitals. The reports from each governor sounded the same. They had set up various safe zones for civilians to go to, and the state capitol was in operation but obviously limited due to no power. Each governor had reported that their surplus supplies were running short and soon they would be out. They had reported that violence against civilians had increased dramatically. The only advice they could give their people was to stay indoors. The one word they all told the VP was that the situation was becoming "hopeless." Cruz tried to reassure all of them, but he did not make any promises. He told each one of them that the president and new government were working hard with the help of the U.S. military and foreign governments to get aid and supplies to them fast.

"Andrew, thank you. I want to put this out to all here. Please feel free to comment openly," Conner stated following Cruz's briefing. "Who do we resupply first? We have ships just off of our shores now with food, fuel, medicines and equipment. Where should those go first?"

The eight people present around the table just looked around at one another. No one wanted to answer, because the answer meant that someone else would suffer or go without.

Finally Griswald broke the silence. "Mr. President, let's first ask one question: Where will the new U.S. capital be? From there we can look at where we should send supplies."

Conner nodded in acknowledgment of the question. He was thinking about the question. "That is a good question, General. I have given only a little thought concerning the new capital. That would make more sense to build up the governmental infrastructure so that we have a solid base to work from. Where do you propose, General?"

"I believe we should find a coastal city, one that has a large port. This will make it easy to get that city back online and rebuilt. From there we can look at expanding out from there."

"What about here?" someone asked.

"Why not here?" Conner asked too.

Griswald replied. "It is far easier to get the resupplies and new transformers via ship than plane. A city that has a port that can handle large container ships is where we should go."

"That makes a lot of sense, General," Conner said, making some notes.

"We have another problem that I didn't think of till late last night," Griswald said. He leaned forward and said, "I cannot believe none of us had thought about this."

"What is it?" Conner asked, looking concerned.

"When we select our new capital we should ensure it's nowhere near a nuclear power plant."

Gasps came from in the room. No one needed him to explain further, they knew exactly what Griswald was talking about.

Conner leaned forward and rested his head in his hands. He too knew what Griswald was talking about. "How could we not think about this before? As if we needed another problem."

"How many sites do we have across the U.S.?" Houston asked. He was sitting next to the president.

"I don't know. Does anyone?" Griswald answered.

Everyone in the room shook their heads no. Griswald turned to his aide and ordered, "Go find out, we must have that information here somewhere." Griswald's aide didn't hesitate. He departed the room with urgency.

"It appears we are premature in discussing the location of the new capital. Please alert the governors and our forces about this new threat. We will need to see what we can do to attempt to evacuate people away from those reactors," Conner said. He was clearly upset by the new revelation.

"Sir, forgive me for even mentioning this, but what can we really do? What aid can we deliver and how exactly can we evacuate people?" Houston asked.

"General, we have to try something; we cannot sit around and do nothing. Let's inform the governors and we'll go from there," Conner said.

"I can't believe we all overlooked this," Griswald stated.

"Mr. President, I don't think it's premature to have the question about how we will distribute resources. Let's be realistic here. This country is huge and with the limited resources we have we can't get to everyone; we'll need to focus on a small area and work from there. We have to put all of our focus, energy, and resources into one city and work from there. In essence what I am saying is we need to abandon parts of this country and hope we will be able to get them back up later," Houston said.

Conner just sat and reflected on Houston's comments. He knew that in some way the general was right. The task before them was overwhelming, and if they took what they had and spread it across the country they would never chip away at the problem. They would have to commit to one city and work from there. But what city?

"General, I hear you; let's discuss this topic when we have the info we need."

All in the room agreed and Conner moved on the meeting.

"General Griswald, since we never heard back from Barone we have to assume he is carrying on with his treasonous path. What have we done about that?" Conner asked.

"We have alerted our forces in Hawaii to intercept them; we have also contacted the commander of the USS *Topeka*, an attack submarine that is operating in the Western Pacific."

"Just one sub?" Conner asked, surprised.

"I was in error when I said we had three at our disposal. That is what we have to spare right now."

"Okay, fine. Sorry, not meaning to question you. I just want the colonel stopped and want to make sure it happens," Conner said to Griswald apologetically. He then continued on with his thoughts. "I have to admit that after each meeting, I get more upset and I feel useless," Conner said, standing up. He started to walk around the room. "There isn't much we can do but talk. We don't have enough food to go around; we don't have the equipment or parts to get our grids back up. We now are faced with nuclear meltdowns on an apocalyptic scale. We have lost our entire infrastructure and there isn't much we can do but sit here, talk, and wait. I cannot stand this feeling. We haven't responded to our enemies, we just talk. We sit a mile in a mountain, we are safe and have enough food to last us years, while our countrymen right this minute are struggling to survive. Many will die, they will starve, they will be raped and murdered." All in the room just watched him pace. The more he talked the more he was getting upset. "How many will die before we stop talking and start doing something? The ultimate question I have for all of you is, will our country survive this?"

USS *Makin Island* off the southern coast of the Philippine Islands

"We made it through the Malacca Strait and past Singapore with no trouble. Now we're about to enter the Western Pacific. I don't know what to expect from here on," Barone said after taking a drink of his coffee.

He and his son, Billy, had been getting together almost daily. Barone enjoyed his son's company and felt blessed that they were able to be together during this time.

"I'm sure we'll be fine. I can't imagine the president would attempt to attack us," Billy said, taking a bite of toast.

"I wouldn't be so sure, son. He's been a tough talker all of his life while in Washington. Who knows, maybe he's a chicken hawk."

Billy chuckled. "Hopefully he is."

"If all goes well we should be spending New Year's with your mom and sister."

"I'd like that. I hope they're okay."

"Oh, I'm sure they are fine. It will take a lot to take out that old gal. Your mom is a tough cookie and she has Megan locked down I'm sure." Barone openly talked with confidence about his wife and daughter's safety, but inside he was deeply concerned.

Barone looked at his son as he ate. Billy reminded him of his wife, Mary. He looked like her a lot and had her fire and strong will. As he looked at Billy, he now wished to himself that he had been home more with him when he was growing up. He now longed for the days when Billy was young. He never really had too many intimate and deeply private conversations with Billy or Megan. He wondered if they resented that he spent so much time away. He wondered if Billy resented that he never went to his baseball games or missed those moments to comfort him when he had a nightmare growing up. Barone had given most of his adult life to the Marine Corps and his country. Now all that time invested was given for what? Why did he make a decision that could prove fatal if he were wrong? He finally admitted to himself that his country was gone and that the Marine Corps he knew died along with it.

"Son, what is the talk among the Marines you're with?"

"Dad, everyone is with you, they are just anxious. We all want to get home as fast as possible," Billy said, looking up from his plate.

Billy's words brought comfort to him. He knew his son was smart and in tune with what was happening on the ship.

Their conversation ended when the General Quarters alarm sounded. Both men looked at each other and didn't say a word. Barone jumped up and ran out of the mess hall. The corridors were alive with activity as men rushed back and forth on their way to their assigned duty stations.

He climbed the last ladder well and entered the bridge. Inside he encountered a hub of activity. The radio operator was contacting the other ships in the flotilla.

"Why has General Quarters been sounded?" Barone asked.

"Colonel, we have a submarine on sonar," a junior naval officer answered.

"Where is it?" Barone asked.

"The sub is approximately . . ."

"I see it, sir!" yelled a Marine on the bridge looking through binoculars.

"Where?" Barone asked. He hurried over to the Marine holding the binoculars.

"Approximately three thousand meters out on our starboard side, sir!" the Marine said, pointing to where he saw the submarine floating on the surface.

Barone grabbed the binoculars, focused them, and saw the submarine.

"Use all channels and hail the sub!" Barone commanded.

Moments passed as the communications petty officer attempted to contact the submarine. The ships kept getting closer and closer. Barone had ordered that all ships not engage the sub but to stay vigilant in case the sub took aggressive action. As the ARG moved closer they saw the top hatch of the sub open and a couple of men come out and stand on the sail. Barone stayed glued and curious as to what was happening. He was not sure himself what flag the submarine flew or why it was on the surface of the water.

"Anything yet?" he asked the communications petty officer.

"Nothing, sir."

The two men on the sail started to wave.

"How close can we pull the *Makin Island* up to the submarine?"

"Sir, we can get close, but I would recommend not doing so," the first officer on the bridge said.

"Tell the rest of the ARG to move away from our position and to slow down. I want to pull alongside the submarine and see what's going on."

"Yes, sir," the first officer said.

The USS *Makin Island* pulled alongside the port side of the floating submarine. By the time they had gotten within a couple hundred meters, the submarine struck colors. Fear and apprehension filled the men on the bridge of the *Makin Island* when they saw it was a U.S. flag.

Barone was alone in not being fearful. If the sub had meant them harm it would not have surfaced. He stood along the railing with a bullhorn in hand, ready to communicate with the men on the sub's sail.

"I am Lieutenant Colonel Barone of the USS *Makin Island* and Commanding Officer of the Second Battalion Fourth Marine Regiment. Are you in need of any assistance?" Barone said, his voice amplified from the bullhorn.

One of the men on the ship looked at the other and said something that no one could hear. He left and went back inside the submarine. The other man raised his hand to gesture for more time.

"What's he trying to say?" the first officer asked out loud. He was standing next to Barone.

"I think they want us to hold on for a minute," Barone responded.

A moment passed and the man who had left reappeared and handed the other a bullhorn.

The first man took the bullhorn and said, "Colonel Barone, what was the name of that blonde from Fremantle back in 1999?"

"What?" the first officer asked out loud. He put down his binoculars and looked at Barone.

Barone was stunned by the question; he kept looking through the binoculars to see if he knew who just asked him the question.

"Who are you?" Barone asked.

"Maybe this will help," the man said. "A half pint for a half pint?"

Barone's eyes lit up. He knew who it was.

"Captain White! What the hell are you doing bobbing in the water?" Barone asked.

"We're waiting for you."

Barone was shocked to hear that. He looked around and saw other puzzled looks on the faces around him.

"Get your ass over here," Barone said.

Captain White gave a thumbs-up.

"Sir, who is that?" the first officer asked.

"Why, Lieutenant, that is Captain David White of the USS *Topeka* and an old dear friend of mine. We go way back. Now get the captain over here without delay," Barone told the first officer.

• • •

Barone poured White another drink and sat down. He looked at his old friend, whom he had not seen in five years. The years had not been good to David. His black hair had been replaced with thick white, his eyes sagged, and his skin was blotchy. There was sadness in his eyes that was not present before. Barone did not know where the years had gone since they had last spent time together. How easy it had become to move on from friends and colleagues. How could you spend each day with someone, then one day say good-bye and not see them for five years?

"I appreciate all the bourbon," White said before taking another sip.

"You're welcome, old friend."

"Let's talk about the eight-hundred-pound gorilla in the room."

"Eight hundred pounds? More like an eight-hundred-million-pound gorilla to me," Barone joked.

White took another drink and put his glass down. "A few days ago we received word from the secretary of defense that we were to patrol the waters out here looking for a rogue colonel and his band of mutinous Marines." White chuckled and continued. "Our orders were to track you down and destroy the ships, take no prisoners, do not negotiate, just sink your ships."

"I guess the president wasn't joking when he said he wanted to stop me."

"I've known you for a long time; we had the pleasure of working together years back on that Wes-Pac. You're a gung ho Marine. I know your wife, I know your children. You're a good man." White paused for a moment to collect his thoughts, then continued. "When they told me it was you, I knew you wouldn't just do something like this without a damn good reason. I couldn't just destroy these ships and kill you and those Marines and sailors without hearing from you what's going on."

"First, let me thank you for not sinking my ships. Second, what I'm doing is taking my Marines and these sailors back home to their families. Our initial orders were to go back and assist the others in the recovery effort back east. With the intelligence we've received, it seems as if the entire power grid is down across the country. This leaves our families vulnerable. I could not in good conscience take the men to the opposite coast from their families to help dig up dead bodies. What has happened at home is catastrophic and we may not fully recover for years. If we don't get back to California soon and help our families there, there may not be a home or family to go back to."

White just nodded and looked at Barone.

"I thought about this carefully, and our country is gone. It was destroyed within seconds. You know these scenarios; you take away food, water, medicine, law and order, and every city will destroy itself within weeks. We may not be able to help everyone when we get home, but we'll protect our families and there we can start to rebuild with what we have. David, there is a ninety-nine percent chance that our country will not look the same in a year; hell, could be less time. The way I look at it, I'm not committing treason or mutiny when there is no country to mutiny against," Barone finished, then took a drink.

"Well, I've had a few days to ponder what the hell you were doing and I knew you wouldn't just do something foolish. I knew you had a plan and a damn good reason." White reached over and grabbed the bottle and poured himself another drink. He took a sip and exhaled loudly. "As you know, the *Topeka*'s home port is San Diego, and we have family back there too. Colonel Barone, may we join your pack of wily mutineers?" White lifted his glass in the air to toast.

Barone was shocked and overjoyed. He lifted his glass and tapped White's glass and said, "Captain White, you and your men are welcome to join us."

"Thank you, Tony. Now let me tell you how lucky you are we found you first."

That comment sparked Barone's interest. He leaned forward and asked, "What do you know?"

"I know that they have a few destroyers looking for you. They also have Hawaii on alert and plan on using land-based aircraft and even missiles to stop you."

"I guess I'm not getting close to Hawaii, then. Is there a way you can keep tabs on where the destroyers are by communicating with them till we are in a safe area?"

"Exactly my plan," White responded with a grin.

"Cheers again, my friend," Barone said, lifting his glass.

San Diego, California

Gordon and his team had just returned from outside the gates. Each day brought lighter loads and more news of the destruction and collapse of the city. Every new day they pushed farther and farther into areas they had not gone before only to find few supplies but more death. They constantly encountered hungry bands of people begging for food. Gordon was sympathetic, but he would not budge and commanded his men not to assist anyone unless they could offer value to their community. Resources were tight and adding more people would only take away from their own. It was tough as he looked upon the gaunt faces of those hungry and dehydrated women and children, but he would remind himself of his own children and the responsibility he had to them. His teams also were encountering more executions and more graffiti that said "Villista." He knew now there was a group operating that was organized and lethal. A new startling development had started a couple of days ago; smoke plumes on the skyline were becoming a common sight to the south. No one knew the reason, but someone was setting buildings on fire.

The dwindling food supplies started to create stress on the community. There were some in the community who never had much food in their pantries to start, and with the rations being limited and not adequate those people were going to bed hungry. His security force had already broken up three altercations between neighbors over food rations. Gordon knew it was going to get worse unless they could find more large caches of food. The gardens were planted but would not produce food for some time. He had created hunting teams to help supplement but after a few days of hunting they had only brought back a couple of coyotes, which most of his neighbors refused to eat.

Gordon started to see the physical decay in the community now. The grasses had just now started to brown and many of the previously well-maintained flowers were starting to look wilted. Dust and dirt were slowly starting to gather on the abandoned cars. The smell of feces was becoming more prominent as people were not disposing their human waste properly in the backyards. The one fortunate statistic after twelve days after the attack was that only one person had died.

Seventeen families had left the security of the gates to try their luck outside. Gordon never attempted to convince anyone if they decided to leave; he felt it was their choice. He did warn them of the dangers on the outside, but he never would work hard to get them to stay. The thoughts of leaving had also come across Gordon's mind more frequently now. He did not know how long they could maintain what they had. If the size of the loads that were coming back continued to get smaller, they would run out of food. However, before that happened the community would probably turn on itself.

Ever since he had been subjected to Mindy's "court," Gordon had started to work on an alternative plan. He kept thinking of their place in Idaho. Their mountain cabin was located in the town of McCall. The town was surrounded by tens of thousands of acres of public land. It was pristine alpine country and the wildlife was abundant. He had discussed this idea with Samantha, who was supportive of whatever he thought was best. Because of his quick response immediately after the attacks, he had secured enough food to last his family months. Fuel was not an issue; he now had a vehicle himself and sufficient medical supplies. Making the journey to Idaho would be tough, but if he could get a convoy to go with him they just might make it. Gordon had yet to discuss his plans with Nelson or Jimmy.

Gordon had not seen Jimmy for days and was concerned for him. He thought of them often and hoped that he and Simone were doing okay. Gordon also thought often about his brother; he was curious how far the attacks had gone. Every time someone knocked on his door, every time he was called to one of the gates because a stranger had approached requesting aid, he'd look up and expect to see Sebastian. The thought that he'd never see him again also crossed his mind. He'd never see a lot of people again. So many people were a part of his life before. The girl who was a clerk at the grocery store or his daughter's dance teacher, where were they now? His clients whom he'd chat with regularly over the phone, how were they making out? Samantha's many friends were scattered throughout the county, their situations were unknown and would most likely remain that way. She had remained relatively calm about her parents; he assumed she knew there wasn't much they could do for them. The Midwest might as well be halfway around the world. So much had changed in a blink of an eye, it sometimes was overwhelming.

The past few days, Gordon had been teaming up with Max. It didn't take long for Max's smugness and arrogance to wear on him. His nonstop talking, specifically talking about himself and all the women he used to get. He would complain that the attacks "fucked up his play." Gordon missed Jimmy and couldn't wait for his return to the teams.

After that day's run, Max had dropped Gordon off at his driveway. Gordon was excited to be done with him and to see his family. He missed them terribly each day he was gone. Just before he made it to his front door, a voice he was familiar with and equally detested came from a few feet away.

"Gordon?"

Gordon stopped. He looked down, shook his head, and turned around.

"What?" Gordon asked, clearly not happy.

"I am quite aware that I'm probably the last person you want to talk to right now, but I want to say a few things," Dan said, slowly walking up to Gordon.

"You're right, Dan; you are the last person I want to see."

"Do you have a minute or two?" Dan asked sheepishly.

"Not really, but go ahead," Gordon said, looking down at his watch.

"What happened a few days ago—" Dan paused. "You see, I'm not like you; I saw what happened at the hospital and was freaked out by it. I am now aware that this is a new world we're living in and it requires new tactics and a new moral code."

Gordon just looked at Dan and nodded in agreement. He then made a comment about Dan's face.

"What happened to you?"

Touching his face, Dan replied, "An altercation on the outside. We ran into a small gang." Dan had a black eye and bruises on his lips and cheek.

"How come I'm just now hearing about it?"

"It wasn't anything, typical bullshit. Tim and I took care of them."

"Is Tim okay?"

Pausing before he answered, Dan finally said, "Yeah, he's fine."

"Okay, go ahead, how can I help you?"

"I wanted to apologize and see if we could start new. We need to work together," Dan said, then put out his hand.

Gordon just stared at Dan and then his outstretched hand. He paused for a brief moment then reluctantly took Dan's hand and shook it.

“Is that it?” Gordon asked.

“No, it’s not. I wanted to discuss something that we encountered in the field today.”

“Go ahead,” Gordon said impatiently.

“We were operating south near Mira Mesa Boulevard when we came across what I believe is that group calling themselves the Villistas.”

As soon as Gordon heard the name, his curiosity perked up.

“I happened to see four vehicles pull into a Lowes. I thought it strange when I noticed all the barbed wire fence around the store. We set up in a blind and conducted surveillance on them for about an hour.”

Gordon was really listening now.

“They had vehicle after vehicle going in and out of the place. A couple of times we heard screams and gunshots coming from the store. I think they are caching a large amount of supplies there.”

“How many men did you see?” Gordon asked.

“We counted a total of twenty-four different vehicles go in and out in the hour we watched. Each vehicle had two people in it and the site had what looked like seven guards along the perimeter.”

Gordon was thinking, but his thoughts soon gave way to reality. He realized he did not have the means to conduct a successful attack on them and take their precious food supplies.

“Gordon, if we could plan a raid I think we might be able to replenish our supplies and give us a boost in the arm,” Dan finished. He was very excited about what he’d seen and thought it valuable.

“Dan, this is all very interesting. Let me sleep on it and we can reconvene in the morning.”

Dan looked almost sad. He had wanted Gordon to be very excited and wanted him to recognize him personally for this information.

"Okay, let's finish the conversation in the morning," Dan said, then turned around and left.

Gordon watched him go. He didn't know what to think of Dan's apology, but the intelligence on the Villistas was a good break for them. Gordon was tired and would think more about it later. The one reprieve from the insanity was his nightly arrival back home. The door wouldn't close shut before he would be greeted by the happy squeals of Hunter and Haley. Their innocence and tenderness was a sanctuary from the horrors outside the gate.

DECEMBER 18, 2014

• • •

A good decision is based on knowledge, not on numbers.

—Plato

San Diego, California

The banging on the front door startled Gordon awake. Whoever was on the other end was in need of his attention urgently. He ran downstairs as fast as his feet would take him. He unlocked and flung the door open to find Max standing in front of him sweating and breathing hard.

"What's going on?" Gordon asked, concerned.

"We had a few people attempt to break into the clubhouse and steal food," Max said.

"Did you catch them?" Gordon asked. He was now putting his boots on in the foyer.

Still unable to catch his breath, Max answered, "Yeah, we got them."

Gordon stood up, grabbed his jacket and shoulder holster, and stepped outside.

"You all right?" Gordon asked, looking at Max, who was leaning against the front of the house.

"Yeah, I'll be all right."

Gordon looked at Max and thought to himself that he still looked chubby. Even with all the food rationing, Max looked like he wasn't losing weight. Gordon didn't give anymore thought to it.

"You ready? Let's go," Gordon said.

"Gordon, that's not it."

"What do you mean?"

• • •

When Gordon reached the end of the street he saw the flames. The clubhouse was aglow with twenty-foot flames. A dozen people had gathered and were running buckets of water to put out the intensely hot flames shooting out of the clubhouse.

Eric ran up to Gordon and asked, "What the hell?"

Gordon just stared at the clubhouse.

"What happened?" Eric asked again.

"Some assholes broke into the clubhouse to steal food. When they were confronted there was a fight and somehow a lantern was turned over. The place went up in no time."

"Oh my God," Eric gasped.

The flames illuminated the sky with an orange glow. More people began to show up; many just stood and watched in horror at what food rations they had go up in flames.

Gordon could see one of his sentries talking to a few people who were sitting on the ground. He knew those must the people who attempted to break in.

He began to march over to the suspects with a defined purpose in his step. When he reached the first one, a middle-aged man, Gordon reached down, grabbed him by the throat, and yanked him off the ground. He pushed him against a tree and began to choke him.

"What the fuck were you thinking? Who do you think you are?" Gordon yelled at the man. The man could not defend himself because his hands were tied behind his back.

The man just gargled as he attempted to speak. Gordon pressed the man's body against the tree with even greater force. Gordon was in a rage. He reached down to grab his pistol but was stopped when Eric came up behind him.

"Gordon, that's enough!"

Eric's voice brought Gordon back from his rage. He let go of the man, who then fell to the ground coughing and hacking.

"Who was on post here tonight?"

"Him right there," Max said, pointing to a man in his twenties who was standing a few feet away.

"Gordon, I'm sorry but—"

"What happened, where were you?" Gordon snapped at him.

"I haven't been feeling well, like diarrhea, and I wanted to go home to use the bathroom. I thought this would be safe for ten minutes or so," the man said. He was nervous and ashamed.

"Whatever," Gordon said looking away, disgusted. He then gave his attention to the four others who had been detained. He didn't recognize a single person. After years of living in the community and even after having closer contact with his neighbors since the attacks, Gordon still did not know all his neighbors.

"So, what's going on?" he asked them.

A man in his mid-fifties with white hair answered, "We're hungry, we have run out of food, and what we're getting daily from the rations isn't enough."

"There's not enough food at all," the woman next to him said.

"We're starving, Gordon, we need more food," another woman quipped.

"I understand that the food rations are smaller than before, but you just can't break—"

"I have two children and they are hungry. What do I say to them?" the fourth person, a man, quickly asked, interrupting Gordon.

"Listen, I understand; but this is everyone's food, not just yours," Gordon responded pointedly.

"When are we going to get more food?" the first man asked.

"We need more food!" the woman next to the man said with emotion in her voice. She started to cry.

Gordon knew it was futile for him to even have this back and forth. He didn't know what to do with them, but he knew now he couldn't trust them.

"Look at what you have done!" Gordon exclaimed, pointing to the remnants of the clubhouse. Gordon knew it was a waste of time to even attempt to put it out; it was a total loss.

"We're sorry, we didn't mean for this to happen," the elderly man said.

"Intentions are nothing. You've now left us with nothing except what we have in our own homes!" Gordon screamed at the man. He was so disgusted he couldn't look at them any longer. He turned around and approached Eric.

"What are we going to do with them?" Eric asked.

"They don't belong here anymore. They leave tonight."

Eric nodded.

Overhearing what Gordon had told Eric, the man with two children screamed, "You can't do that!"

Gordon turned around and answered the man by saying, "Decisions have consequences." Gordon then turned back to Eric and said, "Make it happen."

All of the detainees began to cry out and beg not to be thrown out of the community.

Gordon ignored their pleas and walked off.

Cheyenne Mountain, Colorado

"General, what you're proposing is treason," Houston said with a concerned tone.

"I like the president, but I don't believe killing millions of people without the full knowledge of who attacked us is the correct plan of action. He constantly has emotional outbursts and doesn't seem to be in command of all his faculties. I don't believe he has the moral authority to lead," Griswald answered with passion.

"I just don't know," Houston said. He rested his arms on his legs and put his head in his hands.

"The information we're getting from the Aussies isn't conclusive. They've been told by one of the terrorists that they were trained in Iran, but they don't know where the missiles or the nuclear warheads came from."

"Why won't you tell the president that intel? You seem worried that he'll nuke everyone but if you tell him we have evidence it was Iran like you say, then he'll just respond to them."

"You're right, he'll respond and he'll kill millions of innocent Iranians."

"But they just killed millions of our people and even more millions will die. I don't understand the fucking problem." Houston was upset with Griswald and frustrated by the conversation.

"That's just it, he'll nuke them. Will he just nuke Tehran or will he nuke all the cities? Where will he stop, how big of a nuke? Once we unleash this type of weapon, where will it lead?"

"Are you kidding me right now? That type of weapon has already been unleashed against us. What is your problem with doing something?" Houston shot back.

"There has to be a different way, one that doesn't up the ante and kill more people," Griswald said. He was also getting frustrated with the conversation. He was now regretting that he had opened up to Houston about this.

"Gris, I disagree with you one thousand percent. We have an obligation to protect this nation, or what's left of it. We have a job to do. If our president says jump, we answer, how high?"

"So you are not with me on this?"

"I'm afraid not. Who else follows your line of thinking?"

"I have six others who agree that we need to take more time and look at other options of retaliation, plus they have expressed desire to replace Conner."

"Well, you can count me out. I cannot go along with this. If we know that Iran was a party to this attack, then we need to strike them now and the fact you're talking about overthrowing President Conner is crazy." Houston stood up. "This conversation is over."

"Where are you going?" Griswald asked him as Houston stepped by him to go to the door.

"Gris, I need to inform the president of this situation. You are a good man but you are making a bad decision here," Houston said, standing next to the door.

Griswald stood up just then and walked up to Houston.

"I'm really sorry to hear that, but I understand. You are a loyal and trustworthy officer."

"Sorry, Gris," Houston said, then turned around. He reached for the door handle but was stopped by Griswald, who put him in a stranglehold.

Houston attempted to break free of the choke hold, but Griswald's tall stature and strength prevented it. Griswald took Houston to the floor and began to apply greater pressure to the hold. Houston was kicking and punching, but his resistance was futile. Griswald had a solid hold on him.

"I'm really sorry. I truly am," Griswald said softly to Houston as he applied more pressure.

Houston continued to kick and punch, but his attempts to pry Griswald's arms from around his neck would not work. The struggle seemed to last forever, but in reality Houston's body went limp within twenty seconds. Griswald did not relent even after Houston's body became lifeless. He wanted to ensure that he killed him, not just knocked him out. Griswald held him in this deadly embrace for another thirty seconds before dropping him to the cold, hard concrete floor. Griswald checked for a pulse but found nothing. He was now fully committed to his plan to stop the president, even if it meant killing for it.

USS *Makin Island*, Pacific Ocean

"Hey, Tomlinson, come here," Sebastian called out. He was just finishing his dinner when he saw Tomlinson walk into the mess hall.

Tomlinson nodded and proceeded over to his table.

"So what's up with this slop?" Tomlinson remarked, tossing his tray onto the table.

"You should feel fortunate that you have something to eat," Sebastian reminded him.

"Not another pep talk, okay?" Tomlinson quipped back.

"I'm just saying, there are people in our country starving now."

"Well, they can have this shit," he said as he pushed food around on his tray with his fork.

"I wanted to talk to you about something," Sebastian said, looking around at the other tables to see who was in the mess hall or who might be listening. With the ship having to feed twice as many Marines as usual, the mess hall was full and loud.

Looking down at his food in disgust Tomlinson answered, "What about?"

Sebastian leaned in close and whispered, "What do you think about all of this?"

"What do you mean?" he said, looking up at Sebastian.

"I mean this whole mutiny thing, now that it's been a week plus and the raid on DG, all of it. What do you think?"

"I'm cool with it, it makes sense. Let's get back to Cali and take care of everyone's family."

"I was cool with it too until Diego Garcia. I mean, what's next; we're going to attack Hawaii? I'm not feeling too comfortable about it all."

"I trust the colonel, so I've got his back. Why you asking, anyway?"

Sebastian looked around again before answering. "As soon as we hit California soil, I'm gone."

"Why?"

"I just don't like this anymore. If our country is gone, then I don't want part of all of this." Sebastian gestured with his arms, pointing to everything around him.

"You're fucking crazy, Corporal Van Zandt. I always knew you were," Tomlinson responded. He shook his head and went back to picking at his food.

"I'm serious, shithead, this isn't a joke. I'm asking you if you want to come with me."

"No way, man. If you want to take off and go UA, that's your choice. My family lives back east and I don't much like them anyways. The Corps is my family, so I won't be going with you. Hey, I'm not hungry so I'm going to take off," Tomlinson stood up, grabbed his tray, and left.

Sebastian watched as he walked away. He then caught Gunny looking at him from an adjacent table. Gunny was just staring at him. Sebastian looked at him briefly, nodded, and broke his gaze. He picked up his tray and started to head for the exit when Gunny called out.

"Corporal Van Zandt, you got a minute?"

"Ah, yeah," Sebastian answered nervously.

"Sit down, Corporal," Gunny said, motioning toward the seat across from him.

Sebastian took a seat. "Yes, Gunny?"

"You okay, Corporal?"

"Yeah, Gunny, I'm fine."

"You don't seem fine. It looked like you and your spotter were having a lover's quarrel over there." Gunny was talking with food in his mouth.

"Ah, no, Gunny, we are five by five, all good."

"This new mission should make you happy. Now you get to go home and check on your big brother," Gunny said, taking another forkful of food and stuffing it into his mouth.

"Yes, Gunny, going back to California is exactly what I wanted."

Gunny stopped chewing and looked at Sebastian. He stared into his eyes. Sebastian forced himself not to look away.

"You sure you're all right, Corporal?"

Sebastian paused. He wondered if he should open up to Gunny about his reservations about what took place on Diego Garcia and his uneasiness with the direction the new mission might be going.

"Gunny, I'm fine. Just tired."

Gunny Smith stared again for a few seconds, then said, "Okay, Corporal, that's all. Go hit the rack and get some shut-eye."

Sebastian said good-bye and got up. His instincts told him Gunny knew something was up. Sebastian walked quickly for the exit, praying that Gunny wouldn't call him back.

San Diego, California

Dan had gathered all the men from the scavenger teams in the central park. He was excited that Gordon had listened to him and was going to act on it.

As Gordon stood in front of them, he thought that every day he sent them out into harm's way. This new mission would be different. They needed to have a plan; they needed to train and be prepared for this. He could not risk sending them into this situation unready. He wasn't dealing with highly trained Marines; he was dealing with attorneys, accountants, shop owners, sales people, realtors. Many of them had never picked up a gun before the attacks, much less trained for close-quarters battle.

"Here is the situation. Dan located what appears to be some type of operating base of the Villistas. They have occupied the Lowes on Mira Mesa Boulevard and I-15. Now, we don't have much more information than that. We know they have cars going in and out. More than likely they have stores of food and other supplies there that we need desperately now. We need this to go well, gentlemen. With what happened last night we need this."

All eyes and ears were on Gordon. They all knew the gravity of the situation. They weren't just scavenging; this was to be an assault.

"I know this mission could result in us having armed conflict with these Villistas, and by what we've all found on the roads, these people are not nice. However, this is the world we now live in. If we don't do something soon to find a large cache of food, then our nice little community will soon turn on itself. I'm not ordering you all to go, I am asking. If we conduct this raid there is a chance that some of us will not come back. What I am asking now is for you to think about it. After today's runs I want us all to meet up again here, and you tell me if you're in or not. For those that are in, we will begin to train. I will personally go to their location and recon the area. I will not send you into something unless I feel we can accomplish it. Does anyone have any questions?"

Jerrod raised his hand and asked, "If this mission becomes a green light, when do you estimate we'll go in?"

"I plan on going out there today with three teams to start the recon. I would like to conduct this raid in three days. That should give us enough time to get a feel for the lay of the land and to train. Anyone else have any questions?"

"What happens if we don't volunteer for this mission?" a member of one of the teams asked.

"Nothing; I don't want you unless you're fully committed. I appreciate what you all do now and it's risky, but what I'm asking now is for you all to become soldiers."

"You can sign me up for anything. I'm in!" said a familiar voice from the back of the room.

Gordon looked back and saw his good friend Jimmy.

Gordon smiled and responded to Jimmy, "Good, because you and I are going out there today."

"Well, the truck is fueled up and ready," Jimmy said. He walked up to Gordon and gave him a big hug.

"Good to see you, buddy, really good to see you," Gordon replied.

"I'm ready to get back in the saddle, as they say."

"Does anyone else have any questions?" Gordon asked again.

He paused to see if anyone did, but their silence provided the answer he was looking for.

"Okay, good. I need a team to volunteer to go with us," he said to the group.

Jerrod raised his hand. "Count me and Eric in."

"Sounds good. Dan, you're coming too, get your team ready. Everyone else, go out there and do your runs today. We'll meet up afterward."

All the men got up and left the room.

Gordon turned to Jimmy and said, "Damn glad to see you."

"Same here, buddy; sorry I took so long," Jimmy said.

"No problem at all, you needed the time," Gordon replied.

"After last night, I thought you could use the help."

"You're right. I need you out there with me today."

"I missed what's happening," Jimmy queried.

"I'll fill you in on the way there."

Gordon briefed the teams on how the recon would go. He wanted Dan to lead them there. Once on site, he would split the teams up so they could go set up and gather information from all sides of the Villistas location.

With everyone knowing their responsibilities, the three teams headed out. All were nervous, but all were equally determined to provide for their people no matter the personal cost to them.

The drive took them south along Interstate 15, which had become a graveyard for cars and a migration route for starving San Diegans. As they approached the exit Gordon could see the smoke plumes coming from the vicinity of the Lowes. He wondered what they were burning.

Dan put his arm out the window and pointed to the exit for

Mercy Road. He wanted to approach the Villista hideout carefully. They drove down Mercy Road and took a left onto Black Mountain Road and headed south. As they drew closer he saw more and more Villistas graffiti spray painted on the sides of buildings, houses, and retaining walls. They definitely were in the Villista territory now.

With Dan's vehicle in the lead, Gordon and Jimmy were second, followed by Eric and Jerrod. They had slowed their speed considerably; to Gordon it felt like they were barely crawling up the hill.

"Why is he going so slow?" Gordon asked, curious as to why they were going unusually slowly.

"I don't know why, we're still a good mile from our destination," Jimmy said to Gordon's question.

They were slowly weaving around abandoned cars. The smoke plumes were getting closer and closer. Gordon noticed he hadn't seen anyone walking since they turned onto Black Mountain Road. The whole area made him feel uneasy. Gordon was beginning to have a sense of déjà vu from Fallujah. Up ahead he saw movement; some people were standing on a pedestrian. Gordon leaned forward as if getting a few inches closer to the windshield would help him see better.

"What are they—?" he asked, but was interrupted when Dan's car veered off the road and sped off.

"What the fuck?" Gordon yelled as he watched Dan's car accelerate down Longridge Road.

When he put his attention back to the people on the bridge he knew then they were Villistas and that they had been led into an ambush.

"Turn around now!" he yelled at Jimmy.

But before Jimmy could make the turn, a rocket-propelled grenade exploded in front of them on the street. The explosion threw asphalt and debris onto the truck. Gordon couldn't see anything. The shock of the explosion made Jimmy hit the accelerator. Blinded by the blast and smoke, Jimmy jerked the truck hard to the left and hit the median curb.

"Go, go, go!" Gordon yelled.

Gunfire began to rain down on them. Gordon could hear the bings and bangs of the truck being hit. Jimmy hit the accelerator again and jumped the curb. Crossing over to the northbound lane was difficult, but they cleared the median. As he made the turn to head north, another rocket hit the bed of the truck. The force of the blast threw Gordon and Jimmy into the dash of the truck.

"It won't move, the truck won't move!" Jimmy screamed in anger.

"Get out! We have to make a run for it!" Gordon opened the door and stepped out with his M-4 ready. He placed it in his shoulder as soon as both feet met the pavement, turned, and immediately started to fire upon the people on the bridge.

"Jimmy, let's fucking go!" Gordon commanded, not looking away from the targets he was engaging.

"My door won't open!" Jimmy cried out in a panic.

Gunfire was now coming from both sides of the street and the bridge. Gordon managed to get a few shots off before he felt the sharp burning pain in his side.

"Damn it!" he screamed in pain. "They shot me!"

He turned to locate the shooters on his left in the houses but he could not see anyone. All he could hear was the cracking of gunfire and whizzing of bullets as they passed by him.

"Jimmy, come on!"

Jimmy stopped his futile attempt to open the driver's door and crawled across the bench seat and came out the passenger side.

Jimmy had a pistol in his hand and immediately started to shoot at the people on the bridge.

"Where is Jerrod?" Jimmy asked while shooting.

"Go take cover behind the truck!" Gordon commanded, not answering Jimmy's question.

The slide on Jimmy's pistol locked to the rear. "Damn it! I'm out of bullets!"

Gordon, using his left hand, reached in his pocket and handed Jimmy another fully loaded magazine. Jimmy took it and reloaded quickly. Gordon had managed, even though wounded, to hit a few of the Villistas. The gunfire was coming from everywhere now; Gordon didn't know who to engage because there were so many.

"Jimmy, I'll cover you. Run!"

Jimmy listened this time and started to run north down the street, away from the gunfire.

Gordon saw more men on the bridge. Reinforcements were arriving.

With all the confusion, he had lost track of where Eric and Jerrod had gone. He slowly started to walk backward, still shooting as he went. Feeling the warm blood flowing down his side was not a welcoming sign. The pain was also increasing in intensity. Reaching in his cargo pocket he grabbed another rifle magazine and pulled it out. The second bullet hitting him made him drop it. The impact felt like someone had smacked him with a bat. His left arm went limp.

Gordon started to think to himself, Is this it? Is this how I go out? What about my family?

More determined than before, he tactically transitioned to his pistol. His rifle lay slung to his chest. Taking aim, he managed to shoot a couple of more Villistas.

Like the 7th Cavalry, Jerrod and Eric came across the median about twenty feet in front of him. Eric was hanging outside of the car with his rifle, taking shots. Jerrod turned the wheel hard left and accelerated just as another rocket came screaming in from the bridge and smashed into Jerrod's car. The rear of the car exploded, throwing Eric from the car before it flipped over onto its hood.

Gordon could see Jerrod was still in the car. He started to make his way to the car, but bullets rained down around him. Determined, Gordon pressed forward in an attempt to reach Jerrod. As he marched toward Jerrod he emptied his pistol. Gordon thrust the pistol under his armpit and pressed the magazine release. The empty magazine dropped to the ground with a clang. As he reached for another magazine, the third and final impact did its job. The force of the shot took him to the ground. It struck him just below the collarbone.

As he laid on the hard pavement the trauma from the three shots was taking a toll. His vision began to get blurry and vertigo set in. Looking to his left he saw Jerrod; his now dead body was crushed under the weight of the car. Gordon could not see Eric through the heavy black smoke coming from Jerrod's burning car. The gunfire now seemed distant as his thoughts drifted to his wife, Samantha, and then to his two children. He thought about how he would miss them, their little laughs, and their sweet and gentle hugs. Gordon tried to move, but the weakness from the blood loss prevented it. Feeling what he called the darkness, he struggled to stay awake. Now the sounds around him seemed to go away. All he could hear was his shallow breathing. More thoughts came of his children. He loved them so much; he longed to be in his family's arms. He longed to kiss and hold his wife. As his breathing became shallower, the tears began to fall down the sides of his face. Visions of his family without him took over and he knew the darkness was coming. If he could just keep thinking about them, the darkness wouldn't come. Gordon managed to bring his right arm to his neck. Grabbing the chain he had around it, he pulled the necklace out from underneath his shirt. Attached to the chain was a sterling silver compass. Samantha had given this to him years ago when they were dating. When she gave it to him, she told him that it would always show him the way home. Holding it tightly, he openly cried. Transporting himself there, he could see her like she was then, her long blond hair and pouty lips, the doe eyes and sweet smell. Tears ran down his cheeks as he felt the darkness coming over him. As he slipped away he muttered softly, "I love you."

Cheyenne Mountain, Colorado

Conner was covered in dripping sweat as he fumbled with his keys to his room. His new routine of running at the gym was paying off; he was leaning up and relieving some stress. While the office of president came with huge responsibilities, it offered many luxuries that most did not have anymore. So before each daily run, Conner would say a small prayer acknowledging his gratefulness for his and Julia's safety.

Passing his bedroom, he saw Julia sitting on the edge of the bed. Her seclusion had become commonplace since the death of their son, but something seemed different. He stopped what he was doing and went into room.

"Hi, sweetie, is everything okay?"

She turned to him and said, "Brad, please sit next to me."

She had a gentleness in her voice that he had not heard in a long time. He missed her and did not hesitate when he heard that long-missed tone.

"Of course."

She grabbed his hand, turned, and faced him.

"Brad, I know we have been through a lot together, I know you personally have a huge responsibility. I love you and respect you. You didn't choose this but you have stood up and taken charge like the man I know you are. I'm so proud of you. You are a good man, a good husband, and a good father. I know that over the past couple of weeks I've been very distant. I hope you forgive me for that. I know that it must have been hard for you too and that you haven't had the chance to truly mourn because you've been called upon to lead our country."

Conner just held his wife's hand tight and looked at her. The more she talked the more tears started to well up in her eyes. He had wanted to interject his thoughts, but this was the most she had talked to him since Bobby's death. He let her continue uninterrupted.

"Brad, I know you love me and I know you want the best for me."

Conner nodded.

"Brad, we are good people, we are good, decent people; we are loving parents, or I should say we were. With everything that has happened, from Bobby's death to the attacks. We have to start over."

Julia paused. Tears flowed down her cheeks; she looked down and wiped her cheeks. Conner reached over and placed his hand on her cheek and raised her head so he could look at her.

"I love you too. I have missed you so much. I am so sorry that I couldn't save our son."

"Stop, please. I don't want to revisit that. Bobby's death wasn't your fault. Others are to blame and I know you will deal with them in time."

"I will, I promise you."

"Brad," Julia said softly, breaking her gaze again and looking down.

"Yes, sweetheart? What is it?"

"I want us to have another baby," she said, lifting her head and looking at him.

Conner was shocked; he would have never guessed this is what she had been thinking about. He did not answer. She kept looking at him for an answer, but he kept silent.

"Brad, did you hear me? I want us to try to have another baby."

"I heard you, Julia. Don't you think it might be a bit early?"

"No, I don't. I have thought about this for almost two weeks. Our country has suffered a horrible attack, millions will die, our son is dead, and we must rebuild our country. We, more than anyone, should be having babies. We have all the resources to ensure a baby will survive."

"Julia, sorry to interrupt, but shouldn't we take some time before we contemplate this?"

"No, Brad. I want to have another baby." Julia was now getting upset.

Conner decided to be cautious about the next thing he said. He knew how fragile she was and the last thing he wanted was for her to relapse. He thought about the idea. He did love babies and children and they did have the resources.

Julia kept staring at Conner, her eyes red from crying. Looking into her begging eyes, he could not resist her. All he wanted was to make her happy.

"Julia, I agree; let's have a baby."

"Are you sure?"

"Yes, I'm sure."

She quickly hugged him tightly. She kissed him on the cheek, then the lips. She pulled away from the kiss to look at him and say, "I love you, Brad, thank you."

"I love you too, Julia."

She kissed him, again this time more passionately. She stopped only to say, "There's no better time to start trying than right now." She reached over and brought him closer to her; they both laid back on the bed.

After saying yes to Julia, Brad felt better about his answer. Having another child would give them a family again. The new baby could never replace Bobby, but Julia deserved to be happy and he would do anything to make her so.

San Diego, California

Nelson ran to the door as fast as his legs could take him. The banging and yelling at the front door portended something of great concern.

He unlocked the door and flung it open to find Jimmy and two people he did not know wearing uniforms carrying a bloodied stretcher. They proceeded into the house without a word and headed straight for the dining table. Nelson thought to himself how convenient no one else was home at the time to witness this.

As he followed the men, he peppered them with questions. No one would answer him. He could not see who was on the stretcher, but the fact that Gordon was not carrying it and wasn't in the room gave him enough info to guess that the bloodied person on the stretcher was his good friend.

"Jimmy, what happened?" he asked.

"We were ambushed."

Once the three made it to the dining room, they pushed everything off the table onto the floor and placed the stretcher on the table.

Nelson rushed to Gordon's side and immediately placed his hand on his neck to confirm if he was still alive. Finding a faint pulse, he began to do what came normal for him as an EMT.

"Does anyone know how many times he was shot?" Nelson asked.

"No, it was so loud and so many bullets were whizzing by. I wasn't focused on him. I'm sorry," Jimmy said. The other two did not say a word; they just stood there staring at Nelson.

Nelson saw the wound in Gordon's left arm. He then ripped open Gordon's shirt and saw the wound in his upper chest.

"Go get me some fresh bandages!" Nelson commanded.

"Where?" Jimmy asked.

"Just go into the kitchen and get me a clean towel. Don't grab the ones on the counter."

Jimmy rushed off.

"It's going to be okay, my friend," Nelson said to Gordon.

Nelson rolled Gordon over onto his side to see if the bullet had exited. He was pleased to find that it had.

Needing to thoroughly examine Gordon, Nelson ordered the two men to help him strip Gordon of his boots and other clothing.

Fortunately, Nelson located all the wounds. The wound in his chest looked bad, but the main issue was the blood loss and potential infection. They could handle the infection with antibiotics, but if he needed blood he would have to find out if someone had Gordon's blood type.

"Jimmy, do you know Gordon's blood type?"

"No," Jimmy answered.

"Here's the situation. I think these wounds can be mended, but

Gordon needs blood. We obviously don't have any in our supplies, but we can give him some when we find someone who is a match. We need to do this quickly."

"What do you want us to do?" Jimmy asked.

"I need you to go find Samantha."

"Okay, I'm gone," Jimmy said, and raced off.

"You two are like sticks in the mud. I need one of you to go to the clinic and get some antibiotics, bandages, tape, gloves—just bring me a trauma kit."

"I'd go but I don't know where the clinic is located," one of the men answered.

"Who are you, anyway?"

"I'm Sergeant Holloway and this is Lance Corporal Fowler. We rescued your men."

"I'm Nelson. Now whoever is going to make the run, here is how you get to our clinic. Exit the front door, turn right, and go to Calle Cristo. Turn left, and on the right is our large clubhouse—or was our clubhouse. The house two doors down is our clinic. Just tell the guard that I sent you and that the meds and bandages are for Gordon."

"Okay," Sergeant Holloway answered. "Lance Corporal Fowler, stay here and do whatever the man asks." Fowler nodded and replied, "Yes, Sergeant."

Holloway took off at top speed.

"What can I do?" Fowler asked.

"You can help by telling me what happened," Nelson said.

"We were on patrol to the west when we heard the gunfire. We have been in the area doing reconnaissance on the Villista Cartel."

"Cartel?" Nelson asked.

"Yes, sir, that is what we're calling them. They are an offshoot of the Tijuana Cartel that has now crossed over and is operating in San Diego County. We believe they are using the name Villista to help draw support from the local Hispanic community."

"What's up with the name 'Villista,' by the way?" Nelson asked while he wiped the blood off of Gordon.

"Sir, it—"

Looking up, Nelson said, "Hey, Marine, no need to call me 'sir,' okay?"

"Ah, okay. Sorry, just trying to be respectful, Doctor."

"By the way, I'm not a doctor; I'm a paramedic, that's all."

"Ah, okay."

"So, Villista?"

"Yes, the Villista name comes from the early twentieth century, when Pancho Villa and his revolutionary guard were at war with the United States. We believe that the Tijuana Cartel is taking advantage of the situation and attempting to secure a foothold here."

"So how did you happen upon Gordon and Jimmy?"

"We heard the gunfight from about a click away. When we arrived, we saw your friend here get shot in the chest and fall. We opened fire on the Villistas with our .50 cal. We took most of them out. Then out of nowhere came the man who was just here and he told us we needed to help his friend here."

"So you saw no one else?"

"We saw another one of your guys and he was dead, I don't know who he was."

Just then, Gordon started to move his head back and forth. Gordon briefly opened his eyes but just as quick as he opened them they were closed.

"Hey, buddy. You're going to be okay," Nelson calmly said to him.

Gordon just nodded slowly and attempted to say something, but his voice was unintelligible.

"You have nothing to worry about, I haven't started drinking yet," Nelson said with a grin. Nelson's humor and cool temperament were always available, no matter the situation.

The front door burst open; Samantha came running in. Seeing Nelson in the dining room standing over Gordon, she wasted no time and ran to him.

"Oh my God!" she said, grabbing Gordon's hand.

Gordon opened his eyes and looked at her.

She leaned over and kissed him several times on his face.

"Oh, baby, what happened?" she said, caressing his face.

He kept looking at her but the fatigue from the loss of blood made it difficult to stay conscious. His eyes closed again as he slipped back into the darkness.

Nelson interrupted and asked, "Samantha, what is Gordon's blood type?"

"Ah, what?" she responded with a question. Her focus was on Gordon.

"What is Gordon's blood type?" he asked again.

"Oh, ah; he's B positive."

"Great, thank you."

Pulling Jimmy aside, he explained the situation. Nelson needed Jimmy to literally go door-to-door to find someone who had either B positive or O negative blood. There was no time to waste, as the blood loss would eventually kill Gordon.

Jimmy took off.

"Will he make it?" Samantha asked, turning to Nelson.

"Samantha, you've known me for a long time and you know I don't bullshit around when it come to things like this. I feel that he will make it, but our window is closing. He's lost a lot of blood and if we don't get him some, he will die. Jimmy is out finding someone who is a compatible donor now."

Samantha was a very emotional woman, and typically something like this would have caused her to start crying, but she needed to be strong. She looked Nelson right in the eyes and told him, "Do what you have to, do not let my husband die. Do you hear me? Do whatever you need to."

"I will, Samantha, I promise you. I will."

DECEMBER 25, 2014

• • •

Man is the cruelest animal.

—Friedrich Nietzsche

USS *Makin Island*, Pacific Ocean

"Call General Quarters!" Barone yelled as he heard the news that the USS *New Orleans* was no longer under his control.

"What do we know? I need information, people!" he barked on the bridge of the ship.

He grabbed a set of binoculars and looked at the USS *New Orleans*. The ship had slowed down and started to pull away from them, headed in a southerly direction.

"Get whoever is in charge over there on the radio now!" Barone yelled.

"Sir, we have someone," the communications petty officer said.

Barone walked over to a handheld and picked it up.

"This is Lieutenant Colonel Barone, commander of the Second Battalion Fourth Marine Regiment, who is this?"

"Colonel Barone, this is Captain Newsom, the commanding officer of the USS *New Orleans*. I have retaken my ship."

Barone's anger welled up inside him. He wanted to yell at the captain, but he needed to remain calm and think critically.

"Captain, what have you done with my men?"

"Sir, your men are all being held in their berthing areas under arrest for treason and mutiny."

"I don't want trouble, Captain Newsom; all I want are my men."

"Colonel Barone, that is not going to happen. We are heading toward Hawaii, there your men will be dropped off and be held accountable for the acts they have committed against the United States. I only wish that you could be brought to justice with them."

"Captain Newsom, all we wish to do is go home and protect our families. So I am asking you as an officer and a gentleman, let my men go. We can have them transported over to the *Makin Island* or other ships under my command in exchange for men we have."

"That will not happen, Colonel."

"Listen, Captain, I don't have time for your bullshit hero stuff. If my men are not turned over to me, we will attack your ship."

"What will that get you, Colonel? If you destroy the *New Orleans* your men will die."

"Do I look like a man that will bluff, Captain? You are talking to someone who has seized a United States naval amphib group and attacked a U.S. military installation. I mean what I say. Now you have fifteen minutes to get back to me or I will launch my Harriers." Barone slammed the receiver down.

Barone looked around; all eyes were fixed on him with anticipation of his next command.

"Mr. Montgomery!" Barone barked.

"Yes, sir."

"Prepare our jump jets for an attack on the USS *New Orleans*."

• • •

"What I hate the most is being locked up during GQ. I mean, what if the ship gets hit with a missile or something? We'll drown down here," Tomlinson said, lying in his bunk.

"I have to agree with you. It always makes me a bit nervous too," Sebastian replied.

"What do you think is going on now?" Tomlinson asked.

"God knows, the whole fucking world is turned upside down. This doesn't surprise me."

"I guess you're right."

The berthing area hatch opened up. A Marine officer stepped in and walked over to Gunny Smith.

"So do you—"

"Shhh."

"Huh?"

"Shut up!" Sebastian snapped at Tomlinson. He was trying to overhear Gunny's conversation.

"Corporal Van Zandt, get over here," Gunny yelled.

"Yes, Gunny." Sebastian shot up out of the bunk and walked quickly over to Gunny.

"Sergeant Jennings, you too," Gunny said.

Jennings was new to the unit; he had transferred over from the 1st Battalion 1st Marine Regiment when Sebastian's unit came on board. He was tall, lean, and when he spoke there was no mistaking that he hailed from the Deep South.

"I need you two to get your sniper teams in place. We need one team on the starboard and the other on the port side. We need you to assist in watching over the boats that are transporting Marines from the *New Orleans*."

"What's going on, Gunny?" Sebastian asked.

"Apparently we lost the USS *New Orleans*; the captain of the ship was able to retake it. Men loyal to the colonel are being transported here in exchange for those who don't want to be here. You both will just be another set of eyeballs out there. If you see anyone who wishes us harm and have a shot, take it."

Sebastian thought that God was playing a trick on him. This was exactly the opposite situation he wanted to be in.

"Grab your spotters, gear, and get your ass topside," Gunny commanded.

"Yes, Gunny," both Sebastian and Jennings said.

When Sebastian and Tomlinson made it topside they were welcomed by the noise of Harrier jets taking off. They quickly proceeded to their position and set up next to the flight deck. Sebastian looked through his scope and he could see the USS *New Orleans* and estimated it was a mile away. He could barely make out people on the deck, but he could see the aft ramp was down. Assault amphibious vehicles were in the water heading their way. He kept peering through the scope and spotted two LCAC hovercrafts also heading their way. The plume of water put out from the hovercrafts made it easier to spot them versus the AAVs.

• • •

An hour had gone by and the operation to remove all those loyal to Barone from the *New Orleans* was going smoothly. The Harriers were making runs past the *New Orleans* in a show of force and the LCACs and Amtracs were going back and forth between the two ships. Sebastian thought to himself that it would be nice to go without any incident today.

"How long do you think this is going to take?" Tomlinson asked.

"As long as it will take, T."

Just then, gunfire broke out below them.

"What the hell?" Tomlinson asked out loud.

They both stood up and tried to look down from their position back into the ship's well deck. Whatever was happening had taken place inside the belly of the ship. The gunfire lasted only twenty seconds before it was silenced. But the short-lived silence was broken by the sound of General Quarters. Sebastian and Tomlinson were trying to see something, but their position prohibited a good view back into the ship. Within moments following the call to General Quarters, a blast shook the ship behind them. Sebastian turned around and saw smoke coming from a hatch on the superstructure of the ship. More gunfire broke out, but they could not identify its location before it stopped as quickly as it had started.

"What do we do?" Tomlinson asked.

"Just hold tight; if we can get any shots, we'll take them."

They could hear the rapid gunfire of the Phalanx antiship missile system followed by an explosion just off the port side of the ship.

"Oh my God, they shot a missile at us!" Tomlinson screamed.

Sebastian didn't respond. He was whipping his head around trying to see if anything was coming his way or if he had a target he could shoot.

The Harriers that had been making runs past the *New Orleans* had pulled away from the ship and were flying above it in the clouds. Sebastian could hear them but not see them. Then, without notice, a missile was launched from the *New Orleans*; it went straight up. Both he and Tomlinson watched it travel into the clouds and out of sight. The seconds that passed seemed like forever, but an explosion echoed across the wide-open ocean. Debris rained down from the clouds into the vastness of the water below.

The rapid fire of the Phalanx from the *New Orleans* then sounded. It was attempting to knock missiles from the Harriers out of the sky. Fortunately for the *New Orleans*, their Phalanx did its intended job and destroyed the incoming missiles.

"Can you believe this?" Tomlinson asked.

"Yes, I can. This is what I was talking about." Sebastian was now getting upset again.

As they were watching the fighting near the *New Orleans* they had all but forgotten the fighting on their ship. It had been quiet for minutes now.

Another missile launched from the *New Orleans* with a similar trajectory as before. It disappeared into the clouds, but this time no explosion followed its potentially lethal flight.

Barone's Harriers responded with another volley of missiles, but the *New Orleans*'s Phalanx destroyed them.

Moments had passed with no missile exchange when an explosion like nothing they had heard yet echoed from across the ocean. They both turned their attention to the *New Orleans* and saw that the ship had been hit on the starboard side.

"Oh my God, did one of the jets finally hit it?" Tomlinson yelled out.

Another explosion followed on the same side as the other; flames shot out of side and the ship started to list. The damage done to the *New Orleans* was not from a Harrier but from the USS *Topeka*.

Taking advantage of the damage to the ship, several Harriers fired again. This time, the Phalanx was only able to take one missile down. Two found their way to their deadly destination, the bridge of the *New Orleans*. More flames and debris came from the ship. The ship was taking on huge amounts of water and began to list even more. Heavy black smoke poured out of the gaping holes on the side and from what had been the bridge.

"Did you see that? That was fucking awesome!" Tomlinson said. He was smiling behind his binoculars.

Sebastian looked at Tomlinson in disgust. He reached over and grabbed the binoculars and scolded him.

"What's wrong with you? Those are Americans. Those are our countrymen. This is not funny!"

"Corporal, I'm tired of your whiny bullshit. Stop complaining. You wanted to go home and this is what it takes to go home."

"I don't think that the end justifies the means for me."

"Stop being a bitch, Corporal. I am so sick of you whining about this shit. If you don't like it then you have a choice."

Sebastian didn't answer Tomlinson, because in some way he was right. All he was doing was complaining and if he felt this strong about it he'd do something. He thought to himself, What can I do? Where would he go now?

"Here," Sebastian said to Tomlinson, handing him back the binoculars.

Tomlinson snatched them out Sebastian's hands. He leered at him for a second, then went back to watching the battle across the water.

Sebastian leaned against the bulkhead and looked through the railing as the smoldering and smoking *New Orleans* lay on its side. He could see all the lifeboats and rafts being deployed. The Harriers overhead kept making passes near the ship, but the fighting was now over. The *New Orleans* was a complete loss; hundreds of men were dead. Sebastian wondered what damage his ship had taken. The smoke from their ship billowed out of the well deck and the superstructure behind him.

"Do you think they'll serve turkey today for Christmas?" Tomlinson asked.

Sebastian just turned away and shook his head.

• • •

"I need a damage and casualty report," Barone ordered, walking into the CIC. He had just been on the bridge overseeing the final loading of the survivors from the *New Orleans*. The ship's first officer, Navy Lieutenant Montgomery, his executive officer Major Ashley, Lieutenant Colonel Pelton, the VMA-214 Attack Aircraft Squadron Commander, and Sergeant Major Simpson were already in the briefing room.

"XO, what do you have?" Barone asked Ashley.

"Sir, our damage was limited. We lost one LCAC, which has been replaced by one from the *New Orleans*. We have three KIAs and twenty-two wounded."

"Give me what you have from the *New Orleans*," Barone then ordered.

"Between us and the *Pearl Harbor* we were able to rescue four hundred and sixty-eight Marines and three hundred and thirty-seven sailors. Unfortunately, Lieutenant Colonel Silver was lost, as was Captain Newsom," Ashley said, reading off a pad of paper.

"Any new word from the *Topeka*?" Barone asked.

"Sir, the *Topeka* has proceeded ahead of us to provide overwatch."

"Well, I am damn glad we had them on our side. In my entire career, I have never seen a submarine in action and now I have a newfound respect for them," Barone said, sounding upbeat.

Barone had not wished for this incident but was happy with its outcome.

"You're goddamn right, sir. I couldn't believe my eyes when the first torpedo struck the *New Orleans*, just incredible," Sergeant Major Simpson said.

"Sir, we also lost one Harrier today," Ashley said with apprehension as he interrupted the joyful mood in the room.

"I saw, who was it?"

All the men looked around at one another and no one said a word.

"Gentlemen, what's going on?"

"Sir, the pilot on board was First Lieutenant William Barone."

"That's impossible; his jet was not called up. I know this."

"Sir, he was called up after Lieutenant Holland was injured on his way to the flight deck. Lieutenant Barone took his place and jumped in Holland's aircraft," said Lieutenant Colonel Pelton.

Barone sat stunned; he could not believe what he was hearing. You could hear a pin drop, it was so quiet in the room. Barone started to shake his head in disbelief.

"Are you sure of this?" Barone asked, his voice now subdued.

"Sir, we were just as shocked as you are now. I personally went down to confirm," Pelton said.

"Gentlemen, if you'll excuse me." Barone stood up quickly. A feeling of sickness overcame him. He needed to leave the room immediately. Without saying another word, he left and walked as fast as his legs would take him back to his stateroom.

The entire walk back was torture; he kept picturing his son's young, handsome face. His mind wanted to deny what he just heard.

Finally making it to his room, he stumbled inside and headed for the toilet. He fell to his knees and threw up. He had been in the Marine Corps a long time. He had witnessed death many times and had even taken life, but this was too personal for him, this was too close to home. His son was now dead. How would he explain this to his wife?

After minutes of dry heaving and exhaustion, he sat down on the floor. Seeing the bottle of whiskey, he stood up and grabbed it and poured the entire contents down his throat. He looked at the empty bottle, then smashed it against the bulkhead. Looking at the thousands of tiny fragments of glass he thought of Billy. A memory was all he was now. He had been blown into a thousand unrecognizable fragments like this bottle.

"Goddamn you, Newsom, goddamn you!"

Barone wanted to blame Captain Newsom, but deep down he blamed himself. The emotional pain was now too much; he could not resist and finally gave in and started to sob.

Cheyenne Mountain, Colorado

President Conner sat alone and motionless in the cold briefing room. The solitude felt appropriate in the current circumstances. Christmas morning had started out perfect. He and Julia had spent the early hours feeling like teenagers, lying in bed and making love. This bliss was shattered with the news from New York.

The fears he had about another attack had come true. At 9:23 A.M. Eastern Standard Time a low-grade nuclear bomb was detonated in Manhattan along the east side, destroying most of the city. Feelings of inadequacy and failure competed with the strong feelings of anger and revenge.

Griswald, senior staff, Dylan, and Cruz came into the room and immediately took seats around the long table. Conner looked around and noticed that General Houston was absent. He was tempted to ask about his whereabouts but didn't want to waste any more time and began the meeting.

"By now you all have heard what's happened in New York."

Everyone looked somber and acknowledged Conner by nodding.

"First let me begin by saying that because we have failed to act our country has been attacked again. This new attack wasn't coincidental; this was a planned attack on a national holiday," Conner said, then paused. "General, it has been three weeks since we were initially attacked and still you have nothing but excuses. If we had done something we might have prevented this. We have sat in this mountain for weeks and all we do is talk and talk. I know you oppose my plan. I listened and gave your counsel great respect and deep consideration. Retaliating against our known enemies with the use of our nuclear arsenal is something that should not be taken lightly, I understand that. However, it's not as if we haven't been attacked with the same type of weapon. There are those out there that want to exterminate us. We know who they are; we have been dealing with them for over a generation. Many of my predecessors have had to deal with them. We have taken action before by putting troops on the ground and slogging it out slowly over years and years. Have we had some success? Yes, but we can never win this unless we do to them what they want to do to us. We must wipe them off the map! We must completely and utterly destroy them. Like Lincoln over one hundred and fifty years ago realized that he could not win the war against the Confederacy unless he decimated them—that is what we must do now to our enemies. We can no longer waste time talking; we can no longer waste time attempting to find out who did this. We know who did it." Conner stood up and started to slowly walk around the room. "General, you have been a trusted counsel during these trying times, but I have given you enough time. I do not wish to hear your objections." Conner was looking at Griswald the entire time he spoke. He then began to address the rest in the room: "I brought you all in here today not to talk but to inform you of what we will do today. Today we strike back! Today we once and for all destroy our enemies! We eradicate them from this planet. I am not concerned about what the world thinks. Today, we take real action and begin the reconstruction of our country." Conner made his way back to his seat but did not sit. He again turned his attention to Griswald. "General Griswald, I hereby order our nuclear forces to strike the following cities: Tehran, Baghdad, Islamabad, Kabul, Mogadishu, Pyongyang, Damascus, Tripoli, Aden; I also want all military installations in the countries of Iran, Iraq, Syria, Libya, North Korea, Afghanistan, Yemen, Somalia, and Pakistan destroyed with nuclear weapons. If that means dropping a hundred bombs on each country, I don't care. I don't want them to have the means to come back; I want whoever survives to be sent straight to the Stone Age. You have my orders and I expect them to be carried out immediately."

The room was quiet; no one said a word. They all stared at Conner. They knew the gravity of the situation and what was about to happen.

"Sir, I cannot do what you ask," Griswald said, breaking the silence.

"Excuse me, General?" Conner asked.

"I cannot follow an order that allows for the murdering of millions of innocent people."

"General, enough of the innocent people talk. The days of innocent people are over. The people in these countries hate us. Look at what we have wasted over the past decade attempting to win their hearts and minds. They want us dead. They only use us for their benefit, then discard us. If you will not carry this out, then I will find someone who will."

"Actually, sir, you will not be doing anything like that," Griswald said defiantly. He stood up; he was at the opposite side of the table from the president.

"What was that, General?"

"Sir, we will not let you."

Looking around the room, Conner asked, "And exactly who will not let me?"

"Sir, I have been working behind the scenes to prevent this type of holocaust from happening. I am sorry to say that there is a consensus among those here." Griswald looked at a few around the table. No one would look at him. They all turned away.

"Who exactly is willing to stop me? Please stand," Conner asked of the group around the table.

No one responded, everyone looked at one another. No one would even look in Griswald's direction.

"General Griswald, I was briefed some time ago that you might be up to something, so I planted the idea in others to make themselves available to your potential plan. As you can see, no one agrees with you and there is no consensus," Conner said.

"You cowards, do you not understand what's at stake here?" Griswald screamed.

Conner looked out the main window of the briefing room and nodded. Within seconds, Agents Davis and Jackson stormed into the room. Griswald turned and drew his pistol. Everyone sitting ducked under the table except for Conner, who stood his ground. Griswald aimed his pistol at Davis and shot him in the chest; Davis fell to the ground, dead. Jackson had entered the room just behind Davis, and Griswald was able to shoot him too. The bullet hit Jackson in the head; Jackson's lifeless body fell to the floor with a loud thud. Griswald then turned and faced Conner.

"General, put the gun down."

"I'm sorry, Mr. President, but I cannot allow this to happen," Griswald said, raising the pistol and taking aim at Conner.

"General Griswald, I am the president of the United States! What are you doing? Your name will go down in history as a traitor, as the man who killed a president. Do you want that?" Conner kept looking toward the door and the main window. With the gunfire he was wondering where the Air Force security forces or the command post personnel were.

Noticing Conner's glance toward the door, Griswald said, "Mr.

President, no one is coming. I gave them all orders to vacate the CP upon our coming into this meeting. I knew what orders you would be giving, so I made sure that no one would interrupt us. It appears we were both planning for this confrontation," Griswald said, grinning. "I know what I am doing; by killing you I can save millions."

"You don't honestly think that killing me will stop us from acting?"

Griswald didn't answer. He began to apply pressure to the trigger.

A gunshot rang out in the room. Conner flinched and looked down at his chest, expecting to see blood but found nothing. Looking back at Griswald he saw him waver, then fall onto the table. His pistol fell from his dying grasp and slid across the table toward Conner, who grabbed it. Conner took aim at Griswald, who lay gasping. Cruz then appeared from behind his chair holding a pistol. He too was aiming at Griswald, squirming on the table. When Griswald attempted to speak, blood poured out of his mouth. He grasped the table in an attempt to pull himself up, but Cruz stopped him with one more shot to the head. Griswald shook briefly and then lay motionless, his eyes wide open, with blood pouring out of his mouth.

Conner looked at Cruz.

"I have to admit, I never expected that from you."

Cruz, still holding the pistol, turned toward Conner and pointed the pistol at him.

Conner looked stunned as he took a step back.

Dropping the gun, Cruz said, "Sorry, I'm a bit in shock. I didn't mean to point it at you."

Conner smiled awkwardly. "Mr. Vice President, you scared me for a second."

"Mr. President, we have a job to do. Let's go do it."

Conner and Cruz left the briefing room and walked into the command center.

"Dylan, follow me," Conner said on the way out of the briefing room.

Dylan crawled out from underneath the table and cautiously walked around the table, avoiding the bodies.

"Yes, sir," Dylan said, clearing his throat.

"Two things. First, find General Houston, and second, set me up to go on a live broadcast across all frequencies in forty-five minutes."

"Okay, Mr. President," Dylan answered, and hurried off.

Conner turned to Cruz. "Here's what going to happen just in case something happens to me. Once I am able, I will order a full-scale nuclear attack against those countries I mentioned. Once the attack has started, I will brief the American people the only way we can, and that is via radio."

• • •

The search for Houston was successful; they found his body in Griswald's closet. While Conner prepared for his speech to the country, the Cheyenne Mountain base commander communicated all the launch coordinates to the nuclear subs around the world.

The time came for Conner to give his speech. The attack was under way and now was the time to inform his fellow Americans. He wasn't sure how many would hear his broadcast, but some would, and hopefully the word of their country's retaliation would spread. Conner felt nervous, not because he had just ordered the total annihilation of several countries but because he was speaking directly to the American people. He had only done this three other times, but this time it was to inform them that he had taken his first major step as president of the United States.

Dylan smiled from the production booth and gave the president a smile and thumbs-up. Conner nodded and looked at the large microphone. A voice then boomed in the room telling him thirty seconds. He looked down at the quickly crafted speech, thinking that one day this sheet of paper would be in a museum. Drifting into such deep thought he missed his cue. Dylan's tapping on the glass pulled Conner back to the present. Looking up he saw the red light meaning that the microphone was live.

"My fellow Americans, this is President Conner. I am addressing you this Christmas night not to express holiday wishes but to inform you that another tragedy has befallen our great country. This morning, the enemies of the United States attacked New York City with a weapon of mass destruction. The information we have received so far is that many of our fellow citizens have paid the ultimate sacrifice and have perished in this heinous and cowardly attack. Today's attack, along with the initial attacks three weeks ago, has prompted me to finally take action. This decision did not come lightly, but after much thought and prayer I decided that we must finally act. I gave the order an hour ago for a full-scale nuclear retaliation against those who are responsible for the attacks against us. I can now report that our nuclear forces successfully struck targets within the following countries: Iran, Iraq, Syria, Yemen, Somalia, North Korea, Pakistan, Afghanistan, Egypt, Tunisia, and Libya. I believe this action was justified and will prevent these countries from conducting further attacks against us. Let me be clear to those who may be still out there who wish us harm. We will not just bring you to justice, we will destroy you. Do not tread on us! I know the past three weeks have been extremely difficult and your way of life is now different, but I can assure you that we are working tirelessly to get our power grid and infrastructure back on line. In the meantime, we can help support you by food and medical shipments as we get them from our allies. Your government has not forgotten you. So, as this Christmas comes to a close, we must all come together and remember that life is difficult right now but we are Americans and we, like others before us, will persevere through these dark times. We must not lose hope and must not give in. We will make it and we will rebuild, that I promise you."

Conner paused for a few seconds, then finished his short statement with the traditional ending of all presidential addresses.

"May God bless you and may God bless the United States of America."

JANUARY 3, 2015

• • •

Once we have a war there is only one thing to do. It must be won. For defeat brings worse things than any that can ever happen in war.

—Ernest Hemingway

USS *Makin Island*, Pacific Ocean

Sebastian just stared at the ceiling of the berthing area. His conscience could not allow him to continue to support Barone and their mission. His patience was running thin with the pace they were taking to get home. It had been more than a week since the battle with the USS *New Orleans*, and nothing new had been reported about conditions back home or their arrival. He was not idle with his time, though; he used it to craft a plan. All of those with family would be allowed to take a day to go find their families and return to the ships or go directly to Camp Pendleton. Barone was also allowing Marines who did not want to continue with them past California to go on their own. This is what Sebastian intended to do, but he wanted more than his rifle, water, and a few MREs. He planned on taking a Hummer with enough food and ammunition to last him months. Sebastian did not know what he'd find upon landing back in California and hoped that Gordon was fine. Not wanting to go it alone, he needed to convince Tomlinson to come with him, but the past few conversations didn't sound promising. Not one to give up, he thought he would try one last time. As if Tomlinson was reading his mind, he walked up to Sebastian's bunk.

"Hey, Corporal."

"Hey," Sebastian said, sitting up in his bunk. "I was just thinking about you."

"I hear that all the time, but mainly from the ladies. So what's up?"

"Let's go find a quiet place to have a chat."

"A quiet place? Have you turned homo on me?

"No, I just don't want to share what I have to tell you with twenty other jarheads!" Sebastian exclaimed.

"Hey, did you hear the latest?"

"What?" Sebastian asked while putting on his boots.

"Apparently we have been sailing around in circles. The coast is only a day out. The colonel has been sending SEALs and MARSOC to probe for landing sites and to make contact with Marine units back at Pendleton."

"Really?"

"Yeah, man, we're close now."

"What about the conditions? What's going on?"

"It sounds bad—"

Interrupting Tomlinson, Sebastian asked with urgency in his voice, "How bad? What's going on?"

"The recon teams are saying that nothing is working at all except old cars. There's dead bodies everywhere, wandering bands of starving people, and a Mexican cartel has moved into San Diego with an army."

"Really?" Sebastian's concern grew for Gordon and the family the more Tomlinson talked.

"Yeah, the shit has really hit the fan back there."

"When are we landing?"

"I don't know, days I hear."

"Days? Why aren't we going in now?" Sebastian asked, frustrated.

"I hear ya, but I trust the colonel."

Sebastian shook his head in frustration.

"So where do you want to go?" Tomlinson asked.

"Let's go out to the forward deck."

On their way out, Sebastian noticed Gunny having an in-depth conversation with Sergeant Jennings. Gunny looked briefly at them as they left, but Sebastian did not maintain the eye contact. He could not help but to feel that Gunny knew something was going on.

The chilliness of the air told Sebastian that they were definitely in the eastern Pacific. Tomlinson followed him and lit a cigarette right away. The smoke from his first drag covered the salty smell of the sea air. They made their way around the side of the ship and took a seat on a box out of view of the hatch.

"So what's up, Corporal?" Tomlinson asked, then took another long drag.

"Once we land you know we'll be able to go find family members. As you know, my plan is to go find my brother and his family. I wanted to know if you wanted to go help me find them."

"Of course I'll help you."

Sebastian smiled. He knew that was the easy question; now came the difficult one.

Before he could ask, Tomlinson asked, "Is that it? You wanted to take me out in the dark and cold to ask me that?"

Sebastian paused; he did not answer. The darkness masked

Tomlinson's blank stare. Not until he took another drag was Sebastian able to see him waiting patiently for an answer.

"Here's what I wanted to discuss with you."

Tomlinson took another drag and said, "Go ahead, Corporal."

"I'm not going to beat a dead horse but you know I'm not happy about everything."

"Wait a minute, Corporal. Did you bring me out here to preach about the same shit? I don't have time for this, bro, I really don't," Tomlinson said, irritated, flicking the cigarette butt over the railing.

"Hold on, hold on," Sebastian said urgently.

"Corporal, I'm willing to help you find your family, but I don't want to go through another lecture about what we're doing. You know how I feel. If you don't like it, then leave."

"That's what I'm going to do."

"Seriously?"

"Yes, as soon as we hit the beach, I'm gone. I brought you out here to ask if you wanted to go with me."

Tomlinson did not respond. He stood with his arms crossed and thought.

"I know you don't agree with everything I've said before, but I don't want to keep doing this. Once I find my brother, I'm not coming back. I wanted to know if you wanted to go with me and leave all this shit behind."

"I don't know, man, I really don't know," Tomlinson finally responded.

"I know this may not be an easy decision for you, but I could use you. You're a great Marine and a great sniper and I want you to come with me."

"Are you so pissed about what's happened that you want to bail? We have a good thing here."

"No, we don't. The entire world is turned upside down, we've spent the past few weeks doing things that go against the code of conduct we swore to uphold, we have committed treason, we have killed Americans, for God's sake we have waged war against other Americans!" Sebastian said, raising his voice.

"We have done what we needed to do!" Tomlinson yelled back.

"Well, this isn't what I signed up for!"

"Corporal, I think you're making a mistake. Plus, you won't have anything but a rifle, some water, and a few rations."

"Not true—that's where I need your help. I'm taking a Hummer along with as much food, water, and ammo I can get."

"So you're going to steal from us?" Tomlinson barked.

"I'm sorry you feel that way, but the colonel's actions are wrong."

"Wrong? You're hilarious."

"You can think what you want."

"Whatever, man, I don't give a shit what you do. But I am staying right here," Tomlinson said, pointing toward the deck.

"Well, I do give a shit!" said a gruff voice from the darkness.

Sebastian and Tomlinson turned quickly to see who was talking, but it was too dark. Sebastian felt fear enter his body, as he had said things that he wanted no one else to hear. The sound of footsteps grew louder but the darkness still hid the identity until he spoke again.

"Corporal Van Zandt, you want to abandon your position as a trusted Scout Sniper with our platoon because you don't agree with how things have gone. You came to me the day we heard about the attacks and complained about our initial mission. Our commanding officer put it all on the line by turning these ships around and heading them in the direction you told me you wanted to go," the voice said.

Sebastian now knew who it was. Gunny Smith stepped right in front of Sebastian, so close that Sebastian could smell the smoke on his breath.

"You think you can just leave with precious equipment and resources? Well, Corporal, I can tell you that's not going to happen," Gunny said defiantly.

"Gunny, let me explain," Sebastian said desperately.

"No more explaining. In fact, no more talking from you, Corporal. I heard your entire conversation with Lance Corporal Tomlinson. Apparently he's also tired of hearing you talk. Here's what's going to happen, Corporal: You're not going anywhere; as of this minute you're under arrest," Gunny said. Then, out of the darkness two figures came forward, each grabbing one of Sebastian's arms. Sebastian attempted to struggle but he soon stopped, knowing the futility of it all. Even if he broke free, where would he go? Defeated, Sebastian dropped his head.

"Men, take him to the brig. I'll be down shortly," Gunny ordered. Just as they were walking him away Gunny stopped them. "Corporal Van Zandt, I knew your brother and you're not him."

Sebastian didn't have the physical or emotional strength to even respond.

"Take him below," Gunny commanded.

Both men escorted Sebastian from the deck and into an unknown fate.

San Diego, California

Gordon's eyes hurt when he opened them. Finding it hard to focus, he rubbed his eyes. Trying to focus again, he could make out the ceiling in his bedroom. The sharp pain on his left side prohibited his movement initially, but he forced himself to roll over on his right side. The sun was coming through the slits in the plantation shutters. He wasn't sure what time or what day it was. Managing the pain, he pushed himself up into a sitting position on the bed. Glancing down he looked at the bandages.

"Damn, I look like a mummy," he grunted.

His left shoulder, arm, and side were bandaged, and by the looks of them they were fresh. Everything looked normal around the room. He knew he had been out but wasn't sure for how long. The memories he had after the firefight were cloudy and gave no time frame. Anxious to find Samantha he slid off the bed and stood on his feet. He felt the pain but it was manageable. Taking a few steps, he felt how stiff and sore his body was. He paused and began to walk toward the door when it opened. Samantha stood there with folded clothes and a joyful expression on her face at seeing Gordon awake.

"Gordon! You're awake!" she said happily, walking over to him. She put her arms around him and hugged him.

"Hi, sweetie," Gordon responded. He hugged her with only his right arm.

"Honey, you need to keep resting, please get back into bed. Where were you going?" Samantha asked, looking at him with concern. She gently pushed him back toward the bed.

"I'm hungry," he said, resting back against the pillows.

"How do you feel?" she said, touching his forehead.

"Sore, and my wounds are painful," he said, reaching over and grabbing her arm. "What happened? What day is it?"

Samantha sat on the bed next to him and took his hand. "Gordon, there's a lot to tell. You were rescued by a couple of Marines who were on patrol."

"Really? What happened?"

"They heard the gunfire and were close by so they came and helped out. They found you lying on the road and brought you home along with Jimmy."

"Jimmy's okay?"

"Yes, he's fine. He's been quite busy since you've been out."

"What day is it?" Gordon asked curiously.

"It's January third."

"What? Are you serious? I've been out for over two weeks?"

"Honey, don't get excited. You still need to rest. You lost a lot of blood. But it was the infection and high fever that had us concerned. You have been in and out of consciousness since the incident. Today is the first day you're awake and talking coherently."

Gordon calmed himself down and asked, "How are the kids?"

"They're great, they've been praying for you several times a day. Every day they come in and hold your hand. They've been so sweet and, I have to say, supportive."

"We have great kids, don't we?" Gordon stated, smiling at Samantha.

"Yes, we do. That's because they take after me," Samantha said with a wink.

Gordon held her hand tighter and said, "I love you, baby."

"I love you too. I'm so happy you're okay. I was scared there for a bit. Nelson did a great job and took such good care of you."

"So, what happened with everyone else? That day is foggy for me."

Samantha looked down for a second before she responded. "Jerrod was killed and Eric is missing still."

"Shit, really? How's Melissa?"

"She's not doing well at all. I've been trying to help out as much as I can but she's a wreck."

"Has Jimmy sent out search parties for him?"

The look on Samantha's face changed dramatically with Gordon's last question.

"What is it?" Gordon asked, concerned.

Samantha would not respond; she kept looking down.

"Sam, what's wrong?"

"No search parties have been sent out," she said, still looking down.

"Why? What's going on?" Gordon asked. He was beginning to get frustrated. "Sam, talk to me, tell me."

"Right after the incident Jimmy attempted to get a party to go out for Eric, but he was stopped by Dan."

"What?"

"Mindy and the board appointed Dan as the head of the security forces. Jimmy objected and he was removed from the teams all together."

"Goddamn it!" Gordon said loudly.

"Gordon, it's gotten really bad. It didn't take them a day to take over and change everything you had started. The food shipments are nothing now, they mostly come back empty. There has been fighting between neighbors over food. Mindy and the board are now saying they want everyone to open their homes for inspection to see if anyone is hoarding food. If they are, they want to take it and redistribute it."

Gordon sighed deeply and shook his head.

"I need to get up."

"Wait, there's more," Samantha said, stopping Gordon from getting out of the bed. "Quite a few families have left. A couple came back and told of a sickness that has hit people to the north."

"A sickness, like what?"

"The way they described it was that everyone they had encountered from south Orange County had burns on their arms and were losing their hair."

"Where did they encounter these people?"

"They came across them in Oceanside; they were heading south to get away from the sickness. As soon as they heard about a sickness to the north they turned around and came back."

Gordon sat quietly, thinking.

"What do you think it is?"

"Sounds like radiation sickness," Gordon responded flatly.

Hearing Gordon's response, Samantha gasped.

"Sam, we need to get out of here. I need to speak to Jimmy now." Gordon sucked up the pain and pivoted out of the bed and onto his feet.

"Gordon, you do need to rest, though."

"Samantha, we don't have time. Go find me some heavy duty pain meds and go get Jimmy."

Samantha knew that when Gordon was serious there was no saying no. She left the room promptly.

Gordon walked over to the window and looked out. He could see smoke coming from over the hillside about two miles south. He knew who that was. Their time attempting to survive in San Diego had finally come to an end. Knowing the road to Idaho would be challenging, it provided hope and a chance to continue. If they stayed in San Diego, they would perish.

Cheyenne Mountain, Colorado

Conner's day had been full of good and bad news. He had become accustomed to bad news, so when he received good news it made his day special. With a smile from ear to ear he could not wait to see Julia. His daily briefings always left him feeling helpless, but the news that Julia had shared with him earlier kept his spirits high. Knowing it was early for any accurate testing, Julia's belief that she was pregnant filled him with joy. One very positive thing that had happened out of the loss of their son and the catastrophe that had befallen the country was that he had grown closer to his wife. With his hectic schedule and time away as a career politician they had drifted apart and at times he wondered if their marriage would survive. Now he felt that his best friend, his wife, had become his closest confidant and soul mate. Trying times can work in two ways: They can drive people apart or they can bring them together. The love he was feeling for her resembled the love they shared in their first few years of marriage. He wasn't positive she was pregnant, but the hope buoyed him.

Stepping to the door of their quarters, he could hear music playing inside. He opened the door and what he saw took him back to his days in college. Julia was dancing around the room and singing loudly. When he first met Julia, he was drawn to her distinct feminine energy. That femininity had been lost over the years as their lives went in two different directions, mostly because of his intense schedule.

Finally noticing him standing there, she ran and jumped into his arms. He held her and walked into their bedroom while they kissed passionately. They both dropped onto the bed and continued to kiss.

"I love you, Brad," she said after taking a pause from kissing.

"I love you too, Julia," he responded, with a softness in his voice.

"Sorry for the loud music," she said, caressing his face.

"Not a problem. I actually loved walking into the room and seeing you so happy."

"I feel like a little girl. I know we've been through a lot, but the chance of becoming a mother again makes me feel alive," she said with a glimmer in her eye.

"I know this might seem horrible to say, but your happiness makes all the bad things happening seem distant. Coming home to you gives me a break from the harsh realities of what's happened."

Holding his face in her hands, she responded, "I'm glad that you fully support this."

"Of course."

"So, tell me about your day. Any good news?"

"Why, yes, there was," he replied as he rolled onto his back. She laid her head on his chest and listened to his breathing. "We finally made a decision on the location of the new capital."

"That's definitely good news. So where will it be?"

"Without rehashing the issues of logistics, it came down to two choices, the first being Portland, Oregon, and the second San Francisco. After much discussion and analysis, we decided to go with Portland. It has everything we need. The port and airport are adequate and the population is manageable. San Francisco had positives but the concentration of people was too much. We know we will have some issues, but it's the best choice. If we didn't have the reactor meltdown problems we would have gone somewhere else."

"So what happens next?"

"We go out there. We, meaning a team of us, to go get things set up. That brings me to the bad news."

"Oh no, I know that tone, Mr. Conner," Julia said, raising her head and looking at him.

"I'm going to lead the team," he said.

"What? That's not your job. Send others to ensure it's safe," Julia said, concerned.

"Not this time; I need to go. I'm their leader, and I need to go see exactly what's happening out there."

"You're too important, what if something happens to you?" Julia said as she sat up, looking upset about the news. Her glow had gone and had been replaced by dread.

Conner understood her concerns, but the idea of him leading the team was his. He was tired of being pent up inside the mountain, plus he believed a true leader leads from the front. Brad also thought it would send a powerful statement that their government was real and they were doing something.

"Julia, I knew you were going to be upset, but you have to understand that things are different now. We have limited resources and personnel. I need to lead like leaders of the past and be on my horse leading the charge, not cowering in a bunker somewhere."

"I don't agree with you; you're too valuable to lose. Your country needs you safe, not running around like a cowboy on the frontier."

"I appreciate your concerns, but I'm going. I need to be out there. I need to see exactly what is happening. I will be safer than most; I'm not going alone. I'm taking a large entourage of security. I might be daring, but I'm not foolish."

"Brad, you're going to be a father again. I can't afford to lose you."

Conner paused before responding. He knew he needed to tread lightly.

"Sweetheart, I hear you, but this trip will not be long. I'm going out there to get things started, then I'll return. I'll be gone no more than two weeks."

"Brad, I think you're being foolish, but when did that ever stop you?"

"There's one more thing," he said sheepishly.

"What could be worse?"

"We leave tomorrow morning."

She just looked at him and then abruptly stood up and left the room. He followed her to attempt to console her, but she avoided him. He reached over and touched her arm.

"Don't touch me!"

"Julia, please," he pleaded.

Wanting refuge from him, she went into the bathroom and locked the door.

"Julia, come out, please," he said after he knocked softly on the door.

"Leave me alone."

"Please, open up."

"Brad, leave me alone. I need time to think about this."

He leaned on the door, hating that the past couple of weeks of bliss had been wiped away. Her crying brought doubt to his most recent decision. The sacrifice of being president was becoming something he didn't want anymore. If he could change it, he would. But fate doesn't work that way and he had a responsibility. Backing away from the door, he went to his closet, grabbed a bag, and started packing for his trip.

San Diego, California

"Gordon, what the hell are you doing here?" Jimmy asked, surprised to see his friend up and about.

"We need to pack up and get out of here," Gordon said, walking into Jimmy's house.

"What's up, man?" Jimmy asked, surprised. He hadn't seen Gordon awake for weeks, and here he was now telling him they had to leave.

"Samantha told me about what happened with Mindy and Dan.

I know that any day now they'll come for our food and resources. We have the issue with those Villistas and now I think we have another huge problem with some type of radiation exposure north of here."

"Radiation? Where? Gordon, slow down," Jimmy said, reaching out and patting Gordon on the arm.

Looking irritated and tired, Gordon snapped back, "I don't have time to slow down. It will take us a couple of days to get squared away before we can leave. We don't have the luxury of slowing down! I need you to trust me! We need to act fast!"

"Okay, okay," Jimmy said, putting his hands up.

Gordon quickly explained to Jimmy his plan of driving to Idaho. After years of knowing Gordon, Jimmy had learned not to interrupt Gordon when he focused like this.

Gordon's plan called for them to leave in two days with whoever wanted to come, albeit they had their own supplies and vehicles. The route involved traveling off the main freeways by taking older state highways and surface roads. Avoiding major cities and heavily populated areas was important.

"How are we doing for vehicles?" Gordon asked.

"You still have that truck you took from the man you shot at the hospital, and Nelson still has his vehicle. Mine was blown up."

"What about trailers?"

"I have the camper we can tow and besides that we have the horse trailer we can use, especially since the horses are gone."

"What happened to the horses?" Gordon asked, although he had his suspicions as to what might have happened to them.

"They were killed and eaten about a week ago."

"Well, the trailer will come in handy. Who else do you think will want to come?"

Jimmy gave his opinion on who he thought might want to join their convoy to the north. They discussed the merits of each person or family to determine if they would be a good fit.

"Your idea of who can go and not is kinda harsh!" Jimmy exclaimed.

"What's wrong with it?" Gordon asked.

"The way you put it, sounds like no one can go except for us. Your criteria even excludes Melissa and her baby."

"If Melissa wants to go, I'll take her, but that's it. Everyone needs to have their own vehicle and food. We don't have enough of our own supplies to go around and feed a large convoy of people."

"I hear what you're saying, but there are some good people here who don't have what you deem necessary but would be an asset."

"I don't care, Jimmy; they're not coming unless they have the supplies to take care of themselves," Gordon said sternly.

"You're jaded. You have always been a bit rough around the edges; I suppose that came from the war."

"You keep bringing that up. Let me explain to you why I'm not here to take care of everyone. I was once idealistic and believed in taking care of everyone who couldn't take care of themselves. I took this blind idealism with me when I dropped out of college and joined the Marine Corps after Nine Eleven. I thought it was my generation's calling to support this country and to promote freedom. I left everything behind and went to war. I did the best I could over there and the thanks I received from many in this country was ridicule and hatred. I was used as a political pawn after an incident in Fallujah by those who looked down on me. I was over there risking my life to bring freedom to a people who don't understand it and now hate us. I risked my life to protect the freedoms that many take for granted here. I ended up being the poster child for everything wrong with our war in Iraq. I was headline news when they accused me of murder, but when I was acquitted that never made the news. So, yes, I am jaded! I don't believe that it's my responsibility to help everyone anymore. I only have the moral responsibility to take care of my family and loved ones. I have lived a life believing that it's a man's responsibility to have the tools to ensure his family is safe and secure. Some men didn't think that was necessary; they thought owning dozens of expensive watches and designer jeans was more important than having a gun or even a damn knife. If people didn't take the time to prepare because they thought that was someone else's responsibility, well, my friend, they can now figure it out. I don't have the time nor do I care. It's already hard enough for us to survive without having to sacrifice my resources for others," Gordon exclaimed, his face flush.

Jimmy just stood there looking at him, not knowing how to respond. He knew he had struck a nerve with Gordon and didn't want to get him further upset.

"Hey, I didn't mean to get you upset. We've all had a lot to deal with, some more than others. Let's get working on this plan, okay?"

Gordon wanted to get moving, so he nodded and said, "Okay, let's get this done and get out of here."

JANUARY 4, 2015

• • •

If you are not prepared to use force to defend civilization, then be prepared to accept barbarism.

—Thomas Sowell

USS *Makin Island*, Pacific Ocean

Barone had called an emergency meeting with all of his commanders to discuss the landing in California. The ships were close, and based upon the intelligence from their reconnaissance forces he had a better idea about how the entire operation should proceed.

He had not been himself since his son's death. What little sense of humor and kindness he had was now shut down. He had become hard and unforgiving. He poured himself into ensuring nothing else could go wrong. He became hyper-focused on getting his men to California. The preparations for the landing consumed most of his waking hours. The only other thing that frequented his thoughts was how he would tell his wife about Billy's death. He dreaded that future date when he would stand in front of her. The promise he had made to her years ago was now broken. He had promised that he would do what he could to ensure Billy was always safe. While it was an unrealistic promise, he had made it. It was the reality of his death that made the promise feel truly broken. Billy had been under his command, so he could have prevented it. The guilt he felt ran deep inside him, and what came out of him wasn't depression anymore but anger. He was angry at himself for not monitoring the flight plan more carefully and he was angry that the battle between them and the USS *New Orleans* even had to take place.

The vibe and feel on the ship had changed; everyone was careful about what they said and no one made any mistakes. The word given to them from their unit commanders was that the colonel would not accept mediocrity. If any Marines or sailors wished to change their minds, then they would be arrested and locked up. No more excuses, no more complaining, each and every Marine and sailor had a job to do and it was expected they do it.

As unit commanders walked into the briefing room, Barone looked at each one. No one said a word to one another; very few looked directly at Barone. There was no small talk. Everyone took a seat quickly in the small room. The seats were set in a series of six rows all facing forward toward a map and screen.

Barone looked down at his watch and then looked at the men assembled before him. By his count, all were present.

"Gentlemen, I called this emergency briefing to cover our plan for landing in California. We have had reconnaissance teams going into Southern California for three days now. The intel they have brought back has given critical information for us to draft the plan I am about to detail. However, before I go into this plan, I want to set rules for this briefing. I will not take questions as I go. Once I have explained everything I will then open the floor for any questions you may have. Is that understood?"

In a chorus, all the men responded by saying, "Yes, sir."

"Great. Let me start by covering the ground truth of what is happening in Southern California. Our teams went to these locations." Barone turned around and pointed to a map that showed Southern California. "Coronado, Thirty-second Street Naval Base, Point Loma, and Camp Pendleton. They reached them safely. They were able to make liaison with the base commanders except for Camp Pendleton. I'm not going to break down what each base commander told us but will jumble it all together as a lot of the information is similar. They report that all electronics were down, no vehicles except older vehicles were operating, aircraft, ships, and the entire power grid are down. Each commander has been feeding their personnel on stockpiled MREs after they had consumed what food rations they had left in their specific mess halls. They also expressed that they have had trouble with some of their personnel going UA. They have been operating at a lockdown and not allowing civilians onto the base unless they were family members of personnel. They have been monitoring the situation on the outside and report that mass deaths are starting to occur from dehydration, starvation, and civil unrest. They have reported roving gangs taking advantage of the situation. The city has descended into chaos, gentlemen. There is no law enforcement and there are rumors that the mayor of San Diego has fled the city. They did tell us that they have been receiving communication from the U.S. government now headquartered in an undisclosed location via the SIPRNet, or in layman's terms the government's own secret Internet. The federal government has promised that they soon will be sending supplies, but to date they have received nothing. There are two pieces of confirmed intel that we received that changed our plans from what I had first detailed a few weeks ago. We will not be staying in Southern California. We will only be landing to go retrieve our families and can only stay for a week. After that, we must depart and head north. The reason for this change in plan is because the San Onofre nuclear plant is in full meltdown and radiation has contaminated an area about ten square miles. Most personnel at Camp Pendleton have evacuated and moved east to Twentynine Palms. Our teams there met with a few Marines who were remaining from the I MEF command element. The other situation we have is a former Mexican drug cartel that has moved into the area. They are expanding quickly across the county. According to reports from Coronado and the few elements left at Camp Pendleton, the cartel's numbers are growing and they are well armed. So here is what we are going to be doing: We will conduct an amphibious landing on the beaches of Camp Del Mar here. We will set up a presence at the camp and will operate out of there for a week's time. We will also conduct a simultaneous operation a day later on Coronado Island. There, those sailors who have families in and around San Diego can go get them. By now you have compiled a list of which Marines or sailors will be going onshore to find their families. We will set up a rotation so that everyone has a twenty-four-hour period to go locate and bring back those family members. We want them to bring back what resources they may have. Those resources are on the list that Simpson is handing out now. We will not be allowing personal possessions such as furniture, trinkets, et cetera. Understood?" Barone looked around and, seeing nods of assent, finished his briefing. "Gentlemen, this mission will be tough, as not all those looking for loved ones will find them. I fully expect to lose some people to possible fighting and to those who will decide to go UA and not return. I want a full count of your men now and upon departure a week later. Where we have openings, I will fill them with Marines and sailors who wish to join us from

Camp Pendleton and the other bases I mentioned earlier. I do understand that the amount of time we are now giving is not a lot, but with the realities on the ground, specifically from San Onofre, we cannot stay here. Those going ashore at Camp Del Mar will do so in full MOP gear. We will begin operations at zero-five-thirty January sixth. Please have those lists updated so we know who needs to go ashore. We do not want anyone going ashore who wants a joy ride; this is not a liberty port. Tell your men this is now hostile territory and to expect hostile contact. The ROEs for this mission are every Marine and sailor going ashore will have weapons and ammo, they will return fire if fired upon, and if they see an incident where they can defend innocents then they can engage the hostiles. Now I can take questions."

A dozen men sitting in front of Barone threw up their arms.

"Go ahead, Major," Barone said to an officer in the room.

Standing up, the major asked, "Colonel, you didn't mention the civilian population. We will be encountering them and they will look to us for food, water, et cetera. What do we do with them? What are the SOPs?" The major sat down after asking his question.

"Good question, Major. We will avoid the local civilian population; we cannot help them. We do not have the surplus resources to give them anything. Your mission, and it cannot deviate, is that we are here to secure those family members and bring them back. Just family members, not friends, not random people; I need you to make this clear to the men. Those caught bringing back stragglers will find the stragglers left adrift at sea, and they may join them if they wish to not follow orders," Barone said sternly. He then pointed to a captain in the back.

Standing up, the captain asked, "Can you cover in more detail the rules of engagement?"

"Captain, the ROEs for this mission are simple. Every Marine and sailor going ashore will have weapons and ammo, they will return fire if fired upon, and if they see an incident where they can defend innocents, then they can engage the hostiles. I do not want our men going out looking for a fight; we have a short window here and we must have them get to their families and return directly. I want to stress that this mission is to just go directly to residences or locations of their family members, pick them up, and come directly back. I do not want our troops out on a joy ride or fucking off. We don't have time for that."

One by one he went through and picked each and every officer and senior NCO who had their hand up. He would not let anyone leave this room until they were all clear about the mission ahead. He was now down to the last two Marines.

"Go ahead, Master Sergeant," Barone said, pointing toward the center of the room to a tall and bald older man.

"Colonel, what are we going to do with the prisoners? They are using up resources and there are a lot of them," the Master Sergeant said.

"Master Sergeant, let me just be blunt. Those Marines and sailors who are in the brig now will not be joining us after we depart. We are going to dump their asses on the beach with some MREs and water. We will provide them with the means to defend themselves because in the end they are still our brothers, but we will not be taking them with us. We will wish them well and that will be it. I think that answered your question."

The master sergeant nodded and said, "Yes, sir, it did. It was crystal clear."

Looking around the room there was one last hand raised and Barone called on him. "You there, Captain . . . Ah . . . Smiley,"

Barone said, hesitating then grinning when he read the captain's name.

"Thank you, Colonel. Where are we going after we depart San Diego?"

"Another good question. Captain, once we complete Operation Homestead we will be departing San Diego and heading north toward Oregon. We have spotted a good location to conduct an amphibious landing in Coos Bay. After we secure the beachhead we will march toward Salem, the capital, and take it."

Captain Smiley looked stunned when Barone finished what he said. He then asked, "Take it, sir?"

"Yes, Captain, take it. We will need a new place to call home. We will need a new country to start. We have the means, we have the resources, hell, Captain, we have an army! What we don't need are sniveling politicians telling us what they're going to do with what we have. We don't answer to them anymore; we only answer to ourselves. No longer will we be second-class citizens. We will go to Oregon to set up a new country where it's not the politicians or the celebrities who are at the top of the food chain. We will build a country where the warrior is appreciated and where the warrior class is above everyone else. There is plenty of land in Oregon, good land. This is where we will settle down. I chose Oregon because there are no nuclear plants within five hundred miles. The area is easily defended due to the mountains, there is plenty of wild game, and they have four seasons and get plenty of rain, so agriculturally we can be self-sufficient. This will be our new home, gentlemen, and we won't ask permission to come there. We will take what we need and not be sorry for it. We, all of us, have sacrificed a lot. Many of our brothers made the ultimate sacrifice and for what? For a country where half of the people don't even care for them or respect them? We are no longer sacrificing for a lazy people. Does that answer your question?" Barone finished, his face flush.

"Yes, sir," the captain said, starting to sit down. He stopped, stood straight up again, and asked another quick question. "Sir, what do we tell our men this new mission is called?"

"Rubicon, Operation Rubicon."

Cheyenne Mountain, Colorado

Conner stood staring at Julia sleeping; a range of emotions ran through him. Last night had finished better than it had started. She had finally given in and told him that she understood. Realizing that he had a tough job, she decided to support him. She made him promise that he wouldn't do anything foolish and he agreed that he wouldn't.

Before he tore his gaze away and left, he bent down and gave her one more kiss. Pressing his lips against her warm cheek, he held it there for a few seconds while taking a breath through his nose so he could capture and remember her smell. He gently touched her hair and whispered in her ear, "I love you, Julia." It took a lot of inner strength to pull away. While he had made her that promise, he really couldn't guarantee his safety. Standing at the door, he grabbed the knob but couldn't turn it. He turned around and looked at the room. He wanted to create a mental image of everything in there. The trip would take only two weeks, but not knowing what he would encounter he wanted to remember this moment.

• • •

An anxious curiosity gripped him as the gates first cracked open. The more they opened the more he became excited and nervous. He could see the deep blue mountain sky and the dark green of the trees. As the convoy slowly moved out into the warmth and comfort of the sun's rays, it also exposed the harsh realities of life on the surface.

The main gate was riddled with debris, garbage, and signs. By the looks of it, locals had gone to the base to find sanctuary, but obviously those requests were denied. What tore at Conner's heartstrings was seeing a small child's teddy bear lying among the debris and garbage. He wondered where that child might be and if he was safe. As their six-vehicle convoy of Humvees drove down the mountain, Conner sat thinking about that stuffed animal and the child who had once cherished it. He thought about all the people scattered across the country. How alone, desperate, disappointed, and scared they must feel.

The route to Peterson Air Force Base took them carefully across major roads; his security detail wanted to ensure they avoided residential areas. With starvation now taking hold of the civilian population, there was greater risk traveling across the residential surface streets.

As they carefully drove, weaving around abandoned cars and wandering people, Conner could see that the city itself looked dead. He saw no lights, no movement except for the occasional person looking up as they drove by quickly. Conner could see those weary people scavenging through abandoned vehicles; he noticed many of the storefronts had their windows smashed; the streets were covered with debris and garbage. There was an occasional car or truck driving, but the freeways were now a graveyard for most cars.

Seeing a large group to his right he thought it odd. Looking closer, he saw they were chasing two women. The mob was sizeable, about twenty-plus people. He knew the situation was grave and that they should do something about it. When his convoy passed he saw the mob finally close in and catch them.

"I need you to get off at the next exit and go back," he said, pointing back toward the mob of people.

"Sir, we are not to get off the highway for any reason. We must go directly to the base," the young Air Force tech sergeant said.

"I'm the president of the United States, get off now!" Conner yelled at the young man.

"Yes, sir," the tech sergeant replied, looking startled.

He veered quickly off the highway and away from convoy. It was mere seconds before the radio inside Conner's vehicle came alive.

"Sooner One, Sooner One, this is Sooner Command, over."

"What should I say, sir?" the tech sergeant asked.

"Turn right, then straight," Conner said, ignoring his driver and giving directions as best he could.

"Sooner One, this is Sooner Command vehicle, come in, over," the voice over the radio repeated.

"Sir?"

"Hand me the radio," Conner ordered.

Conner took the handset. "This is Conner. I ordered our vehicle off the highway. There are civilians that need our assistance."

"What is your location, Sooner One?"

"We are on Cody and Bradley heading south."

"Roger that, we are en route to provide support. Sooner Command, out."

Conner tossed the handset down and went back to directing the tech sergeant. "Somewhere over there!"

Too busy looking to see where they needed to go, he hadn't seen the corpse hung from a telephone pole at the entrance of the community. Before the attacks, this neighborhood was a haven for middle-class families; now it looked like a war zone.

"Turn there!" Conner yelled.

The tech sergeant turned to the right abruptly. The tires on his Hummer squealed under the stress of the turn. After making the turn, Conner could see the mob of people ahead. They were ripping and tearing at the two women on the ground.

"Do you have another gun, sergeant?" Conner asked.

"Yes, sir," the tech sergeant said, handing Conner an M-9 Beretta 9-millimeter pistol.

"Stop here," Conner ordered.

They stopped a comfortable thirty feet away from the crazed mob. Jumping out, Conner wasted no time; he held the pistol above his head and pulled the trigger. Seeing the mob rip and tear at the two was one thing, but when they stepped out of the Hummer the added dimension of hearing the women scream created a macabre scene.

The sound of the shot made everyone stop and turn around. The mob had been so focused on attacking and brutalizing the women they hadn't heard them pull up. With the mob silent and their attention now on Conner, the only sound was the moaning of the two women.

"Back away from them now!" Conner commanded, pointing the pistol at the mob.

No one moved; they just stared at Conner.

He shot again in the air and yelled, "Move away from them, now!"

Finally obeying his command, they slowly moved away from the women. Conner cautiously moved toward the two victims as the mob moved farther away. At first all he could see were two lifeless bodies on the ground. He could hear them moaning but saw no movement. With each step the reality of the women's fate came into focus. They were lying in a large pool of blood with their clothes stripped from them. A few more steps closer he could see that the bloodthirsty mob hadn't just beaten them; they had literally ripped them apart. One woman's arm was severed from her body. The other had her abdomen torn open and parts of her intestines were strewn over the both of them. Seeing this shocked Conner to the point he had to turn his gaze away. It took every ounce of control for him not to throw up.

Conner knew there was nothing he could do for these women. He reclaimed his composure and without hesitation walked over and mercifully shot each woman in the head. He took a moment to look at them. He wondered who they were. Just five weeks ago their lives were so different.

He turned his attention to the mob and yelled, "What is wrong with you?" No response came from them; they just stared at him. "Why would you do this?" he asked.

"They stole food," someone from the back of the group finally responded.

"They stole food? That was it, so you brutally beat them and tore them apart?" Conner screamed at them.

A shot cracked loudly behind him. Conner turned and saw the tech sergeant fall to the ground. Conner's initial shock was soon replaced with fear as he began to feel that he had made a big mistake by deviating from the plan to go play hero.

"Who are you to come here and so righteously condemn our laws!" a man said from a distance holding a hunting rifle. Working the bolt, he cleared an old casing and loaded a new bullet.

Conner squinted so he could see better. As the man came into focus, he saw what he was up against. The man was large in stature, bald, and there was something ominous about him. The man took long strides down the street toward him. Others armed with guns, bats, machetes, and various other weapons came out of the other homes. Conner saw movement in the corner of his eye and turned to look. The mob he had subdued now started to move toward him. Conner was in an impossible position and ran to his vehicle. His running prompted the mob to do the same as they rushed the vehicle. Making it just in time he was able to close and lock the door. He looked down to start the Hummer then realized he didn't know how to. The mob began to climb all over the vehicle. Fumbling at the controls, he was turning knobs and pushing buttons. Hummers were not like normal cars. There was no key or ignition switch on the steering column or anywhere on the console. Seeing a lever that said "On" to the left of the steering wheel, he turned it till a light appeared. The mob started to hit the vehicle with sticks, bats, and metal rods. Suddenly, in the chaos, he heard gunfire; the mob quickly leapt off the vehicle and ran. More automatic gunfire came as he saw many in the mob fall to the ground. The heaviness of the situation started to lift as he heard his convoy come to his rescue. He could not see what was happening, as the vehicle faced the wrong way. The battle outside sounded fierce, like things he'd only heard on television. Hundreds of bullets were being fired, but as the seconds ticked away the gunfire lessened till there was only silence. He sat there waiting and listening.

"You're an idiot, Brad. What were you thinking?" he said to himself.

Closing his eyes and lowering his head, he prayed that everything was going to be okay. Never again would he go on a fool's errand, he promised himself. It had taken him only thirty minutes to break the promise he had made to Julia. A knock on the window startled him.

Feeling relieved that he'd be on his way out of this sad situation, he started to speak as he looked up. "I really need to learn how to start one of—" He stopped talking as soon as his eyes gazed upon who was standing there. Covered in blood and sweat, the large bald man with the rifle stood towering over the window. Conner's reaction was of absolute fear; he jumped out of the driver's seat and crawled over to the passenger side door. A blast from the man's rifle blew off the driver's side door handle. The man threw open the door and stopped Conner's attempt to escape. The man grabbed his ankle and with brute force pulled him from the vehicle.

"I am the president of the United States, I am the president!" Conner yelled as he was dragged out of the vehicle and onto the ground. Dozens gathered around him like locusts. He knew his fate would be that of the two women. "Wait, I am the president of the United States!"

"Do you think that means anything here?" replied the bald man with a deep and raspy voice as he leveled his rifle at Conner's face and pulled the trigger.

San Diego, California

Gordon, Samantha, Nelson, and Nelson's parents, who had arrived while Gordon had been out, had been packing the truck and trailer since the night before. Wishing they could have more privacy was impossible. Under the watchful eye of every neighbor they loaded box after box of supplies, food, water, medicines, and gear. The next morning they would finally leave Rancho Valentino and head east to get as far away from major urban centers as possible. Knowing they could encounter "road agents" or bandits, they planned on traveling during the day.

They couldn't pack quickly enough; neighbors kept walking by and looking. The word had spread that they were leaving with Jimmy, Simone, and four other families: the Pomeroys, Thompsons, Behrenses, and Jerrod's wife and child. Gordon was also happy to have the two Marines, Sergeant Holloway and Lance Corporal Fowler, join their group. They had provided a lot of good information and had managed to secure two operational jeeps with trailers. Holloway also had a wife and little girl. One family notably missing was Eric's. They all had tried to convince Melissa to come, but she was staying. She believed Eric would return. The prospect of Eric returning was slim, as it had been a long time since his disappearance.

James, the elderly neighbor who lived a couple of doors down, kept watching them. Others would walk by, whisper to one another, and point. Gordon didn't like it and made his displeasure known by asking them rhetorically, "What are you looking at?"

Gordon was back inside the house loading a box of canned food when the door opened and Nelson rushed in.

"Gordon, come outside quick!"

Stopping what he was doing he followed Nelson out into the garage, where he ran into a sweating and exhausted Jimmy.

"Jimmy, you okay? What's up?" Gordon asked, concerned.

He put his finger up to indicate he needed a second to catch his breath, then managed to say, "Eric's back."

"What?"

"Damn, I thought losing a few pounds would make running easier. Yeah, he's back. Speaking of losing a few pounds, he lost some weight and he's tortured, but he's home."

"Nelson, sorry to leave you with this, but I want to go see Eric."

"No problem, you go. I got this," Nelson said, looking around at all the boxes in the garage.

Gordon started running toward Eric's house. His injuries prevented him from keeping a good pace and a heavy feeling started to creep up on him. Not wanting to overdo it, he slowed down to a quick walk. He thought back to the day of the attack. He had been out for a run that day. That was the last day the neighborhood looked manicured. Most of the houses now looked like something out of an impoverished third world country; the hanging tarps and clothes, the strong smell of feces, the dead plants and grass, cars covered in a thick layer of dust. The clean and manicured feel of the community was gone. It had turned from a cute, beautiful family neighborhood to an unkempt, worn survival camp. Houses were no longer homes, they were shelters.

Gordon arrived at Eric's house and banged on the door for what seemed like minutes. Melissa finally answered and didn't look happy to see him.

"Gordon, hi."

"Hi, Melissa; I just heard. Can I come in and see him?"

She didn't answer right away; she turned around and looked back into her house. Gordon could hear Eric say something, but he couldn't make it out.

"Yes, come on in. He's in the kitchen."

Gordon walked directly back to the kitchen. First seeing Eric was shocking. He had lost a lot of weight and his face and arms were covered in a mix of fresh and older wounds.

"Eric, I can't say how good it is to see you. I have to say when I woke up and heard you hadn't made it back, I feared the worst," Gordon said.

"It's good to see you too. I feared the worst too," Eric said slowly.

"Listen, I don't want to put pressure on you but I have to. We have to leave tomorrow. Everything has gone to shit here. It's too much to explain now, but we want you to go with us."

"Okay, we can do that," he said, looking at Gordon with his sunken eyes.

"You can ride with us, we have a camper trailer. I need you to pack up everything that is useful. We're never coming back."

"Okay."

"Gordon, can we wait a day or two? He needs to rest and get back on his feet. Look at him," Melissa said, concerned for her husband. She walked over to Eric and put her arm around him.

"Melissa, we don't have time, we—" Gordon was saying when Eric interrupted him.

"Mel, he's right, we have to leave. Gordon, I have some bad news. It's a big problem. The guys who attacked us, well, they captured me. I managed to escape a few days ago but had to live in the shadows to make it home." Eric paused to take a drink of water and a breath. "Gordon, they know about our community and plan on coming here for our resources soon. I overheard someone when I was there. I think he's their leader; his name is Pablo. They weren't happy about that day. They lost a lot of people."

"How do they know where we are?" Gordon asked.

Eric looked at Gordon again with those dark sunken eyes.

"You don't have to say anything. Really, don't worry about it," Gordon said, anticipating Eric's answer.

"It wasn't me, Gordon, it was Dan. I overheard them talking about capturing Dan weeks ago. He apparently spilled the beans and promised to take them to us because we had stockpiled tons of food and water."

"So that son of a bitch led us into an ambush. He wanted us out of the way to make way for them." Gordon grew angry.

"Gordon, you're right; we need to leave as fast as we can," Eric said as he reached over and grabbed Gordon's arm. "We have to go; they're coming and they have an army of people."

"Melissa, please start packing all food, water, medicines, batteries, gear, equipment, et cetera that we will need," Gordon said in a commanding voice to Melissa. He then looked at Eric and said, "I'm taking everyone to Idaho. We have a place there, we can live off the land and start over."

Eric just nodded.

"We leave at seven a.m. tomorrow. If you need any help packing, let me know. We'll be over in a few hours to pick up your stuff."

"Okay, Gordon, we'll be ready," Melissa said.

• • •

Gordon's day would be full of surprises. When he turned the corner onto his street he saw that the small crowd of people outside gawking had grown into a large unruly crowd. Nelson was standing his ground with a shotgun trained on them. As he got closer, he saw Dan and Mindy at the front of the crowd.

Gordon reached the crowd and pushed his way through till he reached Dan, who was yelling at Nelson. Grabbing Dan's shoulder he pivoted him and struck him in the face. For Gordon, the look on Dan's face was priceless. Dan fell to the ground with Gordon following by jumping on him. Gasps came from the crowd as they backed away from the two men fighting. Seeing what had happened, Mindy started yelling. Gordon heard her but chose to ignore her. He gave all of his attention and rage to Dan. After a series of punches Gordon saw blood. This encouraged him to hit more. Feeling his own wounds reminded him that Dan was the cause. The street justice he was serving to Dan made his pain worth it. Finally, a few in the crowd took action and grabbed Gordon. Resisting vigorously he kept swinging but eventually his resistance was not enough. It took four men to pull Gordon off of Dan, who lay on the sidewalk covered in his own blood. Gordon took pleasure knowing he had broken Dan's nose, which lay flat against his face.

"You son of a bitch!" Dan said, shaking his head back and forth.

"Fuck you, you're lucky. If these people hadn't stopped me I would have killed you! You fucking piece of shit!" Gordon yelled back.

"You son of a bitch, I will get you! I promise I will get you!" Dan yelled, slowly sitting up. He brought his hand to his face to touch his broken nose.

"You won't be doing anything. I am leaving with my family and others; we're done here. You wanted this community, you can have it," Gordon screamed, still struggling to break free from those who had grabbed him.

"You can leave, Gordon, but not until you give us what you stole," Mindy said.

Gordon turned and looked at her. "What are you talking about?"

"All the food and medical supplies you have stockpiled are not yours; they belong to the community. We intend on taking them so we can redistribute to your neighbors."

"You're not taking shit, Mindy. This is my food. I got all of this before any of this happened."

"That's not true!" yelled James from the middle of the crowd.

Everyone turned and looked at James.

"I was here the day of the attack and saw you and your friend come back and forth with food; hell, I even saw you the day after unloading stuff," James said loudly.

James's comments brought on lots of side conversations with many in the group.

"I got some of this food the day of the attacks and even more the morning after, plus I always kept a decent pantry full of food before the attacks. I can tell you that none of it came from our scavenger missions. Whatever you all are thinking is wrong. You have been misguided by Mindy and Dan," Gordon cried out in his defense.

"Gordon, we believe you came by this food illegally and kept it when it should have been disclosed and shared with the rest of us," Mindy shouted at Gordon.

"I don't give a shit what you think, Mindy, you're not taking anything." Gordon finally shrugged off the last person holding him and stood facing the crowd and Mindy. "James is right that I went out the day of the attack and found food. I was smart, I thought ahead. I didn't stand around like most of you, attempting to get your stupid phones to work and complain that you were missing the next *American Idol*. I knew something was wrong and I went out to take care of my family. It's not my responsibility to take care of you, you, or you!" Gordon said pointing at Mindy and others in the crowd. "If you didn't think and react appropriately, that's not my fault. Mindy, you can talk a big game, but you're not taking anything from me or my friends, period!"

"Well, Gordon, I disagree; you're not leaving nor are your friends till you give us our share of the food you have taken," Mindy said defiantly. "We have met with many in the neighborhood and we have their support. Everyone must open their homes for inspection. Anyone who has more than they need will have that taken and spread out." Mindy was not just talking to Gordon; she had turned around and was speaking to the crowd, which continued to grow larger.

"You will not enter this house or any of my friends' homes. This is my food; I secured it before we came together as a community. If you plan on taking it, then you better bring an army."

Mindy turned around and walked up to within a few feet of Gordon. "Gordon, you and your friends will not be allowed to leave through any of these gates till you have surrendered the food you took from us all. I mean what I say, so please be here, ready to open your house for us to inspect, and yes, we will have an army; look around me," Mindy said, staring at Gordon intently and holding up her arms to acknowledge the large crowd behind her.

"If you or any of you out there plan on coming into my house, plan on dying!" Gordon yelled out to the crowd.

Mindy began instructing the crowd to back off. She announced that the situation with Gordon would be handled in the morning. Slowly, one by one or in small groups, the crowd dispersed. Dan was helped up and walked off without saying a word.

Gordon watched and turned to look at Nelson, who still held the shotgun.

"Are you ready for this?" Gordon asked Nelson.

With his typical shit-eating grin Nelson laid the shotgun barrel on his shoulder and said, "Son, I was born ready."

Cheyenne Mountain, Colorado

Sitting on her toilet, crying, Julia was expressing not tears of pain but joy. In her hands she held the physical proof that supported the feelings she had been having for a couple of days. She was pregnant. Overjoyed, she could not wait to speak to Brad. If only he were here, she thought; seeing the look on his face would have been special for her. Wiping the tears from her eyes she placed the testing strip carefully on the counter. Washing her hands, she looked down at the "positive" sign on the strip to make sure she wasn't mistaken. It all didn't seem real in some way. Looking in the mirror, she saw a different Julia; she saw a youthful woman who would soon bless the world with a new baby. Her mind had already started the process of nesting as she went through everything she would have to do for the pregnancy. Then thoughts of what they would name the new baby came to mind too. There was so much to plan, she thought.

Leaving the bathroom, she heard a knock at the front door.

Dylan was at the door. She was not expecting him but didn't take notice of the somberness in his face.

"Hi, Dylan, how are you?" she asked. "Come on in." She turned around and walked back into the room. Walking into the kitchen, she asked, "Can I get you anything?"

"No, thank you, ma'am," Dylan replied, stepping into the room and not moving far from the door after he had closed it behind him.

"Mrs. Conner, can I speak with you?"

"Sure, one second," Julia said as she grabbed a glass of water and walked back into the living room. She was startled when she finally noticed the look on Dylan's face. "Dylan, is everything okay?"

"Mrs. Conner, I am sorry, but can you sit down?" Dylan asked, pointing to the couch.

"Dylan, what is it?" she asked, the joy of moments ago now gone.

"Please sit down, Mrs. Conner," he said, this time not asking but making a point about it.

"Dylan, I'm old enough to know that when someone says to 'please sit down,' it's not good news."

"Mrs. Conner, I am sorry to be the one and believe me, I don't want to be here."

"Just spit it out, Dylan!" she said as tears began to well up in her eyes.

"Ma'am, about forty-five minutes ago the president and his convoy went off course on their way to the air base. They diverted to address an urgent situation when they came under attack. When we received word of the attack, we immediately dispatched reinforcements."

"Is Brad alive?" she asked, her voice trembling.

"Ma'am, when the reinforcements arrived . . ."

She stopped him again and asked, "Is Brad alive or not?"

"Ma'am, when they arrived . . ."

"Answer the damn question, Dylan!" she yelled at him.

"We don't know, Mrs. Conner."

"What do you mean you don't know? How can you not know?" Her entire body was now trembling. She braced herself against a table.

"When the reinforcements arrived they found all of the convoy dead, and the president was not located. We believe this to be a good sign that he may be alive, but we do not know for sure."

Julia's body became weak, and she fell to her knees next to the couch. Dylan rushed to help her up.

"Please rest, I'll go get a doctor."

Julia stopped Dylan by grabbing his arm. She pulled him close and said, "I don't need a doctor, I need my husband. Go find him, do what you have to do. I don't want to hear from you until you find him, do you understand me?" She let go of Dylan's arm and her body gave way as she fell into the couch.

Looking down at her he declared, "Mrs. Conner, I will find him; I promise you. I will do what I can."

She didn't look at him or respond. She just lay on the couch and sobbed uncontrollably. Dylan stared at her for another moment before he turned and left the room. When he closed the door he heard her wail in grief. A tear came to his eye, but he quickly swept it away and briskly walked down the dimly lit hallway toward the command center and his new mission.

JANUARY 5, 2015

• • •

This is not the end. It is not even the beginning of the end. But it is, perhaps, the end of the beginning.

—Winston Churchill

San Diego, California

Tossing and turning in his sleep, Gordon's dreams had taken him back to his final tour in Iraq. He was reliving the brutal horrors of war. He couldn't escape the bodies no matter how fast he ran. Each time he took sanctuary in a bullet-ridden building he would find more bodies. Bullets were raining down on him, but he was not getting hit. The cries, he heard cries. These were the cries of a baby. With every door he opened, the cries would grow louder but he was never closer to finding the baby, just more bodies. In the distance, he heard his name being called out "Gordon, Gordon!" The cries soon morphed into sounds of a different kind of gunfire. The sound of his name being called grew louder and louder.

"Gordon, Gordon!" Nelson yelled, coming into Gordon's bedroom.

Gordon sat up sweating from the dream. The room was pitch-black.

"Gordon, Gordon, wake up!" Nelson yelled urgently.

Gordon looked over in the direction of Nelson's voice, then he heard the crack of gunfire through the window. Grabbing his rifle, which lay next to him, he sprang out of bed and past Nelson.

"Gather the family and have them stay in the master bedroom. I'm going to find out what's going on."

"Are you sure you don't need me?" Nelson asked, following Gordon down the stairs.

"I'm sorry I keep leaving you at home, but there isn't anyone else I would trust with my family's safety."

Holloway and his family had spent the night at Gordon's house. He came out of a lower bedroom with his rifle and asked, "What's going on?"

"I don't know, but come with me," Gordon said.

Gordon took note that the gunfire was coming from the vicinity of Jimmy's and Eric's houses. Grabbing a handful of loaded magazines for his rifle and pistol, he opened the front door to leave.

"No one comes into this house unless you properly identify them, got it?" Gordon exclaimed.

"You got it, boss," Nelson acknowledged.

Before the door shut, Gordon was stopped by Samantha's voice. "What's going on? Gordon, what's going on?" She ran down the stairs and to the front door.

"I think that Mindy and Dan are attacking Jimmy or Eric."

"Don't you think you should stay here?"

"Nelson is here and so is his dad. I need to go help."

Reaching out to him, Samantha hugged Gordon tightly and kissed him. "Be safe, I love you."

• • •

His injuries were still slowing him down, but the pain was numbed by the medications and the adrenaline pumping through his veins. The gunfire grew louder with each step he and Holloway took. Rounding the street corner, he could faintly see the front of Jimmy's house thanks to the half moon in the sky. The garage door was fully open with shadowy figures running in and out. Gunfire erupted from the second floor, followed by screaming.

Not bothering to identify who was running away from Jimmy's house, he opened fire on them. His assumptions were if you were running away then you must be a bad guy. Holloway followed suit and was also engaging those in the street ahead of them.

Gordon made a mental note that they had shot four people before they began to move on Jimmy's house. Screams still echoed out of the second floor of the house.

"Cover me, I'm going in," Gordon commanded.

"Roger that," Holloway replied, taking a knee and scanning the street.

He was not able to take five steps before gunfire rained down on him, followed by a familiar stinging pain in his upper left arm.

"Are you fucking kidding me?" he cried out in pain.

Holloway took aim and engaged whoever had fired the shot. The sparsely lit night made it almost impossible to identify and know if you had hit someone.

"You okay?" Holloway asked Gordon.

"Yeah, I just can't stop getting fucking shot!"

Feeling that the wound was only a graze, he kept moving toward the open garage door. Loose debris and boxes littered the sidewalk leading up to the garage. Entering the garage, he stepped on someone. Whoever it was let out a grunt, then pleaded. "Help me please," he whispered in pain.

Gordon pulled his light out and flashed it in the man's face. It was Gerald, Mindy's husband.

"Please help me," Gerald pleaded.

Not showing mercy, Gordon leveled his rifle at Gerald's face and pulled the trigger.

Flashing the light around the garage he saw that Mindy and her people had ransacked Jimmy's supplies. How they gained access was not important; they had been successful. Jimmy did defend his house, as was evident by Gerald and another lifeless body near the door to the house. Panning quickly over the garage, Gordon also saw the small pit bull that Jimmy had rescued lying dead in a pool of blood.

The screams were still coming from the second floor. It sounded like Simone. Gordon couldn't stall any longer; he needed to make it to Simone as soon as he could. A loud crash came from the doorway to the house. Two men appeared out of the darkness and into the garage. Not wasting time, Gordon pointed his rifle and let the semi-auto do its job. Both men fell to the ground with a thud. Moving with purpose, Gordon stepped over them and into the house. What little light he had outside was now gone. The house was totally dark. Gordon took two steps and tripped over what felt like another body. When he tried to get up, he slipped and fell down again. The tile floor was covered in blood, making it extremely slippery, and with zero light he didn't know where to step.

After he fell the second time, someone shot at him from inside the house. The bullets hit the hallway wall above him. If it hadn't been for him falling down, he would have been hit. Gordon sprayed bullets into the part of the room where he'd seen a muzzle flash. The only sound that followed was a loud crash of what sounded like a body falling over.

Sweat was pouring off of Gordon's brow and his new wound stung. Simone's wailing continued; the stairs seemed like a million miles away, with someone shooting at him every few steps he took. Not knowing what he would be walking into, he stood up and made his way into the living room. Reaching out with his left arm, he felt the wall and followed it to the bottom of the stairs. Gordon took the brief moment at the base of the stairs to transition to his pistol. He slung the rifle and pulled out his Sig 240. The stairs went up halfway, then hit a landing. There he'd have to turn left and go up the remaining set of stairs to the top. With his pistol out in front of him, he began his march upstairs.

Reaching the landing without incident he called out, "Simone, it's Gordon!"

"Gordon, hurry quickly, it's Jimmy—he's been shot. Please hurry."

Gordon raced up the remaining stairs and toward Simone, who was kneeling with Jimmy in her arms. They both were bathed in the light of a lantern. He re-holstered his pistol and began to examine a blood-covered Jimmy.

"Simone, where's he shot?"

"They shot him in the chest; those bastards came in and shot him in the chest," Simone cried.

"Let me see, Simone," Gordon said softly to her. He handed her the flashlight so he could see.

Gordon reached out to Jimmy and took him out of her arms and laid him on the floor. The motion caused Jimmy to moan and cough. Gordon ripped open Jimmy's blood-soaked shirt and saw something he had not seen since his time in Iraq. Jimmy had a small-diameter hole in the center of his chest that sputtered blood with every breath that he took.

"Simone, go get me some clean towels, something to wipe up the blood."

"Simone, don't go," Jimmy said. As he spoke he coughed up blood.

"What, baby? I'm not going anywhere," Simone said, crying.

"Simone, please go," Gordon pleaded.

"No, Gordon, please have her stay," Jimmy said with difficulty.

Gordon looked at Jimmy. His friend's face was pale from the loss of blood. Knowing the wound was bad, he couldn't give up on his friend.

"Please, Simone, I can help, but I need to get something to clean this up," Gordon said, looking at Simone.

Simone kept her attention on Jimmy, who coughed up blood again.

"Gordon, just sit here with me please," Jimmy said with almost a whisper.

Simone pulled Jimmy into her lap as she cried aloud, "No! No, God, please!"

Jimmy reached out and took Gordon's hand and held it with as much strength as he could muster.

"G, you've been a good friend to me and my family. You've always been there for us and I hope you feel the same way," Jimmy said with ever-increasing difficulty. Gordon could hear the blood bubbling in his chest as he breathed.

Knowing that this was it for his friend, Gordon said, "I feel the same way. You're a good man and good friend."

"Take care of Simone for me," Jimmy said, looking over at Simone.

"Baby, please don't leave me, please," Simone cried.

Jimmy's grip on Gordon's hand grew weaker; Gordon knew the time was getting close.

"G, come close, I need to tell you something." Jimmy's voice had become very faint. Leaning over he placed his face next to Jimmy's. "There's a hiding place behind the water heater. Look for the wooden box." Jimmy coughed and finished his time with Gordon by saying, "Now go, let me have a moment."

Gordon honored his friend's wish and left. Simone was crying uncontrollably; she held on to Jimmy and just cried. Gordon took each step down the stairs with heavy sorrow at the loss of his friend.

When he reached the last step, Simone screamed out, "No, oh my God, no!" Gordon knew Jimmy was dead. A cascade of emotions ran through him. Sitting on the last step, he put his head in his hands and grieved. Gordon's grief would be short-lived, as the night's action still was not over. The faint sound of gunfire in the distance penetrated the walls of the house.

"Gordon, something's going on; it sounds like it's near your house!" Holloway yelled from outside the house.

Gordon was running on pure adrenaline now. His left side was aching as the pain meds were wearing off. The gunfire was short lived; no screaming or other noise could be heard except his and Holloway's heavy breathing. Reaching the front of his house, Gordon and Holloway ran up on a body lying outside of his front door. Pulling out his flashlight, Holloway flashed the light on the body. To Gordon's surprise, it was Dan, and he was still alive.

Gordon grabbed the light out of Holloway's hands and pointed it directly in Dan's face. "What are you doing here?"

Dan's eyes expressed the fear that gripped him. Knowing that Gordon was hovering above him, he knew that he was close to death's door.

Gordon examined his body and flashed the light across it. It appeared that Dan had suffered a single shot from a shotgun to the chest.

"What do we do with him?" Holloway asked.

"Nothing, let him bleed out," Gordon said, handing the flashlight back to Holloway, then proceeding to the front door. Banging on it he called out, "Open up, it's Gordon. We're all clear out here!"

Moments later the door opened and Gordon was greeted by Nelson.

"Get your ass in here," Nelson said.

Gordon and Holloway stepped inside and closed the door.

"Is everyone okay?" Gordon asked, concerned.

"We're fine. Dan and about a dozen of his cronies attempted to get in. My ol' man and me greeted them with Mr. Remington and Mr. Glock," Nelson said, holding up his Remington 870 shotgun.

"Where's Samantha and the kids?"

"Here, Gordon," Samantha said from the top of the stairs.

Gordon ran up the stairs and into Samantha's arms. Haley was standing next to Samantha crying. He reached down, grabbed her, and pulled her close.

"You all right?" Gordon asked.

"As good as we can be, considering."

Then Gordon noticed Hunter wasn't there. "Where's Hunter?"

"He's in his room," Samantha answered.

"Is he okay? I want to see him."

"Gordon, he's having a tough time dealing with what just happened," Samantha said, holding Gordon back from going to Hunter.

"What do you mean?"

"Nelson and his father were at the back of the house in the patio stopping some of them from coming in when the front door was kicked open and—"

"And what?"

"I tried to stop him, but Hunter ran downstairs to help Nelson. I told him not to go but he took off. When the front door was kicked open he stopped them."

"Who stopped them? You're confusing me."

"He had run downstairs with your old double-barrel shotgun and when the door was kicked open he turned and shot."

"Hunter shot Dan?"

"I don't know who it was he shot, but I was coming after him when I saw it happen. I heard the door get kicked in and I saw Hunter turn around and then the gun went off. I'm sorry," Samantha said, still shaking from the incident.

Reaching over and touching Samantha's face gently he said, "Honey, you don't need to apologize; it's no one's fault but Dan and his horde's. Let me go to him."

As Gordon attempted to pull away, Samantha stopped him again and said, "Your arm, you're bleeding."

Gordon looked quickly at his bloody left arm. "It's just a flesh wound, no concern."

"What happened? How're Jimmy and Eric?"

Gordon paused for a moment, then answered, "Jimmy is dead. I was there with him just before. I don't know about Eric. I ran here as soon as I heard the shooting."

"How's Simone?"

"She's not good; we really should go back and check on her. Listen, let me go and check on Hunter, please," Gordon pleaded.

"Okay, go," Samantha said, releasing Gordon's arm.

He went to Hunter's bedroom door, gently knocked, then opened the door. The room was lit by an electric lantern, which gave off a yellowish glow. Scanning the room, he didn't see Hunter; he looked to the far side and still nothing. Whimpering from the closet told

Gordon where he was. He slowly walked over and knocked on the closet door.

"Leave me alone!" Hunter cried out.

"Hunter, it's Daddy."

"Go away. Leave me alone!"

"Hunter, can I open the door?"

"No, leave me alone!"

Gordon didn't want to press his son so he sat down next to the closet door. "Mommy told me what happened. I want you to know how proud I am of you. I know you are scared and don't understand what happened. Know this: You did exactly what I would have wanted you to do," Gordon softly said. Hunter continued to whimper. "Hunter, you did nothing wrong, do you understand?"

"I didn't mean for the gun to go off. I'm sorry, Daddy!" Hunter cried out.

"Hunter, please don't apologize; you did nothing wrong. You were scared and that man should not have been in here. If the gun had not gone off he might have hurt you, your mommy, or your little sister. I am proud of you, I really am. Now can I open the door?"

With an answer just above a whisper Hunter said yes.

Opening the door slowly he saw Hunter curled up in the corner. Gordon reached in and touched his arm gently, and Hunter responded by lunging toward him and into his arms. Embracing him tightly, Gordon rocked and kissed his head.

Hunter cried and kept saying, "I'm sorry, Daddy, I'm sorry."

Losing himself in the moment, Gordon was reminded of the long night he still had before him. Samantha quietly stepped into the room and touched him on the shoulder.

"Gordon, we hear some more shooting."

"Hunter, Daddy has to go."

Hunter clung tight and said, "No, Daddy, don't go."

"I'll be back, I promise."

"No, please don't go, Daddy, I need you."

Hunter's need for Gordon at this moment broke his heart. "I'll be right back."

Samantha leaned down and said, "Come here, baby." Hunter grabbed hold of Samantha and clung to her tightly, still sobbing.

Gordon walked out of the room and went immediately downstairs.

"It sounds like it's the opposite side of the community from Jimmy's house," Nelson said.

"I don't think I can go; it might be a ploy to draw me out. The rest of our group might have to fend for themselves right now."

Gordon, Nelson, Holloway, and Nelson's father chatted for a few minutes about the evening and the need to leave first thing in the morning. Their conversation was cut short when Samantha spoke.

"Absolutely not," she said from the top of the stairs.

Gordon looked up at her. "Absolutely not what?"

"You are not going to stay here. You need to go. I want you to go see Mindy and end this," Samantha said, walking down the stairs. After putting Hunter to bed she had overheard their conversation downstairs.

"I don't think it's a good idea, Sam."

"We'll be fine. Go finish this. This is all because of that bitch. You said Dan is out front dead, so she's the only one left to deal with."

"I said he was shot, he's not dead."

Samantha looked surprised after hearing that Dan was still alive. Pressing him further, she said, "Gordon, we can handle this here. I'm telling you to go and finish this. Go now! Once you've taken care of things then go get Simone."

Gordon was surprised by how forceful Samantha was being. "Sam, I really don't think I should go."

She walked up to him, looked at him squarely, and said, "Go finish this!"

Gordon looked at Nelson, who raised his eyebrows and winked at him. Looking back to Samantha, he nodded his reluctant approval.

• • •

Gordon walked into the garage, reloaded his magazines, and wrapped his arm. As he walked to the front to leave he turned to Nelson and said, "Dan was out front bleeding out; can you take care of him?"

"Sure thing, I'll take care of it stat," Nelson answered, pulling out a seven-inch knife he had sheathed on his side.

"Let me go with you," Holloway asked.

"I got this," Gordon answered, stuffing his pockets with more loaded magazines and double-checking his pistols.

Opening the door again, Samantha stopped him. "Gordon."

Anticipating her comment he said, "I love you too."

"Gordon," she said again.

As he turned to look at her, she said, "Kill them all."

• • •

Ensuring that he survived the night, he took his time getting to Mindy's house. Each step he took was careful and calculated. With so much fighting he knew they too were out for blood. When he reached her street he stopped and squatted down to just listen. Taking a moment to listen to his surroundings, he also thought back on what had transpired earlier in the evening. The thought of

Jimmy being dead weighed on him; the loss his group would suffer without him would be great. He vowed he would avenge his friend tonight.

His eyes had begun to adjust to the complete darkness. Only his knowledge of the streets kept him going in the right direction. After spending minutes listening to the eerie quiet, he felt confident that he could move. Walking briskly, he made for Mindy's house. His anxiety grew with each step; his eyes darting from left to right, straining to see anyone. He wasn't sure how long it took, but he finally arrived. He touched the familiar large shrub just outside her house. He took up a position there and listened. The night had finally remained quiet for a long time. The shooting he heard when he left had lasted only moments. It ended as fast as it had started. Not hearing any movement in her front yard, he stood up and walked around the large shrub and into someone.

Startled by his surprise encounter, Gordon reacted by pushing the man away from him. Whoever it was groaned as he fell on the ground. Not taking chances, Gordon raised his pistol and shot toward the man twice. The man yelled out in pain and was moving on the ground. Gordon shot two more times. The man stopped moving and fell silent.

The sound of breaking glass made Gordon move quickly to take cover along the side of the house. Gunfire and yelling now erupted from inside the house. Gordon recognized Mindy's voice but could not tell whom the male voice belonged to. He wasn't sure how he should proceed; knowing her floor plan was an advantage, but if Mindy was smart she would have blocked off doors and hallways with furniture.

Someone was shooting and it was near the middle of the house, which would have been the living room. Hearing only two voices,

Gordon decided he would attempt to enter through a glass door on the opposite side of the house. The glass door was off a side patio and opened onto the formal dining room.

Gordon slowly made his way along the side of the house. Mindy was sounding hysterical inside and was barking orders to the other person in there with her. It took him minutes to make his way to the patio and finally to the door. He first tested to see if by luck it was unlocked. Unfortunately, Mindy was thinking and the door was not open. Gordon's plan was to shoot the glass out and walk right in. Knowing it was risky, he couldn't think of another way to get in unless he was going to kick down the front door. Leaning up against the side of the house, he was hesitating. He was hoping the glass would shatter and fall. Not being an expert on glass, he was hoping it would work. He stood and placed his rifle on his shoulder and was squeezing the trigger when gunfire came from the front of the house. This was different, though; it was coming from outside. Gordon hesitated again and took cover. Mindy and her companion were screaming and exchanging fire with whoever was out front. Sensing an opportunity, Gordon changed his plan and went to a side garage door off of the same patio. It too was locked, but when a volley of gunfire erupted from inside he took the opportunity to kick the door in. He walked in and went directly for the door that led into the house. It was locked, but still seizing on the chaos in the house he shot the doorknob and kicked in the door.

"Someone is at the back door!" Mindy cried out.

More unintelligible chatter went back and forth between her and the man inside. Leaning up against the door frame taking cover, Gordon laid down a volley of fire from his M4.

"I'll get him, Mindy, don't worry," the man said.

Hearing the man's voice clearly now he knew who was with Mindy.

"Hey, Max, I would say that there's not much you can do. You're surrounded and most of your men are dead, including Dan!"

"Fuck you, you prick!" Max yelled.

"We won't hurt you, Max; all I want is Mindy. If you surrender I won't hurt you!"

More gunfire erupted toward the front of the house. Gordon could hear Max and Mindy taking cover.

"Fuck this, Mindy, I'm outta here!"

"Please, Max, don't; he's bluffing. We sent thirty men after them tonight. There's no way they killed them all," Mindy pleaded.

"You sent thirty and we killed thirty, that's why I'm here!" Gordon responded to Mindy's plea.

"Sorry, Mindy, I gotta go," Max said, standing up and tossing his pistol. "I'm surrendering, Gordon!"

"Walk down the hall toward me!" Gordon instructed him.

Taking out his flashlight Gordon flashed it down the hall so he could see Max to confirm. With his arms raised, Max followed Gordon's command and walked down the hallway toward him.

Knowing there wasn't a better time to deal with Max, Gordon stood up and pointed the rifle at Max.

"What are you doing?" Max asked, concerned.

"I said I wouldn't hurt you, I didn't say anything about not killing you," Gordon said, then pulled the trigger twice.

The force of the two rifle shots hitting Max caused his body to fly back and land a few feet beyond where he had previously stood.

Mindy started screaming hysterically. He heard her run from one room into what sounded like the kitchen. Advancing inside, Gordon took up a position just outside the kitchen door.

"Mindy, there's no way out, my guys are out front. You can't escape."

Expecting a response, Gordon was surprised when she didn't say anything.

"You've never been one for a loss of words."

To Gordon's surprise, he heard the front door burst open and someone come in.

"Who is that?" Gordon called out.

"Holloway."

"Roger that. Max is dead and Mindy is holed up in the kitchen!" Gordon informed Holloway.

"I know just what to use," Holloway said.

A few moments passed; Gordon could hear Holloway down the hall in the family room. There was a kitchen door off of that room too.

"Fire in the hole!" Holloway yelled.

Gordon took cover, not sure what Holloway was throwing into the kitchen. A loud bang echoed out of the kitchen, followed by a scream, then silence.

Gordon and Holloway both entered the kitchen from their respective doors. The room was full of smoke as Gordon entered with his flashlight and handgun out in front of him. Both men looked for Mindy but could not find her. They turned their attention on the only other door in the room: the pantry.

"I know you're in there," Gordon said, knocking on the pantry door. He had tried to open it, but Mindy had locked the door from the inside.

"Gordon, you can take what you want, just let me live," Mindy pleaded with him.

The desire to blast the door and pull her out kicking and screaming was strong, but he changed his mind.

"Mindy, I'm not going to kill you," Gordon told her.

With Holloway's help, they pushed in a large china cabinet from the dining room and placed it in front of the door. Once he felt that she could not escape, he informed her of her situation.

"Mindy, I left you alive tonight so that you finally see the reality of the new world we live in. Your good friend Dan let the Villistas know where our pleasant little community was. They will be here any day, and if they find you, you will finally experience what so many have on the outside. When you finally close your eyes and death takes you, remember that it didn't have to be this way. You chose this path."

Realizing the truth in Gordon's words, Mindy cried out, "Let me out, please!"

As he and Holloway walked onto the street and headed back home, her cries and screams grew fainter with each step they took until they could no longer hear them. Gordon knew there was a good chance that someone would release her, but he felt confident that she wouldn't survive the realities of the world outside her protected community.

• • •

Before going to pick up Simone, Gordon decided to check on his family. Exhausted, all he wanted to do was rest, but the day had only just begun.

"Hi, baby," Sam said sweetly, greeting him with a hug and kiss.

"It's done" was all Gordon said. He didn't want to go into everything that had happened at Mindy's house. Kissing her, he asked, "How are the kids? How's Hunter?"

"They're both asleep in our bed. Hunter is doing better; I don't know if he'll ever be the same after tonight."

"He won't," Gordon replied. He paused, then said, "I'm going to go get Simone. I want to leave as soon as the sun rises if that's possible, okay?"

"Sure thing, babe; we'll be ready."

Gordon was very short with Samantha; the night had been long and his strength was waning. As he closed the door behind him, he thought that this would be his last walk to Jimmy's house. He had walked to Jimmy's house hundreds of times over the years, and now this would be the last. Thoughts of his times in Rancho Valentino came to him in rushes: times of celebration, a birthday party, Easter egg hunting, the Christmas Eve nights walking with his family and looking at the Christmas lights. As he looked at his community now, he saw a broken place. Not only had the houses physically decayed, so had the peacefulness and civility. Life was falling apart all around him and he knew their only chance now was outside the gates and in Idaho.

Jimmy's death was just the beginning. He didn't want to admit it, but death now was the norm.

Entering the house through the still-open garage door, Gordon got a better look at the casualties from earlier. He only recognized Gerald of the three dead. He stepped carefully inside so as not to fall again. Now that he could see, he saw that one of the bodies on the floor in the hall was Lance Corporal Fowler, his eyes wide open. He reached down and forced his eyelids closed, then pulled his dog tags off his neck and pocketed them. Continuing on into the living room, he saw another dead body. It was the person who had shot at him just hours before. Gordon had many fond memories of this room; just last year they had watched the Super Bowl from here. The memories now proved depressing and he needed to find Simone, so he pressed on farther into the house looking for her.

"Simone, it's Gordon," he called out.

No response.

He called out again, "Simone, it's Gordon; where are you?" Not hearing a response, he ran upstairs to where he had left them. They were not there. He looked in every room upstairs and couldn't find her.

Then he realized there was one place he hadn't looked; the backyard. His concerns were put to rest when he looked out the kitchen window. There, he saw her kneeling on the ground next to a shallow, freshly dug hole.

Opening the door to the back, he said, "Simone?"

She did not respond. She just rocked back and forth. He could hear her mumbling words, but they were unintelligible. Walking up behind her, he glanced into the grave and saw Jimmy wrapped in a bloody white sheet. For some reason, Gordon took note that the grave was very wide, wide enough to fit two people.

"Simone?" he said again, this time touching her shoulder.

Jumping at his touch, she turned around.

"Hi, Gordon; you're just in time. Do you want something to drink?"

"What? Umm, no. Simone, do you want me to help you finish burying Jimmy before everyone comes over for the ceremony?"

"No, that won't be necessary," she answered. She glanced back to the grave and stared at Jimmy. Her voice seemed oddly calm and subdued.

"I need to get you back to our house and cleaned up before we come back here for your stuff and Jimmy's funeral."

"That won't be necessary," she replied. She stood up and said, "Follow me."

Gordon just looked at her strangely; he had seen shock before, but her behavior was different.

She led him to the garage and pointed to a wooden box on the workbench.

"I heard what he whispered to you, so while you were gone I fished it out for you. Jimmy loved to hide things but I always knew about them." She opened the box and held the lantern above the opened box so Gordon could see its contents. Peering in, he saw several tall bottles and two smaller boxes.

"What is it?" Gordon asked.

"Go ahead," she said, motioning to the box.

Gordon reached in and pulled out a bottle of Macallan thirty-year-old single malt scotch.

"The other two are the same; the two small boxes are little humidors with Cuban cigars. He knew you'd appreciate this but wanted to surprise you once we arrived in Idaho. Now that won't happen," Simone said, then put the cover back on the box.

"Simone, I am so sorry. I wish I could have made it here quicker—"

"Don't say any more; you did what you could. It's just fate. First Mason, now Jimmy; we weren't meant to survive this for whatever reason. God knows I can't figure it out, but there's a reason; it's either that or we're just unlucky," Simone said with a slight smile.

"We don't have a lot of time, so let's get you packed."

"Gordon, I'm not going with you. I'm staying here with my family."

"That's crazy. You have to come with us."

Simone placed her hand on Gordon's arm and said calmly, "Gordon, everything you need from us as far as food and supplies is here in the garage. I took anything you could use and put it out here. There will be no need to go into the house, do you understand?"

"This is crazy talk, Simone, you're coming with us; I promised Jimmy."

She grabbed his hand and looked at him deeply. "Gordon, I have lost everything. My life has lost all meaning. What is there to live for? My life was them."

Gordon pleaded, "Please don't do this! This is not what Jimmy would want."

"Gordon, go. Please go. And when you return, don't come inside the house, do you understand?"

"Just wait, let me get Samantha; let me have her talk to you."

"I've made up my mind; I am very clear about this. Please kiss Samantha and the kids for me," Simone said. Letting go of Gordon's arm, she turned and walked inside. He could hear the dead bolt lock behind her after she closed the door.

He was in total shock. He couldn't move. He stood frozen, staring at the door. Knowing how influential Samantha was, he quickly left to go get her. Simone looked determined, but Samantha could help. The sound of the single gunshot stopped him in his tracks. He knew what she had done and wished it could have gone differently. In one night, two of his closest friends were dead, his son had shot someone, and their life in Rancho Valentino was over for good.

USS *Makin Island* off the coast of Southern California

When the door to the brig opened, Gunny was the last person Sebastian thought he'd see.

"Corporal Van Zandt, stand up! You're coming with me, shit bird," Gunny said in his scratchy voice.

Sebastian didn't hesitate; he stood up and followed Gunny. As they were walking, Sebastian noticed how empty the passageways were. Many questions came to mind at first but he thought it not worth it to ask. One passageway after another was devoid of life. He wasn't sure where Gunny was taking him, and the farther they walked the more concerned he got. After ten minutes of walking, they finally made it to their destination. Gunny opened the hatch and motioned for Sebastian to exit.

Stopping before he crossed the threshold, he turned to Gunny and said, "Gunny, if you're taking me out here to kill me, just let me know. I hate surprises."

"No one is going to kill you, now get your dumb ass out here."

Sebastian took Gunny for a man of his word and stepped out onto the deck. The sun was attempting to make an appearance, but the clouds and fog were keeping its rays at bay. Looking around, he tried to get a fix on where the ship was, but the fog was too thick.

"Where are we?" Sebastian asked.

"Corporal Van Zandt, I like you. I have known you for over a year and I have seen a squared-away Marine. You're a damn good sniper and a good NCO, but you let your emotions get the better of you. Do you know what I am saying?"

Sebastian tried to answer, but Gunny continued to talk.

"Van Zandt, I understand your dilemma. I know you look at all the bullshit and wonder what it's all for. Well, I can say that there's a lot of bullshit in the Marine Corps. I've seen it, but in the end we are an institution of men who come together because we have common values. Now the world has dealt us, meaning the United States, a shit sandwich. Listen, son, the U.S. is fucked, period. I don't know how it survives this; but just because our country falls doesn't mean we have to. I know you don't like the colonel, but he has given us all a chance to make it through this. Now, you could have been a piece in this survival puzzle but no, you had to open your mouth and get stupid. Now look at ya, Corporal. In a nutshell, you're going to get what you wanted. We are leaving San Diego in a week. Once the last of our men are done gathering their family members, we will dump the garbage, meaning you, on the beach. You will be given a weapon, a few magazines, a few MREs, and some water. Then you're on your own. What you don't know is this: You will have two total shit storms to deal with on your hunt for your brother. First, the nuclear reactors at San Onofre have melted down. Second, there is some renegade Mexican militia conquering parts of San Diego. Now, if you manage to make it to your brother's place, you might find him already dead or gone. You'll not only have to deal with two fucked-up situations, but you'll have a million starving San Diegans trying to kill you for a scrap of food. The moral of the story, Van Zandt, is that you should keep your mouth shut. Your chance of survival out there on your own is not high, but let this be a lesson to you."

Sebastian's mind just went blank listening to Gunny bloviate. He thought many times that Gunny liked to hear himself talk. He wondered if now might be a good time to be honest with him and tell him to fuck himself. He decided against being honest. If he wanted to get some kind of advantage from Gunny, then he should take his advice and keep his mouth shut.

"Thank you for the words of advice, Gunny."

"You're welcome, Corporal, now let's get your ass back down below."

"One second, why did you take me up here?"

"I thought I'd show you something, but the fog isn't cooperating."

"What's out there?"

"San Diego, San Diego is right there," Gunny said, pointing over the railing into the fog.

Sebastian leaned forward in hopes of getting a glimpse, but nothing.

"Let's go," Gunny ordered.

Sebastian kept staring, hoping to see something.

"Let's go, Corporal," Gunny said, sounding impatient.

Giving up, Sebastian turned and started to walk back to the hatch. Right before he stepped in he saw something out of the corner of his right eye. He stopped and looked; a break in the fog exposed the hidden city behind it. He kept staring until a landmark that was unmistakable appeared: the Hyatt Towers stood darkened in the distance. The fog continued to clear and more of the city became visible. Sebastian could make out the outline of the buildings but not a single light was visible. The city was completely dark.

"We made it, we're in San Diego!" Sebastian exclaimed.

"That's correct, Corporal, that's San Diego; we made it home."

Sebastian stood looking at the skyline of the darkened city. His journey had taken thousands of miles and had forever changed his position within the Marine Corps. When the ships pulled away in a few days, he would no longer be a Marine; he would be a survivor left alone to fend for himself in this new wilderness.

Anza, California (eighty-nine miles outside of San Diego)

As the sun began its descent on what had been a long day, Gordon was happy that he and his convoy of five vehicles had driven the distance they had. Taking the smaller state highways they had been able to avoid the congestion of abandoned vehicles and the droves of wandering people. He also had pushed his convoy as far east as he thought was safe, but now he was at a crossroads. He and Nelson had been discussing which way to go. Their convoy sat at the intersection of Highway 371 and Highway 74. Right would lead them into Palm Desert, and left would lead them into the mountains. The mountain pass was risky because they could find themselves snowed in. But the route into Palm Desert provided risks too. It took them through a populated urban area, something he wanted to avoid. Nelson thought it best to go through Palm Desert, as he felt the chance of wintry weather could cost them a vehicle.

Gordon finally let his instincts reveal the direction, and that was toward the desert. Nelson was happy with the decision and away they went down the long, car-less highway. As they headed east, Gordon looked in the side mirror and saw the sun just above the mountains. He thought of his brother, Sebastian; they had taken short trips to Palm Springs in the past. He hoped his brother was okay. He wondered if they had been victims of the same fate and were now stuck in Afghanistan. He wondered if he'd ever see his brother again. Just before he departed his house, he had left a note for Sebastian on his desk. He figured the odds of him finding it were slim, but if by chance he made it back to the States, Gordon knew Sebastian would go looking for him, and going to the house would be a good place to start.

Looking again in his side mirror, he noticed the sun had disappeared. It was now hidden by a dark set of clouds over the mountains. Gordon now felt good about his decision to head east, as the clouds to the west portended bad weather in the mountains.

"Look what I found in Jimmy's stuff," Nelson said, pulling out an old cassette player.

"Does it work?" Gordon asked. He looked amused at the sight of the old player.

"Shit, man, I never checked. I just grabbed it when I saw it. There was also a case with old cassettes," Nelson said, picking out a cassette tape. He put it in the player and hit play. The player sprang to life with the soft, subtle strumming sounds of a banjo.

"What is this?" Gordon asked. At first he thought it was some type of bluegrass music, but there was something Irish in the sound.

"Flogging Molly is the name of the band. The song's called 'The Son Never Shines (On Closed Doors).' You want me to change it?"

"No, I kinda like it. It's soothing and almost fitting for our journey," Gordon said.

Both men sat and listened to the music, neither saying a word.

With the clouds to their backs and clear skies ahead, Gordon thought again of everything that had taken place over the past five weeks. In that short time, the city he called home had collapsed into chaos after suffering an attack that destroyed its power grid and made useless all electrical devices. Misery, suffering, and death caused by starvation, disease, and murder had now become the norm for the survivors left in San Diego. For those able to leave, now was the time. For those who stayed, their lives or what days they had left would be marked by horrors not seen in centuries. Reflecting on all of this, Gordon drove into the darkness and the unknown with hopes that a brighter and more hopeful day existed at the end of the long road.

OCTOBER 15, 2066

• • •

Olympia, Washington, Republic of Cascadia

"We have definitely covered a lot so far," John said, looking at his pad. He had been taking diligent notes the entire time.

"I'd like to take a break, if you don't mind?" Haley asked.

"Of course."

"Can I get you and your people a cup of tea or coffee?" Haley asked as she stood up.

The two photographers declined her offer, but John asked for tea.

While Haley was preparing the tea in the kitchen, John walked around her house. He slowly took his time looking at the myriad of framed photographs she had hung along the wall in the hallway. As he examined each one to see if there was anyone of note in them, one caught his eye. It was a photo of Gordon dressed in an old camouflage uniform surrounded by others in similar dress. They were all holding up a worn "Doug" flag. The blue, white, and green striped flag had the words, "First Idaho Infantry, Republic of Cascadia" hand-sewn across the white field that stretched from one end to the other. The Douglas fir emblazoned in the center was faded and showed wear that can only come from war.

He pulled the photo off the wall and walked into the kitchen to get more information on it. The kitchen was empty. He walked into the adjacent room and there he found Haley holding what looked like a necklace.

His abrupt entry into the room startled her, causing her to drop the necklace.

John was curious about what she had, so he stepped forward and picked it up for her. He looked at it and saw that it was a silver compass attached to a silver chain.

"Here," he said as he handed it to her.

"Thank you," Haley responded. She took it quickly and placed it back in a small chest located on a bookshelf. She looked disturbed that John had touched it.

"May I ask what that was?" John asked.

"My brother gave it to me," Haley said, not looking at him. She still had her hand on the chest.

"I didn't know you had a brother until you mentioned him today," John stated, looking confused.

Ignoring John's comment, she asked, "So what do you want to discuss in our next session?"

Taking note that she deliberately didn't comment about her brother, he said, "I want to talk about your time in Idaho."

Haley turned around and faced him.

"Our years in Idaho were some of the best I can remember. Even though the war started not long after the lights went out, I was inoculated from what was happening. We were safe in Idaho. Although the same cannot be said about the journey there, or as Daddy referred to it, 'the long road.' Something happened that changed us all." Haley paused and looked back toward the necklace on the shelf. She reached over and touched it. She then looked back at John and said, "I would like to talk about that next."

Read on for an excerpt from G. Michael Hopf's novel
The Long Road, also available from Plume

Book 3 of the New World Series coming in April 2014

OCTOBER 15, 2066

. . .

Olympia, Washington, Republic of Cascadia

Haley rubbed her thumb repeatedly across the smooth surface of the compass. Touching it soothed her. She needed it after having just spent almost an hour talking about her parents and life in San Diego after the lights went out. The compass brought her such comfort and gave her a connection to her now-distant family.

She knew John was not a fool and had picked up on her not answering his direct question about Hunter earlier. She was hesitating to go back into the living room; she didn't want to face the question, she didn't want to have to relive that time on the road. Even though she'd told him she wanted to talk about it, she now regretted her decision. The road to Idaho had been tough and had become one of those moments her father told her occurs in a life where your course changes.

Deciding she had stalled long enough, she put the compass back in the chest on the shelf and walked into the hallway. She could hear John and the camera crew laughing. Their laughter echoed off of the bare wood floors and the walls of the sparsely furnished home. She thought that these men knew nothing of true hardship. To her, their laughter displayed an innocence and ignorance of years before. She didn't blame them; it wasn't their fault when they were born. However, she did hold a grudge in some ways against those many who now enjoyed the fruits of her and her family's labor but disregarded the cost.

The Great Civil War was not unlike many civil wars in history. It was brutal and hard. It did have one distinction that separated it from those before it: The rules that governed war were gone. The divisions that had been fostered over the most recent generations in America became more pronounced and deadly. Once the last bits of fabric that had held the country together vanished in that instant fifty-two years ago, it took only days for Americans to rip and tear at other Americans.

Haley was only five years old when it happened; she never got to enjoy the typical twentieth-century invention of a child's life. Gone were the birthday parties with abundant cakes and ice cream. Gone were the Christmases with dozens of beautifully wrapped toys. Gone was the innocence. She was forced to grow up quickly and act like an adult. Even though her father did all he could to protect her from the horrors while they were living at Rancho Valentino, he could not shield her from the depravity of life once they made their way to Idaho.

She walked into the living room and just stood there looking at the men. None of them noticed her; they were absorbed in the typical conversations that young single men have.

After clearing her throat loudly, she said, "I'm ready if you are."

"Great!" John said, jumping up. He was surprised to see her. He felt a bit foolish, as he hadn't known how long she had been there and the topic the men had been enjoying was not entirely appropriate.

Haley walked back to her chair and sat down. She smoothed out the creases in her skirt and sat pensively waiting.

John shuffled around and quickly grabbed the pad he had been taking notes on. Taking the seat across from her, he said, "Sorry, one second."

"Take your time," Haley responded.

"I'd like to start with the trip to Idaho. From the sounds of it, a lot happened on the way there, and I think that's a good starting point."

"Very well," Haley answered. She clasped her hands tightly to keep them from nervously fiddling with her skirt or sleeve.

"There is one item I'd like to ask before, though."

"Go ahead."

"Before today I never knew you had a brother. I apologize if I didn't do my research, but like your father and mother, you have been very reserved in sharing details of your past life," John stated, twirling his pen.

"The thing is, my brother is all around us. How many places in Olympia are named Hunter?" Haley asked.

After pausing to think, John blurted out, "You're right; I never thought anything about it before. So what happened to him, your brother?"

"My brother was not unlike my father in his passion to protect his family. He took it quite seriously." Haley stopped talking and looked down. The pitch of her voice changed. She unclasped her hands and again started to pat down the creases in her skirt.

John, noticing her discomfort, chose to move on to something else. "Haley, if you want, let's talk about the trip to Idaho."

"He was a good boy," Haley said just above a whisper. She was still looking down, fidgeting with her clothes.

"What's that?" John asked, leaning in toward Haley.

"Nothing, sorry, nothing," she said loudly, looking up.

"Okay, so let's begin with the trip to Idaho."

"Sure, let's do that. So as to not bore you, let's start on our third day into the drive. That day revisits me in my thoughts often. Let's begin there."

JANUARY 8, 2014

• • •

We must travel in the direction of our own fear.

—John Berryman

Barstow, California

"Run, Haley, run!" Gordon screamed.

Haley stood frozen in fear. She had never seen a person burn to death before, and now she was watching flames dance off of Candace Pomeroy's back as she slowly crawled away from her car.

"Hunter, grab your sister and run over there!" Gordon yelled out, pointing to a dropoff in the road that led to a culvert large enough to provide protection for only the kids.

Hunter ran over to Haley and grabbed her with force, causing her to drop the small teddy bear she held.

"No, my bear!" she yelled out.

"No, Haley, we gotta run!" Hunter screamed.

Gunfire was raining down on the vehicles from a few covered positions up the road. There wasn't much cover for Gordon and his convoy. To either side of the road lay flat, open desert dotted with creosote plants. Even their vehicles didn't provide the protection needed, as was the case with the Pomeroys' car. The initial rain of bullets had hit their fuel tank just right, causing their car to explode into a ball of flames.

Hunter pulled Haley to the small culvert. Gordon and Nelson had hidden behind Gordon's truck. The banging of bullets rattled the truck and their ears. Gordon attempted to look over the truck but was met by a hail of gunfire.

"Fuck!" he screamed in frustration. He looked for Samantha but didn't see her.

"What do we do, Gordo?" Nelson asked. Each bullet that struck the truck caused him to flinch.

The Pomeroys' burning car was draping them in thick black smoke. Sensing an advantage, Gordon ran for the jeep. Holloway had been driving it but was nowhere to be seen. He jumped in the back and grabbed the handles of the .50-caliber machine gun mounted there. Not wasting any more time, he pressed the butterfly trigger and started to fire on the positions the gunfire was coming from. Dirt and debris were flying in the air as the .50 did its work. He transitioned from one position to the next. He remembered seeing three areas from which they were taking fire. Gordon was in a rage as he screamed out while firing the heavy gun. It took only moments on each position to destroy whomever had ambushed them, but he kept firing until the gun ran out of ammunition. Looking over the top of the smoking barrel, Gordon could not see anyone up ahead, but he needed to be sure. He jumped into the driver's seat and put the jeep in gear. As he began to pull away, Holloway came running toward him.

"Where the fuck were you?" Gordon asked, clearly angered.

"I went to my family and made sure they were okay," Holloway answered directly, not intimidated by Gordon's gruffness.

"Jump in, we need to make sure these fuckers are dead," Gordon said.

Holloway jumped in, and both men proceeded cautiously. When they came upon the first position, Holloway jumped out and ran over to discover two dead men; both had been ripped apart by the machine gun. He continued on by foot and discovered a similar scene at the second, but at the third one a man was alive.

"We've got a live one here!" Holloway yelled.

Gordon drove the jeep over to Holloway's position and got out. He stepped over to the wounded man, pulled his handgun out, and put it to the wounded man's head.

"Are there any more of you?"

The man didn't respond but coughed up blood.

"Answer me, you piece of shit!" Gordon screamed, pressing the barrel against the man's sweaty forehead.

Gordon began to slowly squeeze the trigger but stopped when screaming rang out from behind him. He stood and looked; the screams gave way to gunfire. He could tell people were moving, but the dark smoke was making it impossible to see what was really happening. He took a step, then remembered the wounded man. He turned, took aim, and shot the man.

• • •

"I'm scared. Where's Mommy? Where's Daddy?" Haley cried.

Not answering his little sister, Hunter could see a few men marching toward them and the convoy from the eastern desert.

Haley began to cry loudly.

"Ssshh! Haley, be quiet!" Hunter commanded.

"I can't, I can't, I'm scared!" Haley whimpered, her body trembling uncontrollably.

"Mommy and Daddy will come soon, I promise."

"What if they're dead, what if Mommy and Daddy are dead?"

"Haley, you have to be quiet."

More gunfire rang out from the men approaching. Haley screamed.

Hunter reached over and put his hand on top of her mouth. She attempted to pull away, but he forced his hand with pressure equal to her resistance. "Stop, just stop!" Hunter demanded.

Looking into her brother's eyes, she calmed down, but tears were still flowing and she was having a hard time controlling her breathing.

He could no longer see the men in the distance, but he could hear gunfire coming from them and from the convoy. He wanted to know where the men were, so he pulled away from Haley and started to crawl toward the entrance of the culvert.

"No, stop, where are you going?" Haley cried out.

"I'm checking to see where those guys went."

"Stop, don't leave me."

"I'm just going to poke my head out."

Haley began to cry loudly, making Hunter stop and go back to her. He held her close and told her things would be okay. Reaching into his pocket, he pulled out a silver compass and gave it to her.

"Here, take this. Dad gave it to me. He said it would keep me safe, and if I give it to you, it will keep you safe."

Taking the compass in her trembling hands, she looked up at her brother.

He smiled and said, "I'll be right back." Hunter crawled away to the opening of the culvert and peered out. He looked left and then right. Seeing one of the men not two feet away, he attempted to duck back inside, but the man grabbed him and pulled him out. Hunter kicked, but he wasn't a match for the man, who punched him once in the face, knocking him out.

Haley began to scream, knowing that something bad had happened to her brother.

The man peered into the culvert and said, "Come here, little girl."

USS *Makin Island* off the coast of Southern California

Sebastian's patience was at its breaking point. As each day passed without notice of his departure from the cold gray walls of his cell, he grew more agitated and restless. Knowing that his brother's house was only twenty miles away made the wait worse. After having traveled thousands of miles and enduring hardships, not to be able to just leave was unbearable. Since Gunny had taken him topside three days before, he hadn't seen the light of day. His treatment was fair, but this now was feeling like torture. One advantage the wait gave him was the ability to establish a plan. Gunny had allowed him to have a map, paper, and a pencil. He mapped several routes and identified waypoints. Knowing that traveling the highways could be bad, he plotted surface streets and natural trails to lead him to Carmel Valley.

It had been six weeks since the attacks, and the last intelligence he had on San Diego was days old. In a nutshell, the city had collapsed into chaos. The Villista Army was now occupying large parts of the city. Some Marine squads who had gone ashore to gather family had encountered them. Barone had no intention of securing San Diego but at the same time was not about to allow an organized mob to harass his Marines. He attacked many of the Villista strongholds and encampments, destroying resources and killing many of their people. Sebastian supported this approach and appreciated anything Barone did that would increase his chances for survival.

The welcome sound of keys unlocking his door echoed off the walls of cell.

Sebastian stopped what he was doing and stared at the door; he knew it was too early for chow, so someone was coming to pay a visit.

The large metal door opened, and Gunny stepped inside.

Sebastian stood up, excited to see Gunny because his appearance might portend his release.

"Van Zandt, how ya holdin' up?"

"Good, Gunny."

"I have some good news and some bad news. What ya want first?" Gunny said, standing tall with his arms crossed.

Sebastian's eyes widened with anticipation. He was nervous about what the bad news was, but he wanted to save the good news for last.

"Bad news."

"Well, Corporal, San Diego is a total cluster fuck. It's worse than Fallujah back in '04."

"I kinda figured it would be bad," Sebastian answered.

"Not sure if this is good news based upon the bad news, but we're leaving early and so are you. The colonel wants all the prisoners dropped off by sixteen hundred hours. So, you finally get what you want, Corporal. Your precious California awaits. Now grab your shit, you're coming with me."

"Ah, now!" Sebastian exclaimed, not quite prepared. Just moments before he'd been grumbling to himself about the wait; now the reality of navigating in the chaos of what was San Diego took him off guard.

"Yes, Corporal. Get your trash, a bird is waiting for you and the other scumbags," Gunny barked.

Nervously grabbing what few items he had been allowed, Sebastian followed Gunny out of the cell and down the narrow passageways toward the flight deck.

"Are you giving me everything you mentioned before?" Sebastian asked.

"Don't worry, Corporal, we're not cruel. We will give you enough to get by."

"Thank you."

Stepping out on the flight deck, Sebastian thought that he'd never see this ship or Gunny again. He had a flash of nostalgia. He really wished that things had gone differently, but the path Barone was on was not one he could follow. Gunny escorted him to the ramp and patted him on the back.

"This is it, Van Zandt. I brought you up first; there's another handful of Marines joining you on this one-way trip. I wanted you to get first dibs on the gear on board," Gunny said, pointing inside the helicopter.

"Thank you, Gunny," Sebastian said, putting out his hand.

Gunny looked at his hand, hesitated, then grabbed it firmly, "God damn you, Van Zandt, I really wanted you to come with us; but no, you had to go renegade. Listen, I couldn't let you go without some goodies and a surprise. Grab the pack with the black strap tied on the top."

"Roger that," Sebastian said; he still had Gunny's hand.

"If you find your brother, and I hope you do, tell him Smitty says hello, okay?"

"Will do, Gunny."

They stared at each other for another brief moment before Sebastian turned and walked onto the helicopter. Packs with rifles were lined up on the webbing on both sides of the chopper. By a rough count, he totaled a dozen. This gave Sebastian some encouragement; he hoped he could convince some of them to come with him. He located the pack Gunny had mentioned and sat down next to it. Picking it up was not easy; the pack had to weigh sixty pounds.

He wanted to see what surprise Gunny had for him, so he opened the pack up and started digging around. Inside he found the familiar tools of the Marine trade. MREs, a tent, can opener, matches, tarp, poncho, extra bootlaces, extra set of clothes, rope, compass, two flashlights with spare batteries, a Ka-Bar knife, extra boxes of 5.56-mm ammunition, two boxes of 9-mm ammo, and four grenades, two high explosive and two smoke. He just assumed that the grenades were the surprise, but then he felt something in the bottom of the pack. He pulled it out and knew that these would come in handy: night-vision goggles with spare batteries. Hearing others coming on board, Sebastian repacked everything and sat back. He checked his rifle and put on his shoulder holster for the 9-mm while the others boarded.

As each one boarded and sat down, he tried to see if he recognized them. No luck, he didn't know one of these men; not that it mattered, he just wanted in some strange way to have a familiar face with him. Once everyone was aboard, the crew chief came on and raised the ramp. As the turbines of CH-53 chopper began to spin, Sebastian thought back to his time in the Marines. He loved the Corps, and the way he was leaving it made him sad. When the chopper lifted off the flight deck, he said his typical prayer, this time with meaning. Finishing, he looked over his shoulder at the ship below. He wished the best for the Marines of his battalion and hoped that wherever they ended up they could find peace. Settling into his seat for the short ride, he thought about what he might encounter on the ground in San Diego. He couldn't lie to himself; he was anxious, but knowing he'd be able to complete his long journey gave him solace. He just hoped that Gordon and his family were still alive.

Cheyenne Mountain, Colorado

"Nothing? Nothing is not an answer! It's an excuse! It's a cop-out!" Julia screamed at Cruz and Dylan.

"Mrs. Conner, please understand that until we can get some more intelligence, there's nothing we can do," Cruz tried to explain with a cautious tone.

"You listen here, Andrew, you're my husband's best friend and his vice president. You need to have men out there every second of the day looking for him,"

"We don't even know if he's alive, Julia; you have to understand," Cruz said, defending himself.

"All you have are excuses. I want results!"

"Mrs. Conner, if you would just listen to the vice president," Dylan attempted to interject.

Waving a finger, Julia scolded him. "Don't even tell me what I should do. I've listened long enough. It's been three days and nothing has been done. You all just sit here and talk. This is exactly what Brad hated about this group. You just sit around and talk all the time."

"Julia, we have limited manpower, we can't have them going door-to-door," Cruz said.

"Yes, you could. I'm not asking for you to search every building from here to where he went missing, but you should have teams going door-to-door there."

"We tried, but we were repelled by a superior force," Cruz exclaimed. "We even sent two-man teams; neither team has come back."

"Don't we have any resources here to do something? Are we that helpless?" Julia asked. She was getting increasingly frustrated by this back-and-forth.

"We have more men coming soon, and when they arrive, we will have a plan."

Julia looked tired and frustrated. She finally sat down at the table. The waiting was wearing on her physically and emotionally. It had been three days since Conner had disappeared. Cruz had sent a team to find him, but when they attempted to conduct a search, they were fired upon by the locals. Cruz had requested support from the handful of military installations that still had operations. But with only two aircraft, it would take some time before they could have those men on the ground.

"Julia, believe me when I say that if I could go get Brad I would, but we are vulnerable now. I'm making my decisions based upon what I think Brad would do," Cruz said. He sat down next to her.

Lifting her weary head, Julia responded, "Thank you for saying that; you're right. Brad would look at the big picture, and if searching for someone would jeopardize the greater good, he would not do it." She reached over and touched his hand. Cruz responded by placing his hand on top of hers.

Gripping her hand a bit tighter, he said, "I will not rest until we find him, please trust me; I will find him."